Praise for Ryan Steck

Ryan Steck delivers again! Redd and Decker are locked, loaded, back in action and coming in hot! *Target Down* belongs at the top of everyone's 2026 reading list. From its first page to its last, this is a thriller that never lets up. Clear your calendar on publication day and prepare to strap in. It's a wild ride you won't forget!

JACK CARR, #1 *New York Times* bestselling author of The Terminal List series

Ryan Steck is the real deal! *Gone Dark* powers forward, with each scene slamming into the next like colliding freight cars. Matthew Redd is my new favorite thriller hero.

ROBERT CRAIS, #1 *New York Times* bestselling author of *The Big Empty*

Things have Gone Dark up in Montana, but Mathew Redd has his hand on the switch and is about to shed some light on the subject. . . . The fourth in Ryan Steck's pulse-pounding novels, *Gone Dark* fans the flames of a wildfire of a series!

CRAIG JOHNSON, *New York Times* bestselling author of the Walt Longmire series

Gone Dark is wildly entertaining—Steck keeps raising the stakes, putting his characters into increasingly impossible situations, but Matthew Redd is a hero equal to every challenge. Vivid imagery, pulse-pounding suspense, and an all-time great dog—everything we read thrillers for.

JOSEPH FINDER, *New York Times* bestselling author of *The Oligarch's Daughter*

Set in Montana's breathtaking Big Sky Country and packed with intense, hard-hitting action, *Out for Blood* reaffirms Ryan Steck's prowess in the thriller genre, demonstrating once again why his character, former Marine Raider Matthew Redd, is a force to be reckoned with. If you're looking for action, this one's coming in hot!

JACK CARR, former Navy SEAL sniper and #1 *New York Times* bestselling author of the James Reece Terminal List series

Matthew Redd, introduced in Ryan Steck's debut novel *Fields of Fire*, is back and ready for trouble. Redd, a former Marine Raider turned Montana rancher, takes on a gang of outlaw bikers where the buffalo roam. The Wild West has never been wilder. Intense, brutal, and faster on the draw than a gunslinger; *Lethal Range* delivers a fresh take on your grandpa's Western.

NELSON DEMILLE, #1 *New York Times* bestselling author of *The Maze*

Intense, riveting, and ultimately wild escapist fun, *Lethal Range* is a powerful modern Western. It's *Sons of Anarchy* crashing into *Yellowstone*. Steck is a talented cinematic writer and has created a character in Matthew Redd that is both larger than life and remarkably relatable. Buy this book!

DON WINSLOW, #1 bestselling author of *The Force* and *The Border*

Matthew Redd is a hero many readers will find comfortingly familiar while refreshingly different, and Steck wields him with precision in *Lethal Range*—a spectacular follow-up to his stellar debut. If you're a skeptic who thinks Ryan Steck can only write about thrillers, you're missing out on one of the hottest new authors in the genre. You'll be far from disappointed in this installment and eager for more.

JACK STEWART, *USA Today* bestselling co-author of *Silent Horizons*

Ryan Steck's *Fields of Fire* busts out of the chute with nonstop action and it never lets up until the final page. A magnificent debut with a terrific sense of place in Big Sky Country and a hero to root for in Matthew Redd.

C. J. BOX, #1 *New York Times* bestselling author of *Shadows Reel*

Ryan Steck hits it out of the park with his debut, *Fields of Fire*. Part military thriller, part spy novel, part good old-fashioned Western—Matthew Redd has cemented himself as the go-to man in a bad situation. It starts off with a literal bang and never lets up, with an ending that will leave readers scrambling for more.

BRAD TAYLOR, *New York Times* bestselling author of *End of Days*

A flawless story with a stellar cast of memorable characters . . . *Fields of Fire* is a twisty, electrifying thriller reminiscent of the very best of Brad Thor that will keep readers flipping pages well into the night.

SIMON GERVAIS, former RCMP counterterrorism officer and bestselling author of *The Last Protector*

TARGET DOWN

RYAN STECK

TARGET DOWN

A MATTHEW REDD THRILLER

Tyndale House Publishers
Carol Stream, Illinois

Visit Tyndale online at tyndale.com.

Visit Ryan Steck online at therealbookspy.com.

Target Down

Cover design by Dean H. Renninger

Interior design by Laura Cruise

Edited by Sarah Mason Rische

Published in association with The John Talbot Agency, Inc., a member of The Talbot Fortune Agency, LLC, 180 E. Prospect Ave. #188, Mamaroneck, NY 10543.

Library of Congress Cataloging-in-Publication Data

A catalog record for this book is available from the Library of Congress.

ISBN 979-8-4005-1090-8 (HC)
ISBN 979-8-4005-1091-5 (SC)

Printed in the United States of America

32 31 30 29 28 27 26
7 6 5 4 3 2 1

For Bryan Tema—pastor, mentor, and friend. Bryan, your encouragement and teaching have meant far more to me than you will ever know. Thank you . . . for everything.

Prologue

KYIV, UKRAINE
FIFTEEN YEARS AGO

Sergei Konstantin caught sight of the figure stepping out onto the upper span of the bridge—a lone silhouette backlit by firelight and moonglow, gliding over the unfinished superstructure like a ghost—and felt adrenaline surge through him.

It was the American.

Finally, he told himself, *we've found him.*

Volkov had been livid when Konstantin had called in to report the man's escape. The trap at the warehouse had been the perfect kill box—every exit blocked, no way out—and yet somehow, one of the Americans had made it through not just the warehouse fire but the outer perimeter. Not only had they all looked incompetent, but if the American survived, reported back to his superiors, then it would only be a matter of time before he or someone else started pulling threads, and the whole operation would unravel.

There was only one way to make sure that didn't happen.

The American has to die.

Volkov had sent all his soldiers, along with a dozen hired guns, to monitor every possible exit from the peninsula. Konstantin had been sent to guard the Podilsko-Voskresenskyi Bridge—the half-finished span of concrete and steel that stretched across the Dnieper like a broken promise. Construction of the bridge had languished in a state of perpetual delay for years, and the prospects for it being completed in Konstantin's lifetime were not good.

At first, he'd been annoyed with the assignment. The bridge was too long—nearly four miles across—and too open. No professional would be dumb enough to try crossing it on foot. Konstantin figured he'd spend the night cold, bored, and irrelevant, guarding a monument to bureaucratic failure, while somebody else would gain Volkov's favor by bringing back the American's head.

But now it seemed luck had favored him.

The American had chosen to cross the bridge after all.

It'll be the last thing he ever does.

The man was already well out onto the span, a hundred meters at least, moving fast and with purpose. Somehow, the American had slipped past Konstantin's position in the shadows below the ramp. That realization sparked a flicker of irritation, but it passed quickly. The man was on the bridge with nowhere to go. That was all that mattered.

He was too far away for a clean pistol shot. Even with a steady hand, beyond fifty meters, scoring a hit with a Makarov was more a matter of luck than skill. A shot from this distance would just waste ammo and alert his target.

I need to get closer.

Konstantin slipped from cover and started up the ramp at a run. Ahead, the steel arch rose like a sentinel in the dark, its ribs gleaming under moonlight. The basic structure of the bridge was in place, but there were still gaping voids in the deck, scattered scaffolding, and skeletal lanes open to wind and sky. As Konstantin reached the top of the ramp and crested onto the main span, the deck changed beneath his feet—concrete giving way to steel plates bolted into place over open air. His footsteps rang out sharp and hollow, like a hammer beating a gong.

He winced.

But the American hadn't looked back. He was still moving at a fast walk, though not in a straight line. Instead, he was randomly weaving back and forth, no doubt hoping to make himself a more difficult target for a sniper. Yet, for all his caution, he remained seemingly oblivious to the sound of approaching footsteps.

Konstantin closed the distance at a sprint.

Seventy-five meters . . .

The Russian's lungs were burning from the exertion. He wasn't a runner.

Fifty meters . . .

Close enough.

Konstantin took a couple more steps, then stopped and raised his Makarov in a two-handed grip, took aim at the American's back, and fired.

The report thundered across the span, shattering the quiet.

The American staggered as if he'd been shoved from behind but didn't fall. Instead, he veered to the right, even as Konstantin pulled the trigger twice more. He couldn't tell if either of the follow-up shots scored a hit, but he knew his first round had found its target.

Konstantin continued tracking the man, chasing him with the front sights, trying to line up another shot. But the American veered again, this time stumbling toward the edge.

Two more shots—snap decisions, no time to refine the aim. One may have hit; both might've missed. He couldn't tell.

Konstantin cursed aloud.

The American reached the edge, one hand slapping out against the guardrail. Then, without warning, he pitched forward, over the side.

Konstantin lowered the pistol and jogged toward the spot, breathing hard. There was a dark smear on the rail, glistening in the moonlight. He pulled a compact flashlight from his coat, snapped it on, and tilted the beam to reveal a bloody streak on the metal, right where the American had gone over.

He's bleeding. Good.

Thirty meters below, the Dnieper rolled wide and black in the moonlight, its surface broken only by wind and current. The man had gone over the north side, the upstream edge of the bridge. That wasn't good—it meant that when the American surfaced, the current would carry him back under the structure and out of view.

Konstantin scanned the surface, looking for any sign of movement. A ripple, a splash, the glint of skin catching moonlight. But there was nothing.

No sign of the American.

Konstantin knew the bullet hadn't killed him outright, but the injury, perhaps combined with the shock of hitting the water after falling thirty meters, might easily have stunned him, leaving him unable to swim back to the surface.

He's dead, Konstantin tried to convince himself. *He has to be.*

But that wasn't good enough.

Volkov will want confirmation. He'll want the man's body.

Konstantin waited a full minute, then another, playing his light back and forth across the water, expanding his visual sweep to adjust for the current, but the river refused to give up its secret.

× × ×

It would be two weeks before Volkov would finally get confirmation of the kill, in the form of a bloated, partially decomposed body washing up on the bank of the Dnieper, thirty kilometers downstream. The identity of the victim was never made public, but Volkov had contacts—men and women embedded in various agencies, well-placed enough to learn what official channels would not disclose.

The dead man had been an American named Daniel Keene. Military background, attached to a task force so secret it didn't officially exist. His remains had been quietly repatriated, shipped home on a military transport, along with three other badly burned and similarly "unidentified" bodies.

The last member of the American ops team known as Rogue Unit was dead.

Officially.

Privately, however, the man's name was *not* Daniel Keene.

The American's real name was Aaron Decker.

That's all they ever knew.

And the *unofficial* story was much, much different.

WARSAW, POLAND
PRESENT DAY

"I just saw a ghost."

There was a pause on the line, then the gravelly voice of Grigori Volkov filled Konstantin's ear. "A ghost?"

"I saw Aaron Decker."

Konstantin glanced over his shoulder, scanning the terminal, checking to make sure that the man—the *ghost*—wasn't now following him.

It was him, he thought again. *But how?*

He'd been sitting at the airport bar, halfway through his second vodka, preparing for a long flight home, when he saw the man walking openly through Chopin Airport like he didn't have a care in the world—the same man he'd shot and killed on a bridge in Kyiv, fifteen years ago. The American had aged a little, grown his hair and beard, but it was him.

Alive.

Konstantin had moved quickly, jogging ahead to stage himself near a boarding gate to get another look at him, just be sure. Then he'd made the call.

"He's dead," Volkov said when Konstantin had finished his report. "You killed him."

"I know." Konstantin lowered his voice. "But I tell you, he's here. In Warsaw."

"Kostya, they found his body. Matched his DNA. Whoever you saw, it wasn't him."

"I'm telling you, it *was*," Konstantin said, his voice flush with irritation. "He walked right past me, didn't even look. But I know it was him. Same face. Same walk. I'll never forget how he moved. He's older, sure, but it's him."

There was another long pause. Konstantin could hear Volkov's breathing over the line. "If it is truly him . . ." He trailed off. "The body. The DNA results. Someone helped him do this. And yet, there was no blowback from that operation. He didn't just survive. He went underground. Why?"

Konstantin knew it was a rhetorical question. He had not been privy to the reasoning behind the decisions his boss had made those long years ago, but he knew it involved powerful men in sensitive positions. Men who stood to lose everything if the truth about what happened that night ever came to light.

Volkov waited a beat before continuing. "I want you to find out who he is, Kostya. Who he *really* is."

Konstantin felt a flicker of unease—not from the fear of reprisal, though that lingered too, but from the simple fact that he had no idea where to begin looking for that information. He could reach out to one of his informants in the Polish security service, get the American's name from passport control. He would almost certainly be using an alias, but it was a place to start. "And when I find out who he is?"

"You do what you should have done fifteen years ago," said Volkov with grim finality. "And this time, Kostya, make sure he's dead once and for all."

ONE

WASHINGTON, DC

Gavin Kline sat two seats from the end of the polished conference table, the placard in front of him like a place marker at a wake. *Acting Director, FBI.*

The title carried just enough weight to get him in the room—but not enough to mean anything.

His role as director was always going to be temporary, an interim appointment until a presidential nominee was approved by the Senate. The directorship was a political appointment, reserved for loyalists—champion fundraisers with law degrees. But while he had the job, he made the most of it, rooting out corruption and generally improving the Bureau's public image. Washington being Washington and politics being politics, a few months had become six, and then twelve, and now, almost two years later, he was still at the helm.

Nevertheless, he knew his days were numbered. The White House had put out its short list and he wasn't on it.

That was fine. Kline wasn't even sure he wanted the job. At the end of the day, he was a cop, not a politician. But what bothered him most was the uncertainty of his future. Where did he go from here?

His first choice would be to take his old job as head of the Intelligence Directorate back, but whether he would be able to do that depended on who actually took over the top spot. It wouldn't be unusual for a new director to clear out the old guard. There were of course plenty of other jobs out there for someone with his experience, but Kline had trouble imagining a life outside the Bureau. And retiring? He couldn't see himself doing that at all.

Although . . .

Lately, he'd been thinking an awful lot about spending more time in Montana. Not some middle-aged cabin-in-the-woods, fly-fishing fantasy. He spent enough time there to know there was a dark underbelly beneath that Big Sky. But Montana was where Matthew lived, with Emily and the kids.

His grandkids.

The thought of him, Gavin Kline—unrepentant, lifelong bachelor—having *grandkids* still boggled his mind. He had assiduously avoided being a family man, but the older he got, the more he understood the appeal of those things he'd always written off as distractions. Not Christmas cards or birthday parties—he wasn't built for that. But just the idea of being part of someone else's life.

Part of Matty's life.

Matthew Redd. His son.

Just thinking about him made Kline's chest swell with pride. Matthew had grown into an extraordinary man, despite all of Kline's mistakes and squandered opportunities.

They would never have a traditional father-son relationship, and they were both reconciled to that. What they had was something else. They'd fought together, shoulder to shoulder. Saved each other's lives. And had come to develop a bond that had nothing to do with bloodlines. Not father and son, but brothers-in-arms. And he had convinced himself that was enough.

Mostly.

Some part of him had always believed that he could persuade Matthew to come work alongside him at the Bureau. They'd done it in the past, with Matthew working as a civilian contractor advising a fly team, on an ad hoc basis. But with the success of that endeavor behind them, Matthew had turned his focus to home and family, striving to turn a profit with the ranch and raising his two babies, along with the latest addition to the family, a young boy who had practically fallen out of the sky and into their arms. If Kline was going to pull

Matthew away from ranch life, get him to move the family east, he would need a pretty powerful incentive.

It was probably a moot point anyway. Once he turned the reins over to the next director, his ability to create the right job for Matthew Redd would be severely limited if not eliminated altogether.

For now, though, he was still the director of the FBI, and that meant enduring afternoon meetings like this one—a closed-door interagency security council convened inside the West Wing's Situation Room. The official topic was cross-domain threat convergence. In practical terms, that meant looking at where national security and law enforcement priorities overlapped, especially in the gray areas where organized crime, cyber activity, and geopolitical maneuvering blurred together.

Russia was the driving concern today. Not the war in Ukraine exactly but the strategic noise surrounding it. The president claimed to want a comprehensive policy—diplomacy, force projection, law enforcement—though his choice to delegate oversight to the national security advisor made Kline question whether the leader of the free world actually wanted to solve the problem or just give the appearance of caring. So far, the meeting seemed like typical Washington wheel spinning.

The president's man had just finished a rundown of the latest intelligence: arms traffic moving through the Black Sea corridor, shell companies in Cyprus laundering funds for unnamed buyers, a fresh wave of ransomware attacks pinned to Eastern European syndicates. All of it with fingerprints that pointed back—indirectly—to Moscow.

"The question," the advisor said, "is how much of that activity is directed—not just tolerated—by elements inside the Kremlin."

The table stayed quiet for a beat, then the director of national intelligence broke the silence. "If you're asking whether Russian intelligence is controlling these actors directly, I'd say no. But enabling them? Absolutely. These networks have reach, liquidity, and plausible deniability."

A deputy from Treasury—mid-forties, tightly wound—jumped in. "We've traced four separate crypto funnels back to entities flagged by Europol. All laundering through art holdings and real estate. The scale of it . . . This isn't just a few bad actors freelancing. Someone's coordinating the movement."

The advisor nodded. "Which is why we need consensus—how do we treat this? As an intelligence matter? A financial crime? Or as hybrid warfare?"

A low murmur passed around the room. Kline resisted the urge to roll his eyes. This was the part where everyone picked their jurisdictional turf and dug in.

The secretary of defense leaned forward, fingertips pressed together. "We need to be careful about conflating organized crime with state policy," he said calmly. "The Russians have long relied on criminal intermediaries as unofficial assets. It's a legacy tactic. That doesn't mean they're being micromanaged. Sometimes chaos is just . . . useful."

Kline regarded the man. He hadn't expected the SecDef to be the one pumping the brakes. Most of the DOD people he'd known saw every crisis as a nail begging to feel the hammer of the United States military.

After that, the conversation splintered into side exchanges—intel-sharing agreements, Treasury warrants, NATO liaisons. Typical interagency churn. No one wanted to own the problem, just to make sure their agency wasn't left holding the bag.

Kline paid attention, taking mental notes. There were a few sharp minds at the table who understood the problem, but no one put forth anything remotely resembling a comprehensive plan for dealing with it.

Finally, the national security advisor turned to him. "Director Kline, does the FBI have anything to add?"

Kline straightened in his chair. "Our policy is, as it has always been, to vigorously prosecute organized crime on American soil, regardless of whether it's state sponsored. But we recognize that the lines are getting blurrier—and that these networks don't stop at borders, physical or digital."

He let that hang a moment, then added, "So let me say this clearly. The Bureau is committed to working hand in hand with our partners across the interagency community. We'll share what we know and follow the evidence where it leads. No silos. No turf wars. That's the commitment. While I'm still in the chair, at least."

A few heads nodded. No one objected.

He stood with the rest of the room as the meeting adjourned. Outside, aides began swapping notes and blocking out time for the next round of briefings. Kline stayed back, watching the knot of suits shift and re-form like chess pieces. He could already see a future where his seat was filled by someone less interested in nuance and far more interested in optics.

But for now, it was still his Bureau, and that made it his problem.

TWO

RICHLAND, MICHIGAN
THREE MONTHS LATER

The townhouses formed a neat row along one side of the cul-de-sac. On the other, bare-limbed trees—venerable oaks and maples, their branches just beginning to bud after the first spring rains—sheltered the residences from the main road, hiding their presence from passing motorists. A single streetlamp near the turnoff cast a pale amber cone across the pavement, but aside from that, and the pale light of the waning half-moon rising out over the lake, all was dark and still.

The watcher, perched high in the upper branches of an oak tree, had no difficulty penetrating those shadows. All was revealed in the objective of the AN/PVS-22 Universal Night Sight scope clipped onto the upper rail of his Knight's Armament SR-25 rifle. The scope was an older model—a Gen III image intensifier, relying on ambient light amplification to render the world in crisp gradients of green. Not exactly cutting-edge technology anymore, but it sufficed.

His scope settled on the third house from the left. The target.

Nothing stirred within. No movement behind the curtains. No silhouettes pacing past upstairs lights or television sets playing late-night talk shows. Everyone was asleep, or at least doing a good job of faking it.

He remained motionless for a while, watching. Listening. Then, satisfied with his original assessment, he began scanning, sweeping down the lane and back up the tree line—

There you are.

Four figures were advancing from the direction of the main road. They wore dark attire. Not tactical combat gear, but . . . were those tracksuits?

The realization elicited a faint chuckle from the watcher.

Russians.

They moved in a close single file, making a show of being stealthy, but it obviously wasn't their strong suit. As they came even with the corner of the row, two of them peeled off and headed in the direction of the lake, obviously intending to come up on the rear of the townhouse, where they would be hidden from his view.

Can't be helped, he thought.

The other two continued forward, staying near the tree line opposite the townhouses until they were standing across from the front door of the target. They hesitated, checking the street, then started across—quick, low steps meant to look like trained movement. But their footwork was sloppy. No coordination. No awareness of the camera mounted above the garage door or the faint red glow of the sensor beneath the eaves.

Amateurs.

The moment they stepped onto the walkway, the porch-mounted floodlight snapped on, bathing the men and most of the front yard in a swath of brilliance. The watcher in the tree winced as the night scope flared brightly, its image instantly blown out. He blinked, shifted off the rifle, and continued watching, unaided by technology, as the fireworks began.

THREE

The man sleeping alone in the upper story front bedroom of the townhouse registered the sudden change in light and opened his eyes a fraction of a second later to confirm it. The motion-activated front flood had just switched on.

There might have been a perfectly innocent explanation for this—a feral cat roaming the yard, a plastic bag or some other bit of litter carried on the wind, a neighbor receiving a late-night DoorDash delivery—and were he an ordinary homeowner, he probably would have dismissed it as such, rolled over, and gone back to sleep.

Aaron Decker, however, was not an ordinary homeowner.

His gut told him that something was wrong, and he hadn't lived as long as he had by ignoring it.

He sat up, swung his bare feet onto the carpeted floor, and moved quickly to the walk-in closet, where he shoved aside several shirts on hangers to reveal what looked like a closed electrical panel inset in the back wall. When he lifted the latch, however, an entire section of the wall swung out, revealing a narrow vertical shaft, illumed with recessed lighting. A steel ladder was mounted to the back of the shaft.

Decker did not mount the ladder, though. Instead, he swept out of the room and crossed the hall to one of the smaller bedrooms.

Under normal circumstances, he would not have entered his seventeen-year-old daughter's room without knocking and asking permission first. He respected both her privacy and her increasing autonomy. He also trusted her implicitly.

These were not normal circumstances.

He crossed to her bed, where she lay on her side, curled up under the covers, earbuds in, phone screen dark on the nightstand. He laid a hand on her shoulder. "Brynn, honey. Wake up."

She startled under his touch. "Dad? What—"

"Fire drill."

She groaned but, to her credit, didn't question or protest. This was a procedure they had rehearsed dozens of times over the years, and while she often complained about it after the fact, when he spoke those two words, she took it seriously.

He turned away before she could throw back the covers and darted back into the hall, then took three quick steps to the next room. As he reached for the doorknob, he heard a loud thud from below, followed almost simultaneously by an equally loud bang.

Someone had just kicked open the front door, causing it to slam into the wall.

The twin impacts were followed immediately by the loud, rhythmic beep of the alarm panel registering a breach.

Decker crossed to the bed where his ten-year-old son lay, sprawled sideways across the mattress, blanket wrapped around one leg. Decker shook him gently but firmly. "Mitch, buddy. Fire drill."

The boy stirred. "What? *Now?*"

"Let's go, buddy. Just like we practiced."

Mitchell was still young enough to think that the readiness drills were pretty cool, but the middle of the night was the middle of the night. He sat up groggily, then seemed to perk up. "Is that the alarm?"

"No questions. Time to move."

Decker took his son's hand and pulled him along, back toward the master bedroom, where he found Brynn standing just inside the open closet door.

"Dad, is that the alarm?" she asked, her forehead creased with real concern.

"No time," replied Decker, his voice taking on an uncharacteristic urgency. "Down you go."

Brynn pivoted, moved inside the walk-in, and stepped onto the ladder. As soon as she had descended below floor level, Decker nudged Mitchell forward.

The boy, now fully awake, stepped onto the ladder and scurried down. Decker lingered only long enough to pull the closet door shut, then entered the shaft as well, activating a switch to close the hidden door behind him.

The ladder dropped down nearly fifty feet, below the level of the garage floor and directly into an underground room with roughly the same dimensions as the living room two stories overhead. Brynn and Mitchell stood just to the side, staring at him wide-eyed.

Brynn spoke first. "Dad, what's going on?"

"I don't know yet, baby girl," he replied, moving past her to the back wall of the shelter where a large high-def television displayed on its quartered screen the feed from four of the nearly two dozen hidden security cameras placed both inside and outside the townhouse. One of them revealed a pair of figures moving up the stairs to the top level.

Two men, wearing dark clothes and balaclavas, carrying pistols.

Decker blinked, processing what he was seeing.

Another of the split screens abruptly flashed, changing to display the feed from another of the motion-activated cameras. Two more gunmen had just come in through the slider on the back deck.

Four shooters.

Decker knew this wasn't just a random home invasion. They were here for *him.*

He cursed his own complacency.

For a decade and a half, he'd lived as though the past had been buried with the nameless body fished from a river in Eastern Europe. He'd convinced himself that the men who set up the ambush in Kyiv—and the still-unidentified traitor inside the unit who had sent his team to die—had completely bought the deception, called off the hunt, and moved on.

Now he knew better.

He couldn't fathom what had changed, what had put him back on the radar, and ultimately, it didn't matter. All that mattered was that the genie was out of the bottle. This life he'd built for himself, for his family, was over. There would be no going back.

He glanced over to the entrance vestibule and the steel vault door—six inches thick, weighing nearly a ton, and operated by a quiet hydraulic piston system hidden within the reinforced frame. The door locked with a set of interlocking steel bolts designed to withstand forced entry, shaped charges, or thermal tools. Once sealed, it could only be opened from the inside.

The smart move was to button up the shelter and stay put with his kids. The house alarm had already triggered. His phone was probably ringing upstairs right now, the monitoring service calling to ask if he needed emergency assistance. When he failed to answer, the police would be dispatched. There was little chance that the men currently moving through his home would happen upon the hidden entrances on each floor that afforded access to the ladder. After they completed their sweep of the residence and found only empty rooms, they would vanish into the night before the police cruisers showed up.

It would be over in five minutes, nothing left to do but give a statement to the police and turn in insurance claims.

But that wouldn't be the end of it.

Whoever sent these men wouldn't stop just because this team failed. Next time, they'd be smarter. Maybe their next attempt would come when he was away from home, away from the refuge of his shelter.

And they would keep coming until he, and everyone he loved, was dead.

"Dad?"

He turned.

Brynn was sitting on one of the futon couches that served as the shelter's only furnishings, her arms wrapped protectively around Mitchell, once again assuming the role she'd stepped into the night her mother died.

She was seventeen going on thirty.

Christine would've been proud.

He knew what he had to do.

Staying put would win them a night—maybe even a few days—but it wouldn't stop what was coming. The only way to protect his children now was to go on the offensive.

Fight back.

Send a message.

"It's going to be okay," he said softly.

Then, before either of them could question this bland assertion, he crossed to the corner of the shelter, where his gun safe—a Liberty National Magnum series, outfitted with a biometric lock—stood bolted to the concrete floor.

When she'd learned that she was pregnant with Brynn, Christine had demanded he get rid of his guns. *"I won't have them lying around the house where the kids can get at them. It's too dangerous."*

Of course, she'd had no idea what he did for a living. As far as she knew, he was a veteran, now working as an insurance adjuster. She thought the guns were a hobby. A holdover from his time in the Marines.

She would have been horrified to know the truth.

The safe had been a compromise she had grudgingly accepted, but only with his promise that he would always—*always*—keep the firearms locked up tight.

And even though she was four years gone, he kept that promise.

He placed his hand on the fingerprint reader, heard a soft chirp, followed by the click of internal bolts disengaging. He swung open the door to reveal a small arsenal.

Decker quickly scanned the selection, dismissing the heavier pieces—a Daniel Defense MK18 chambered in 5.56 NATO, a SCAR 17S in 7.62, a Benelli M4 Tactical 12-gauge—and moved down to the handguns. This would be a close-quarters battle.

He decided on the Glock 19, which was already outfitted with a Dead Air Ghost 45M suppressor. He slid in a fifteen-round magazine loaded with Federal Premium HST, 147-grain subsonic 9mm, and released the slide, racking a round into the chamber, then grabbed two more magazines. It was only when he reached to stuff the spares in the back pocket of his pants that he realized he had no back pocket, and for that matter, no pants. All he was wearing was a pair of navy blue boxer briefs.

Well, that's unfortunate, he thought.

He slipped one of the spares in the elastic waistband, left the other behind, and then turned to leave . . .

And saw Brynn and Mitchell staring at him . . . or rather at the pistol in his hand, eyes wide in disbelief.

The look felt like a knife to the heart. His job was to comfort them, make them feel safe. Not terrorize them.

But that's not the world they live in anymore.

"I'm going up," he said, moving past them. "Do not open this door for anyone but me."

Brynn shook her head. "Dad—wait. What are you—"

He didn't stop. As soon as he reached the doorway, he activated the switch to close the door, slipping through as it began to close with a hiss of hydraulics.

"Dad!" Brynn cried, leaping to her feet.

He glanced back, meeting her eyes through the diminishing gap. "It's going to be okay. I'll be right—"

The door slammed shut, sealing the two children inside, and locking him out.

With the men who had come to kill him.

FOUR

Brynn stood frozen in place for a long moment after the vault door sealed with an ominous final thud. Mitchell leaned against her, confused but trusting, the way little brothers always were when they didn't know what else to do. She kept an arm wrapped around him, partly for his comfort, partly because if she let go, she wasn't sure what she might do.

He left us.

That thought looped on repeat in her head.

It didn't make sense. The whole point of the fire drills and the shelter and the camera system was to *stay put.* Her father had drilled that into them more times than she could count.

"If someone breaks in, we stay right here where we're safe. Nobody's getting through that door."

But he hadn't called the police. Instead, he'd grabbed a gun and gone out to meet the intruders like some kind of cinematic action hero.

Brynn glanced over at the door of the safe. Her father, in his haste, had failed to block his collection from her view before locking it shut. Her heart began to race.

She had known that he owned guns but, until this moment, had not realized how many or how varied. These were the kind of firearms she'd only seen in movies. Brynn didn't like guns. Didn't like shooting them, and didn't like the fact that there were so many of them out there in the world. Her father had taken her shooting once—just a handgun—and the experience had only reinforced her opinion. She hated the noise, the recoil, the *smell* . . . But more than anything else, she hated that ominous feeling of having the power to snuff out someone's life in the palm of her hand.

She tore her gaze away from the safe and instead looked over at the TV. The screen, divided into four frames, flickered every time a new camera was activated. The infrared images looked grainy, washed-out, and the rooms—*her* living room, *her* kitchen, the hallway outside *her* bedroom—looked completely alien. It didn't help that in each one, a figure clad head to toe in black moved through the frame, holding a gun.

One of them opened her bedroom door and went inside.

Brynn suddenly felt nauseous. Violated. Her room was her sanctuary, and some stranger had just walked in like he owned the place.

Mitchell didn't say anything, but kept hugging her tight, his eyes also on the screen.

A flash of motion in one of the lower frames distracted Brynn. She glanced down just in time to see the man in the kitchen jerk suddenly, as if touching a live wire, and then collapse. In the adjoining frame, the man in the living room pivoted toward the kitchen, gun raised. He managed half a step before he too folded and went down like a sack of concrete.

Then another figure appeared in the kitchen feed, darting past the man lying there and out of the frame. He reappeared in the living room feed, stepped over the second unmoving form, and kept going, flashing into view on another frame, as he began ascending the stairs.

Dad?

For a heartbeat, Brynn didn't understand.

And then she did.

She pressed a hand over her mouth, but it was too late. The knowledge hit her like a punch to the gut. She had just watched two men shot dead.

Not in a movie or a TV show, but right here in her house.

And it was her father who had done it.

Brynn felt the world tilt under her feet, as if the very laws that governed it—right and wrong, safe and unsafe—had been quietly rewritten when she wasn't looking. And in that new, broken world, her father wasn't just the man who tucked her in at night.

He was the man people feared in the dark.

Mitchell shifted beside her, small and warm and utterly defenseless, and the sight of him was enough to snap the thread of panic coiling inside her. She twisted, putting her body between him and the screen, shielding him from what she could never unsee.

"Hey," she said, forcing calm into her voice. "Let's not watch right now, okay?"

Mitchell didn't argue. He just leaned against her.

Brynn hugged him tighter, unable to tear her eyes away as her father reached the top story landing and kept going.

FIVE

Decker swept through his own home like the angel of death.

The upstairs landing was empty. No movement.

He cleared Mitchell's room—*bed empty, closet door ajar but no one inside.*

The hall bathroom—*empty.*

Brynn's room—*clear.*

Only one place left.

Decker edged through the open door to his own bedroom. Two flashlight beams shone from within, one near the bed, the other illuminating the walk-in closet. He sighted fast and fired again. The first man dropped instantly, collapsing forward onto the bed. The second started to turn, requiring a slight targeting adjustment, then he too fell.

Suddenly, the smoke detector shrieked to life overhead, triggered by the muzzle gases swirling through the air of the enclosed space, adding one more discordant note to the symphony of chaos. Decker tuned out the cacophony, focusing on the immediate task of identifying the would-be killers.

He'd seen four intruders on the camera feed, but they might not have come alone. Even now, reinforcements might be making their way up the drive, coming in through front or back doors, ready to finish what their ill-fated comrades had started. There wasn't a second to waste.

He went to the man sprawled across his bed, flipped him over, and did a quick pat down. No wallet. No phone.

No surprise.

At least they got that right.

He picked up the man's flashlight—a little LED number not much bigger than a tube of Chapstick—and held it in his gun hand, shining it on the dead man's head as he peeled up the balaclava. The rough-shaven face beneath it had blunt features, Slavic cheekbones, dark hair cropped close to the scalp. He looked to be middle-aged, with a thick build like a heavyweight boxer gone to seed.

A thug, thought Decker. *Not an operator.*

Still holding the flashlight pinned awkwardly against his pistol grip, Decker stepped around the bed and reached for his phone on the nightstand with his free hand, noting the missed call alert on the lock screen—the alarm company, no doubt. He ignored it, opening the phone and scrolling to the camera app, framing the man's face in the display.

In the sudden brilliance of the auto flash, Decker spotted something on the man's neck just below the ear—a smudge of ink, half hidden by the collar of the track jacket.

He saved the photo to the cloud, then set the phone aside in order to tug down the man's collar and reveal the neck tattoo. The ink was old, the image faded, but nevertheless distinct—a crude eight-pointed black star, almost like a compass rose, with a ribbon of Cyrillic letters beneath it: ВОР В ЗАКОНЕ.

"Vor v zakone," he muttered. *Thief-in-law.*

Russian mob.

Any doubts he might have had about the connection between this attack and that incident fifteen years earlier had just evaporated.

His past had finally caught up to him.

The house, the quiet life, the evenings spent helping Brynn with calculus homework or tossing a football around the backyard with Mitch—all of it was over now.

The fantasy that he could ever escape the life he'd lived—the blood he'd spilled—had been just that. A fantasy. The past hadn't been dead after all; it had just been biding its time.

He let the regret settle for exactly three seconds.

Then he buried it.

There was no time for grief now. No room for anything but cold, ruthless action.

First priority: Protect the kids. Go off-grid, somewhere they won't even know to look for us.

Easier said than done.

The enemy shouldn't have known to look for them *here*—should never have learned Decker's real name. But somehow, they had. And if that most closely guarded secret wasn't secret anymore, where could he go? Who could he trust for help?

He couldn't turn to Gavin Kline again. The enemy would almost certainly have learned of his connection to the interim director of the FBI. In fact, it was probably one of the off-the-books favors he'd done for Kline in recent months that had pinged him.

Sloppy, Decker. You did this to yourself.

But thinking about Kline put him in mind of someone else. Someone *outside* the system.

Someone who owed him a favor.

First things first.

He moved to the dresser, pulled on a T-shirt emblazoned with the logo of Grolier Recovery Services and a pair of jeans, stuffing the Glock into the waistband, then grabbed his trail runners from under the bed and headed back into the closet. He stepped over the body sprawled there and opened the panel that hid the ladder shaft.

Still barefoot, he slid down the ladder, entering the vestibule to the shelter, and pressed the intercom panel beside the massive steel door.

"Brynn, it's Dad. You can open up now."

The door didn't move.

After waiting nearly thirty seconds, he pressed the button again, keeping his voice even. "Brynn, it's me. It's safe. Open the door."

Nothing. What was going on in there?

Decker fought back a surge of impatience. They didn't have time for this. He was about to send another prompt when, finally, he heard the bolts disengage. The door swung open to reveal Brynn and Mitchell standing just beyond the threshold.

Decker stepped through, moved past them to the gun safe. He unlocked it, crouched, pulled a soft-sided carrying case from the bottom shelf, and began stuffing weapons into it. No time to be choosy. In went the MK18 carbine, the shotgun, and all of the handguns. He added a Kevlar plate carrier and chest rig, several boxes of ammunition, and two prepaid cellular phones. As he worked, he spoke over his shoulder. "We're leaving. Don't worry about packing."

No answer.

He zipped the case, hefted it onto a shoulder, and finally turned to look at them.

They were still standing near the door, frozen like statues, staring at him like he was some kind of monster. Then Mitchell's eyes left him, flitting to something behind his father. Decker looked in the same direction and realized Mitchell's gaze had gone to the flat screen, which was still displaying the camera feeds.

The living room. The kitchen.

The bodies of the intruders.

They'd seen everything. They'd seen him kill.

Brynn's voice broke the silence. "Who are you?"

Decker just stood there, the gun case weighing him down like an anchor. Brynn's question hit him harder than any bullet ever could. Because in her eyes, he didn't just see fear. He saw betrayal. And for a sick, aching moment, he thought he was looking at Christine.

"Who are you?"

Christine would have asked him that if she had ever learned the truth about him. He had kept that part of his life separate—secret—to protect her, or at least that was what he had tried to believe. But really, hadn't he done it to protect himself, from something exactly like this moment?

For a second, the urge to explain—to *justify*—rose in him. But there wasn't time.

Later. If there is a later.

"I'll explain everything," he said, meeting her stare. "But right now, we have to go."

For a moment, Brynn didn't react. Then something changed in her eyes. It was as if something clicked inside her, stiffening her spine. She might not understand what was happening yet, but she recognized the urgency of the situation. Whatever she was feeling about him, about what she had just seen, would have to wait. Right now, keeping Mitchell safe was her highest priority.

She's not just Christine's daughter, Decker thought grimly. *She's mine too.*

Brynn released Mitchell from her embrace and took his hand. "Come on. It's time to go."

Mitchell looked up at her in confusion. "I'm in my pajamas."

Brynn squeezed his hand. "So am I, buddy. Dad will take care of it later."

Her acceptance snapped Decker back into action. As soon as they were outside in the vestibule, he went back in just long enough to activate the shelter's lockdown sequence. He slipped through as the thick steel door began to swing closed, and just before it slammed shut, he tossed his phone inside. Then, with the gun case once more slung over his shoulder, he mounted the ladder.

"Follow me," he said, and began the climb.

Brynn waited just long enough for him to clear space, then urged Mitchell onto the ladder, by which time Decker was already activating the switch for the garage-level entrance. He emerged cautiously, ready to engage any hostiles that might have found their way inside during the brief interval. Seeing none, he stepped off into the garage, where an older-model charcoal-gray Honda CR-V—Brynn's car—and a silver Toyota Land Cruiser SUV were parked, the latter with its front end facing the garage door.

Decker grabbed the key fob for the Toyota from the hook by the door and keyed the back hatch. Behind him, Brynn stepped off the ladder and hustled Mitchell toward the passenger side of the Cruiser without needing to be told. As soon as the rear hatch was up, Decker set the gun case on the floor of the cargo area and took out one of the prepaids—an Alcatel Go Flip 3—and powered it on as he stepped back and moved forward to the driver's door. As he slid behind the wheel, he saw Brynn already buckled into the front passenger seat.

"I want you in the back," he said, in a tone that made clear it wasn't a suggestion. "On the floor, head down until we're on the road. Mitch too."

She blinked at him, processing the request, then unbuckled without argument and climbed into the back, pulling Mitchell down with her into the footwell.

Decker placed the phone in the center console and the Glock across his lap, then closed the rear hatch, started the engine, and hit the button on the garage door remote. As the door slowly rolled up, he lowered both front windows so that, if he had to use the Glock, he wouldn't be shooting out the glass, then put the Cruiser in gear.

Headlights dark, the Toyota rolled forward, down the short driveway, and onto the narrow lane leading out of the cul-de-sac. Decker kept one hand on the Glock, scanning the street, the tree line, everywhere for any hint of a looming ambush, but nothing happened.

He let the Land Cruiser roll to the corner, then made a slow right onto the main feeder road. Only once he was several blocks clear, merging onto the highway that would eventually funnel him toward Kalamazoo, did he thumb the headlights on and roll up the windows.

"Okay," he said over his shoulder. "You can get up now."

Brynn immediately scrambled back into the front passenger seat without asking permission. She didn't look at him as she buckled her seat belt. Her gaze was fixed forward, jaw set in a line of fierce determination. "Where are we going?"

"I'm still working on that." He eased the Glock down into the footwell, then took the Go Flip from the console and began dialing a number—one he'd memorized but never thought he'd need to use.

"Please tell me you're calling the police."

Decker winced just a bit. "Not quite."

"Then *what* are you doing?"

Hitting the call button, he looked at his daughter as the line began to ring. "I'm calling in a favor."

SIX

BOZEMAN, MONTANA

Matthew Redd hefted the suitcases from the back of Emily's Tahoe and set them down on the curb in front of the departures entrance to Bozeman Yellowstone International Airport. The terminal, a blend of stone and timber that looked more like a mountain lodge, was eerily quiet, with just a handful of travelers hurrying to catch the day's last flight out. In a few minutes, Mikey Derhammer, Redd's best friend in the world, would be joining them.

Earlier in the day, Mikey's wife, Liz, had gotten the call that her mother, who lived in Utah, had suffered a stroke. Mikey and Liz had scrambled to book tickets on the last available plane—BYI to Denver, where they would make a connection to Salt Lake City. While Liz packed, Mikey called Redd, asking for a ride to the airport.

There had never been a question of whether he would do it. That was just how it worked—when your friends needed you, you showed up. And Mikey, more than most people, understood that. He'd run to Redd's aid more times than Matt could count, putting his own life in danger without ever giving it so much as a second thought.

I owe him a lot more than a ride to the airport.

Redd and Emily had dropped the kids off with her folks and then picked up the Derhammers and made the drive to Bozeman, more than an hour away.

Emily joined them on the curb now, wrapping Liz in a lingering hug. "Call when you get there," she said. "No matter how late."

"I will." Liz's voice caught, just slightly, but she forced it steady. "Thank you both. For everything."

Redd wasn't much for long goodbyes, but Liz hugged him nevertheless. Theirs wasn't always the warmest of friendships. There had been a time or two, in the past, when Liz didn't want her husband to risk so much to help Redd, but when it mattered most, Liz understood that all of them were stronger together than apart, and *that* was what made them family.

When Liz finally let go of Redd's big frame, Mikey passed their sleeping son, Lucas, to his wife and threw his arms around Redd as well.

"Better get going," Redd said quietly.

Mikey pounded his friend on the back. "No world-saving missions without me."

Redd chuckled as he let go and stepped back. "I'm still recovering from the last one," he said, only half joking. "So, deal."

"Seriously, Matt, don't go getting into trouble while I'm in Utah. Who would have your back?"

Redd shrugged.

"I know you're not going to call your father-in-law. He'd be the first one to shoot you, dude."

Everyone laughed, including Redd.

The truth was, much like his relationship with Liz, Redd had once been at odds with his father-in-law, Reverend Elijah Lawrence. Though, now that Redd had a daughter of his own, he more than understood the good reverend's initial objections.

The last thing I want is for Lauren to fall for a guy like me.

Thankfully for Redd, Elijah had proven to be a man who, quite literally, practiced what he preached, and had found it in himself to forgive Redd for sins of the past, of which there were plenty. And only a few weeks ago, Redd—who'd grown in his faith, in part because of Lawrence's teaching—had been baptized by his father-in-law, with Mikey assisting, in a creek behind the small church where Elijah still preached.

"Dad loves you now, Matty. Don't listen to Mikey."

"Yeah, sure." Mikey smiled. "But he loves his daughter more, and he still loves his rusty old shotgun too, which he keeps conveniently within reach at all times just in case you—"

Liz elbowed her husband playfully in the gut.

"I mean, just in case *something* goes down."

"I'm gonna miss you, Mikey."

"You too, brother."

And then, just like that, they were gone, disappearing through the sliding doors, Liz still carrying Lucas, Mikey rolling the bags along.

Redd and Emily stood for a beat longer, then climbed back into the Tahoe for the long, lonely ride home.

"It's going to be strange without them around for a little bit," Redd remarked, filling the silence after they'd been driving for a while.

Emily's eyes lit up. "It's been good for us. Having them close. Good for you too."

"Yeah."

"Seriously, Matty. I'm so proud of the person you've become."

The compliment made Redd uncomfortable, and he didn't know what to say. "I love you, Em."

"So," she said, settling all the way back into her seat, "what are we going to do now?"

Redd hadn't given it much thought. "Business as usual. I've got a ton of chores to do around the ranch."

"What if we took a vacation?"

"A *vacation*? To where?"

"I don't know," Emily said absently. She was looking out her window, and Redd glanced over just as she adjusted her seat belt and turned back to him. "Utah?"

"Em."

"Kidding. I'm just kidding, Matty. I mean, I miss our besties already, but they'll be back soon, I hope. We've got to keep praying for Liz's mom. Poor thing."

Redd just nodded.

"But it would be nice to get out for a few days. Don't you think?"

"Maybe we could finally take that camping trip we've talked about?"

"Hmm. I was thinking more like flying to Washington to see Gavin on his turf, where he lives, and what his life is like out East, but camping might be fun."

"Good thing," said Redd. "Because DC is about the last place I want to go."

"Where would we camp?"

Redd gave it some thought before answering. "Well, we've talked about Yellowstone, right?"

"Oh, now I'm in! You know I *love* Yellowstone."

In fact, Redd did know that his wife loved Yellowstone, so the suggestion had been a calculated one, and thankfully, it had worked.

"I might even have a spot in mind that would be perfect for all of us," he added.

"We should talk about it more at home. Plan it out, and *actually* do it. We could all use a little peace and quiet for a while. It's been a tough few years, Matty. For all of us."

"Deal," said Redd. "We'll plan it out at home, think about what the kids would want to do."

"This is going to be so much fun," replied Emily, her voice now a full octave higher than it had been. Seeing his wife so happy brought a smile to Redd's face.

They fell into silence again, the dark sky filled with bright stars that just barely illuminated the tips of mountains to the west. They were finally approaching Wellington when Redd reached for the dial on his center console and spun it to the right. Mac Powell's "New Creation" was just coming to an end. A heartbeat later, the opening chords of "Hard Fought Hallelujah" blared through the Tahoe's speakers.

Though he wasn't the sing-along type, Redd was fond of the song, a collaboration between Brandon Lake and Jelly Roll, which almost perfectly articulated how he felt inside.

He was deep in thought when the music suddenly stopped, the sound replaced by the default ringtone on Redd's iPhone, which was buzzing from inside the cup holder next to him.

He glanced down at the glowing screen, but before he could reach for it, Emily picked it up. She looked at the display for a moment, then regarded him with one eyebrow arched in a look of mock suspicion.

"Who do you know in Michigan?"

SEVEN

MICHIGAN

Forty minutes later, on the outskirts of Battle Creek, Decker turned into a run-down, no-name twenty-four-hour self-storage outfit. He punched in the gate code and then drove down the rows until he found the one he was looking for. With Brynn and Mitchell looking on silently, he got out, unlocked unit D-236, and raised the roll-down door.

Inside, surrounded on three sides by large black Rubbermaid Action-Packer storage boxes, was a dark green 2018 Jeep Cherokee Trailhawk, which he had purchased years earlier using the same alias printed on the Michigan driver's license and passport that now sat in the Jeep's glove box.

He started the Jeep and eased it out of the unit, then directed Brynn and Mitchell to get in. He pulled the Land Cruiser inside the unit and, after transferring the soft case containing his weapons to the Jeep along with several of the storage boxes, locked it up again. Five minutes after arriving, they were back on the road, heading northeast on Interstate 69.

Mitchell fell asleep somewhere along the way and lay curled up in the back seat under a sleeping bag retrieved from one of the storage boxes. Brynn, however, remained awake, quietly gazing out the windshield as the miles rolled by. Decker gave her space, dreading the inevitable moment when she would break the silence. Shortly after making the turn onto US Highway 127, she did.

"So, are you going to tell me what's happening?" she asked, not meeting his gaze.

Even though he had his answer ready, Decker let the question hang in the air a moment. "You know that I was in the military," he began.

"The Marines."

He nodded. "Well, I was assigned to a special activity team. Our missions were beyond top secret."

Her eyes finally swung toward him, regarding him with unmasked skepticism. "Dad, seriously?"

He lifted a hand off the steering wheel. "Scout's honor. But all that was a long time ago."

"What kind of missions? Like, are we talking about assassinations and Jason Bourne kind of stuff?"

Decker blinked. He'd thought he was ready to explain, but he hadn't expected her to ask *that.* He wasn't sure what startled him more—the bluntness of the question or how she hadn't asked it like a teenager, but like someone who already knew the answer.

"I . . . uh . . ."

"That's a yes." She exhaled slowly, processing, and then turned her eyes forward again. "So, what was that tonight? Someone settling a score? Or do you know too much?"

"I think you've seen too many movies."

She whirled on him. "Really? I just watched you kill two men. *Kill* them, Dad. And don't take this wrong, but it looked like you've done that before and that it . . . that it . . ."

"That it what?" asked Decker.

"I dunno. That it didn't even bother you."

"Brynn—"

"Don't treat me like . . ." In the back seat, Mitchell mumbled something, prompting Brynn to lower her voice, but the fire of her anger remained undiminished. "Don't treat me like I'm the crazy one, Dad. Don't sit there and act like this is just another Tuesday night."

Decker's hands stayed loose on the wheel, but inside, something twisted. Something deep.

She's not being unreasonable, he told himself. But even so, he wasn't ready to share everything with her. He might never be ready for that.

"They came into our house," he finally said quietly. "They were after me, but they would have killed you too. You and Mitchell. I did what I had to do. Nothing more, nothing less."

"Yeah, well, it looked like you've done *that* plenty. You probably just never thought you'd have to do it *in front of us.*"

Her words hit like body blows. Decker didn't flinch physically, but he might as well have. He opened his mouth, then shut it again. What could he say that wouldn't sound like a lie?

Brynn turned back toward the windshield, wrapping her arms around herself like she could hold her body together through sheer force of will. "Did Mom know?"

He knew the price he would pay for telling her the truth, but also knew that the price of a lie, even a well-intentioned one, would be so much higher. "No."

"So, you lied to her. The whole time you were together?"

"Brynn, it's not like—"

She held up a hand to cut him off. "I don't even know who you are anymore," she said, voice low and shaking. "And I don't think I want to know."

Decker swallowed against the sudden rawness in his throat. He kept his eyes locked on the road ahead.

"You know who I am, Brynn," he said at last, almost a whisper. "I'm the man who would do anything—*anything*—to keep you and your brother safe."

"Dad . . . you're the reason we're in danger. *You.*"

He hung his head. "I know. And I am going to find a way to fix this. But it's going to take a little time."

Brynn didn't answer. She just stared out into the dark beyond the windshield, arms still folded tight.

"I didn't . . . keep this secret from your mom because I didn't love her," he said. "I did it because I thought . . . if she knew what I'd done, what I was capable of . . ." He trailed off.

"That she'd leave you?"

"I kept that part of my life separate. Maybe that was the wrong thing to do.

I don't know. But, honey, I left that life behind when you were still a baby. Shut that door. Locked it. Threw away the key. I did everything I could to make sure it wouldn't follow me."

"But it did."

"Yeah," he said. "Somehow, it did."

She considered this for a moment. "You've been out? For real?"

He nodded. "For a long time."

Even as he said it, he realized that he wasn't being completely truthful. He had left Rogue Unit behind, but he'd continued the work with his *favors* for Gavin Kline.

"It didn't look that way tonight. You were *ready.*"

"I guess I knew there was always a possibility that something like this might happen. That's why I took precautions."

"Like the shelter? And the guns?"

He nodded. "Like the shelter and the guns."

She sighed, and he sensed some of her earlier anger ebbing. "Well, at least you're one of the good guys, right? I mean, you're not into anything, like, illegal."

Decker hesitated. Did he dare tell her everything? Could he risk not telling her? "Some people," he said, choosing his words carefully, "might say otherwise."

She cocked her head to the side. "Let me guess. You were doing the wrong thing for the right reason."

Decker shrugged. "Sometimes that's what you have to do to make the world a safer place."

"By killing people."

"Look, Brynn, the world isn't as black-and-white as you think. What you saw tonight, as much as I wish you hadn't, that's what happens in a war. And believe me, that was war. These weren't good people. They were all very bad men—period."

She turned to look at him again. "Okay, so who were they?"

"Mob muscle, Russians. Settling an old score."

"So, what happens now?"

"We're going off-grid. Do you remember your grandpa's cabin up in the UP?"

Her forehead creased as if trying to access a memory. "Kind of. We went camping there once, didn't we?"

He nodded. "You were six. It was the summer before Mitchell was born."

"I remember there were a lot of bugs."

"That's putting it mildly." He allowed himself a small grin in return. "It's not exactly the Four Seasons. No electricity, no plumbing. Just a couple of rooms and a woodstove. It's way off the road in the middle of nowhere. Which is exactly why we're going."

The cabin had belonged to Christine's father—a battered A-frame tucked into the woods north of Seney, surrounded by sugar maples and long-forgotten logging trails. When they'd first gone up there as a family, Christine had been adamant that they'd fix it up one day. She'd talked about putting in solar panels, restoring the dock, maybe even turning it into a seasonal rental. But then Mitchell came along. And before he was old enough to swing a stick at the lake's edge, Christine got sick.

After she died, they never went back. And when her father passed not long after, the cabin became an afterthought—its ownership buried somewhere in probate paperwork and half-settled estates. Decker wasn't sure who it belonged to anymore.

"We're going to stay there?" asked Brynn, dubious.

"Just for a couple days. It'll take them a while to even realize it's an option for us, and by then, we'll already be gone."

"You really think they'll keep coming."

"I know they will."

Silence settled over the car again, this time heavier. Then, softly, she said, "Okay."

Decker glanced at her. "Okay?"

She nodded once, still staring out into the dark. "Just . . . promise me you won't keep any more secrets from me."

His throat tightened. "I promise."

"Even if they're bad."

"Even then."

She didn't say anything else. But she didn't pull away either. And that, for now, was enough.

EIGHT

RICHLAND, MICHIGAN

Konstantin wanted a drink.

No, he *needed* a drink. Desperately. Something to fortify him for the phone call he knew he had to make. Unfortunately, he was stuck here, in the front passenger seat of a black Mercedes GLE 450, in the parking lot of a suburban office complex, watching the turnoff to the cul-de-sac and wondering what was going on.

And what had gone wrong.

Because things had definitely not gone according to plan. The hit team should have been in and out in a matter of minutes—five at the most.

Get in, get it done, get out. That was what he had told them.

But now, nearly three hours later, he had no idea if they had succeeded.

What he did know was that fifteen minutes after the shooters got out of the car, the first police cruiser had arrived. Another showed up a few minutes later. After that, it was as if the floodgates had opened. The entire cul-de-sac had been cordoned off within half an hour. A mobile command unit showed up next, along with crime scene techs and uniforms with long guns.

No ambulances, though.

Whatever had happened inside the house, it hadn't gone smoothly for the hit team.

He'd warned them that the man was formerly part of an elite military team, but the shooters—all soldiers in Chicago's *Vory v Zakone*—what Americans called the *Bratva*, "the Brotherhood"—had dismissed his concerns.

And evidently, they had paid a steep price.

But what about Decker?

He pinched the bridge of his nose, frustration boiling just under the surface. The only thing worse than a botched operation was a botched operation with unanswered questions.

When he'd first begun investigating the "ghost" of the man he'd killed in Kyiv, he'd quickly found himself at a dead end. The passport the man had used at the airport had led nowhere. At least, not for Konstantin. Volkov, however, had access to deeper channels. How deep, Konstantin still didn't know. Maybe a contact inside one of the Western intelligence agencies. Maybe something even more elaborate than that. Whatever it was, it had produced results, albeit slowly. Finally, nearly three months after the initial sighting, Volkov produced a name: Aaron Decker. And more importantly, an address in Richland, Michigan.

"You're going to America, Kostya," Volkov had told him. *"Coordinate with the avtoritet in Chicago. It's his home, so be respectful."*

Konstantin hadn't liked that arrangement. He didn't know the players in America. Didn't know if he could rely on them or trust them. Unknown quantities were a complication. But that was the way of it. The *avtoritet*—Yegor Petrovich—controlled the territory, and there was no operating on his turf without his blessing. Naturally, Petrovich insisted on using his own men.

"They're good," he'd told Konstantin over the phone. *"Loyal. And they know their way around."*

Loyal or not, Konstantin had his doubts the moment he met them. Too much flash, not enough discipline. The kind of men who cared more about gold chains and Instagram followers than getting the job done.

Still, what choice did he have? At least using locals would eliminate any trails leading back to Moscow.

So, the five of them—Konstantin and the four shooters—had loaded into the Mercedes and made the three-hour drive from Chicago to Richland, where they'd idled away the evening at a steakhouse, moderating their vodka intake somewhat. After a quick drive-by to familiarize themselves with the target location, they'd pulled into the parking lot, where they'd wait to make their move.

Konstantin had stayed behind in the car. He didn't know these men, hadn't worked with them, and wasn't willing to put his life in their hands. When the authorities eventually investigated the slaughter, he needed to be sure that nothing would lead back to him. Or Volkov.

Either way, it would be over in a matter of minutes.

But not one of them had returned. And now the place was crawling with cops.

Konstantin didn't know whether to drive away or stay put. Would the police notice a vehicle pulling away? Would they be curious enough to follow? He decided it wasn't worth the risk. That drink would have to wait. The phone call, however, could not.

Volkov would be awake—it was just after noon in Moscow—but that didn't make the call any easier.

He exhaled and tapped the screen. The line clicked once, then twice, and then Volkov answered. "Yes?"

"It's me," Konstantin said, his voice low. "We have a problem."

There was a beat of silence. Then, "You failed."

"I don't know," he said quickly. "The men went in, but they never came back out. Cops are everywhere now. Whatever happened, it wasn't clean. For all I know, they killed each other."

"We should be so lucky," Volkov rumbled. "You didn't go in with them? I told you to make certain he was dead."

"You told me to coordinate with the *avtoritet* in Chicago," Konstantin said, forcing calm. "It's Petrovich's turf. He made the decision."

"And you have no idea if Decker survived," Volkov said, then sighed. "All right. Let me make a call."

Konstantin leaned back in the passenger seat, staring out through the windshield at the pulsing blue lights beyond the tree line, and rubbed a hand across his face. What now? He couldn't stay parked here all night, but he couldn't leave without knowing what had gone wrong.

A minute passed. Two.

Then his phone buzzed.

He swiped to answer, pressing the phone to his ear.

"The police found four bodies in the house," Volkov said without greeting. "All dead of gunshot wounds. All of them soldiers of the Vory—identified by their tattoos. No one else alive or dead inside."

Konstantin felt his guts begin to churn. "He got out?"

"Obviously," Volkov snapped. "And now he knows someone is after him."

"Then we've lost the element of surprise."

"Yes," Volkov said darkly. "*You* lost it."

Konstantin bit back his instinct to argue. "What do we do now?"

"We go after him. This doesn't end until he's dead."

"How do we find him? It took almost three months to get this far."

"Three months ago, we didn't know who he was. Now we do." He paused as if debating whether to say more, then added, "You'll have a new target location within twenty-four hours. Be ready."

The line went dead.

Konstantin stared at the dark screen for a moment longer, then lowered the phone to his lap.

Decker was alive. Worse, he was aware that he was being hunted. And now the hunt would be that much harder.

NINE

UPPER PENINSULA, MICHIGAN

The road had stopped pretending to be a road five miles ago. Now it was little more than a narrow dirt track, rutted and overgrown, snaking its way through a dense tangle of spruce, birch, and pine. The Trailhawk bumped and rocked as it pushed forward, branches scraping against the sides like skeletal fingers. Brynn sat in the back seat with Mitchell, watching the foliage blur past, her arms once again folded tightly across her chest.

They hadn't seen another house in at least an hour.

The nearest town was Seney—barely a dot on the map—almost thirty miles to the south. That was where they had stopped briefly for groceries earlier that morning. Cell signal had dried up not long after that.

This is a nightmare, thought Brynn.

Mitchell, by contrast, was practically vibrating with energy.

"This is so cool," he whispered, nose pressed to the glass. "It's like we're the last survivors of a zombie apocalypse."

Brynn didn't share his enthusiasm. She wanted to be supportive. She'd told her father she was on his side. That she understood. That she was grateful.

But every time she closed her eyes, she saw those men. The way their bodies had collapsed. The way her father had moved through the house with such brutal calm. Efficient. Detached.

He wasn't the man she thought he was. And while she was trying to accept that, it wasn't coming easy.

The trees broke at last, revealing a clearing cut long ago from the forest. The cabin stood in the center—a squat, weathered structure of gray logs and moss-covered shingles. The windows were small and shuttered. A hundred feet from the cabin, a small wooden structure half swallowed by tall grass leaned at a questionable angle.

Please tell me that's not an outhouse, she thought.

"Wow," Mitchell breathed. "Is this it?"

Decker nodded from the driver's seat, cutting the engine. "This is it."

They climbed out. The air smelled of pine needles and loam. But that was about the only positive thing Brynn could say about the place. There was no satellite dish. No solar panels. No power lines.

"Tell me there's a bathroom," she pleaded.

Decker nodded toward the leaning shack.

"Nope," Brynn muttered. "Absolutely not."

He laughed. "Relax. I brought along a portable compost toilet. We can fill the water jugs from that." He pointed to an old iron pump beside the front porch.

Mitchell jogged toward the pump and gave the handle a try. Nothing. He leaned into it with both arms, and after a few creaks and groans from the mechanism, water sputtered from the spout. "Awesome!"

Brynn turned in a slow circle, feeling the isolation press in. Trees in every direction. No neighbors. No help.

And no escape.

Her father was already unlocking the cabin door.

She followed him up the steps. The air inside the cabin was stale and musty, the space lit only by the pale morning light filtering through moss-streaked windows. A cast-iron stove squatted in one corner of the main room, flanked by a pair of weathered Adirondack chairs and a table on which sat an old-fashioned kerosene lantern. A mouse-chewed blanket hung limp over the back of a pinewood couch. Dust coated every surface.

Brynn's nose wrinkled. "Okay, gross. When was the last time anyone came out here?"

Her father set the duffel of gear down beside the door. "Probably the last time we were here."

Brynn shook her head, then rolled up the sleeves of the hoodie Decker had purchased for her in Seney and leaned out the door. "Mitch, grab the paper towels and cleaning wipes from the Jeep."

"What are you going to do?" asked Decker.

She shrugged. "Try'n make this place suck less."

She found an old broom by the hearth and started sweeping, stirring up clouds of dust that caught the light like fog. By the time Mitchell returned, she had the windows open and the stale air was finally beginning to freshen.

Brynn looked over her shoulder at the old cast-iron stove. "Can you get a fire going in that thing so I can make breakfast?"

Decker shook his head, amused. "Brought a camp stove. It's cleaner. Easier."

"Then set it up," she said, all business. "I don't know about you and Mitch, but I'm starving."

He stared at her for a long time, the ghost of a smile on his lips.

"What?" she asked, bringing her hands to her hips in a show of defiance.

"It's just . . . right now, you remind me so much of your mom, it hurts."

TEN

MOSCOW, RUSSIA

Grigori Volkov sat alone in the office of his penthouse apartment, an untouched tumbler of vodka—chilled when he'd poured it, now probably lukewarm—on the desk beside him. The room was silent except for the ticking of a brass carriage clock on the mantel. Ticking away the remaining seconds of his life?

Maybe.

This situation was not good.

The call to Nightshade had gone about as well as he'd expected, which was to say not well at all. He'd dreaded having to make it. No, *dreaded* wasn't the word. He'd *feared* it, and that was no small distinction. Volkov feared nothing—not the Kremlin, not the Bratva, not even death. But Nightshade . . . He wasn't too proud to admit that he feared Nightshade.

That fear had been earned.

Their history went back more than twenty years, to a time when Volkov had been a rising predator in a sea of sharks. Moscow was still reeling from the collapse of the old regime, and the vultures were circling. He had rivals then—older, crueler men with deeper roots and bloodier reputations. He'd fought hard, clawing his way toward the top, and it might have ended there—another ambitious killer swallowed by the machine.

But then Nightshade found him.

He'd offered Volkov a bargain—impossibly lopsided, dangerously tempting. The destruction of his enemies. The keys to the kingdom. Influence beyond his imagining. All in exchange for one thing.

Fealty.

Unquestioning. Absolute.

Volkov had been skeptical. The man wasn't even Russian. What did he know of Volkov's world? But then, Nightshade had delivered.

A week later, Volkov's primary rival had died in a car bombing. No one claimed responsibility. Two more enemies went missing within the month. It was like a scythe had swept through the upper echelons of the Moscow underworld, clearing a path only Volkov could walk.

There was no longer any question that Nightshade had reach . . . power. And secrets. No one knew who he truly was. He was nothing more than a rumor, rarely spoken of. It was almost as if he was a devil, and saying his name aloud might summon him from the underworld.

Volkov hadn't questioned his good fortune. He'd accepted his place, his power—and the unspoken cost. Then, fifteen years ago, Nightshade asked a favor. A very specific one. There was a team of American operatives operating in Eastern Europe. Off the books, unofficial, effective. Nightshade wanted them taken off the board.

And when Nightshade asked, you didn't say no.

Volkov arranged the trap in Kyiv. A perfect kill box. Or so he thought. There had been a little drama at the end when one of the Americans had briefly slipped the noose, but it had been dealt with.

But then came the call from Konstantin, months ago, reporting that the lone survivor of the warehouse wasn't dead after all.

Reporting the news to Nightshade had been the first time Volkov had known fear.

Nightshade had shown restraint. He hadn't punished Volkov, not yet. Instead, he'd instructed Volkov to stand by while *he* took the lead in tracking down the elusive American operator. That exhaustive search had yielded a name. Aaron Decker. And more—an address. A precise location in the American Midwest.

That should have been the end of it. All Konstantin had to do was kill one man. *One man.* Who was asleep in his bed.

Was that really so much to ask?

Apparently.

Konstantin had failed. The hit team was dead. Decker was gone. And now Volkov was in the most dangerous position imaginable: standing between Nightshade and a still-breathing target.

The call to Nightshade still haunted him.

"What's the problem?" Nightshade's voice was tight, contemptuous. Of course, he knew there was a problem. Why else would Volkov be calling?

"He got away."

"Got away," Nightshade repeated. He didn't sound angry exactly. More like . . . incredulous. "Escaped?"

"The men we sent in . . . underestimated him."

"The men you sent." Nightshade seemed to ponder the words like some ancient riddle. "Why didn't you take care of this personally?"

"It was a mistake," Volkov admitted.

"One of several, it would seem," Nightshade said slowly. "I told you what this man was capable of. I laid it out in no uncertain terms. Did I not?"

"Yes, sir. You did. It was a matter of access. The *avtoritet* in Chicago—"

"I am not interested in the politics of your Brotherhood." Nightshade's voice hardened, every syllable perfectly clipped. "I gave you the name. I gave you the location. I practically handed him to you gift wrapped."

"I take full responsibility."

"This is not a minor setback. Now he knows. And a man like Decker, once he knows he's being hunted . . ." He let the sentence hang like a noose.

"I can fix this," Volkov promised. What else could he say? "I just need to know where he is."

"Do you know how difficult it was to find him the first time? When he didn't even know he was being hunted? He was a ghost, Grigori. His identity was buried so deep we had to peel back a dozen layers of falsehood just to find out who and where he was. And now?" His voice dropped to a venomous whisper. "Now, he knows we're coming for him."

Volkov swallowed. "I don't have the resources to find a man like that."

"That's been made abundantly clear." Nightshade's voice snapped like a lash. A long pause followed, a silence that Volkov knew better than to disrupt.

Finally, Nightshade said, "I will see what I can do. Make whatever preparations you need to make to ensure that you don't fail again."

And then the line had gone dead, and all Volkov could do was wait.

Something Nightshade had said still burned in his mind. *"Why didn't you take care of this personally?"*

The truth was, *personally* had meant sending Konstantin. His most reliable lieutenant. A man with a track record of quiet, efficient violence. A man he trusted—at least, more than most. But in Nightshade's eyes, *personally* had meant something else. It meant that *he* should have been the one to pull the trigger.

And now, he couldn't help but wonder—should he have gone?

Not to literally carry out the hit. He hadn't done anything like that in years. But to take charge. Call the shots.

Maybe I still should.

The idea sat uneasily in his mind. He was powerful—*respected*—in Moscow. But power was a fragile thing. And Nightshade did not forgive.

His phone buzzed.

He snatched it up, heart suddenly hammering. It was a text message from Nightshade. No words. Just numbers.

GPS coordinates.

He copied the numbers and entered them into a mapping application. A pin dropped onto the map with a dull, clinical beep—Michigan, again. This time, farther north. Much farther. Almost in Canada.

Volkov zoomed out first, trying to orient himself. The pin hovered in the middle of a vast green swath, ringed by the bluish-gray contours of Lake Superior and speckled with patches of low-lying towns. No cities. No interstate highways. The nearest recognizable name was a dot labeled *Seney*—a place that looked like it might have three streets and one gas station.

He zoomed in.

The image resolved slowly, revealing a tangle of forest roads that narrowed to nothing more than tire tracks. The pin itself was buried deep in the woods, with no visible structures. No roads, no power lines. Just trees.

Exactly the kind of place someone would go if they didn't want to be found.

Volkov stared at it, jaw clenched. How had Nightshade tracked Decker there? It beggared belief.

He leaned back in his chair, then picked up the phone and dialed Konstantin.

"I have a location," he said when the call connected. "I am texting it to you."

He pasted the GPS coordinates into a text message and sent it.

There was a long pause, then, "This is out in the middle of nowhere."

"Exactly where a man like Decker would go."

"What do you want me to do?"

Volkov's voice dropped, every syllable clipped and deliberate. "I want you to put together a team. Not those street-level fools from Chicago. No more *Vory* muscle with gold chains and tracksuits. *Real* killers."

"Understood."

"I want men who know how to move quiet and kill fast. Ex-Spetsnaz, GRU—anyone who's been wet. No hesitation. No mistakes."

"Professionals," Konstantin said.

"The best you can find," Volkov confirmed. "You tell them nothing except what they need to know. No names. No history. Just the target and the kill zone. Get this right, Kostya. You don't get another chance."

There was a beat of silence.

Then Konstantin said, "I'll make it right."

"You'd better." Volkov ended the call without another word.

He stared at the map for a long moment, then picked up the glass, downed the vodka in a single swallow, and reached for the bottle.

ELEVEN

UPPER PENINSULA, MICHIGAN

The mosquitoes had won.

Decker had been looking forward to an old-fashioned wienie roast over an open fire, followed by s'mores, but the swarm that had arrived just before sunset had other ideas. Abandoning the planned cookout, which in hindsight probably wasn't the smartest idea from a tactical point of view, Decker pulled them all inside to eat their dinner of hot dogs and baked beans in relative comfort, under the golden glow of an old Coleman white-gas lantern. Later, he'd fire up the woodstove to toast marshmallows.

After the cleanup earlier that morning, the day had taken on a pleasant rhythm, almost like a family camping trip. Mitchell had spent most of it exploring near the woods behind the cabin, bounding back every hour or so to report his findings like a junior park ranger. Brynn, to Decker's quiet surprise, had stayed inside reading, working her way through the tiny shelf of swollen, dog-eared paperbacks that her grandparents had brought there ages before, and which had somehow survived years of neglect. One of those paperbacks—a tattered Louis L'Amour Western—now sat open and face down beside her plate.

Decker, however, had not allowed his vigilance to lapse. While the kids settled into the illusion of peace, he'd spent most of the day out in the surrounding woods, planting sensors along the road and establishing a secure perimeter. No one would get within a square mile of the cabin without his knowing it.

Not that it would make much difference if the Russians found them. At best, his electronic fence was a feel-good measure.

Decker leaned back in his chair, letting the quiet settle. Through the cracked windows came the sounds of rustling leaves, a breeze moving through the trees. The crickets had taken up their nightly chorus. Mitchell was finishing the last of his second hot dog, mouth full, ketchup on his cheek. Brynn was staring at her empty plate as if trying to decide whether to have another helping.

"Admit it," Decker said, looking between them. "This hasn't been the worst day of your life."

Brynn looked back at him from under one raised eyebrow. "Ask me tomorrow."

Mitchell snorted. "I think it's awesome. We should live like this all the time."

Decker laughed. *If only we could,* he thought. But they would no more be able to stay here than return home. The cabin could only be a temporary refuge.

Because sooner or later, the people hunting them would find this place. He didn't know how close they were, or how many were coming, but it would happen. When it did, they would be long gone. This was no place to make a stand. His priority was getting Brynn and Mitchell somewhere safe.

After that he would go hunting.

But not tonight.

Tonight, he would give his children one last good memory.

He stood, collecting the empty plates. "Let's do s'mores," he said. "Woodstove marshmallows aren't traditional, but I promise they'll taste just as good."

Mitchell whooped and scrambled up, already rummaging through the grocery bag for the chocolate and graham crackers. Brynn rolled her eyes, but Decker saw the faint smile she was trying to hide.

He turned toward the stove—

Decker stopped, frozen in his tracks.

A low rumble reached his ears, distant, but unmistakably the sound of an aircraft engine. Probably just a small plane out of Escanaba or Marquette. Maybe a float plane carrying some fly-in fisherman heading to a remote lodge.

But the noise was growing, resolving. It wasn't the smooth whine of a fixed wing but the throaty roar of a jet turbine, undercut with a faint but steady rhythm.

Rotors.

Decker's heart sank. "I thought we'd have more time," he murmured.

"Dad?" Brynn asked, sensing the change in him.

He turned to her. "Come with me. *Now.*"

Mitchell jumped to his feet, startled. "What is it?"

"Outside." Decker grabbed the lamp off the table and the soft case from the corner, slinging the latter over one shoulder. "Move."

Brynn hesitated just a moment, then grabbed Mitchell's hand and moved toward the door. Decker pushed through ahead of them, emerging onto the porch. The sun had fully set, plunging the surrounding woods into a sort of fairy-tale gloom. The sound of the helicopter was unmistakable now, cresting above the treetops, still distant—but not distant enough.

He led them around back to the root cellar. It was nothing like the shelter at the townhouse. Just a stone-lined chamber excavated beneath the cabin, originally used for storing potatoes and canned goods through the long UP winters. The hinges on the heavy bulkhead door groaned as he pulled it open, revealing steep steps descending into cool, earthy darkness. Cobwebs, just visible in the lantern's low light, hung from the naked ceiling beams. He handed Brynn the lantern.

She recoiled. "You want us to go in *there*?"

"I'm not asking, baby girl."

"But it's filthy. And—"

"It's safe." The assertion felt like a lie. Nowhere was safe. "You need to protect Mitchell. Stay quiet."

Mitchell peered down into the musty dark. "I don't like it . . ."

"I know, buddy." Decker crouched and touched his son's shoulder. "But you're brave, right?"

Mitchell nodded solemnly.

Decker straightened and then reached into the carrying case, took out the Benelli, and proffered it to Brynn.

She stared at it, horror flashing in her eyes. "I—I can't—"

"You can. Safety's here." He pointed to the small cylindrical button just behind the trigger. "Push it from right to left." He demonstrated, revealing a little red dot. "Red means ready to fire." He pushed it back. "Keep it on safe until you need to use it, and don't put your finger on the trigger until you've got no other choice. There's a round in the chamber already, so all you have to do is slide the safety off, point, and shoot. You'll only get six shots, but it's loaded with buckshot, so you don't have to worry about aiming."

He put the shotgun in her hands. "Anyone comes through that door, you shoot."

She looked back at him, wide-eyed. "What if it's you?"

It won't be me, he thought, *because I'll already be dead.*

But he couldn't say that to her, so instead he tried for a reassuring smile. "Well, obviously, don't shoot if it's me." He put a hand on her shoulder. "You've got this, Brynn. Keep Mitch safe."

He waited, just long enough for the kids to climb down into the dark hole, then closed the doors behind them and prepared himself for the fight.

TWELVE

The roar of jet turbines and the low thrum of rotors grew louder by the second, but the watcher did not turn his head to search for the aircraft. Instead, he remained still, nestled in the crook of a tree nearly twenty feet above the forest floor, wrapped in a homemade ghillie suit crafted from strips of camouflage netting, keeping his focus on the man moving along the exterior of the cabin, visible to him in the objective of his sniper scope.

Aaron Decker.

Phantom.

He hadn't thought about that call sign in years. Like everyone else, he'd just assumed that Phantom was dead. End of story. And, all things being equal, he would have been content to leave it that way. Nothing good ever came of raising old ghosts.

But Phantom hadn't really died. And someone had figured it out.

The realization had shaken him more than he wanted to admit.

He'd been surprised when the news had popped up on his radar. He had been out of the game for a long time but still kept a weather eye out. He had too many secrets in his head to ever really retire. Listening to the chatter was a matter of self-preservation.

Phantom, alive and living in suburban Michigan. Real name Aaron Decker, a widower, raising two kids.

Kids?

He shifted slightly, tracking Decker as he moved toward the tree line and then disappeared beyond it. Even now, fifteen years out of the game, the man moved like an operator.

He's still got it.

It had been curiosity about that point, more than anything else, that had motivated him to travel to Richland, arriving just ahead of the Russian hit team. Not that they had posed much of a challenge to Decker.

Tonight would be a different story.

Decker might not survive this.

The noise deepened as the aircraft came in low and fast, and finally the watcher shifted his gaze from the scope. It was just a silhouette in the twilit sky, moving over the treetops a hundred yards north of his position. It looked a lot like a Black Hawk, but bigger—probably a civilian variant like the Sikorsky A-92. Seating for nineteen, give or take. There were no external lights—not even a red anti-collision beacon. The pilots were running dark, which meant they were using night vision devices, and that told him all he needed to know. Whoever was flying had military training. So, he felt certain, would the men riding in the back.

The rotor wash bent the tops of the trees as the helicopter slowed, nose tilting back slightly. It hovered for a beat, then dipped toward a clearing about two hundred yards from the cabin, the downdraft raising a cyclone of dust and pine needles as it descended the last fifty feet.

The side doors were already open, and as soon as the wheels touched down, dark figures began to pour out.

The watcher settled back, returned his eyes to the scope, and resumed scanning.

Now it begins.

THIRTEEN

There were twelve of them in all. Full kit. Body armor. Suppressors. NODs mounted to their bump helmets. Targeting lasers attached to the Picatinny rails of their assault carbines. Moving like they knew what they were doing.

No tracksuits tonight.

As soon as the last man was on the ground and out of the rotor sweep, the bird lifted again, nose pitching upward as it climbed out of the trees and banked north.

Decker exhaled slowly and lowered the infrared spotter scope.

So much for the early warning system.

The men on the ground split quickly into two groups, six each, spreading out into paired echelon formations—a forward-swept V, like open jaws reaching out to devour the cabin. Classic kill-box doctrine. There was just one flaw in their plan.

Decker was nowhere near the cabin.

Lying prone behind a moss-covered log about seventy-five yards northeast of the cabin, hunkered down behind the stock of his MK18 carbine, Decker watched the dual formations flowing through the woods toward their objective, maintaining an interval of about ten yards. If they stayed on course, the right flank would sweep across his position—the second man from the end would practically step on him—and with their NODs activated, it seemed impossible that they wouldn't see him. But Decker knew how to become part of the landscape, blending into the shadows. He slowed his breathing, sank deeper into the camouflage of leaves and shadow, and waited for them to come to him.

The formations drew closer, each step of their advance precise, disciplined. Weapons at the ready, invisible infrared lasers no doubt already searching for a target. Decker didn't move, didn't even blink, as the footsteps grew louder.

The lead man of the right flank moved past, just a few yards from his position, and then the second man was right beside him, exactly where Decker had anticipated he'd be. And as the man's boot crunched softly on the forest loam, Decker moved. In one fluid motion, he was on his feet, left hand clamped around the man's mouth and jaw, twisting violently upward and to the right, while his right hand brought his Karatel Maestro fighting knife across the man's exposed throat, cutting spine deep. The man stiffened, hands coming up in a futile effort to break free of his assailant's grip, his carbine falling away to hang from its sling. He did not struggle long. Decker held the man close, guiding him soundlessly to the ground, melting both of them back into the shadows as quickly as he'd emerged.

The man in the center of the formation paused mid-step, sensing something amiss. He pivoted cautiously, searching the darkness, and then began subvocalizing an urgent query into his lip mic. Decker was already in motion, launching from the underbrush like a guided missile. No time for subtlety. His hand clamped down on the radio man's throat even as he jammed the blade under the helmet, behind the man's jaw, driving it home as his body weight bore the man to the ground.

Two down, he thought but knew better than to believe his luck would hold.

The takedowns hadn't gone unnoticed. He could hear the others reacting—soft curses, the tempo of footsteps changing, the rising awareness that danger was in their midst. He stripped off his victim's helmet, then rolled away into the underbrush, shrinking into the darkness behind the formation. Once behind the cover of a white spruce bough, he settled the helmet onto his head and put his eye to the cup of the night optical device—an old school Gen 3 PVS-14 monocular. The tilt switch had kicked the unit off when its former user had gone down, so Decker toggled the power off, then back on again, resetting the system.

The green glow flared to life. The woods materialized before him—tree trunks, branches, tangled undergrowth, all rendered in ghostly monochrome. But it was the spears of infrared laser light, slicing through the spaces between the trees, that got his attention. The gunmen were adjusting their formation, spreading out in pairs, scanning every direction, looking for him.

The time for knives had passed.

Decker considered his options. Once he opened fire with the MK18, the hostiles would quickly home in on his muzzle flashes. Switching to his suppressed Glock would mostly eliminate the latter problem, but stopping power was a consideration. The men wore body armor; he would need to score head shots, and that meant getting a lot closer.

I can do closer.

He let the MK18 hang on its sling and drew the Glock, then went prone again, burying himself in a shallow grave of loam and pine duff. He let his head settle into the crook of his elbow and waited.

He didn't have to wait long.

A pair of lasers—brighter, more focused than the others—lanced over his head, cutting shorter arcs. Decker could hear the tread of their boots on the soft earth, the sweep of ferns against their legs, the murmur of voices as they discovered their fallen comrade. He couldn't make out what they were saying, or if it was even English.

One man knelt over the body. The other was keeping watch, head on a swivel. Decker sighted in on the kneeling man, aiming at the narrow sliver of exposed neck, just above the top of the plate carrier, and pulled the trigger once.

He didn't wait to see what happened. Even with the suppressor, the report of the shot echoed loudly through the woods, sending a clear, unmistakable message.

It's on.

Decker was already moving, rolling sideways into a shallow depression and crawling fast beneath the sweep of tangled spruce limbs. A burst of automatic fire cracked through the trees behind him, rounds punching into bark and branches. Woodsmoke swirled in the laser-lit air. Splinters showered his back as he ducked behind another tree, only to roll out onto the opposite side with the MK18 now in hand. He sighted down one of the lasers, taking aim at the emitter, and loosed a burst, then ducked and crawled again, staying low, keeping the trees between himself and the enemy.

More fire raked the space he'd just left. They'd seen his muzzle flash. They knew where he was. Or rather, where he had been.

He found new cover behind a different tree, eased out again.

Aimed.

Fired.

Moved.

Then one by one, the beams vanished, swallowed by the dark.

Decker froze, cheek pressed to the forest floor, scanning dead space. Nothing. No lasers. No movement.

The gunfire had stopped too.

He waited. Five seconds. Ten.

Still nothing.

They were staying down now. Holding position. Waiting for him to reveal himself.

He caught the faintest flicker of movement between two trees off to his left, but as he turned toward it, a burst of gunfire erupted from somewhere off to his right. He ducked reflexively, though judging by the muffled sound of the impacts, none of the shots were even close. It was covering fire, designed to make him stay down while other shooters moved in for the kill.

He rolled right, came up on a knee, and fired—three quick shots—at the last place he'd seen movement. Then he was crawling again, ducking behind a fallen pine slick with sap.

Another burst. Different angle.

They were working in tandem, one team firing, the other advancing with every exchange. Classic infantry movement techniques. This was where their superior numbers would make all the difference.

He waited, breathed, fired another burst—short, disciplined—then moved. No time to check if he hit anything.

Shoot and move.

Reload.

He was burning through ammo now, with almost nothing to show for it. He had to keep moving, but he couldn't just run away. Brynn and Mitch were still in the root cellar, and if the enemy found them . . .

They won't, he promised himself. *Not while I'm alive.*

He crabbed sideways, came up behind a windfall, and loosed another burst.

Three rounds, snapped into the dark toward a muzzle flash. He couldn't tell if the shots found their target, couldn't linger to find out.

Every time he found new cover, the pressure followed—sustained bursts of fire, bounding pairs flanking wider and wider. He was staying ahead of them, but just barely.

A cluster of rounds chewed into the log he'd just cleared, hurling slivers of bark across his retreating back. He pivoted hard, rolled away, then fired from the prone. Spent brass rebounded from a nearby tree to land on the exposed flesh of his arm, the hot metal searing his flesh.

He caught a blur of movement, swung the muzzle of his weapon toward it. Fired. Moved, even as another fusillade was unleashed at him.

He dropped flat a moment later, rolled, snapped off another burst, felt the bolt lock back. Empty.

Decker dropped the mag and jammed in another. His last.

He was maybe thirty yards from the cabin now. Thirty yards of mostly open ground. Too far to crawl. Too exposed to sprint. But what choice did he have?

He surged to his feet, rifle shouldered, and sprinted for the cabin. Rounds sizzled through the air all around him—short, controlled bursts. No more wild suppressive fire. They were aiming now. Tracking him.

He half turned mid-stride, fired a long burst without slowing. The cabin loomed ahead, angular and black in the display of his NOD. Ten more yards. Five.

He threw himself flat, sliding for the corner of the A-frame like a runner stealing second. As he passed the corner, he flipped over, bringing the carbine up to loose another burst, even as incoming rounds tore into the shingles right above him.

The cabin offered some protection, but he was still partially exposed, so he wriggled back several feet. From this vantage, he could see the driveway cutting through the trees and barely visible figures moving along its edge, careful not to linger in the open. Decker lined up his shot, aiming at the point where he knew one of the men would reappear, and took up the slack in the trigger, waiting . . . waiting . . .

Now.

The MK18 bucked against his shoulder, but in that instant, two things happened simultaneously.

Decker saw the gunman stagger and drop.

And he felt the bolt lock back again.

He let the rifle drop on its sling and drew the Glock. The weapon wouldn't be much use until the hostiles were practically on top of him, and by then, it wouldn't much matter.

He thought about the cellar door, just around the back corner, a few feet away . . . pictured Brynn and Mitch inside, huddled together, waiting for the noise to stop.

When he died, would his children be spared? He was the primary target, after all. Once he was dead, the job would be finished, wouldn't it?

He couldn't quite bring himself to believe it.

Out on the driveway, the gunmen began emerging from the woods, tentatively at first, as if trying to draw fire, and then with more confidence as they realized he was black on ammo. Seven men, striding down the driveway, rifles at the ready. They weren't even bothering to stay behind cover.

They thought they had him.

He raised the Glock.

Well, come on then.

FOURTEEN

He'd hoped Decker could handle it on his own, and for a little while there at the beginning, it looked as if he just might.

From his vantage in the trees—which on further reflection probably wasn't the best place to observe a gun battle—he'd watched as Decker lived up to his original call sign, moving like a wraith, silently dispatching three of the assaulters before they even realized that they were under attack.

After that, however, the situation had developed in a more predictable fashion. It was a simple numbers game. Twelve . . . well, nine . . . against one. Nine men, each carrying in the neighborhood of three hundred rounds of ammunition, against one man who, from what he could tell, had only three or four thirty-round mags for his assault weapon.

The math did not favor Phantom. He had managed to subtract a couple more, but at the cost of the last of his ammo. Now, the odds of his surviving the night were no longer long. They were nonexistent.

Decker was down to a sidearm and whatever grit he had left in his bones. The remaining gunmen—seven now—were advancing on his position like the Earps and Doc Holliday moving down the streets of Tombstone. They smelled the end. They knew their target was out of ammo, out of surprises.

The watcher let his scope drift across their line, picking out targets. He could tag the lead man easily. Maybe the second one, too, if he transitioned quickly enough. That might buy Decker a few more minutes.

But then what? Trade fire with the rest until they triangulated his position?

Still, the question wasn't *could* he help Decker; it was *should* he.

Taking the shot would mean taking sides, something he'd assiduously avoided doing, both during and after his extended journey into the world of shadow warfare. It was like that thing with the cat in the box . . . Schroder's cat? Something like that. The cat wasn't alive or dead until you opened the box. As long as he didn't open the box, confront the truth, he could go on living. And living with himself.

Except that, if he was honest with himself, he'd known the cat was dead. Known that someone in the upper echelons of Rogue Unit was dirty and had sent four men to their deaths all those years ago. The fact that the Russians had found Decker so quickly confirmed it.

So what was he going to do about it?

If he chose sides, intervened on Decker's behalf, it would be a declaration of war, and not just to the men hunting Decker here tonight. His name would be added to the target list.

And yet, that part of him that had once been a patriot . . . the young man he had once been who had proudly raised his hand and sworn an oath to defend his country and the Constitution, bear true faith and allegiance, *"so help me God . . ."* That part of him knew that there were worse fates than death.

He settled the reticle once more on the leader and inhaled, finger on the trigger, taking up slack as he let out his breath slowly.

Then something flashed across the scope's field of view, an enormous black shape, there and gone in a heartbeat, and when it had passed, the lead gunman was gone as surely as if God Himself had reached down and erased him from existence.

"What the—" Startled, he jerked back, pulled away from the scope, and looked down with both eyes to see a vehicle—a big lifted four-wheel-drive pickup, its matte-black finish rendering it virtually invisible in the darkness. The truck was running dark, and after all the shooting, the assaulters probably hadn't even heard it coming.

In the instant that he looked, the truck skidded to a stop, slewing sideways across the driveway, with the driver's side facing the cabin. Bodies littered the drive behind it. Three at least, scattered like bowling pins, limbs twisted at unnatural angles.

The driver's door flung open, and a hulking figure erupted from the cab.

The watcher brought his eye back to the scope, glassing the newcomer.

The man was huge. Not just tall, but big. Thick through the chest and shoulders. He wore a ball cap pulled low, hiding everything but his short beard from view. What caught the watcher's attention, however, was the man's gun—a big Magnum, outfitted with a rail system—though in the hand of the man who wielded it, it didn't look quite so impressive.

He extended it across the hood of the pickup, and then a tongue of flame licked out from the muzzle. The report was deep and loud, echoing off the trees like a sonic boom. The watcher swung his scope down the driveway just in time to see one of the remaining gunmen knocked off his feet as if he'd been hit with a wrecking ball.

There was another detonation, and the head of the last assaulter seemed to disintegrate under his bump helmet.

And just like that, it was over.

The hulking figure stood beside the truck, his Magnum still extended, smoke drifting from the barrel, but there was no one left to kill.

Well, that's new, thought the watcher. Decker, it seemed, had a few surprises left after all.

FIFTEEN

Decker had been resigned to his fate, determined to go down fighting, but under no illusions about the outcome. So when the black truck came barreling out of the darkness and turned the advancing gunmen into hamburger, he struggled to process what was happening.

Then the realization washed over him like a tsunami, and as the adrenaline ebbed away, he had to hyperventilate to keep from throwing up. When the urge finally passed, he rose slowly from behind the cabin's corner, both hands lifted, and shouted, "Friendly coming out!"

The big man by the truck spun toward the sound of the voice, leading with the Magnum, but then just as quickly tilted the barrel skyward.

"Come out," he called back.

Decker shoved the Glock into his waistband, stripped off the captured helmet and tossed it aside, then stepped into the open, his eyes fixed on the man who had just saved his life.

It had been over a year since they'd met for the first and—until today—only time, but Matthew Redd was hard to forget, and not just because of how physically imposing he was. The man was indefatigable.

Redd had been targeted for elimination at the same time that a kill team had come after Gavin Kline—at the time, a deputy director of the FBI—very nearly killing him. Decker, naturally, had taken exception to the assassination attempt on his former CO and benefactor, and had gone on the warpath. That alone might not have brought him into Redd's orbit at just the right moment to save his life, if not for one other consideration: Matthew Redd was Gavin Kline's son. So, when Kline had learned that a second hit team was on its way to Montana, he'd called an audible, summoning Decker to the rural battlefield. Redd had already done most of the hard work, but Decker had arrived just in time to save Redd from certain death.

Later, when Kline had introduced them, Redd had made a promise. *"You saved my life. You saved all of us. I owe you one, Aaron."*

Decker had tried to downplay his role, but Redd had insisted. *"If you ever need anything, give me a call."*

It was a marker Decker never expected to call in. He wasn't that guy. He didn't need help . . . didn't need rescuing. He was the guy *other* people called for help.

But then the Russians showed up at his house.

Even that was something he could deal with . . . *had* dealt with. He knew, of course, that the *brati* he'd splashed would only be the first wave. That didn't frighten him. He would eliminate the problem by going to the source.

There was just one issue.

The kids.

Decker had to keep them safe while he did what needed to be done. And he couldn't just leave the kids in the care of trusted family friends, as he did when taking the occasional "business trip" for Kline. The unknown enemy behind this attack would find them, use them against him. No, he had to stash them somewhere *nobody* would think to look, with someone who wasn't in Decker's orbit.

"If you ever need anything, give me a call."

The plan had been to hand the kids off to Redd. Having him ride in like the cavalry had not been an expectation.

Decker hadn't felt this way since Kyiv. Since Gavin Kline had saved his butt.

Like father, like son.

When he was sure that his legs wouldn't shake, he strode out to meet his savior. "Cut it pretty close, didn't you?"

Redd shrugged. "Had to come all the way from Montana. You have any idea how long of a drive that is?"

"I figured you'd fly."

"Thought about it," Redd admitted. "But I'd literally just left an airport, and between waiting for a flight and making the drive out here from Detroit, I doubt it would have saved much time." He glanced over his shoulder at the bodies littering the drive. "Still, if I had known you were going to throw a party for me, I'd have driven a little faster."

Decker nodded. "I'm glad you showed up when you did. Unfortunately, I don't think this is over. They've got a helo. The next wave is probably already inbound."

"They *had* a helo," Redd corrected.

Redd walked to the passenger door, opened it, and yanked a man out by the collar. In the scant illumination from the truck's interior light, Decker saw that the man was wearing the same tactical attire as the other assaulters. He was also trussed up tight, hands behind his back, face bloodied, eyes full of hatred and confusion.

"Who's this?" asked Decker.

"One of the guys I caught climbing into that helo just as it was setting down out on the main road."

"You jumped the bird?"

"When I saw them coming in for touchdown, I parked and came up on their blind side and . . . well, let's just say I introduced myself."

Decker looked past him, peering into the Raptor's interior. "So, where's the rest of the crew?"

Redd winced, and his expression flattened. "They were, uh, uncooperative. Told them to power down"—he shrugged—"and they didn't. Long story short, you don't need to worry about the helicopter or any of the guys on it. I held on to this one, though. Thought you might have some questions for him."

Decker looked down at the bound man, who was trying to look defiant through the pain of his injuries. He crouched, meeting the other man's gaze.

"Let me guess," he said. "Bratva." He yanked up the man's sleeve, exposing a faded tattoo—barbed wire twisted around a skull. "You know what this says about you where I'm from?" he went on. "You've done time. You've spilled blood. You're a killer. Well . . . so am I."

The Russian didn't respond, just continued glaring.

"But I'm not interested in the Bratva," Decker went on. "I want to know who you're *really* working for. Who sent you? Who wants me dead?"

The man's face curled into a slow, smug grin, then he spat a bloody gobbet straight into Decker's face and muttered a familiar curse in Russian.

Decker wiped the spittle away with the back of his hand, stood slowly, and drew the Glock from his waistband. He pressed the business end of the suppressor to the Russian's forehead. "Last chance."

From the corner of his eye, he saw Redd watching intently, his face registering neither approval nor disapproval.

The Russian laughed. "You won't do it."

Decker pulled the trigger. The man's head snapped back, and he toppled backward. In the low light, Decker could see the small round hole in the center of his forehead, a dribble of blood welling from it.

Redd frowned. "Well, I could have done that."

"He was never going to talk."

"Maybe I should have saved a couple more?"

Decker shook his head. "There are plenty more where he came from. I'll find someone to answer my question." He gave Redd a sidelong glance. "In case I forgot to say it, thanks. I suppose I owe you an explanation."

Redd shrugged again. "You don't *owe* me anything. I owe you, remember? But I wouldn't mind knowing what I just stepped into."

Decker nodded in the direction of the house and started walking. "How much has Gavin told you about me?"

"Just that you do favors for him. Off the books. I'm guessing you used to do that stuff for one of the alphabet soup agencies."

Decker chuckled. "The unit I was in wasn't part of any agency. We handled the stuff that couldn't be resolved through official channels. Anyway . . . long story short, as you might say, the unit was compromised. There was a traitor . . . someone near the top. We . . . my team . . . we were starting to figure it out, but then whoever it was set us up. Sent us into an ambush."

Decker felt his throat suddenly growing tight with emotion. It had been years since he'd thought about the events of that night, about his teammates being cut down . . . one of them practically dying in his arms. And a lot longer than that since he'd told anyone.

"I made it out," he went on. "But I knew I couldn't go back . . . give whoever it was another chance to take me off the board. So I went to Gavin and asked him to help fake my death."

"How did you know Gavin?"

"He was my CO, back when I was in the Corps. And we did some *work* together after that, too."

Redd—himself a Marine, having served as a Raider—raised an eyebrow, then extended a fist. "Semper fi."

Decker chuckled again and lightly bumped his fist against Redd's.

"So how do the Russians figure into this?"

They reached the cabin, and Decker led the way along the side of the structure. "They were working with the traitor. They were the ones who ambushed us. Somehow, they must have figured out I was still alive. Maybe I got a little complacent."

"You don't seem like the sort of person who would slip up like that."

"This all happened fifteen years ago. And I was dead, remember? No one was even looking for me."

Redd nodded slowly. "So, the Russians found out you're still alive, and now they want to finish the job."

"The Russians are still just the blunt instrument. It's the traitor in Rogue Unit that wants me dead. He knows I can bring him down."

"Rogue Unit? Cute. So, who is this traitor?"

"I have no idea."

Redd folded his large arms across his chest. "You must have suspected someone."

Decker shook his head. "The unit wasn't structured like that. No one involved used their real names. Minimal contact between the operational side and leadership."

"Still, this traitor saw you as a potential threat."

"Yes, he did," said Decker. "And I intend to prove him right."

Redd seemed to consider this for a moment. "So, we start with the Russians. Find out who in the Bratva was the go-between with your traitor, and then lean on him until he gives up a name."

"I appreciate the offer, Matt, but there's no 'we.' This is my problem. I can handle it."

Redd gave a meaningful glance over his shoulder. "Seems to me like you were the one getting handled tonight."

"I was playing defense. Now I'm going on offense. But the thing is, I can't do that and keep my family safe. Not at the same time."

"Family?"

"My kids. I brought them up here with me. Stashed in the storm cellar just before the shooting started." He nodded toward the cellar door. "Obviously, I can't take them with me where I'm going."

Redd studied him for a long moment. "You don't know how to ask for help, do you?"

The remark stung. Mostly because it was true.

"Yeah, me either," Redd went on. "Doesn't come natural to me. Thing is, I got this best friend who's a real pain in my . . . well, you know. Anyways, his name's Mikey, and he's always on me about asking for help. Come to think of it, so's Em—"

"This story have an ending?" Decker asked.

Redd's eyes narrowed. "Just tell me what you need, Aaron."

Decker hesitated, then said, "I want you to take my kids with you. Keep them safe until this is over."

Redd blinked. "You want *me* to babysit?"

"I don't trust anyone else to do it."

Redd took another long moment to process this. "That's a waste of the favor. Let me really help you. We'll take the kids back to my ranch. Em will look after them. Meanwhile, you and me—we'll solve this permanently."

Decker shook his head. "I appreciate the offer, but I work better alone."

"Alone? Dude, you'd be dead right now had you been alone." Redd gripped Decker's shoulder, looking down at him. "I've been where you are right now. In fact, that was where you found me. Outnumbered and outgunned. I nearly died trying to go it alone. I've tried the whole 'lone wolf' thing, and you know what? It doesn't always work. Not for wolves, and not for us."

Decker looked away, jaw working as he stared out into the trees. Redd wasn't wrong. The road to finding the traitor who had betrayed him and his team, and who now wanted him dead, would be a long and bloody one. And the truth of the matter was that he wasn't as dialed in as he used to be.

He didn't like the idea of leaning on anyone—but Redd wasn't just anyone.

Still, he hesitated. "I need to think about it."

"Fine. You can think about it on the drive."

Decker raised an eyebrow.

"We'll take the kids back to the ranch together," Redd said. "Regroup. Catch our breath. You can plan your next move from there."

Decker looked at him for a beat longer, then gave a reluctant nod. "All right. Fair enough."

Redd grinned and let go of Decker's shoulder. "Now," he said, stepping over to the cellar doors. "Let's go meet the family."

As he reached for the handle, Decker's heart skipped a beat. "Wait!"

He flung himself at Redd.

Despite outweighing Decker by a good hundred pounds, Redd yielded to Decker's urgency, letting the smaller man push him out of the way a fraction of a second before the cellar door exploded in a spray of splinters and buckshot. The echo of the shotgun's report cracked across the clearing like thunder.

Decker rolled to a stop in the dirt. Redd came up beside him, hand already on the grip of his Magnum. Decker covered the big revolver with one hand, preventing Redd from raising it, even as Brynn, backlit by the lantern glow emanating from deep within the cellar, emerged, the Benelli braced against her shoulder, sweeping the muzzle from side to side, looking for a target.

Just like he'd told her.

Decker threw his hands up, shouting, "Brynn! Stand down."

She blinked, eyes narrowing as she examined the two figures on the ground. "Dad?"

Decker breathed a sigh of relief. "It's me, baby girl. I'm all right. It's over for now."

Beside him, Redd let out a chuckle. "Well, this one needs no introduction. She's definitely your daughter."

SIXTEEN

MOSCOW, RUSSIA

Not for the first time, Grigori Volkov was waiting for a phone call.

He seemed to spend an inordinate amount of time lately waiting on phone calls. Waiting for Nightshade to provide necessary intelligence, waiting for Konstantin to report back with the news that Aaron Decker was finally dead. The longer he waited, the more a familiar dread settled in his gut.

It should have been finished by now. The mercenary company Konstantin had contracted—Sibir Zashchitniki, a breakaway cadre of Wagner-trained professionals operating out of Belarus—was supposed to be the best money could buy. The operation had cost him tens of millions—dollars, not rubles—most of it to expedite the trans-Arctic deployment into Canadian territory from where they would launch the assault. The helicopter alone had tripled the budget. But returning to Nightshade's good graces was worth any expense, while all the money in the world would do him no good if he screwed this up.

Volkov checked his phone again. Still nothing.

It had been more than two hours since the kill team launched their assault. More than enough time to confirm the kill, exfiltrate back across the Canadian border, and report success.

He scrolled to Konstantin's contact. The call connected, but then a robotic voice informed him that the person he was calling had a voicemail box that had not been set up. Scowling, he rang off and dialed the number for the CEO of Sibir Z, Mikhail Artyomovich Skvortsov.

Volkov didn't know Skvortsov personally, only by reputation. By all reports, he was a brute, an animal—and while sometimes an animal was exactly what the situation required, Volkov preferred to keep men of Skvortsov's ilk at a distance. But right now, he needed answers, and with Konstantin gone dark, there was no one else to turn to.

The line rang once, twice, then connected.

"Da?" the man growled. His voice sounded like it came from a pit of gravel and cigarettes.

"It's Volkov."

"I know who it is," Skvortsov replied.

"I can't reach Konstantin. Have you heard from your men? Was the operation a success?"

"I've had no contact with the team since insertion. That area of United States is a black hole for mobile phone coverage."

Volkov's jaw clenched. "I don't care about your communications problems. I paid for results."

"And you will get them. Be patient." Skvortsov ended the call before Volkov could offer a retort.

Volkov laid the phone on his desk and sat back, fuming. He could not afford another screwup. It was unthinkable that this man—Aaron Decker—could have stood against a dozen hardened mercenaries, and yet he had proven exceedingly difficult to kill in the past.

Still, Skvortsov's answer made the most sense. That part of the United States was almost like Siberia for remoteness. No doubt Konstantin would call as soon as—

The phone vibrated on the desktop. Volkov glanced at the displayed number—Skvortsov again—and then snatched it up and accepted the call. "Yes?"

"I . . . have news." The gravelly voice of the mercenary executive was subdued, humbled, and Volkov felt his guts twist. "One of my men called in. He's badly wounded but alive."

Volkov gripped the edge of the desk. "What did he say?"

There was a beat of silence.

"Things did not go . . . according to plan. Somehow, this man Decker was forewarned. Our surprise was not quite the surprise we had hoped for. Even so, the numbers were on our side. But then someone else showed up. A big man in a black pickup truck. He hit several of my men. Crushed them. Then he got out and shot the rest."

Each word sent a chill through Volkov's bloodstream. "One man did that?"

"There's more. Your man, Konstantin, was captured. Decker executed him."

"What?" Volkov hissed.

"Bullet to the head. Then they got in the black truck and drove away."

Volkov's mind recoiled. *Kostya dead? Decker still alive?*

He didn't dare call Nightshade to report another failure, couldn't ask him for help in finding Decker one more time. "You assured me of results," he said slowly, barely managing to keep his voice even.

Skvortsov didn't argue. "Yes. And I will deliver them. I will kill this man Decker. And the man in the black truck." He paused a beat and then added, "I will see to it personally."

Volkov swallowed hard, eyes fixed on nothing. "So will I."

SEVENTEEN

UPPER PENINSULA, MICHIGAN

Matthew Redd was tired.

His back was tight, and his eyes full of grit. He wasn't sure if the dull buzz in his skull was exhaustion or adrenaline—or both. The Raptor's shocks were handling the pitted two-lane with ease, but he could still feel every bump.

He'd been on the road for the better part of twenty-four hours, running on caffeine and obligation, crossing half the country without rest. Just gas stops, bad truck-stop coffee, and worse radio, only to land with both feet in the middle of a minor war. And now, barely half an hour after arriving at Decker's cabin, he was behind the wheel again, heading home.

Neither man had said much since getting on the road, not because of any lingering tension, but just mutual exhaustion.

"You realize we're both running out of steam," Decker observed now from the passenger seat. "This is how people wrap themselves around trees."

"You saying you want to drive?"

"No. I'm saying I want to sleep. But I guess I can't, can I?"

Redd glanced over, a tired half smile forming. "You catch a few hours; we'll trade off."

Decker didn't return the smile. "Who's gonna keep you awake?"

Redd flexed his jaw, eyes fixed on the empty road ahead. "I'll manage."

"With my kids in the car?" Decker shook his head. "I think I'll just push through."

"I can drive," Brynn said from the back seat. It was the first thing she'd said that didn't sound like an accusation.

Redd managed, barely, to keep his expression neutral. "I appreciate that," he said evenly, "but I've got it covered."

"I'm a good driver," Brynn said defensively. "Tell him, Dad."

"You are, baby girl," replied Decker. "But I'm with Mr. Redd on this one."

Brynn let out a breath and slumped back in her seat, folding her arms across her chest. "Whatever."

"Where are we going?" the boy, Mitchell, asked.

"We're all going to Mr. Redd's place. He has a ranch in Montana."

"A *ranch*? With horses and stuff?"

Redd couldn't help but smile. "That's right. I've got a horse named Remington, and a dog named Rubble who's almost as big as a horse."

"Are you a cowboy?"

"I guess I am, sort of."

Mitchell laughed. But not Brynn. Her voice quiet but direct, she asked, "Do you kill people like my dad does?"

Redd didn't flinch. "Not if I can help it. But sometimes, to protect the people you love, you make some hard choices."

"You're helping my dad so he can go do something dangerous, aren't you?"

Redd shot a helpless glance at Decker, who addressed his daughter. "That's something Mr. Redd and I are going to have to talk about. But right now, we need to keep moving."

An hour and a half later, Redd pulled into a Circle K in Harvey, Michigan. The place was quiet, without even the sound of highway traffic to supply background noise. The canopy lights cast a cold, steady glow over the empty lot. Redd went in and grabbed an assortment of energy drinks and bottles of water, along with chips and protein bars for sustenance.

Back at the truck, Decker was already climbing into the driver's seat.

"I'll take the next leg," he said, helping himself to one of the energy drinks. He cracked the tab and took a generous swig, then made a face. "How do the kids drink this crap?"

Redd chuckled. "You sure you're up for it?"

"Yeah. Get some shut-eye."

Redd didn't argue. He walked around and eased into the passenger seat. It felt a little strange handing the reins over to Decker—a virtual stranger—but he was desperate for a break. As the engine rumbled to life once more, he reclined the chair, closed his eyes, and tried to surrender himself into the arms of sleep.

It didn't happen. His body ached, his muscles buzzed with tension, and his mind wouldn't quiet. Too many unknowns. Too many variables. Too much at stake.

He cracked one eye and glanced over at Decker, who appeared alert and focused on the road, then sat up and glanced into the back. Mitchell was out cold, and Brynn was finally asleep too, her head resting against the window, her arms still crossed, defensive even in sleep.

Decker noticed the glance in the rearview mirror. "She's had to grow up fast," he said, answering a question Redd hadn't asked. "Since her mom . . ." He trailed off, the memory clearly painful.

"I'm sorry," Redd said solemnly. He couldn't imagine going on without Emily. He let the sentiment hang for a moment, then added, "She doesn't seem too happy with us right now."

"She's still getting used to the idea that I'm not just Mr. Mom."

Redd didn't have an answer for that, so he let it go. He glanced back to ensure that Brynn was still asleep, then, lowering his voice, asked, "So what's your next play?"

"Well, like you said before, I'm going to figure out who sent those guys tonight. There will be a trail, and it will involve the Russian mob. Once I figure out who sent them, I'll lean on him until he gives up a name. Then I'll move up the chain until I figure out who's really behind this."

"You're going to need help." He saw Decker start to respond and raised a hand. "I don't mean me . . . Well, I do, but that's not what I'm talking about. You're going to need intel . . . Unless you already have someone inside the Bratva."

Decker grimaced. "Alas, I am not as plugged in as I used to be."

"Have you considered calling Gavin?"

Decker shook his head. "If there's one thing the acting director of the FBI doesn't need right now, it's a scandal. He can't afford to explain why he's diverting Bureau resources to protect his personal assassin. Not if he wants that top spot."

"Fair enough. Still, couldn't hurt to let him know what's going on."

Decker pondered this for a moment. "I'll take it under advisement. Right now, I just want to get the kids somewhere safe."

"Safe," echoed Redd. As a father, he understood that impulse. But he also knew that sometimes the only way to keep your kids safe was to hunt down and eliminate the threats to their safety. Especially against an enemy like this. "You do realize they found you twice in twenty-four hours."

Decker gave a quiet nod. "That's been bothering me too. I don't know how they found the cabin so quickly. I know I didn't leave any breadcrumbs that could have led them there."

"The traitor?" Redd said.

"Has to be. But even so . . ." Decker shook his head. "I'm good at this, Matt. I know how to cover my tracks. Finding me at home? Okay, that would have taken some doing. But finding the cabin? The odds of them stumbling across it in less than twenty-four hours are astronomical. Especially since *I* didn't even know I'd be going there."

"Could they have tracked your movements?"

"I don't see how. I swapped vehicles. Dumped all my technology."

"What about a satellite? Or a drone? If they had eyes in the sky, they might have seen you leave your place. Seen you swap rides. Tracked you all the way up here."

"I guess it's . . . possible? But they would need a bird with persistent overhead—thermal, radar, loiter time. Civilians don't have access to aircraft like that. And flying it over domestic airspace without raising red flags?"

"Homeland Security could do it," said Redd, recalling how rogue elements within the agency had once tracked him through a blizzard, sending wave after wave of killers. "Maybe your traitor is still on the inside. HSA, or some other government agency that can task them to conduct surveillance."

"If so . . . they could be watching us right now."

"Something to think about." Redd paused a beat, then went on. "But if that's how they found you, there will be a paper trail. Gavin could sniff that out for you."

Decker was quiet for a long moment. "If you're right about that," he said finally, "then even your ranch might not be safe."

Redd had already considered that. "Then we don't stay long. Em can take the kids somewhere else. Somewhere with no connection to you. And Gavin can send some agents to provide a protective detail. That's how you keep your kids safe. Then you and me can get down to the business of finding this traitor and putting him out of business permanently."

Decker stared back at him. "You don't owe me this, Matt."

"It's not about what I do or don't owe you," said Redd. "It's about what's right. And you know as well as I do that this won't end until either you're dead or they are. I'd just as soon it be them."

Decker held his gaze a moment longer, then nodded. "All right. We do this together. Maybe for starters, you can get some shut-eye. We've got a long road ahead."

Redd didn't argue. Instead, he tipped the bill of his New Era cap down to cover his eyes and reclined in his seat again. This time, sleep came easy.

EIGHTEEN

They drove into rain somewhere near the Wisconsin state line, and while the shower didn't last, the road surface seemed to ooze in the Raptor's headlights. A long snaking stretch of US 2 unspooled ahead of them, flanked by pine trees and the occasional distant farmhouse. The dashboard clock marked the passage of time—nearly 5 a.m. now—and the miles just kept coming.

Taking another turn in the driver's seat, Redd surprised himself with a jaw-cracking yawn. He knuckled one eye and shook his head in a futile effort to banish the sleep monster. If he didn't stop, and soon, he was going to fall asleep at the wheel. "I'm pulling over," he announced, braking and steering onto the shoulder.

Decker, sleeping lightly in the passenger seat, sat up and rubbed his face. "I'm running on fumes, Matt. Don't think I could keep it between the lines right now if I tried."

Redd heaved a weary sigh. "You and me both. I think we're going to have to just sit here for a bit."

Decker straightened in his chair, his expression hardening. "I don't think that's a good idea. If they are tracking us, we have to keep moving."

From the back seat, Brynn spoke up. "Let me drive."

Redd glanced at Decker, who was looking back at his daughter.

"I appreciate the offer," Redd began, striving for a diplomatic tone. "But I think—"

"I'm serious," Brynn said, sitting up straighter. "I've had my license for a year. I'm a good driver. Better than you in your current condition."

"She's not wrong." Decker sighed. "Honestly, she might be a better driver than you even when you're fully rested."

"She's also seventeen," Redd replied as gently as he could manage, ignoring the joke.

"Seventeen and wide-awake," Brynn shot back.

Decker shifted in his seat, casting Redd a look that was somewhere between amusement and resignation. "She is a good driver. Drove us halfway to Milwaukee last summer. Highway speeds. Heavy traffic. Handled it just fine."

Redd breathed out slowly, gripping the wheel. "This isn't the freeway. We're in the middle of nowhere out here. What if a deer jumps in front of us?"

"I would never hit a deer," said Brynn.

"And this is not a Honda Civic," Redd went on. "Or whatever you're used to driving. The Raptor's bigger, handles differently."

"She's driven my Land Cruiser," Decker interjected. "She can handle your rig. And right now, her reaction time is a lot better than ours. You know I'm right. We can't afford to stop, and we can't afford to crash."

Redd hesitated, drumming his fingers against the wheel. The rational part of him agreed—*barely*. The rest of him recoiled at the idea of anyone else behind the wheel. Especially a teenager. Especially in *his* truck. He'd bought it with cash, scrupulously saved from his USMC pay. Wrecked it twice, rebuilt it twice, each time better than before, thanks largely to the expertise of Mikey Derhammer, who managed the body shop in Wellington. He did not want to have to rebuild it a third time.

"I'll be careful," Brynn said, as if sensing the pitch of his resistance. "Fifty-five tops. I won't even mess with the radio."

Redd looked between the two of them, then up at the stars just starting to fade into the bruised blue of morning. He sighed. "One hour. No more."

Brynn was already sliding forward in her seat, a grin spreading across her face. "One hour. Got it."

As they swapped seats, Redd growled, "You scratch her, and I'll make your dad ride the rest of the way in the bed."

Brynn laughed. "Deal," she said, hands already on the wheel, adjusting the seat.

Redd climbed into the back, taking the seat Brynn had vacated. Beside him, Mitchell dozed on, oblivious to his sister's victory. To her credit, Brynn pulled the Raptor smoothly back onto the road, her hands at ten and two, eyes scanning the road ahead like a seasoned long-hauler.

Redd leaned his head against the cool glass and let his eyes close. The sound of the tires over wet pavement, the rhythmic hiss and low engine hum . . . it was almost enough to lull him to sleep. *Almost.* He could almost feel the steering wheel in his hands, his foot hovering above an imaginary brake pedal. He didn't doubt Decker's estimation of his daughter's abilities, but trust had to be earned.

Still, as ten minutes passed, then twenty, with no hint of uncertainty in her handling of the big pickup, Redd's exhaustion won out over his apprehension. Hovering on the edge of sleep, Redd's thoughts drifted. He thought of Emily. Of home. And of the storm that lay ahead.

He was all in now. He wasn't looking forward to dropping Decker's kids in Emily's lap. She'd understand—of course she would—but it was still a big ask, even for someone as rock solid as his wife. She'd handle it, though. He had no doubt. She always did. It was just one of the many reasons why he loved her.

But how on earth were they going to track down the mysterious traitor? Both Redd and Decker knew that they'd have to lean on the Russians, but that sounded like something easier said than done. Redd didn't know anything about the Bratva, much less where to begin looking for them. They were going to need help. No matter what Decker said, this wasn't something they could do alone.

And that meant calling Gavin.

A few years ago, the thought would have been anathema to Redd. J. B. Thompson was his father; Gavin Kline was a stranger. Someone who didn't even care enough to give Redd his name. But in the ways that mattered—trust, respect, reliability—Gavin had slowly earned something like the title of father.

It wasn't fatherly wisdom that Redd needed right now, though. It was information that only the head of the FBI could provide. Information about the Russian mob, information about the traitor.

And maybe information about Aaron Decker. Kline knew better than anyone what Decker was up against, and more importantly, what he was capable of.

Yes, he was going to have to have a long talk with Gavin just as soon as—

"I think someone's following us!"

Redd's eyes snapped open. He sat up straight, heart pounding. "What did you say?"

Brynn didn't take her eyes off the rearview mirror. "There's a car back there that's been behind us since we left Duluth. Hanging back. I tried slowing down to get them to pass, but they just slow down and match my speed."

Redd craned his head around, blinking away the last traces of sleep as he stared out the rear window. The sky outside was streaked with silver and coral, the earliest wash of sunrise bleeding through the tree line. And there, maybe a hundred, hundred fifty yards back, was a pair of headlights.

Decker, sitting in the passenger seat, was already swiping his fingers across the screen of the dash-mounted GPS, scrolling the route ahead. "There's a road coming up," he said. "Looks like a farm road. Hard left. Take it. We'll see if they're really tailing us."

"What?" protested Redd. "Aaron, she hasn't trained for this. Brynn, pull over. I'll drive."

"No," said Decker, calm but firm. "There's no time for that. If we stop and they are gunning for us, we'll be an easy target." He returned his attention to Brynn. "It's coming up, baby girl. Slow it down."

Redd saw there was no point in further arguing the issue, so he instead focused on the trailing vehicle.

"Slower," Decker repeated, with slightly more urgency. "It's a hard turn. There. See it?" He pointed to the approaching intersection, which, while broad, angled away from the highway almost to the point of doubling back.

Redd felt the deceleration as Brynn braked harder, heard the faint rhythmic clicking of the turn signal—*She's using her turn signal? Are you kidding me right now?*—and then felt the truck swinging to the left. He clenched his fists against his thighs, resisting the urge to crawl forward and take the wheel.

But Brynn made the turn smoothly and was already accelerating again, heading down an unstriped but paved two-lane that wended through farm country.

Now came the test. Would the trailing vehicle follow, or keep going on the highway?

With the Raptor now moving in the opposite direction along the adjoining road, Redd got a side-on view of the other vehicle—a black SUV of indeterminate make. As it passed by, he saw its brake lights flash red.

Slowing.

Making the turn.

"Well, that answers that," he murmured, reaching for his gun.

NINETEEN

"Brynn," said Decker, "you just stay steady. Don't worry about them. Focus on the road. And do exactly what I tell you."

"Got it." Her voice was tight, knuckles white on the wheel.

The pavement ended without warning, giving way to a rough gravel road that sliced arrow straight into the heart of farm country.

The Raptor jolted and rumbled, and Redd was glad for the suspension upgrade Mikey had installed. Still, it was like riding a jackhammer on wheels.

"Go faster," said Decker, his attention divided between the GPS and the road ahead. "Mr. Redd's truck can handle it."

Redd had to stifle a protest. Brynn, however, just gave the truck a little more gas.

Redd checked their six again and saw the headlights of the SUV, growing brighter behind them, closing the gap, no longer content to merely follow.

Redd's fist tightened on the grip of his Korth NXS .357 Magnum. He wished it was the steering wheel in his hand.

"What's going on?"

Redd turned to find a sleepy-eyed Mitchell looking around in bewilderment.

"Hey, bud." Redd tried to keep his voice calm. "Everything's okay. But let's have you get down on the floor, all right?"

Mitchell stared back at him, eyes widening as confusion gave way to alarm.

"Do as Mr. Redd says, Mitch," said Decker, calmly, without looking back.

Mitchell unbuckled his seat belt and slid down into the footwell.

Redd kept looking over his shoulder. The SUV was closer now, maybe fifty yards away, headlights seeming to vibrate as it shuddered along the rutted track. He lowered his voice. "I don't think this is going to end with us outrunning them."

"I know," Decker said gravely.

"So you also know what we have to do."

Decker didn't answer right away, but Brynn did. "What's he talking about?"

"Just stay focused on the drive, baby girl. There's a bend coming up in about a mile and a half. A hard right. You're going to have to slow down for it. Remember how I taught you. Brake going into the turn, then accelerate coming out of it."

"Aaron," Redd said, insistent. "Tell her to stop. Let me out."

"Stop?" asked Brynn, her voice edging up.

"Not yet," said Decker. "We need to make some space."

"I'll manage," Redd said.

"We might only get one shot at this. I want to make it count."

"You guys maybe want to loop me in here?" said Brynn.

"No," said Decker, in a tone that brooked no argument. "Just keep driving."

The Raptor jounced over another patch of washboard gravel. Brynn kept the wheel steady, but Redd felt the truck fishtailing just a little. He checked back again, just as the SUV surged forward, swerving to the left.

"They're making a move," he called out. "Driver's side."

Decker glanced back, saw the headlights swing to the left and then disappear as the SUV began drawing even with the Raptor. "Split the road, Brynn," he urged. "Drive down the middle. Don't give them space."

Brynn complied without looking. The Raptor swung to the left and clipped the front end of the SUV. The impact was negligible, a glancing blow between the Raptor's rear bumper and the SUV's front fender, but it was enough to send a jolt through the truck.

Redd winced.

"Oh, my gosh," Brynn gasped. "I hit them. I hit them."

"You're fine," Decker cut in, calm and clear. "Don't worry about it. Just keep driving."

"But the truck—"

"Is a tank," finished Redd, trying to hide his chagrin. "You're doing fine, Brynn."

The SUV had fallen back but remained so close that its headlights were almost completely eclipsed by the Raptor's tailgate. Redd half expected the other driver to make another attempt, but their pursuers opted for a different solution. As Redd watched, he saw an arm extend from the SUV's passenger-side window. An arm, and something else.

"Gun!" Redd barked. He leaned over the seat Mitchell had vacated and hit the button to lower the window. Dust and cold air rushed in.

He leaned his upper body out, the NXS braced in his right hand, his left gripping the doorframe for stability as he curled around to line up his shot, drawing a bead on the SUV's windshield, right where he thought the unseen gunman's head would be, and pulled the trigger.

Even though the Magnum was not actually inside the cab, the report boomed like a thunderclap. Anticipating the recoil, Redd held the big gun steady, even one-handed, but the constant vibration from the road spoiled his aim. The round went high, punching into the top corner of the SUV's windshield, spiderwebbing the glass. The SUV nevertheless jerked back, the shooter vanishing into the dark cab, but not before squeezing off a shot that struck the tailgate with a resounding thump.

Redd pulled back inside and saw Mitchell shaking in the footwell, hands clamped over his ears. He patted the boy's shoulder, murmuring, "You're doing fine, kid. Just stay down."

In the driver's seat, Brynn had gone ashen. Wind continued to whip in through the open window, filling the cab with the din of rushing air and road noise. Redd considered raising it, shutting out the clamor, but decided to leave it down, in case he had to use the NXS again.

His plan had been to have Brynn stop just long enough for him to get out so that he could use the Magnum against their pursuer. A single round through the engine block would put the SUV out of commission and still leave him enough in the chamber to deal with the vehicle's occupants, but he needed to be on the ground. Shooting from a moving vehicle on a gravel road was worse than worthless; it was dangerous. More importantly, he didn't want to draw return fire to the truck. Not with Decker's kids inside.

But to make that happen, they needed distance that their pursuers weren't going to give them. He needed a different plan.

"That bend is coming up," Decker said, not even acknowledging the exchange of gunfire. "About two hundred yards."

"Okay." Brynn's voice was taut with panic and adrenaline.

"You've got this, baby girl. Trust yourself. Trust the truck."

Brynn eased off the gas and applied the brake just as they reached the bend. The Raptor responded, nosing into the corner with a growl from the tires. As the big truck slewed into the turn, Redd felt the tail end slip—not quite a fishtail, but close. Brynn feathered the wheel left, then right again, maintaining control.

"Back on the gas," Decker coached, calm as ever. "Smooth and steady."

Brynn obeyed, and the Raptor surged forward, chewing up the curve and leveling out on the far side. Her breath was coming in short gasps, but her grip on the steering wheel remained steady.

"That was textbook," Decker said.

But the SUV was still behind them, bouncing in their wake, sliding into the turn. It swayed hard, the suspension fighting to stay grounded, but then the driver gunned forward again, surging out of the turn to make another attempt to pull alongside, this time snaking up the passenger side. There was barely enough room—a sliver of gravel between the truck and the drainage ditch that separated road from field.

"Right side!" Redd shouted, hitting the button to lower that window.

From the front, Brynn glanced over, caught sight of the vehicle in the side mirror. Her eyes widened, but then, for the first time since the ordeal began, she didn't wait for her dad to tell her what to do. She swerved right, closing the gap, cutting off the SUVs path. The Raptor's tires chewed into the loose gravel at the margin.

Redd barely had time to brace himself before the vehicles made contact. As before, it was a glancing blow, the sturdy rear bumper of the pickup hooking into the fender of the SUV, right above the left front wheel, but it was enough. The Raptor shoved the SUV sideways.

The other driver tried to brake, but his vehicle had too much momentum. It skidded through the loose gravel, then its right front wheel dropped into the ditch. As it heaved over and bottomed out on the edge, its momentum carried it forward. The vehicle flipped, the rear end leaving the ground, the front end slamming down into the bottom of the ditch. The impact crushed the hood like an accordion, launching the SUV skyward. It tumbled once, then twice, then caught a stump hidden in the tall grass. That final blow twisted the entire chassis sideways and sent the vehicle corkscrewing into the tree line, where it collided with a thick birch tree with a final thunderous crack.

Brynn drove on, the Raptor barreling on down the gravel road, leaving the carnage in its wake.

"Brynn," Decker said gently. "You can stop now."

She didn't respond. Her eyes were wide and fixed ahead, knuckles white against the wheel.

"Brynn," Decker repeated, louder, sharper. "Stop the truck."

This time, his words got through. Her foot came off the gas and slammed down on the brake pedal. The Raptor skidded on the gravel, fishtailing, before finally coming to a jerking halt. As if a switch had been thrown, all was suddenly quiet; the only sound was the faint rumble of the idling engine.

Brynn let out a shaky breath. Her arms dropped from the wheel and she curled forward, pressing her forehead against it, shoulders beginning to tremble.

"I didn't mean to . . . I wasn't trying to—" Her voice cracked. "Did I kill them?"

Decker reached across the console and gently took her hand. "Look at me, Brynn."

She didn't.

"Brynn," he said, softer this time. "Look at me."

Redd heard the calm in his voice, saw the quiet in his face. Every word, every syllable, radiated reassurance and empathy.

Slowly, Brynn turned her head. Her eyes were glassy, tears welling up at the corners.

"You did good, honey," he said. "You're safe. Mitchell's safe. It's all going to be okay."

She blinked once. Then nodded, just slightly.

"You did good," he said again. "Now stay here. I'll be right back."

He opened the door and climbed out, drawing the Glock from his waistband. Redd slid out as well, joining him, Magnum in hand.

As they started down the road, Redd glanced over at Decker. The face of the loving father was gone, replaced by something harder, colder. Yet Redd didn't mistake the change for the lowering of a mask. This wasn't a different man. The same love that steadied Brynn's shaking hand now powered each step down that gravel road. This was the other side of fatherhood, Redd knew.

The part that would do whatever it took to protect his family.

TWENTY

The SUV looked like a crushed soda can, wrapped around the trunk of a stately birch. The frame had twisted from the impact. The glass was mostly gone, passenger door peeled open like the lid of a sardine can.

Despite the catastrophic nature of the damage, Redd and Decker approached cautiously, weapons ready.

"Cover me," Decker said, moving ahead.

Redd nodded, aiming the NXS at the vehicle while taking care not to flag the other man. Decker moved in low, kneeling and sweeping the interior with his Glock before leaning in for a closer look. A second later, he glanced back. "It's clear. Come up."

Redd lowered his weapon and moved forward to join Decker. The smell hit his nostrils—hot metal, radiator coolant, blood.

Death.

There were two men inside. The passenger was sprawled across the dash like a discarded puppet, his neck twisted so far around, it looked backward. He hadn't been wearing a seat belt, and when the vehicle flipped, he'd been flung around the interior like the marble in a can of spray paint.

The driver was alive, but just barely.

Redd took note of the man's appearance. Overweight, his round florid face beaded with sweat. No discipline in the eyes, no trace of training. This man wasn't cut from the same cloth as the shooters he'd fought outside Decker's cabin.

He was wedged against the wheel, gasping through blood-streaked teeth, cradling his right arm with his left. His pants were saturated with blood. Decker was leaning in close to him, his left hand jammed against the man's groin.

"You've torn open your femoral artery," Decker was saying, his voice clinical and cold. "I'm holding pressure on the wound right now, but that's only a temporary fix. You need immediate medical attention, but unfortunately, it's going to take a while for the paramedics to get here. If I move my hand, you'll bleed out in a couple minutes. Maybe less."

The man's head rolled toward him. His face was a mask of pain, but even so, he managed to spit something out in Russian.

Redd didn't need a translator.

"Suit yourself." Decker shifted his posture, giving the appearance of easing the pressure on the wound, while actually pressing harder.

"No!" the man cried, gasping. "Wait! Please!" He spoke English, his accent thick but not unintelligible.

Decker nodded. "That's better."

"These guys don't look like the same crew that came after you back at your place," Redd said.

"They're not. This guy's local mob muscle." Decker looked at the driver again. "Isn't that right? Working out of . . . where, Chicago?"

The man seemed to consider his answer, weighing the cost of loyalty. Then he spat out a chuckle. "Duluth."

Redd raised an eyebrow. "The Bratva is in Duluth?"

The man winced, lips pulling back from blood-streaked teeth. "Big port. International. Lots of freight. But out of the way. Easy to move . . . anything."

Redd nodded. "Makes sense."

"Who sent you?" pressed Decker.

"I . . . I don't know his name."

Decker's hand moved. "Try again."

The man groaned, eyes fluttering. "The Russian."

"You're all Russian."

"No. He's *Russian* Russian. From Moscow. Big man. *Vory v Zakone.*"

"Is that like a Bratva godfather?" asked Redd.

"Something like that." Decker nodded to the driver. "How did you find us?"

"We were told . . . big black truck with tinted windows and dark rims. Might be coming through. Watch the highway. That's all."

Redd leaned closer. "You were just sitting there on the roadside? Watching for us?"

"He told us to, so we did. We saw you." The man's breathing hitched. "We follow. That's all. I swear."

"Someone must have seen us leave the cabin," said Redd. "A survivor. Called this Russian with a description of my truck."

"That means they aren't tracking us," said Decker. "It was just dumb luck that these two spotted us." He turned back to the driver. "I'm guessing you called this in?"

Before the man could answer, the distinctive hum of a vibrating phone was audible. Decker reached his free hand into the man's jacket pocket and took out a mobile phone. The screen was smeared with blood, but he wiped it clean on the man's lapel and then held it up to the man's face. It took a moment for the device to recognize its owner, but then the screen revealed a chain of text messages in Cyrillic. Decker began scrolling through them.

"That him?" Redd asked. "The Russian?"

Decker nodded. "First message was about spotting us on the highway. Next few are updates . . . *Trying to lose us* . . ." He paused, brought his gaze to the driver again. "Last message: *Stop them. Kill everyone.*"

He tapped out a response with his thumb and sent it.

"What did you say?" Redd asked.

Decker looked up at him, a hint of a smile touching the corner of his mouth. "I said, *It's done.*"

He flung the phone away, into the woods, and then lifted his hand from the driver's thigh. The sodden fabric of his pants immediately began to pulse with arterial spurts.

The man gasped, eyes going wide. "No! No—wait! Please!" He let go of his injured arm and pressed his good hand against his groin but had neither the strength nor the leverage to stop the bleeding.

Decker stood, ignoring the man's pleas. "That'll buy us a little time, but we should get moving."

He turned and began moving back to the road. Redd glanced at the pleading driver. The man's face was going gray with shock, eyes bulging. Blood was already pooling beneath him, soaking into the crushed upholstery.

"Please. Help me. I told you what you wanted to know."

Redd almost felt a twinge of pity. This man wasn't a soldier, wasn't a professional. But then he thought about Mitchell huddled in the footwell, Brynn's hands shaking on the steering wheel.

This man hadn't hesitated when he got the order to kill them.

"Live by the sword, die by the sword," he murmured. "Ever hear that one?"

"Please." The man's pleading eyes were full of tears.

"Nothing I can do." Redd used the barrel of his gun to lift the man's shirt. "Your only shot is to take off your belt, wrap it around your leg as tight as you can get it, and hope it slows the bleeding enough to get to a hospital."

The man wasted no time. Fingers shaking, he reached for his buckle, unfastened it, then started pulling frantically on his belt.

"Of course, let's say you do survive," started Redd. "What happens when the big Russian bad guy finds out that you failed your task, *and* that you gave us his info?"

The man stopped, dropping the end of his belt, seemingly resigned to his fate. "I'm already dead."

Redd nodded. "But let me warn you . . . If you do somehow defy every odd and walk away from this, you'll wish you did die if you ever come near me"—he thrust his free thumb toward Decker and his Raptor—"or him."

Not waiting for a response, Redd turned and hurried after Decker. The man's cries followed him but grew fainter by the second.

"I still don't think they're tracking us," Decker said as Redd caught up with him. "Not with drones at least. This was a Hail Mary play that got lucky."

"Yeah, well, if they're watching the roads, they might get lucky again. It's a long way to Montana."

"They can't watch all the roads. They know that we were here, in Minnesota, but they won't know where we're going. If we stay off the main highways, stick to back roads, I think we'll be okay."

"That'll add hours to the trip."

"I don't think we have a choice."

Redd frowned but then nodded toward the truck. "You think she's going to be okay driving after this?"

Decker raised an eyebrow. "I think *she* will. The question is, will you be okay with her driving?"

Redd gave a grunt that was half laugh, half sigh. "I guess we'll find out. Let's just hope she doesn't have to do anything like that again."

They reached the Raptor. Brynn had gotten out and climbed back into the rear cab, where she was holding Mitchell in her arms. Both of them looked up as the two men approached.

Redd glanced at the scrapes on the rear quarter panel and shook his head. "Mikey's gonna tear me a new one when he sees this."

"Sorry about your truck, Mr. Redd," Brynn said. She looked like she might burst into tears.

"Don't worry about it. You did good." He managed a smile. "But I think I'll do the driving for a while."

TWENTY-ONE

Decker plotted a route into the GPS that wound across the Midwest, along rural highways and farm roads, snaking westward across Minnesota, the Dakotas, and into Montana, bypassing major population centers entirely. It wasn't the fastest route, but it was quiet, anonymous, and hopefully hidden from the searching eyes of the Russian mob.

They took turns behind the wheel. Redd, Decker, and Brynn rotated in shifts—one driving, one navigating and keeping the driver awake, the third catching what rest they could. No one spoke much unless necessary. The driver got to choose the music.

The rest of the trip was uneventful. Small towns blurred past the windows, their main streets empty but for grain silos and blinking stoplights. Mitchell was fascinated at first, calling out cows, tractors, and even a bald eagle gliding low over a frozen pond. But the landscapes grew repetitive, the novelty wore off, and eventually he sagged back in his seat, arms crossed, announcing his boredom.

No one blamed him. Twenty-seven hours was a long time to spend cooped up in the cab of a pickup.

Night came down on them in eastern Montana. The road narrowed, empty but for the occasional distant rig, its running lights glowing like stars against the black. A few miles outside Jordan, Redd called for a break. They pulled into a gravel turnout surrounded by scrub brush and got out, all except Mitchell who was already curled up in the back seat, snoozing. Brynn, who had been driving, gazed up at the sky. The moon, a thumbnail of silver, hung just above the dark horizon to the west, but with so little artificial light, the night sky was almost bright enough to read by.

"I've never seen so many stars before," Brynn said softly.

Redd, recalling his first night in Big Sky Country so many years ago, couldn't help but smile.

They took turns relieving themselves behind a roadside bush and then climbed back into the Raptor for the final push. "We should make it to Wellington around dawn," said Redd, trying to inject a hopeful note.

Dawn was still eight hours away, but nobody complained.

They drove on under the canopy of the Milky Way. Gradually, twilight pulled back the curtain, letting the mountains gently materialize on the western horizon, the rising sun behind them washing the foothills in a pale orange glow. Redd soon began to recognize familiar landmarks. Junctions. Farmhouses.

They hit the outskirts of Wellington just after sunrise, approaching from the east. The road narrowed as they left town, climbing gradually into the hills. Redd turned off onto a paved service road that gave way to gravel, then steered the Raptor onto a long winding track. He slowed to cross the narrow wooden bridge spanning the creek, feeling the planks clattering under the tires and the vibration as they rolled over the cattle guard. On the other side, the entry gate came into view: two weathered upright posts, each hewn from a lodgepole pine, topped with the hand-painted sign reading *Thompson Ranch.*

Through the screen of trees, he could see several head of cattle grazing in the pasture, and then, he saw the house.

Redd felt a flicker of something rare and fleeting.

Satisfaction.

He'd built the house with his own hands. Every bit of it, from the foundation to the cabinetry.

With a little help from Mikey. And his father-in-law.

A couple of years ago, the old place—the one where J. B. had raised him—had burned in a fire. This one, like a phoenix, had risen from the ashes. It was where *he* would raise his children.

He eased the Raptor up the final rise and parked beneath the oak tree that shaded the turnaround.

"Well, this is it," he said. "Home, sweet home."

Mitchell was the first one out of the truck, launching himself from the back seat before Redd could shut off the engine. His eyes were wide, sweeping over the house, the barn, the pasture, the distant cattle.

"Whoa," he said, half to himself, half in wonder. "This is a *real* ranch. Can I see your horse?"

Brynn slid out after him, slower, her nose wrinkling a little as she got her first whiff of cattle manure. Her gaze moved from the porch to the barn to the tree line beyond, assessing it all like the terrain of a distant planet.

The front door banged open, and a blur of muscle and fur bounded down the porch steps and hit the ground at a run, ears back, tail swishing, paws kicking up a spray of gravel as it quickly closed the distance.

"Rubble, sit," Redd said sternly, but the massive rottweiler paid no heed. He reared up, placing both front paws on Redd's shoulders, and tried, rather successfully, to lick his face.

"All right, all right. I missed you too, Rub."

Rubble dropped to all fours, tail still going, and barked once, a deep-chested whuff.

"Who's a good boy?" Redd scratched his ears. "Now behave. We've got company." He turned to the others. "This is Rubble. He's a big teddy bear. Well, for the most part."

Mitchell was already down on one knee, grinning ear to ear as Rubble sniffed at his outstretched hand. Brynn stayed back, regarding the dog warily.

"I've never seen a dog this big," she said. "He's almost as big as my dad."

Redd laughed. "Yeah, but the dog smells better."

A moment later, the screen door swung open again, and another figure emerged onto the porch.

Emily.

She stepped into the early light with a coffee mug cradled in both hands, the sleeves of her wool sweater pushed up to the elbows. Her chestnut hair was pulled into a loose braid over one shoulder, a few strands catching the dawn breeze.

Redd never failed to be amazed by her effortless beauty. Nothing seemed to diminish it, not work or the many trials they had faced together over the course of the last few years. Yet his love for her went much deeper than mere physical attraction. The bond between them, which might have been dismissed as mere puppy love—a fleeting high-school romance—had endured across time, distance, and Redd's own pigheadedness.

Emily was, quite simply, his everything.

From the porch, her eyes moved from him to the others, then came back to him. "Matty, you didn't tell me you'd be bringing friends for breakfast."

Her tone was half joking. She knew him well enough to know that he had his reasons for keeping radio silence.

He had wanted to call her, had thought about it a dozen times during the drive, but if the Russians had even a partial bead on his identity, there was a chance—however slim—that they might connect the dots and start monitoring her phone. It wasn't likely, but it wasn't impossible. Better to show up unannounced than to draw trouble to their door. Again.

"Sorry, babe. It just sort of happened."

She gave him a look of mock exasperation then broke into a smile. "Well, are you going to introduce me?"

"You remember Aaron?"

Decker gave a quiet nod from the gravel. Emily returned it. "Of course I do. Hard to forget the man who saves your husband's life. Though, I think you kind of . . . *vanished* . . . before we got to actually, you know, *officially* meet."

Decker spoke up. "This is Brynn and Mitchell."

Mitchell gave a shy wave. Brynn, still standing a little behind her brother, offered a polite smile, wary but respectful.

Emily regarded them with a physician's eye, not merely looking at them, but assessing them, reading the weariness in their faces. Then she stepped aside and pulled the screen door open. "Well, don't just stand there. Come on in. I'll get breakfast started."

As they filed into the house, Brynn followed Emily into the kitchen. "Need a hand?"

"I'd love some help! Don't get a lot of that in the kitchen, if you know what I mean." Emily winked playfully at Brynn.

"Hey, I help cook meals and stuff," said Redd.

Emily chuckled. "Matty, grilling steaks isn't making a *whole* meal."

"Speak for yourself," said Decker.

Emily reached for a mixing bowl, then slid that and an egg carton toward Brynn. "Want to help me scramble some eggs for everyone?"

Redd smiled at the exchange then filled two mugs of coffee, handing one to Decker, who had taken a seat at the breakfast bar.

Decker accepted the mug but stared into it with a bemused expression. "Got creamer?"

Redd laughed. "You're kidding. Big tough guy like you?"

Decker gave a guilty shrug.

Redd shook his head and circled around to the refrigerator to grab a carton of half-and-half.

Just then, a squall erupted from the baby monitor on the counter. Redd started to rise, but Emily waved him off. "I got it, Matty. Drink your coffee. I can tell you need it . . . and maybe a shower." She turned to Brynn, handing her the shredder she had been using to make hash browns. "Can you hold down the fort for a minute?"

Brynn nodded, smoothly taking over while Emily headed into the other room. A few minutes later, she returned with a much-soothed baby Lauren in her arms, followed by a bleary-eyed Jack who wore his favorite, if somewhat outgrown, Buzz Lightyear pajamas. The sight of his adopted son, looking healthy and happy, never failed to bring a smile to Redd's face. The kid had been through so much in his short life; he deserved a little happiness.

Jack brightened when he saw Mitchell. He flashed a big smile and went over to him. "Hi!"

Mitchell, looking a little surprised to see another boy, albeit one slightly younger, reacted with unexpected shyness. "Hey."

Redd quickly interceded. "Jack, this is Mitchell. Why don't you show him your room?"

Both boys seized on this idea, with Jack grabbing Mitchell's hand and dragging him toward the stairs as he launched into an inventory of his toys.

Emily, with Lauren still cradled in her arms, slid onto the stool on the other side of Decker. "Matty's not in the habit of bringing surprise guests for breakfast, and while you're a hard read, Mr. Decker, you don't seem like the type to hit the panic button without good reason. So, tell me, how bad is it?"

Decker stared back at her for a moment, then glanced at Redd as if asking for permission. Or help.

Redd decided to throw him a lifeline. "There are some rather unsavory people trying to cause trouble for Aaron. He asked us to watch Brynn and Mitchell while he deals with it."

Emily looked at Decker, her expression now more welcoming. "Of course. We're happy to help. Mitchell can have Jack's room. Jack and Little Matty can share a room. Brynn can take the guest room. What else you need?"

Decker looked at Redd again.

"Aaron needs my help with this, Em. I gotta go with him."

Emily raised an eyebrow. "So when you said *we* would watch the kids, what you really meant was that *I* would watch them."

"Em, I—"

She raised a hand. "You're lucky I love you, Matthew Redd."

"Don't I know it."

Emily began rocking back and forth, soothing the baby with gentle motion. "I get it, Matty. You're obviously going to be more good to Aaron out there than you would be puttering around here. Between the two of you, I'm sure you can wrap this up."

She glanced over at Brynn, who was watching the exchange with intense interest, completely forgetting about the potato she had been in the process of shredding. "I'm sure Brynn and I can manage the boys. Besides, it'll be nice to finally have a young woman around the house. I could use some girl time."

Redd smiled. This was why he loved her.

"Just make sure," she went on, "that whatever trouble you two are dealing with doesn't find its way here. While you're gone, I mean."

Decker gave a helpless shrug. "I really can't—"

Redd cut him off. "We're not going to give them a chance to do anything like that. But all the same, I'm going to call Stuart. Have him keep an eye on you."

Stuart was Sheriff Stuart Blackwood. Despite their initially frosty relationship, Blackwood had become one of Redd's closest allies over the past few years. The lawman made no secret of wanting Redd as one of his deputies and had even hinted at having Redd take over for him when he retired.

Emily looked unconvinced. "If these 'unsavory' folks are bad enough to spook you, then I have to wonder if Stuart can handle them."

"There's no reason to think they know where the kids are. Or that we're involved in this." Sensing that he had failed to make his case, Redd went on. "If you feel even a little bit nervous about this, I can give Gavin a call. Get him to send a couple agents from the Bozeman FO."

Even the thought of having FBI agents watching over them did not appear to completely ease Emily's concerns, but after considering it for a moment, she nodded. "All right. I suppose that will have to do. Besides, if all else fails, I've got Rubble."

"The dog? I thought he was a giant teddy bear," said Brynn.

Emily chinned toward Redd. "He said that, huh?"

Brynn nodded.

"Well, he *is* a giant teddy bear. But he can also turn into a war dog real quick."

"He isn't going to attack me, is he?"

"Nah." Emily shifted Lauren in her arms. "I can tell you're one of the good ones, sweetie. You and Rub Man will be friends before you know it."

"Thank you," Decker said gratefully. "Both of you."

Emily rose and handed the baby to Redd, then moved to take over for Brynn. "What are friends for?" Her eyes met Redd's. "But you better come back to me in one piece, Matty."

"Always."

"Good." Emily took a deep breath and placed her hands on her hips. "Then let's eat."

TWENTY-TWO

CHICAGO, ILLINOIS

Volkov ground two antacid tablets between his teeth and swallowed the chalky grit. He'd been going through them like candy, but so far, they had done little to quell the acid fire burning in his gut.

He couldn't remember the last time he'd slept. Really slept. He'd nodded off a few times on the flight from Moscow—twilight naps in the leather recliner aboard Skvortsov's Gulfstream V—but those had somehow left him feeling even more drained.

It had been a little over thirty-six hours since the failed attempt to eliminate Decker at the cabin in northern Michigan. Thirty-six hours since Konstantin died with a bullet to the head. Thirty-six hours since Decker had disappeared again like smoke through a screen door.

Duluth had been a fleeting ray of hope. Two local Bratva soldiers had spotted a black truck roughly matching the description of the one that had crashed the party at Decker's cabin. They'd followed it and then, on Volkov's orders, run it off the road, killing the occupants.

Or at least that was what they had reported. After that, the two men had gone silent. Several more hours had passed before the truth had come out. Both men were dead, and there was no sign of the black pickup.

Now he was in Chicago, holed up in one of Yegor Petrovich's properties in River North. Petrovich, an *avtoritet* with roots in Chelyabinsk and reach into every port and warehouse from Milwaukee to Indianapolis, had known better than to refuse to help him with the search for Aaron Decker, but that didn't mean he was happy about it. Volkov could feel the man's contempt with every tight-lipped update.

The Chicago Bratva was a blunt instrument. The first failed attempt on Decker's life had amply demonstrated that. The disaster in Duluth had nailed it home. Skvortsov had promised better. In addition to a small army of shooters, the CEO of Sibir Zashchitniki also managed a cadre of elite cyber operatives who could hack into social media accounts, trace credit card activity, and penetrate CCTV networks with ease. But so far, their efforts had turned up nothing. No phone pings. No credit card hits. No facial recognition matches.

If Decker had been a ghost before, now he was . . . vapor.

Thirty-six hours of dead ends. Thirty-six hours in which the trail had gone from lukewarm to a block of ice.

He stepped into the adjoining room and found Skvortsov hunched over a laptop, headset on, screens casting a bluish glow across his hawkish features. A grainy video feed flickered to life on the main display—two young men in hoodies speaking rapid-fire Russian. Skvortsov raised a finger without looking, signaling Volkov to wait.

"No. The timestamp doesn't match. Check again." He listened a moment longer, then killed the call with a muttered curse and leaned back in his chair.

"Well?" Volkov asked.

Skvortsov shook his head. "Nothing. We've scraped toll road data, security cameras, flight manifests, even cross-referenced metadata from every phone ping within fifty miles of that cabin. But still . . . nothing."

Volkov stepped closer, knuckles whitening around the edge of the desk. "You said your people are the best."

"They are. But this man is"—he shook his head—"like no one. He has no digital presence. Who lives like that?"

Volkov's hands clenched into fists. "We need something," he said. "What about his kids? Kids can't live without their phones."

"Evidently, these kids can." Skvortsov shrugged. "Be patient, Grigori. He will make a mistake eventually."

"Patience is not one of my virtues," Volkov shot back. *Nor is it one of his.*

As if in response to the unspoken thought, Volkov felt his phone buzzing in his pocket.

Please, he thought, as he pulled it out and glanced at the illuminated screen. *Anything but—*

The blood drained from his face.

Skvortsov glanced up, his expression sharpening. "Bad news?"

Volkov didn't answer. He turned away and accepted the call.

"Grigori," Nightshade said, his tone eerily smooth. "It's been almost two days. I thought I would have heard back from you by now."

Volkov worked moisture into his mouth. "I sent men to the location you gave us. Decker was already gone." It was only a partial lie. Skvortsov had sent in a second team to sanitize the scene, and there had been no trace of Decker beyond an abandoned vehicle. "It looks like something spooked him."

A pause. Then the voice came back, quieter—and far colder. "Don't think for a second that you can deceive me, Grigori."

Volkov closed his eyes.

"I know all about what happened," Nightshade continued. "You failed. Again."

Volkov felt the air in the room tighten. "I didn't mean to mislead you."

"Didn't mean to?" Nightshade said, almost musing. "I suppose you also didn't mean to botch the easiest kill of your career? Or fail to clean up the mess after?"

Volkov bit down the reply that rose to his lips. He wanted to flip the accusation back on Nightshade. After all, it had been his faulty intelligence that had sent Skvortsov's men into the meat grinder. But he knew better than to speak in anger to this man. "Decker had help."

"Help," Nightshade echoed. "Interesting. What kind of help?"

So, you don't know everything after all.

"A man in a big pickup truck. Came out of nowhere. Killed several of my men. Including Konstantin."

There was a silence on the line. Not total—Volkov could hear something faint in the background. Tapping? A keyboard.

"The truck was later spotted passing through Duluth. In Minnesota. The men who were sent to follow weren't able to confirm whether it was the same truck that showed up to save Decker, but . . ."

"But?"

"They're dead," Volkov said, knowing better than to dress it up.

Nightshade gave a long, disappointed sigh. "I must say, Grigori, this is not what I expected when I gave you that address. I thought you understood my expectations."

"I do."

"Do you?" The voice turned ice edged again. "Because it seems to me you've mistaken your position in our arrangement. You don't get to fail quietly. You don't get to sweep your incompetence under the rug and hope I won't notice."

Volkov bowed his head. "I was wrong."

"Yes," Nightshade said. "You were."

Volkov's gut clenched. *Here it comes.* He swallowed. "Do you want me to fall on my sword? Fine. I will." He tried to sound defiant—if he was going to die, at least he'd go out on his own terms—but the quaver in his voice betrayed him.

On the other end of the line, Nightshade just chuckled. "Oh, Grigori," he said. "If I wanted you dead, we wouldn't be talking."

Volkov exhaled, tension bleeding from his shoulders in a rush of cold sweat.

"There's still a path forward," Nightshade continued, voice tightening again—but this time with purpose. "One last chance for you to redeem yourself."

Volkov swallowed again, sensing a trap, but nonetheless daring to hope. "What would you have me do?"

"Have you ever heard the saying, 'The definition of insanity is doing the same thing over and over again, and expecting a different result'? That's the lesson here, Grigori. You keep thinking that Aaron Decker is a nail you can pound into oblivion with a sledgehammer. This will require finesse. Can you do finesse?"

"Finesse?" Volkov glanced over at Skvortsov, who was following the call with rapt attention. "Yes, I can do finesse."

"Good," Nightshade said. "Then pay attention. I know where Decker will go next. In fact, he's likely already there. But I don't want you charging in like a rabid bear and ruining what will probably be your last chance to end this cleanly."

"Just tell me where he is."

"He's in Montana. With the man who owns that truck. His name is Matthew Redd."

TWENTY-THREE

STILLWATER COUNTY, MONTANA

When the last of the dinner dishes were loaded into the dishwasher, Redd grabbed two cans of Coke Zero from the fridge and joined Decker on the front porch. He left the light off, partly to avoid attracting insects but mostly so that they could watch the stars poke through the lavender sky, and handed one of the cans to Decker.

"To Big Sky Country," said Redd, offering the top of his can for the toast.

Decker, however, just stared at the can Redd had given him. "Got a glass?"

"A glass?" replied Redd, speaking slowly as if slightly offended by the question.

"I hate drinking from a can. Plus, pouring it helps release the carbonation so it doesn't sit like a rock in your gut."

Redd rolled his eyes and leaned back in his chair. "I think there are some Solo cups in the pantry. Help yourself."

Decker gave the can a small shake, then shrugged. "Never mind." He clinked his can against Redd's. "To Big Sky Country, and the people who make it home."

"Amen."

Redd took a pull, savoring both the flavor of the cold Coke and the sunset.

He had a feeling it would be a while before he would be able to enjoy another. The house behind them had settled into a peaceful rhythm. Emily and Brynn were inside, watching a rerun of *The Big Bang Theory* with Jack. Lauren had gone down first, then Mitchell and Little Matty had crashed hard after a long day of trailing Redd through chores. They had helped muck Remington's stalls and feed the animals, and as a reward, Redd had let Jack ride Remington around the corral. All in all, it had been a good day.

Which made what they would have to do next that much harder.

Redd took another swig then set the can down on the arm of his chair. "So, how are we gonna do this?"

Decker rolled his can between his palms. "We've got three real problems right now. The Russian. The traitor. And staying off the radar while we go after all of them. We'll start with the Russian."

"Back to Duluth?"

Decker chuckled. "More like Chicago. It's the major regional hub for all Russian mob activity. Whoever this Russian is, he'll be working with the Bratva *avtoritet* there. We just need to find the person inside their operation who can give us a name."

"And once we get a name?"

Decker shrugged, spreading his hands. "We pay him a visit and get him to give up the traitor's name."

Redd blinked. "And if he's in Russia?"

"Then we go to Russia," said Decker with another shrug.

"Russia," echoed Redd. "That's your plan?"

"It's not ideal, but—"

"Not ideal? It's suicide." Redd shook his head. "I get that you've got all these mad ninja assassin skills, but Russia? That's not just behind enemy lines; that's another planet altogether. We go over there, we've got no backup, no allies, no extraction. One wrong move and we disappear forever."

"There's a reason I prefer to work alone."

"And when was the last time you did that kind of work in a place like that?"

"I was in Belarus just a few months ago," Decker shot back. Yet, even as he said it, a light bulb seemed to flash over his head.

Redd raised an eyebrow. "Belarus? Well, isn't that an interesting coincidence."

Decker frowned but said nothing.

"Look," Redd went on. "I'm not exactly known for subtlety, but I do know that it's better to work smarter than work harder."

"Meaning?"

"Meaning, if we can get a name for this Russian, maybe we can slip it to Gavin. Have him put it into the FBI computer . . ." He wiggled his fingers as if doing a magic trick. "Connect some dots."

Decker leaned back. "Having him send a couple agents to watch the kids is one thing. Telling him to start digging into the Russian mob will tip our hand. The traitor is going to be watching for red flags like that."

"Gavin knows how to be discreet. He kept you a secret for fifteen years."

Decker frowned, unwilling to cede the point, but Redd pushed on. "Now, to your third problem . . . staying off the radar. Have you given any thought to how we're getting to Chicago? I'm not sure I'm up for another marathon road trip."

"We'll fly," Decker said, as if it were the obvious choice. "I'll be using an alias, of course, but my travel ID will get me through security. I've got a storage unit in Chicago with everything we'll need. Weapons, cash, burner phones."

"You might have a fake ID handy. I don't."

Decker waved that off. "The Russian isn't looking for you."

"Whoever told the Russian about my pickup might have got a look at me. I'm not exactly easy to forget. And fake papers or not, there's no shot they won't have people at O'Hare and Midway watching arrivals, just in case."

Decker gave a thoughtful hum and took another sip. "We could hire someone to fly us. A charter."

"That could be a little pricey."

"Money's not a problem. The challenge would be finding someone trustworthy. Some of these private operators have been known to pick up a side hustle now and then. I'm not saying they're all criminals, but a lot of them *know* criminals. And pilots love to talk." Decker gave him a measured look. "Know any local flyboys? More importantly, anyone you trust?"

"The only local flight I've made was in a Forest Service whirlybird that dropped me off in the middle of a wildfire . . ."

Redd trailed off as the memory took root. He took out his phone and began scrolling through his call history. It took several seconds—the call he was looking for had come in months ago—but he hadn't deleted it.

"There you are," he muttered, and tapped the call icon.

It rang twice before a voice answered, alert but guarded. "Thornhill."

"Hey, Frank, it's Matthew Redd."

He almost added, *Remember me?*

Redd had met Frank Thornhill, the Forest Service fire management officer for the region, during the previous year's wildfire in the Elkhorn Mountains. After Redd's actions during the fire, Thornhill had called to thank him personally.

But there was no need for a prompt. Thornhill's manner immediately relaxed. "Matthew! Great to hear from you. How have you been?"

"Busy," Redd said, which was true enough. "But still vertical, so I can't complain."

"Good, good. So, to what do I owe the pleasure?"

"Well, I was wondering if you could help me out with something. You work with a lot of contract pilots, don't you?"

"Several. Why? You need someone to fly a search for you?"

Redd considered the dodge for a split second. It would be easy to let Thornhill believe that, but he decided that honesty was the best policy. "Not exactly. Me and a buddy need to get to Chicago. ASAP. I'm just looking at all my options."

"Chicago, eh? That's a bit of a jump. Flying United would be a heck of a lot cheaper, and probably faster too."

Redd winced. "My friend wants to take the scenic route." *So much for honesty.* "And he's paying for it."

Thornhill accepted this with a knowing grunt. "Chicago," he repeated. "You'll want fixed-wing then." He seemed to consider the question for a moment. "Okay, I know someone who might be interested in picking up a charter. Toby Marquez. Everyone calls him Skids."

"Skids?" asked Redd, dubious.

"Pilot humor," Thornhill said with a chuckle. "He's got a Cessna 414. Does reconnaissance flights for us during fire season. Flies hunters and tourists all over the rest of the time. This time of year, he pretty much scrounges for anything. He's a bit of a character, but then most of these guys are. Operates out of Skyservice at Helena Regional. If you like, I'll reach out to him and let him know you're interested."

"I'd appreciate that."

"Sure thing. I'll send you his contact info and let him know to expect your call."

"Thanks, Frank. I owe you one." Redd ended the call and faced Decker. "I think we've got transportation sorted."

Decker raised an eyebrow. "Skids?"

Redd shrugged. "That gets us *to* Chicago."

"I can arrange to have a rental delivered to the FBO." Decker emptied his can and set it on the porch beside his chair. "We'll head to my storage unit and load up, then do some hunting."

"Might take a day or two to figure out who we're looking for."

"Yeah," Decker agreed. "Which is another advantage to hiring a plane. If we draw too much heat, we'll need to be able to go wheels up fast."

Redd's phone buzzed. He glanced down and saw a text message from Thornhill. "That was fast," he muttered, clicking on the message, which contained the phone number for High Country Air. Redd clicked on it and waited for the call to connect.

"High Country Air." The voice was a relaxed baritone. "This is Skids."

"Skids, this is Matthew Redd. Frank Thornhill gave me your number."

"Yeah, he told me to expect your call. Said you're looking to fly to Chicago. That right?"

"Yes. Tomorrow morning if possible."

"Sure, it's possible. How many pax?"

"Two of us. Some luggage."

"All right. Round trip?"

Redd glanced over at Decker who, hearing only Redd's side of the conversation, returned a quizzical look. "Skids, I'm going to put you on speaker so my friend can hear."

Redd clicked the speaker icon just in time to hear Skids give his consent. "Go for it."

"Skids wants to know if it's a round trip."

Decker nodded. "That would be a yes. Not sure how long we'll be staying, though. And there's a possibility that we may need to schedule additional legs before returning."

"Additional legs?" Skids suddenly sounded less relaxed. "How long is this gonna take?"

"I'm afraid I can't give you an exact time frame. Let's say a week, with an option to extend."

"A *week*?" came the incredulous reply. Skids was silent for a long moment. "Look, let's not waste your time or mine. This is gonna cost you. A *lot*."

"How much?" asked Redd.

He nearly choked when Skids gave the answer. Decker, however, took the number in stride. Without missing a beat, he came back with a figure that was about ten percent lower, then added, "I'll be paying in cash."

"Cash?" Redd could hear the wariness in the pilot's voice. "This isn't something illegal, is it? I mean, I gotta ask."

"Of course not," Decker said. That at least was mostly true. Decker let the denial hang in the air for a moment, then, in a decidedly calculated manner, added, "Cash isn't going to be a problem, is it?"

Redd could almost hear the wheels in Skids's head spinning. If they paid cash, Skids could invoice any amount he pleased and pocket the difference. Tax-free income. On the other hand, if it was dirty money—and Skids couldn't afford to take the chance that it wasn't—he would have to find a way to launder it, which would not only put him in dodgy territory, legally, but also cost him a percentage.

"Because if it is," Decker went on, "we can find someone else."

"No, no," Skids replied hastily. "Cash is fine."

"The money *is* clean," said Decker, "though I don't expect you to take my word for it. I prefer to use cash because I'd like to avoid leaving an electronic trail. I trust you can be discreet."

"Of course," said Skids, still sounding a little apprehensive.

"I want you to fly VFR. No flight plan. Once we get there, we'll need you to be on standby. I'll give you an additional per diem to take care of any expenses, and when all of this is done, I'll toss in a bonus. Say . . . another five thousand."

Redd did the math and realized that Decker had effectively given back the ten percent he'd cut off Skids's original quote, only now it felt like he was doing the pilot a favor.

Skids was quiet for another long moment. "You swear this isn't anything illegal?"

"Scout's honor, Skids. And I *was* a Boy Scout." Decker lowered his voice as if confiding a secret. "You seem like a guy who can keep a secret, so I'm going to be straight with you. I can't tell you who we work for, but I will say this: You can't break the law if the guy you're working for makes the law. You get me?"

Skids seemed to brighten at this. "Yeah. Yeah, I read you. Okay, let's do this. Can you be at Skyservice at oh-five-thirty?"

Decker glanced at Redd. "Can we?"

"It's a forty-five-minute drive. I don't know about you, but I was hoping for a little more rack time."

"Better make it seven," countered Decker. "We'll bring coffee."

Skids gave a dry chuckle. "You show up with the cash, and we can leave whenever you want."

"See you then."

Decker made a cutting motion, and Redd ended the call, then let out a low whistle. "You really have that much cash on you?"

Decker made a dismissive gesture. "Rogue Unit didn't exactly have a line item in the federal budget. We self-funded by recovering the assets of the guys we took down."

"You stole from criminals."

"Recovered assets," Decker corrected dryly. "Quiet money. We all invested our shares, made it grow. It's untraceable. I was never in it for the money, but it's nice to have a rainy-day fund, just in case."

Redd didn't say anything, but in his head, he was doing the math again. The kind of cash Decker had just tossed around without blinking represented a solid chunk of Redd's yearly net income. And that was on a good year when nothing broke and the weather held.

He didn't resent it. But it did underscore just how different their lives were. Decker had the means to charter aircraft like he was ordering an Uber. Redd, for all his grit and know-how, was still counting every bale of hay and gallon of diesel.

He pushed the thought away. No good came from dwelling on it.

"We should probably take turns standing watch tonight," he said instead, his voice quieter now.

Decker sighed. "I *was* hoping for at least one good night's sleep, but I suppose you're right. I'll take first shift."

"I'll set a timer." Redd stood, collected the empties, and headed inside. He was already thinking about the early morning ahead. The animals would still need feeding. One last round of chores before he left the ranch behind.

He wondered how long it would be before he saw his home again.

TWENTY-FOUR

HELENA, MONTANA

Early the next morning, Redd eased the Raptor into the gravel lot in front of a hangar adorned with a mural showing an airplane breaking through a cloud like a breaching whale, along with the stenciled legend *High Country Air*.

Before he could shut off the engine, the door opened. The man who stepped out was nearly a foot shorter than Redd, maybe five seven on a good day, but carried himself like someone who didn't care who noticed. Stocky build, wide shoulders, and arms that strained the seams of his green flight coveralls. He had thick black hair, combed straight back from his forehead, held in place more by habit than product, and a grin that was wide and unapologetic. He stood in the doorway, watching the two men approach.

"You must be Redd," he said, making a show of craning his head to look up at Redd as he approached. "Frank said you took up a lot of space." He turned his gaze to Decker. "That means you must be the one with the wallet?"

Decker held up a paper grocery bag emblazoned with the IGA logo. "That's me. Aaron Decker."

Decker had made a conscious decision to use his real name with Skids. No sense in burning an alias this early on.

"Skids Marquez," the pilot said, offering his hand.

As soon as handshakes were exchanged, Decker handed over the bag. Skids accepted it, the grin never leaving his face, though it did tighten slightly as he peered into its depths and took out a stack of crisp, banded one-hundred-dollar bills. He thumbed through it, confirming that it was exactly as it appeared, then raised his eyes to Decker. "Looks like it came right out of a bank vault."

"Something like that," Decker said.

Skids checked a couple more stacks then nodded to the door. "Okay, follow me."

Redd and Decker grabbed their bags from the bed of the truck and trailed Skids into the building. A door in the small reception area took them down a short corridor to a tidy office. A restroom sat across the way, and at the far end, a metal door led into the hangar itself.

"Probably a good time to hit the john," Skids said, jerking a thumb toward the restroom door. "Be right back."

A couple minutes later he re-emerged, now carrying a well-worn canvas backpack which Redd guessed held more than a couple stacks of Benjamins.

"All right," Skids said cheerfully, slinging the bag over one shoulder. "You boys just bought yourselves a whole lotta avgas. Let's get flying."

He led them through the metal door into the hangar where two aircraft waited, noses pointed toward the open bay door. One was a low-slung twin-engine affair. The other was smaller, with a taller stance and broad high-mounted wings that looked more at home in the bush than on a runway. Both bore the same *High Country Air* markings. Skids took them around to the left side of the larger aircraft and opened a door just aft of the wing, deploying a small foldout stairway.

Inside, the cabin was snug. Redd ducked slightly as he stepped in, noting the narrow aisle flanked by two rows of leather seats arranged in a club configuration—two facing forward and two facing aft.

As they settled in, Skids addressed them from the front of the aisle. "Gentlemen, our aircraft today is a Cessna 414 Chancellor. Our service ceiling is just over thirty thousand feet, but as we'll be operating under visual flight rules, we'll be staying below eighteen thousand feet.

"Our destination is Chicago Executive Airport, but we'll need to make a refueling stop en route—Sioux Falls Regional. The first leg should take about two hours and forty-five minutes, and after refueling, the second leg to Chicago will be approximately two hours and fifteen minutes. We should be wheels down in Chicago in six hours, give or take.

"Please keep your seat belts fastened during takeoff and landing. Life vests are located under your seats, though we won't be flying over any large bodies of water. That means if we crash, we all die, rendering the life vests completely and utterly useless."

Decker smiled at Redd. "I like this guy."

"Oh, yeah. He's a hoot," Redd said dryly.

"Emergency exits include the main door we boarded through and an over-wing hatch," continued Skids. "And as always, stay clear of the propellers when entering or exiting the aircraft. Other than that, sit back and enjoy the ride."

With that, he pivoted and ducked into the cockpit, where he slipped on a headset and began his preflight checklist. There was a brief whine, which quickly rose to a metallic crescendo and then a heavy mechanical chug as the port engine roared to life. The propeller blades began to spin, slowly at first, then faster until there was only a blur of motion. Vibrations rippled through the seat back, a low roar settling into a steady thrum that reverberated in Redd's chest. The process repeated as the starboard engine awakened.

Redd felt a sudden stir of apprehension. He'd flown in everything from C-130s to tilt-rotor Ospreys, but he'd always disliked flying, especially in helicopters, because it meant giving up control, putting his fate entirely in the hands of another person, and trusting in a machine that was designed to operate in places humans were not meant to go. In the military, he had come to terms with his anxiety, adopting an almost fatalistic attitude toward flying, knowing that if something did go wrong, there were trained crews and protocols layered ten deep. He trusted those machines because, for better or worse, he'd trusted the institution behind them.

But this? This was different.

He had no frame of reference for what to expect. No institutional trust to lean on. Just Skids and the hope that the same casual confidence the man carried into his flight suit didn't extend to his maintenance log.

The aircraft began to roll. In the front seat, Skids worked the controls calmly and efficiently, guiding the twin-prop out into daylight, picking up speed as they taxied out onto the tarmac.

The engines throbbed in stereo, low and powerful. The military birds Redd was used to made no pretense of comfort. They were noisy, brutal machines. The Cessna—relatively quiet, polished, clean—left him feeling slightly untethered.

Skids brought them to a brief halt at the end of the runway. Redd could see the pilot's head moving slightly, scanning for traffic, one hand already adjusting knobs on the console. After a radio call to the tower, he shoved the throttles forward.

The engines gave a throaty roar as Skids let the RPMs build, and then he released the brake and the Cessna lunged forward. The nose dipped slightly with acceleration before lifting again. The little bumps and cracks in the pavement thudded through the tires and up through every nerve in Redd's body, the rhythm quickening until it was a sustained rattle. His seat back flexed as gravity pushed against his chest. He fought the instinct to brace with both hands.

Through the front windscreen, he could see the far end of the runway racing toward them, getting closer. Closer.

And then, the nose came up and the vibration ceased. Redd's stomach dropped a beat behind the plane. He felt a slight buffeting as they caught a thermal, then the wings leveled, and they were flying.

The tension in Redd's muscles didn't vanish, but it did ease a little. He loosened his grip on the armrest, leaned slightly toward the window, and took in the view. Below, the Montana landscape unrolled in quiet majesty—the prairie, lush and green with spring rain; the pine-dotted ridgelines; the distant shimmer of the Missouri River tracing its ancient course through the valley.

Redd sat back in his chair, finally allowing himself to relax, and glanced over at Decker. "Well. That wasn't so bad."

But Decker was already asleep.

× × ×

Skids touched down smooth as silk at Sioux Falls, where they deplaned and stretched their legs while the ground crew topped off the tanks, then they were back in the air within the hour. By the time they descended toward Chicago Executive Airport, just shy of 2 p.m. local time, Redd was in a surprisingly good mood.

The feeling was short-lived.

As the Cessna's wheels chirped against the runway, Redd took his phone off airplane mode. A moment later, a notification popped up showing a missed call.

Sheriff Blackwood.

Redd had spoken to him the previous afternoon, asking the lawman to keep a discreet eye on Emily and the kids while he was away, and an ear out for any trouble in the county. Blackwood knew that trouble had a way of finding Matthew Redd and so took the request seriously without asking too many questions.

The fact that Blackwood was calling back so soon did not bode well.

Decker noticed the change in his expression. "What is it?"

"Missed call from the sheriff," Redd said. "He's not the type to call without a good reason."

Decker offered no platitudes. His only response was a slight tightening of his gaze.

Redd jabbed the call button and held the phone to his ear, bracing for bad news. "Stuart," he said, when the call connected. "It's Matthew. Sorry I missed your call. I was in the air."

"Matthew," replied Blackwood. A pause, then, "You know how you asked me to keep an ear out for any kind of trouble in the wind? I hope this turns out to be nothing, but . . ."

Redd felt his pulse quicken. "Go on."

"Well, I don't know if this qualifies, but it sure don't smell right. An MHP trooper called in a 'convoy'—his word—of SUVs rolling to the truck stop near Big Timber. Illinois plates. No violations, but the trooper said the occupants looked like bad news. He talked to the attendant at the gas station who said she thought they sounded Russian. Or Eastern European, anyway."

Redd's mouth was suddenly very dry. "Any idea where they're headed?"

"West. That's all I know." Another pause. "Is this something I should be worried about?"

"When was this, Stuart?"

"About an hour ago, give or take. Matthew, is this going to be a problem?"

Redd's gut began to roil. From Big Timber, they could be in Wellington inside of two hours. It seemed impossible that the Russians could have tracked them so quickly, and yet what other explanation could there be? And now, a small army of them were on their way to the ranch, and he and Decker were a thousand miles away.

The urge to act, to move, to race home and protect his loved ones surged in him like panic.

But panic wouldn't help. Not now.

He pushed the storm back down, kept his voice calm. "No, Stuart. It's probably nothing. But thanks for the heads-up."

"You sure?" Blackwood pressed. "I can send a couple deputies out to the ranch. Just to be on the safe side."

Redd almost said yes. Almost begged the sheriff to call in everyone he had, roll sirens all the way to his front gate, and set up a barricade. But that would do more harm than good. Emily wouldn't be able to leave if the place turned into a police cordon. And if this convoy was what he feared, a handful of deputies wouldn't stop them. They'd be cannon fodder.

"No need," Redd said. "I'm sure it's just a coincidence."

Blackwood didn't respond right away. When he did, it was with a tone that said he wasn't buying the calm any more than he was ignoring it. "All right. But I'm going to have my deputies watching the roads for this convoy."

"Sounds like a good plan. Keep me in the loop." Redd ended the call and immediately went to his contact list.

"Well?" asked Decker, his voice edged with concern.

Redd didn't answer. Instead, he tapped the icon to initiate another call. It rang once. Twice. *C'mon, pick up.* Three times. Then, a voice.

"Hey, Matty. You made it to big bad Chi-town?"

"Em, just listen . . ."

TWENTY-FIVE

STILLWATER COUNTY, MONTANA

Emily stood there for a moment, her phone still pressed to her ear like she was waiting for more, even though Matthew had ended the call ten seconds ago. Her mind was still processing, still catching up.

Her pulse thudded in her neck. The living room around her—Jack's scattered LEGOs, Junior's discarded juice cup, the soft hum of the refrigerator coming from the kitchen—suddenly felt surreal, like the quiet before a tornado.

Matthew had sounded relaxed, but she had known him long enough to hear what was going on just below the surface. "Em, just listen. I don't think I'm going to make it back in time for the camping trip."

Her heart had skipped a beat.

"Why don't you take the kids and go on ahead without me. I'll meet you at the spot."

She hadn't missed the meaning.

The camping trip.

Even before discussing a trip to Yellowstone on the way back from dropping Mikey and Liz at the airport, Emily had been considering the idea of a family trip. The timing was just about right. Lauren was old enough now that she didn't have to be held all day long. Jack had mostly settled in. The kids and Rubble could run wild, and they could all sleep under the stars and just get away from the craziness of day-to-day life.

But that wasn't what Matthew was talking about.

Camping trip was code.

It meant *leave.*

Now.

They'd discussed it barely twelve hours earlier, right after Matthew and Aaron had made their travel plans to go to Chicago. *"If I call and talk about the camping trip,"* Matthew had said as he settled into bed beside her, *"you need to drop everything, put the kids in your rig, and go."*

And she'd said, "*Sure thing, babe,*" keeping her tone light even as her stomach tightened into a knot. She knew better than to disregard his concerns. He'd even mentioned a spot they could go, where he'd be able to meet up with them later if needed. Matthew wasn't being paranoid. Bad men had found them before. It could certainly happen again.

But so soon?

She shook off the paralysis of denial and got to her feet. "Brynn!"

After a second shout, she saw the girl emerge from the hall. Her smile fell when she saw Emily's expression. "What's wrong?"

"We're leaving. Right now. Take Mitchell and Jack out to the Tahoe."

Emily saw the change—the light in Brynn's eyes flickering . . . dying . . . as realization dawned. The belief she'd dared to nurture—that the worst was behind her, that the nightmare was over, that this place, this family, was *safe*—cracked like thin ice underfoot.

Then her jaw set. Hesitation evaporated, replaced by steel. Brynn was her father's daughter.

"Should I pack anything for them?" she asked, voice tight.

Emily shook her head. "No time."

Brynn swallowed and then turned away, calling her brother's name. Emily pivoted toward the stairs, bounding up two at a time. She slid the baby gate on the landing aside, leaving it open, and headed into the nursery, scooping Lauren out of the crib. The baby began to wail, startled by the sudden movement. Emily barely heard, urgency superseding her maternal reflexes. She held her daughter close with one arm, grabbed the packed diaper bag off the changing table, and was back in the hallway in seconds.

"Matty!" she called out. "Honey, where are you?"

No answer.

"Matty!"

Then she heard Brynn's voice rising up from below. "I've got him!"

Emily breathed a sigh of relief and headed back down the stairs, descending more cautiously. She found Brynn standing at the front door, holding Little Matty's hand, with Mitchell and Jack beside her. She could see the uncertainty in the boys' expressions—confusion but also excitement—but Brynn's face was a mask of calm. The fear was still there, but she was holding it together, just like Emily was.

"Okay, boys," Emily said, managing a smile. "We're going on a surprise road trip! Go hop in the Tahoe."

Mitchell lit up. "Cool. Come on, Jack."

But Jack didn't move.

Emily crouched, shifting Lauren against her shoulder. "Jack?"

He stood rigid, brows furrowed, fists clenched at his sides.

"Sweetheart, we've got to go."

Jack shook his head. "I don't like surprises."

Tension coiled in Emily's shoulders. Lauren was still crying, her wails escalating with each passing second.

"I know, buddy," Emily said gently. "It's a last-minute adventure."

Jack's feet remained planted. "We aren't supposed to go anywhere."

Emily felt a pang of frustration, quickly suppressed. Jack, normally the shyest, sweetest kid you could ask for, did not handle change well. Some of it was no doubt the result of the trauma he had experienced the previous year, just before he'd come into their life, but Emily suspected that he was also mildly neurodivergent. Regardless of the reason, routine and structure helped him feel safe. Change terrified him.

"Yes, sweetheart," Emily said. "I know. But plans changed."

Jack crossed his arms tightly over his chest. "I don't like *changed*."

Brynn knelt beside him. "Hey, Jack, c'mon—it'll be fun! You can sit next to me and pick whatever music you want."

Jack looked at her, then away. "No," he mumbled. "I don't want music."

Emily's jaw clenched. Lauren was still crying, wiggling in her arms, and the seconds felt like minutes. She tried a different angle.

"Hey, Jack," she said with sudden brightness. "How about this—why don't you run upstairs and grab Buzz? I bet he wants to come too."

His frown faltered. "Buzz?"

"Yeah." Emily nodded, keeping her tone light. "Buzz wouldn't want to miss this adventure."

Jack hesitated, then gave a slow, almost imperceptible nod.

"I'll go with you," Mitchell said, seizing Jack's hand.

"Good man," Emily said. "But hurry back. The rocket's already counting down for liftoff."

As the two boys trundled up the stairs, Emily sighed out her frustration and pushed through the door, heading out to the Tahoe with Brynn in tow. Ignoring the persistent crying, she settled Lauren into her car seat, buckling her in, while Brynn did the same for Little Matty.

As soon as Lauren was secure, Emily raised her eyes to Brynn. "Stay here with them. I'll be right back."

Brynn opened her mouth to reply but Emily was already sprinting toward the house. She ducked inside and went straight for the gun safe. Keying in the code with shaking fingers, she retrieved the 12-gauge shotgun and a box of shells, then went back toward the door.

"Boys!" she called. "Rocket's leaving!"

Waiting for them, standing still for the first time since Matthew's call, she began to process the details. The ranch would be okay. Before leaving, Matthew had asked their neighbor Cal Rigby to swing by once a day and take care of the chores so that Emily would have one less thing to worry about. Hopefully, Cal would keep Rubble in kibble too. She thought about leaving a note to explain their absence, but there just wasn't time.

No time to pack up their camping gear. No time to grab food for the trip. They'd have to pick up what they needed on the road.

But then she remembered what Matthew had said the night before. *"Don't use your debit card. They can track your location with it."*

So how was she supposed to pay for food and gas?

She decided she would use her debit card once. A single cash withdrawal from an ATM. Even if they—whoever *they* were—registered the transaction, it wouldn't tell them anything about where they were going.

How much would the bank let her take out? And how far would that get them?

Matthew had told her something else. *"Leave your phone."*

Her gut twisted at the idea of surrendering the device. *What if I need to reach Matthew? What if something happens to the car? What if—*

She closed her eyes, forced herself to breathe.

Lord, please watch over us. Be with us.

Trust Him, she told herself. *You can do this.*

A verse from Psalm chapter 23, one of her very favorites—and a verse she'd claimed many times over since marrying Matthew Redd and charging headfirst into numerous dangerous situations—suddenly popped into her head.

"Even though I walk through the valley of the shadow of death, I will fear no evil, for you are with me."

Please, Father, be with Matty, too.

She took out her phone and placed it on the table by the door.

Footsteps pounded on the stairs, and Mitchell and Jack appeared a moment later. Jack was clutching his Buzz Lightyear action figure to his chest with one hand. The other was tucked tightly in Mitchell's.

Mitchell's eyes lingered on the shotgun in the crook of Emily's elbow, but he didn't say a word.

Emily gave him a nod. "Good job. Now let's move."

They headed outside in a cluster, the boys piling into the back, Emily taking the driver's seat. She placed the shotgun on the floor, between the doorframe and the front seat, with the business end pointing forward. She wasn't worried about an accidental discharge, but all the same, if it did go off, she didn't want it blasting buckshot into the back seat. Brynn, who was bent over Lauren, trying to soothe her, got out and slid into the front passenger seat. Emily did a quick visual check to make sure that everyone was accounted for and buckled in, then started the Tahoe.

"Wait," Brynn said suddenly, her hand flying to the door handle. "I forgot something. Be right back."

"Brynn—"

But Brynn had already flung the door open and was sprinting back toward the house.

Emily growled under her breath, fingers tapping the steering wheel, each second excruciating.

Leave. Now.

How long had it been? How much closer were the men who were coming to kill them?

She glanced in the rearview mirror, then back at Lauren, who had finally settled down. The boys were talking amongst themselves, speculating about their eventual destination. A surprise road trip could only mean one thing: ice cream.

Then Brynn reappeared, emerging from the house with a small backpack. She ran to the Tahoe and climbed in. "Sorry about that."

Emily didn't ask for an explanation. She just dropped the Tahoe into gear and put her foot on the gas.

"Rubble!"

Jack's cry nearly made her jump out of her skin. She shifted her foot to the brake, more out of reflex than anything else, but then glimpsed movement from the corner of her eye. The rottweiler was bounding across the pasture where he'd been exploring, racing toward the Tahoe like a heat-seeking missile.

Jack's face lit up. "Can Rubble come with us?"

"Jack, I don't—"

But Emily's refusal came too late. Mitchell had already unbuckled his seat belt and opened the door.

"C'mon, Rubble!" he called.

The dog launched himself the final few yards and leapt into the open door, wedging himself between the boys, panting happily. Mitchell pulled the door shut and settled back into his seat, while Jack threw an arm around the dog's neck.

Emily groaned aloud. There was no telling how long they would be away from home, and barely enough room for Rubble in the Tahoe as it was. But explaining that to the boys would take time, and that was the thing in shortest supply.

That, and money.

"Great." She slid her foot onto the gas pedal. "One more mouth to feed."

As they sped down the driveway, Brynn glanced over at her, eyes narrowing. "Is that going to be a problem?" she asked in a low voice.

Emily gave a quick shake of the head. "I'll figure it out."

Brynn must have sensed the uncertainty in her tone. "Just how long are we going to be gone?"

"I wish I knew. As long as it takes Matthew and your father to sort this out." She paused a beat, then muttered, "Or until we run out of cash."

Brynn gave a small, knowing smile and reached for her backpack. "Dad gave me this before he left." She unzipped the pack and took something out. "*'In case of emergency,'* he said. I think maybe this is what he meant."

Emily glanced over and then did a double take.

Brynn was holding money. Two stacks of banded bills.

Bills bearing a portrait of Benjamin Franklin.

"I don't think money is going to be a problem," finished Brynn.

TWENTY-SIX

CHICAGO, ILLINOIS

Redd leaned forward, pressing the phone against his forehead, and closed his eyes. He felt utterly helpless. No, worse than helpless. *Useless.*

His family was in danger. Again. Because of him. And where was he? A thousand miles away.

He took a slow breath, trying to quiet his inner accuser. Emily was strong. She knew what she was doing. He'd given her a head start. Now, he needed to trust her.

It's not enough.

Redd sighed. In many ways, he'd come so far since he first returned to Wellington years ago, and yet, in other ways, he was so far from the man he wanted to be.

Emily is strong, he told himself again. *What's that quote she always tells me?*

Then it hit him.

"My grace is all you need. My power works best in weakness."

No, not *just* a quote. Redd couldn't remember exactly where the passage came from, but he knew it was from the Bible and was likely authored by Paul. *"Most of the New Testament is,"* Emily had told him during one of their nightly Bible studies together.

Well, God, Redd prayed sincerely, *You must be really powerful right now, because I've never felt so weak.*

He made a mental note to ask Emily exactly where that verse was located when he got back home to her and their kids.

You will make it home to them, he told himself.

Then, *Please, keep them safe . . .*

It wasn't a long prayer, but Redd couldn't find any other words.

"Matt?" asked Decker, his voice low, barely audible over the hum of the engines as the plane continued to taxi. "What's happened?"

Redd hardly heard him. His thoughts were still churning. Deep down, he still believed what he had told Decker earlier—that the only way to truly keep their families safe was to eliminate the problem. But it was hard to remember that with the threat about to land on his doorstep.

How did they track me down so fast?

"Matthew," Decker said again, more sharply. "Talk to me."

Redd lowered the phone and met Decker's gaze. "They're coming."

Decker's face went visibly pale. "What?"

"Blackwood called me. A bunch of Russians in SUVs with Illinois plates rolled through Big Timber about an hour ago."

"Big Timber? Where's that?"

"About an hour from Wellington," Redd replied, forcing the answer past clenched teeth. He took a breath. "I told Em to take the kids and go, but . . ." Emotion constricted his throat. He tried breathing again. "How did they know where to look for us?"

Decker didn't answer. He just stared back at Redd, his expression taut. Redd could see the stew of emotions bubbling under the surface, knew what Decker was thinking because he was thinking it too.

The ranch was supposed to be a sanctuary. A place where his children would be safe while he did what needed to be done. He should have stayed with them. Protected them. That was what fathers were supposed to do.

Then Decker blinked. Shook his head as if awakening from a daydream. "I don't know. Maybe they spotted your license plate."

"Those guys in Duluth didn't have a plate. All they had was a description. A black pickup. And if they got a look at the license plate, they never got a chance to send it. There's something else going on here, Aaron. They keep finding you. Finding us. How?"

Decker shook his head again. "I don't know." He ran a hand across his face, his gaze darting out the window before coming back to Redd. "You should go back. I'll have Skids drop me off here, then turn around and take you back to Montana. If he flies IFR with a flight plan, he can skip the refueling stop. Have you back in four hours or so."

Redd's every instinct told him that was exactly what he should do. Rush home, protect his family. But even as he started to nod in agreement, his own words echoed in his head.

This won't end until either you're dead or they are.

That hadn't changed. The bad guys would just keep coming. His family . . . Decker's kids . . . They would never truly be safe until Decker found the man who was giving the orders.

And Decker couldn't do it alone.

Or maybe he could. But the odds of success would be a whole lot better with someone watching his six.

That was the promise he had made. The debt he owed.

The lesson he'd learned the hard way.

Outside the cabin, the engine pitch shifted as Skids eased the plane out of a turn and began the final taxi to the terminal building.

Redd let out his breath. "No," he said. "I'm not going anywhere."

Decker looked at him, confused.

"Our kids are safe. Emily knows what to do. We came up with a plan. She's already rolling out, heading somewhere they'll never think to look."

Decker stared back at him for a long moment. "Are you sure? I mean, this is our kids we're talking about. I can handle this myself."

"Maybe you can, but the thing is, you don't have to. And we both know that this doesn't stop until the people coming after us are in the ground."

Redd could see the battle playing out behind Decker's eyes, the war between his fatherly instincts and the tactical logic of Redd's position. "You really think she can handle this?" he said finally.

Redd didn't hesitate. "She can handle it."

"We shouldn't have put her in this position."

Redd felt the sting of those words. Emily was on her own now, taking their kids off the grid and into the unknown. And he wasn't with her. Wasn't there to protect her and the kids. No matter how much sense his decision made, guilt was a lead weight in his gut.

But wallowing in it wouldn't help. Not now.

"What we should or shouldn't have done is irrelevant. This is what is."

There was a gentle bump as the plane rolled to a stop. Decker glanced out the window then back at Redd. "If something happens to them—"

"We'll never be able to forgive ourselves," Redd finished. He paused, still feeling the weight of his decision. "I can't be in two places. So I have to be in the one where I can make the most difference. But maybe there's something we *can* do to help them."

He brought his phone up and opened his contact list.

"Who are you calling?" asked Decker, visibly tensing.

"Gavin. It's time to bring him into the loop."

Decker's hand shot out, covering Redd's before he could tap the screen. "Wait. Are you sure about this?"

"No," Redd admitted. "But I'm doing it anyway."

"If he starts poking around, asking questions about the Russian . . . or even showing an interest in Bratva activities, someone is going to notice. It will tip them off. We can't take that chance."

"I'm not going to ask him to launch an investigation," Redd said. "Just to send a couple agents from the Bozeman field office to keep eyes on Emily and the kids."

"And when he asks why?"

"I'll tell him that it's a local thing, and that I can't tell him any more than that. He'll go along with it."

Decker exhaled slowly and drew his hand back. "Fine. But don't mention me. At all. Not a word."

Redd nodded and pressed the contact. The call connected almost immediately, and the voice of Gavin Kline filled his ear. "Matty!"

Despite everything, a grin touched Redd's lips. All his life, he'd hated being called Matty. It was what his mother had called him, and that was not a pleasant association, but he was willing to tolerate it from people he loved. Somehow, Kline had finally made his way onto that very short list.

"How have you been?" Kline was saying. "How're Em and the kids?"

"They're okay," Redd said, though the words felt like a lie even as he spoke them. "Listen, Gavin, I need to ask a favor. It's a big one."

There was a pause. "Sounds serious. But of course. Whatever you need."

Redd took a breath. "I'm out of state. Dealing with something. Em and the kids are going camping . . . to that spot I told you about."

This time the pause was longer. He hoped Kline would not only decipher his intentionally vague language but grasp its significance. He didn't want to say Emily's ultimate destination aloud, just in case the Russians had not only figured out who he was but also had the ability to intercept his calls.

"I know the place you mean," Kline said. "Go on."

"The thing is, I'm a little worried about them out there. I've kind of been dealing with . . . a situation. I'm handling it, but I'm worried there might be some spillover—"

Kline cut him off. "You don't need to spell it out, Matt. What do you need from me?"

Matt, not Matty. Redd took that as a sign that Kline understood the seriousness of the situation.

"I'd feel a lot better if I knew someone was looking out for them. At least until I can get things wrapped up and join them. I was hoping you could send a couple agents from the FO in Bozeman to keep an eye on them. I know it's a big ask—"

"I'll do you one better than that," said Kline. "I'll go there myself."

"That's not necessary," Redd started to say. "I think a couple—"

"I know you enough to know that you probably didn't want to make this call. Am I right?" Kline didn't wait for a response. "I could send a few agents, Matt, but tell me the truth . . . Who would you feel better about watching your family: a couple random feds or *me*?"

It wasn't even a question for Redd.

"I just don't want to put you out, Gavin."

"I've been looking for an excuse to come out there and see my grandkids anyways. So this works out just fine. I'll grab a few things and be on my way. Sound good?"

Redd was taken aback, relief suddenly washing over him. Kline wasn't just some desk jockey who happened to carry a gun. No, the current acting director of the FBI was a former jarhead just like Redd, and since reconnecting, Gavin had proven time and time again that he was willing to risk everything—including his own life—to protect his family.

"I . . . I, um . . . I guess I don't know what to say."

"*Thank you* usually covers it," said Kline. "Seriously, though, don't you worry about Em and the kids. I'll keep them safe."

"You won't be able to reach her by phone," Redd added hastily.

"That won't be a problem. You just take care of yourself, got it?"

"Got it. I'll call again when I can." Redd ended the call and let out a deep sigh. The burden that had landed on him with Blackwood's news had finally eased, if only a little. Emily and the kids weren't out of danger—not by a long shot—but at least he had been able to do something for them. "Gavin is going to come take care of it personally."

Decker's shoulders relaxed, the tension in his face easing slightly. "That's . . . good."

Right then, Skids stepped out of the cockpit. "Welcome to Chicago, gentlemen," he said. "Local time is one fifty-five p.m." He regarded them for a moment. "So, you fellows have any idea how long you're going to be here?"

Decker exchanged a glance with Redd before replying, "Not a minute longer than we have to."

TWENTY-SEVEN

It had been years since Redd had spent more than an airport layover in Chicago, or any other city of consequence for that matter, and he was surprised by how foreign it felt to him.

Born in Detroit, he'd always thought of himself as a city boy. The noise, the motion, the *intensity* . . . The city was in his blood. When he'd gone to live with J. B., the quiet of rural life had unnerved him. He'd adapted, exceled even, but had never really purged his inner urban child. Right up until the moment he'd left to join the Corps, he had seen his time there as a kind of exile. When he'd been stationed at Camp Pendleton, he hadn't spent his liberty hiking the rugged trails of the Cleveland National Forest. Gaslamp Quarter had been his oasis.

But something had changed in him since he'd begun this new phase of his life. Being in a city didn't invigorate him anymore. Just the opposite—he felt like he was drowning.

Of course, maybe it was just being in this part of the city. West Humboldt Park wasn't exactly the sort of place that made it into the tourist guidebooks. The run-down stretch of Kostner Avenue bore little resemblance to the Chicago of movies. There were no gleaming skyscrapers here, no riverwalks or museums.

No coffee shops or joggers or mothers pushing baby strollers. Just old brick warehouses and a new grocery store or two.

He had spent the last hour in the passenger seat of Decker's rented Dodge Durango, the engine idling low and steady, the air-conditioning keeping them cool as they surreptitiously watched the front of an auto-body shop half a block away.

The Durango had been waiting for them outside the terminal building. Decker had driven southward, weaving through the suburban sprawl of Wheeling and Mount Prospect. The landscape through which they passed transitioned from manicured lawns and strip malls to the denser, more industrial zones of Cicero, where Decker kept the storage unit containing everything he might need for extended operations in the Windy City.

At Decker's urging, Redd had traded his NSX for something a little more pedestrian but with untraceable ballistics. Redd settled for a Glock 9mm with a filed-down serial number and a suppressor but held on to the big Magnum, as there was no telling whether they would be able to return to the storage unit before leaving town.

Once geared up, they'd headed on to West Humboldt Park, one of the neighborhoods where, according to Decker, Russian gangs were known to have a presence. Decker seemed to have an intuitive grasp of what was going on just below the surface, not unlike, Redd supposed, a skilled hunting guide who knew exactly where to find a herd of elk, simply by reading the signs. They cruised the blocks, noting the patterns of suspicious activity: groups of men loitering near certain storefronts, quick exchanges on corners, and most notably, a black Mercedes-Maybach GLS 600 with blackout-tinted windows, passing through the urban decay and standing out like a sore thumb.

"That's our guy," Decker had announced when the luxury SUV passed by. They tailed it discreetly through several more stops before it finally pulled into the open garage bay of a grungy-looking auto-body shop, a few hundred yards from the spot where they'd now been sitting for just over an hour.

Their patience was rewarded when, finally, the SUV rolled back out onto the street and turned toward them. As it passed, Redd caught a brief glimpse of the driver through the windshield, a big guy whose head and shoulders filled the space above the steering wheel—no doubt both chauffeur and bodyguard. The front passenger seat was empty, but he could just make out a second form in one of the rear seats.

The target.

"Showtime," Decker announced, putting the Durango in gear. He waited two beats, then pulled out, whipping a tight U-turn and following.

They trailed at a cautious distance, letting two cars buffer them as the GLS headed south then west, driving through intersections with little regard for the color of the traffic lights. The SUV continued westward along Division Street, the surroundings gradually shifting from the industrial decay of West Humboldt Park to more residential neighborhoods. As they approached the on-ramp to the Eisenhower Expressway, the Mercedes signaled and merged onto the highway, heading west.

"I think our boy is heading home for the night," observed Decker.

"Where's home?"

"The burbs. He'll have a nice little McMansion in Oak Brook or Hinsdale."

The city's skyline receded into the haze behind them as they joined the flow of late-afternoon traffic on the expressway. Around them, the urban landscape quickly gave way to less densely populated suburbs. The Mercedes veered onto Interstate 88 and continued southwest for several more miles until, nearly half an hour after leaving the auto-body garage, the SUV swung onto the exit ramp.

"Oak Brook," said Decker. "All right. Now's our chance."

Redd raised an eyebrow. "Our chance to do what?"

Decker told him.

Redd was dumbfounded for several seconds. "You're serious, aren't you? That's your plan?"

Decker gave him a sidelong glance. "I thought you'd be more enthusiastic about it. You have a reputation for . . ." He paused, as if trying to come up with the most diplomatic phrasing. "Direct action."

"Direct action is one thing," countered Redd. "This is just crazy."

"It'll work," said Decker. "Trust me, we'll take them completely by surprise."

"It's not them I'm thinking about. It's all the people driving by. With dash-cams and iPhones."

Decker shook his head. "Trust me. They won't even give us a second look. You ever hear of a little thing called normalcy bias?"

Redd was familiar with it. Normalcy bias was the phenomenon where people tended to overlook or dismiss unusual and potentially dangerous events because their brains were wired to assume everything was normal. It was why people tended to dismiss gunshots as backfires or fireworks.

Redd nodded slowly. "So you're counting on the fact that nobody expects to see . . . basically, a carjacking, on a street in the suburbs."

"Exactly," said Decker. "They'll see it and not see it."

Redd still didn't love it. But he didn't disagree that the plan had a certain . . . directness.

Decker turned onto the exit ramp, accelerating to close the distance between the two vehicles, following the curving offramp around to the intersection with West 22nd Street. The Mercedes turned right, the road lined with strip malls and office parks.

"Get ready," Decker said. He eased off the accelerator as he followed the other vehicle through the turn, then dropped his foot again. The engine growled, and the Durango surged forward. As the rear of the Mercedes seemed to race toward them, he whipped the Durango into the left lane, racing past the other vehicle just as they both passed under the interstate overpass. As the shadows engulfed them, Decker yanked the wheel hard to the right, cutting across the Mercedes's bow, and slammed on the brakes.

There was a cacophony of rubber shrieking on pavement, followed a fraction of a second later by the thump of the GLS hitting the Durango's rear bumper. The Durango rocked forward slightly, and Redd felt the seat belt dig into his chest, but the impact was so gentle, there was no danger of whiplash.

"Now," said Decker.

Redd had one hand on the seat belt release and the other on the door handle, and even as Decker shouted, he was moving, releasing the seat belt and throwing the door open. Decker did the same, and in less than a second, both of them were out and moving toward the Mercedes.

Following the collision, the Durango had rolled forward, leaving just enough room for Redd and Decker to pass each other—Redd went for the driver's side of the GLS, and Decker went the other way. As they made the swap, the driver's door of the Mercedes opened and the driver started to get out. He was, as Redd had earlier noted, big. Almost as big as Redd himself. Wide shoulders, barrel chest, no discernible neck. The kind of guy who probably bench-pressed small cars for fun. He looked like a pro wrestler in a cheap suit. His face was screwed up in a mask of indignance, his mouth open to deliver some invective-filled rant.

Redd didn't give him a chance to utter a word much less throw a punch. He clapped cupped hands against the man's ears, hard, creating a pressure spike that drove into the man's eardrums like the detonation of a flash-bang and, in the same motion, shoved the man's head backward into the doorframe with enough force to rock the Mercedes from side to side. As the man started to go down, Redd guided him back so that he fell awkwardly across the driver's seat. Redd then reached down, grabbed the man's ankles, and heaved him up and over the center console. He took a moment to search the man, relieving him of his phone and key fob, flinging both items into the dark reaches of the overpass. Then he closed the door, shutting the now-unconscious driver inside.

He didn't see what was happening on the other side of the SUV, but if Decker was staying true to plan, he would have already wrenched open the rear passenger door, subdued the lone passenger, and yanked him out by the collar. Sure enough, as Redd started back toward the Durango, he saw Decker dragging his unconscious captive toward the passenger side of their vehicle. Redd slid in behind the steering wheel of the idling Dodge while Decker shoved the man into the rear seating area and got in beside him.

From start to finish, the takedown had taken no more than forty-five seconds. Not one of the cars passing them by had even slowed for a look.

"Go!" Decker shouted.

A heartbeat later, Redd hit the gas and sped away.

TWENTY-EIGHT

Redd stood with his back to the closed roll-up door, arms crossed, watching as their captive begin to stir. The guy had the build of a bulldog—beefy arms, a barrel chest—but was plump through the middle with a prodigious gut. He had probably been real street tough in his younger days, not unlike the driver Redd had laid out, but he'd clearly spent too many years drinking top-shelf vodka while his underlings did all the hard work.

After the takedown, Redd had driven back to Decker's storage unit in Cicero—a drive of about twenty minutes—where they had discreetly off-loaded their still-unconscious subject, securing him to a low-slung folding camp chair with zip ties and several wraps of duct tape. As consciousness returned, his sagging head came up, and he squinted as if trying to bring the world into focus. His face twisted through a flickering range of emotions—confusion, anger, fear—like someone cycling through the presets on an unfamiliar car radio, but when his eyes finally locked on Decker, all of that drained away, replaced by something else entirely. Awe.

"You're him," he said slowly, in accented English. "You're *the man*."

The way he said it—*the man*—said all there was to say about Decker's reputation.

"Name?" asked Decker.

The man spat a couple harsh words in what Redd assumed was Russian.

Decker regarded him with a long, appraising stare. "I doubt your mother would have named you that," he replied calmly. "You already know who I am, and I'm guessing that means you know what I'm capable of. Are you sure that's how you want this to go?"

The man just glowered at him.

"Name," Decker said again, this time with an edge.

The man winced as if the word had been a slap. "Dmitri," he muttered. "Dmitri Anischenko."

Decker smiled, but it didn't reach his eyes. "See? That wasn't so hard."

Dmitri refused to meet his gaze.

"I'm not your enemy, Dmitri," Decker went on, his tone softer, conversational. "I apologize for handling you a little roughly. We really needed to talk to you and didn't think you'd accept a polite invitation. But the honest truth is, we don't want to hurt you. We just need a little information."

Dmitri now raised his head. "And then you will let me go? I don't think so."

Decker moved closer. "You know who I am," he said again. "You know that I've put several of your brothers in the ground. That was self-defense. They came into my home, threatened my children." He paused to let that sink in. "I didn't choose this war. Neither did you. Isn't that right?"

Dmitri just stared straight ahead.

"Who is calling the shots? Who really wants me dead?"

Dmitri's expression hardened and he spat another obscenity at Decker. Redd saw a defiant look in the man's eyes—the look of a man who, resigned to his fate, had just decided to die with what passed for honor in his world.

Decker's expression didn't change. He circled wide around the bound figure, approaching from behind, and placed his hands on Dmitri's shoulders. "Matt, can you grab those bolt cutters?"

Dmitri visibly flinched at the request. Redd, hiding a smile, unfolded his arms and reached down for the thirty-inch bolt cutters he'd strategically propped against the wall for just this purpose. As he hefted them onto one shoulder and moved toward the bound man, Dmitri began to squirm.

"Where do you want me to start?" Redd asked, directing the question to Decker.

"Fingers" was the casual reply.

Redd shifted the bolt cutters off his shoulder, gripping a handle in each hand and spreading them apart, opening the jaws of the tool. He worked them back and forth, grinning maniacally as if savoring the rhythmic *snick-snick,* exactly as they'd rehearsed.

"You think you can scare me?" Dmitri gasped.

"I think we already have," Redd remarked, then glanced over at Decker. "Don't you think so, Aaron?"

"Matt's right. You look pretty scared already."

Dmitri swallowed hard, his bravado starting to crack.

"Who's calling the shots, Dmitri?" said Decker. "Who wants me dead?"

Dmitri repeated his vulgar Russian curse.

"Are you right-handed, Dmitri? It matters because . . . Well, like I told you, we're not going to kill you. You have my word. Once you tell us what we need to know, we'll let you go. And you *are* going to tell us. The only question is how high you'll be able to count when you finally do."

Dmitri's only answer was a defiant grimace.

Decker shrugged. "We'll start with your left hand then."

"Very considerate," remarked Redd, lowering the open jaws until they were hovering just above Dmitri's left hand. With forearms bound tightly to the arm of the camp chair, he couldn't pull away, but he did begin rotating his wrist trying to keep his fingers away from the tool.

"Oh, for pity's sake," Redd said with mock exasperation. "Hold still. I want to do this cleanly."

"I don't know his name," gasped Dmitri. "He's *Vory.* From Moscow. That's all I know. He doesn't deal with me."

"Who does he deal with?" asked Decker.

"Petrovich."

"Petrovich?"

"*Avtoritet.* Yegor Petrovich."

"Where can I find him?"

Dmitri spat a laugh. "He will find you, I think. Very soon."

"I can't wait that long. Where is he?"

When Dmitri hesitated, Redd brought the bolt cutters down, brushing them against the back of the man's hand.

Dmitri broke. "Zvezda."

"What's that?"

"His club. Very private."

"Where is it?"

"Back of the Yards. Was old packing plant. Now is club."

"Probably a busy place," prompted Decker. "Lots of security."

"Is fortress. You go there, you never leave."

Decker nodded slowly. "You let us worry about that," he said, and then nodded for Redd to join him in a corner of the storage unit.

"Sounds like this club is going to be a tough nut to crack," said Redd, keeping his voice low so that Dmitri couldn't overhear.

"I've gotten into tougher places."

"Think they've got a dress code?"

Decker smiled. "Just in case they do . . ."

He stepped over to the stack of Rubbermaid totes lining one wall, running his finger across the labels taped to each one like a librarian looking for a particular title. When he found the one he wanted, he slid it out of the stack, carried it to the door, and then came back for another.

Redd watched in silence as a new stack took shape. When Decker set the fourth tote down, he turned to Redd. "This should be enough to get us into Fort Knox."

"I think I'd rather break into Fort Knox."

Decker bent down to grasp the door handle and raised it, revealing the Durango parked and waiting just outside. "Let's load up."

As Redd picked up two of the totes, heaving them into the rear cargo compartment of their vehicle, Dmitri found his voice again. "You said you would let me go."

Decker shoved the remaining totes past the threshold. "When we're done with Petrovich, we'll come back for you."

Dmitri spat a laugh. "You won't be coming back."

Redd turned to him, one hand on the door handle, and shrugged. "Then I guess you won't be going anywhere."

Then he hauled down on the door, slamming it shut.

TWENTY-NINE

GARDINER, MONTANA

The store looked more like a ski lodge than any grocery store Brynn had ever been to, with a big triangular roof, dark wood siding, and a sign that read *Gardiner Market—Family Owned Since 1945*. The parking lot was nearly empty, with just a Subaru, a dusty Tacoma with out-of-state plates, and an ancient Winnebago parked crookedly across several spaces near the pull-in.

"Still early in the year," Emily observed as she pulled into a parking space near one of the store's two entrances. "In two or three weeks, this place will be packed." She shut off the engine. "I'm going to run in and grab a few things. Can you hold the fort here for a bit?"

Brynn nodded, glancing back to the rear seating area where everyone, with the exception of Rubble, was out cold. "I think I can manage."

Emily gave a tired half smile. "Won't be long. When I get back, you can run in and pick up whatever creature comforts your heart desires . . ." She trailed off, glancing thoughtfully at the streaked windows of the grocery, then added, "Though I wouldn't get my hopes up."

Brynn laughed. As primitive as the store—and for that matter, the little rural Montana town—was, she wasn't nearly as horrified by it as she would've expected to be. It was, she decided, a lot more welcoming than her grandfather's cabin in the UP had been.

She tried not to dwell on that memory.

As she watched Emily head into the shop, Brynn's mind drifted to her friends at school and her life back home. Her dad had said they'd be gone for a few days when they first packed up and hit the road, but something deep down told her that timeline was probably wishful thinking.

Even if they could go home, Brynn wasn't sure where "home" was now. Their townhouse was littered with dead bodies. She couldn't imagine taking Mitchell back there.

Everything has changed, she thought to herself, finally processing it for the first time.

She wanted to contact her friends, especially Brooke Tiffany, her bestie since she was eleven, but given that someone had clearly been after them and tried more than once to kill them, she knew that wasn't a good idea.

For her family, or for Brooke.

I miss you, Mom. I wish you were here . . .

She peeked back once more to make sure the kids were all still sleeping, and once she confirmed that they were, Brynn got out to stretch her legs. She was surprised at the brisk chill in the air. It didn't feel like spring here. There was still snow on the distant ridgelines to the south—where they were going next. She stretched, raising her arms high, twisting and arching her back, then leaned against the side of the SUV, breathing it all in.

A few hours ago, when Emily had given the order to evacuate the ranch, Brynn had been almost paralyzed with fear. Everything had happened so fast. No time to pack, no time to think. Just load the kids and go.

Once they'd gotten off the rural back roads and onto the highway heading south, some of her apprehension had eased. She knew from experience that her dad's enemies wouldn't hesitate to attack them on the open road, but it seemed a lot less likely that anyone would be able to sneak up on them.

After only about an hour on the move, they'd arrived in Bozeman, where Emily stopped at REI to pick up camping gear for their trip. While she was inside loading up on tents, sleeping bags, a big camp stove, cookware, collapsible water jugs—basically everything they'd need to stay off-grid for a while—Brynn had taken the kids and Rubble for a walk in the big field out behind the store. They'd grabbed a late lunch from the KFC across the way, and then it was back on the road for the next leg of the trip.

They had taken their time, stopping every half hour to stretch their legs and give Rubble a chance to do his business, and gradually the sense of being on the run gave way to the thrill of exploration. Even Jack seemed to warm up to the idea of being on an adventure. Two hours later, they arrived in Gardiner—the last stop before entering the fabled Yellowstone National Park.

Now, in the parking lot of the little rural grocery, Brynn gazed out at the clouds scudding low over the snow-frosted ridgelines and felt, for the first time in a long time, a sense of wonder. The idea of camping didn't exactly thrill her, but Yellowstone . . . Yellowstone was different.

Even the name had an almost mythical quality to it, more a fantasy kingdom—like Narnia or Oz—than a real location a human might actually visit. And while Brynn wasn't really a fan of the great outdoors, the idea of seeing geysers and bison and whatever else there was to see in the park did have a certain once-in-a-lifetime appeal.

"Hey, gorgeous. You local?"

The voice . . . No, not just the voice, but the proximity, startled Brynn, sending a jolt of pure adrenaline through her nervous system. She whirled jerkily, taking a step back and inadvertently bumping into the side of the Tahoe, and saw a white guy, maybe twenty, about her height, but lean, almost gangly, with a scraggly beard and sharp eyes that moved too fast.

He's a tweaker, she thought reflexively.

He was standing almost at arm's length, though his hands were stuffed into the front pockets of his dingy gray hoodie.

Behind him, two more young guys, cut from the same cloth, leaned against the bed of an old pickup, primer black with a mismatched driver's side door, watching their buddy make his move.

Where did they come from?

She hadn't even heard them pull in, much less noticed the young man's approach.

She heard her dad's voice in her head, admonishing her about the importance of situational awareness. *"Don't let your guard down just because the sun's out."*

She didn't answer the guy, didn't meet his stare. Her eyes darted around the parking lot, looking for an escape route, just in case. The guy was between her and the store entrance, but if she could get past him, make it inside . . .

And leave the kids behind?

The young man spoke again. "I asked if you're from around here." His grin was lazy and didn't hide the hunger in his shifty eyes.

Brynn finally met his stare, keeping her voice even. "Just passing through . . . My dad's inside getting some groceries."

There was just enough hesitation in her tone to betray the falsehood.

"That right?" He nodded. "Going to the park?"

Brynn knew that responding would only encourage him but nevertheless found herself replying, "Yeah. So . . ." She stopped herself, knowing that she shouldn't be telling him anything.

"We're headed up to Chico. Got a cabin, some brews, some crystal. Gonna be a good time. You should come with."

"No thanks."

He took a step closer. "Come on, baby. Ditch the fam and come party with us."

Brynn tried to shrink back, but there was nowhere to go. From the corner of her eye, she saw movement behind the window glass. It was Rubble. His muzzle was pressed against the glass. She could feel his low growl vibrating through the doorframe.

"Whoa." The young man flinched, backing away. "Mean-looking mutt."

Brynn glanced back, looking for the door handle. If she could just get it open, let Rubble out . . .

As if reading her mind, the young guy closed the distance, reaching over her shoulder to jam his right hand against the door. His palm was flat against the window, preventing her from opening the door and releasing Rubble.

She could feel the guy's breath on her, smell his stink—body odor and cigarettes. His lazy smile was gone, and in its place was something colder.

"You're making a mistake," she said, trying to summon steel into her voice.

He leaned in. "Only mistake would be you staying here."

Behind him, the two other guys pushed off the truck and started toward her.

"C'mon, baby." His voice was low now, almost a purr in her ear. "You don't want this to get ugly, do you?"

Brynn opened her mouth to call out, to scream maybe, but something in his expression stopped her. He wasn't bluffing. His hand would be over her mouth . . . or around her throat . . . before she could draw the breath to scream.

Think, Brynn! What would Dad do?

Easy. Her dad would wipe the floor with this animal.

The mere thought of that seemed to switch something on in her head. Without even taking a moment to think it through, Brynn snapped her knee upward, aiming for the one soft target she knew every guy had.

Somehow, he saw it coming, twisting his hips just enough to deflect the strike. Then he slammed his forearm into her shoulder, shoving her hard against the Tahoe. The impact rattled her teeth.

"That wasn't very nice," he hissed. "Now we've got a problem."

The other two were right behind him. One stepped in close, eyes flicking toward the Tahoe. "You got kids in there?"

Brynn didn't answer. Her heart was roaring like a waterfall in her ears. Inside the Tahoe, Rubble was going ballistic, barking furiously, claws scrabbling at the glass. She knew the noise had probably roused Mitchell . . . maybe all of the kids.

What would happen to them if they tried to intervene?

The third guy lifted the hem of his hoodie just high enough to show the butt of a pistol tucked into his waistband. "How 'bout you just come along with us, and nobody has to get hurt?"

"How 'bout you drop that piece on the ground before I spray your brains all over the parking lot?"

Emily Redd stood at the front corner of the Tahoe, her 12-gauge braced tight to her shoulder, muzzle trained on the face of the kid with the gun.

Everyone froze.

"Hey," said the first guy, the one still bracing Brynn against the side of the SUV. "Let's be cool."

Brynn felt him shift closer to her, as if trying to use her as a shield. *Uh-uh. Not gonna happen.*

She dropped, squirming out from under his hold, backpedaling away. The guy started to reach for her, but Emily intervened. "Don't," she snarled. "This is loaded with double-aught buck. I can skin all three of you with one pull, and right now, I'm really tempted."

Brynn's assailant took a step back, hands raised. So did his friends.

"Now," said Emily. "Put that gun on the ground. I won't say it again."

The kid with the pistol reached down slowly, plucked the weapon from his waistband, then bent to place it on the asphalt.

"Anyone else packing?" Emily's voice was flat and cold.

No one answered.

"Shirts up. Show me."

All three complied; hands shaking, they tugged up the hems of their sweatshirts and jackets to show bare stomachs. No other weapons were in evidence.

"Now, get back in your truck and get out of here. Cops are already on their way, but if you hurry, maybe I'll forget to tell them that I saw your license plate."

The threat of police involvement did what even the shotgun couldn't do. The three men practically fell over themselves hastening back to the pickup, and in a matter of seconds, the truck peeled out of the lot, tires squealing as it accelerated north on the main road.

Emily waited until they were gone to lower the shotgun. Right then, Brynn's knees gave out, and she felt herself starting to go down. Emily was beside her in an instant, wrapping her free arm around Brynn's waist, easing her down beside the Tahoe. "It's okay," she soothed. "Just breathe."

Brynn nodded, but instead of a measured inhalation, she broke down sobbing. "I didn't know what to do. I tried—"

"It's okay," Emily said, squeezing her tight. "You did good. You did real good."

She stayed there for a long moment, hugging Brynn until she was finally able to breathe again. "I'm okay," she managed to say. "Help me up."

Emily did, walking Brynn back to the passenger side and opening the door for her. The kids were awake now. Jack and Mitchell had worked together to get Matty and Lauren out of their car seats, and they were all hunkered low on the floor, with Jack cradling Lauren, who was crying but otherwise okay, tightly in his arms. Rubble was still growling softly but no longer looked ready to come through the glass.

"Show's over, gang," Emily said as she took Lauren from Jack. "Everyone back in your seats."

Jack and Matthew Jr. just stared back wide-eyed for a moment, but Mitchell shook off his inertia and began coaxing the other boys to do as instructed. Emily turned to Brynn. "You gonna be okay if I run back inside and grab the cart? It'll only take a second."

"How did you . . . ?"

"I was just coming out when I saw what was going on. Went out the other door and came up on the other side. I guess those guys were so focused on you, they didn't even notice."

"Neither did I."

"Well, it did the trick, thank God." Emily let that hang for a beat, then repeated her question. "You good here?"

Brynn blinked. Was she? "Maybe wait until the cops get here?"

"Oh, honey, I didn't call them."

The revelation hit Brynn like a splash of ice water. "You didn't? They had a gun." She glanced to where the thug's pistol still lay, all but forgotten. "They tried to kidnap me."

Emily laid a hand on her arm. "I know, honey, and if this were any other day, I would have kept them here until they were in handcuffs. But we're trying to keep a low profile. We can't afford to take any chances. If our names show up on a police report, the *real* bad guys might figure out where we are. And I don't think they'll scare off quite as easy."

Brynn stared back at her, struggling to accept the answer. She found the idea of the three punks getting away with what they'd done offensive, but she knew Emily was right. They were fighting for their lives. Justice would have to wait.

"So . . . ," Emily said after a moment. "You good?"

Brynn managed a nod. "Yeah. Go get the stuff. I just want to get out of here."

"Deal."

"Wait!"

Emily stopped and turned back toward Brynn. "What is it?"

"We aren't just going to leave that gun here, are we? What if someone finds it?"

"Way ahead of you. I'll grab it and turn it in to someone in the store when I get the cart."

THIRTY

CHICAGO, ILLINOIS

The packing plant rose amidst the urban decay like the dark tower in some fantasy epic. Five stories of cracked brick and soot-streaked windows, with several street entrances, all but one of which were boarded over and tagged with graffiti. The place looked abandoned, but the periodic arrival of luxury vehicles—an average of one or two every ten minutes during the hour that Redd and Decker spent surveilling the site from the cover of an abandoned car two blocks away—told a different story. The drivers pulled up in front of the one door that wasn't sealed with plywood, let out their passengers—most singletons, a few couples, all dressed for a night on the town—who were subsequently admitted into the darkened doorway, and then drove away, returning the scene to its postindustrial slumber.

"Doesn't look like much," Redd remarked.

"It's not supposed to," replied Decker, peering through a pair of binoculars. "That's the point."

They kept watching for another half hour, identifying a side entrance, used less frequently, and only, it seemed, by people sneaking out for a smoke break.

Only once, right at the beginning of their surveillance, did someone enter through the side door—a young, athletic-looking man wearing casual clothes. Probably an employee, Redd decided, showing up a bit late for his shift.

Occasionally, when a change in the wind coincided with the opening of the front door, they caught the sound of revelry, but the exact nature of the celebration remained obscure.

"So how are we going in? Bluff our way past the bouncers at the front door, or sneak in pretending to be waiters?"

Decker lowered the glasses and gave him a wry look. "You think you could pull off either one?"

Redd laughed. "Heck no. I'm about as subtle as a splitting maul."

Decker chuckled. "That's not really my style, either." He paused a beat. "I haven't seen any cameras. My guess is that whatever passes for security in there is going to focus on the entrances. Ground level. All we need to do is find an entrance they aren't watching."

"You've obviously got a plan. Care to share?"

"See the fire escape? The one at the east corner?"

Redd searched the dark facade, noting the jagged outlines of what remained of the building's exterior staircases, protruding from the brick like bones jutting up from the earth. Most were fragmented, but the one Decker had referenced looked marginally better. A skeleton, but with enough connective tissue to make an ascent, provided it didn't collapse under their weight.

"It's ugly, but I think it'll hold," Decker went on. "We'll climb up to the roof, force our way inside, and clear our way down to the party."

Decker went up first, fixing a safety line at the top in case Redd needed the assist. As it turned out, the precaution wasn't necessary—Redd hauled himself up without trouble. He used a pry bar to pop open the roof access door while Decker, standing behind him with his Glock drawn and pointed at the open doorway, waited.

Nothing.

No, not quite nothing. A sound, something like the roar of surf with a low bass backbeat, was rising up from the depths.

They moved inside, descending the steps without comment. The stairwell didn't appear to have been used in years. At the landing, Decker slowly opened the door to the fifth floor while Redd covered him, but it was immediately apparent that the floor wasn't in use. Dust coated every surface. Exposed wiring dangled from the ceiling. Doors stood ajar, revealing empty rooms filled with old furniture and forgotten equipment.

They moved on.

The fourth floor was more of the same, but the noise rising up the stairwell was more distinct. Cheers. Applause and laughter. Music too, but low, understated. Nothing like the sonic assault of a dance club or rave.

The sound grew steadily as they descended to the third floor, and Redd felt sure that the source of the tumult would soon be revealed. When they reached the third floor landing and Decker cracked the door, that expectation was confirmed.

A long corridor stretched away into shadow. The air of mustiness persisted, but unlike the upper floors, there was evidence of recent activity.

Redd exchanged a glance with Decker. They would have to clear this floor before moving down.

Covering each other, they moved door to door along the short hallway. Each room was unoccupied, though some of them contained stacks of boxes, indicating that they were being used for storage. At the end of the hall, they came to a set of double doors. Light bled out around the seams, and the dull roar of crowd noise and music seemed to pulse against the doors.

Decker tried the handle—unlocked—and then slowly pulled one of the doors open.

Beyond lay a balcony overlooking a cavernous atrium, which seemed to be the source of the tumult. Large light fixtures hung down from the ceiling, shining into the depths but only casting indirect light onto the balcony. Cautiously, the two men moved forward and looked down.

Below, a crude fighting cage constructed of chain link panels dominated the center of the floor. Inside, two bloodied, bare-chested fighters were circling each other, looking for any opening to exploit. One was shorter, thick through the neck and shoulders, a wrestler by the look of him. The other stood taller, leaner, hands floating, dancing just outside the other's reach. They clashed like magnets, the smaller man shooting in low, arms wrapping around the other's waist. The taller fighter sprawled, dropping his hips, hammering elbows into the back of his foe's head.

Redd looked away, widening his gaze to take in the crowd as they roared their approval. There were dozens of them, mostly men but some women, shouting, placing bets. The only people not wholly consumed with the fight were the handful of servers in black tie moving about in their midst, delivering drinks, and the large men in cheap suits stationed at intervals around the perimeter.

Decker tapped his arm and pointed to the far side of the room where a similar balcony extended from the second floor, overlooking both the octagon and the audience. Several plush couches ringed the edge, some of them occupied with well-dressed men and somewhat-less-dressed women.

One man stood out from the others. Late fifties, if Redd had to guess. Broad shoulders. Confident posture. Dark shirt, open at the collar, showing off tattoos and the gold chain around his neck. The women hung on him, and the other men deferred to him like sycophants.

"That's got to be him," Decker whispered. "Petrovich."

Redd nodded.

In the cage, the shorter wrestler had his arm around the other fighter's neck, squeezing. The taller man wriggled and struggled but had neither the leverage to flip his foe nor enough wiggle room to work a hand inside the choke hold. His struggles intensified then ceased altogether as he began tapping furiously against the grappler's forearm. The other fighter just kept squeezing as the crowd erupted.

Decker leaned close again. "If we'd known what kind of club this was, we could've come in the back door, with you posing as the main event."

"Ha-ha."

The crowd was still riding the adrenaline high of the fight's brutal conclusion, but Petrovich already appeared to have lost interest. He detached himself from his arm candy and stood, saying something to one of his looming bodyguards.

"He's leaving," whispered Redd.

"Or just using the head. Either way, this is our chance."

They retraced their steps along the third-floor corridor, then dropped quickly down the stairwell to the second floor. They moved fast but quiet, checking corners, passing through a series of empty rooms and narrow service corridors. Despite being closer to the action, the floor seemed deserted, evidently reserved solely for Petrovich's use.

At the far end, Redd paused, held up a fist, then slowly pied the corner just in time to see Petrovich step into view. The Russian strode down the hallway and entered a door. His bodyguard remained outside, arms crossed and scanning the hall.

"How do you want to play this?" asked Redd.

Decker eased around the corner, assessing the playing field. "We're going to have to rush the guy. Take him down before he can sound the alarm."

"Dicey." Redd took another look. Decker's earlier comment had given him an idea. "Let me try something."

He stripped off his plate carrier and weapons, leaving them on the floor beside Decker, then rose to his full height, rolled his shoulders, and stepped out into the open.

The bodyguard immediately snapped to, taking a step toward him. "Hey! You're not supposed to be up here."

"Yeah, yeah," Redd replied, patting the air in a placating gesture as he continued forward. "Dude, I am so turned around. Where's the locker room?"

The bodyguard bristled, one hand brushing back the tail of his jacket, no doubt a precursor to drawing a weapon. "Stop! You can't be here. Turn around."

Redd felt a tingle of apprehension. Playacting wasn't his strong suit, but he had to stay the course, had to bluff his way past this guy, if only for a few feet. "This way, right?" He took a few more steps, drawing even with the man.

"I said stop." The bodyguard dragged out his sidearm.

Redd brought both hands up now and sidestepped away, managing to move past the man in the process. "Whoa, dude. I'm just trying to find the locker room." He pointed past the guard. "That way?"

The guard's eyes flicked down the hall, and that was when Decker made his move, advancing with the stealth and swiftness of a ninja.

But not stealthy enough. Somehow, the bodyguard spotted him out of the corner of his eye. He spun, bringing the pistol around, aiming it at Decker.

Redd surged forward and drove his fist into the man's jaw. The blow snapped his head sideways and sent him crashing into the wall beside the door with sufficient force to dent the plaster. He slid to the ground, his face trailing a bloody smear.

Redd shook out his hand then knelt to retrieve the man's weapon. "Well, that's not how I thought that was going to go, but I guess I'll take it."

Decker didn't pause to congratulate him but pivoted toward the door and pushed through. Over his shoulder, Redd saw Petrovich, standing at a urinal, his back to the door. He shouted something in Russian but didn't turn his head. At least, not until Decker closed with him and shoved him forward, slamming his face against the wall above the urinal.

Petrovich yelped in surprise, but Decker silenced him by jamming the muzzle of his Glock under the man's jaw.

"Not a sound," he hissed.

Petrovich, his eyes full of both pain and rage, glowered at him but nodded.

Redd quickly dragged the unconscious bodyguard into the small restroom, dumping him on the floor of the only stall, and then turned to Decker. "Where do you want to do this?"

"Let's get him upstairs. No telling how long before someone comes looking for him."

Redd nodded, then turned to Petrovich. "I'd zip up if I were you, dude."

The mobster did just that, and then they hauled him, braced between them, out of the bathroom and back down the hall. Decker kept the pistol tucked firmly beneath his jaw, discouraging any resistance. Redd paused just long enough to retrieve his gear, throwing his plate carrier over one shoulder before continuing toward the stairwell.

They reached it without incident and ascended to the third floor, where they pulled Petrovich into a converted storeroom filled with old desks and battered filing cabinets. Redd dropped Petrovich into a chair and clamped his hands down on the mobster's shoulders to keep him in place.

Petrovich stared up at Decker, eyes widening in recognition. "It *is* you. Volkov's ghost." He studied Decker for a moment with a look that verged on admiration. Then his expression hardened. "You just made the biggest mistake of your life."

Decker ignored the empty threat. "Grigori Volkov?"

Petrovich seemed to realize that he'd just answered a question Decker hadn't even asked and responded with a now-too-familiar Russian curse.

Redd looked over at Decker. "That name mean something to you?"

Decker nodded. "Back when I was . . . *active* . . . Volkov was a rising star. A real alpha in the Russian underworld. A lot of his rivals met with unfortunate accidents. Some of them were our doing. At the time, I wondered why Volkov never showed up on our target list. It was one of the things that made me question the integrity of the unit." He paused a beat, as if lost in thought. "He must have been the one behind the hit in Kyiv."

"If you're right, then this Volkov is probably still working for the traitor. They're worried you're going to figure out who it is and come after them."

Decker met Redd's stare. "I am."

Petrovich chuckled darkly. "Good luck with that. Maybe he'll tell you all about it, right before he puts a bullet in your brain." He narrowed his eyes and added, "First your family. Then you."

Without even thinking, Redd began to squeeze Petrovich's shoulders. The Russian let out a gasp of pain. Redd eased off, but only a little.

Decker leaned in close. "Is Volkov in Montana?"

Petrovich started at the question. "You know?"

Decker ignored the question. "How does he keep finding me?"

Petrovich flinched, and Redd sensed that the Russian was starting to gain control of his responses.

He tightened his grip again.

Petrovich gritted his teeth, trying to endure the pain in stoic silence, but as his collarbones began to bend, his tough guy facade crumbled. "Nightshade!" he gasped.

Decker's eyes went to Redd, a subtle message. *Ease off.*

Redd did.

"Nightshade?" Decker prompted.

Petrovich sagged in the chair, his bravado leaking out like air from a punctured tire. "That's what Volkov calls him."

"I want his real name."

When Petrovich didn't answer immediately, Redd gave him another squeeze.

"I don't know," Petrovich cried. "Nightshade. That's all I know. He calls Volkov. Or Volkov calls him. Tells him where to look for you."

Decker's eyes narrowed in a thoughtful expression.

"Mean anything to you?" asked Redd.

Decker's head shook ever so slightly. He glanced down at Petrovich. "If that's all you know, then I guess we're done." He looked up at Redd. "Kill him."

Redd wasn't a fan of cold-blooded execution, even of someone as vile as Petrovich, but as he was pretty sure this was just Decker's way of eliciting more information from the gangster, he removed his right hand from the Russian's shoulder, drew his Glock, and pressed it to the base of Petrovich's skull.

"You might want to move," he told Decker. "This will probably make a mess."

"Wait!" begged Petrovich. "Just wait!"

Decker cocked his head to the side. "Wait?" He reached out and yanked aside the collar of Petrovich's shirt to expose the tattoos inked into the man's chest and shoulders, a permanent testament to his violent life. "How many times have you been the one holding the gun, listening to innocent people beg for their lives?"

"I'm sorry," Petrovich wailed. "Please, don't do this."

Decker regarded him with a cold stare. "Does Volkov know who Nightshade is?"

Petrovich grasped at the question like a lifeline. "I don't know. I don't think so. But I do know this. He's *afraid* of him. And Grigori Volkov isn't afraid of anyone."

Redd heard a note of awe in the man's admission. The idea that someone like Volkov—a real alpha, as Decker had put it—lived in fear of the mysterious Nightshade cast the situation in a whole new light. Nightshade, whoever he was, was more than just a traitor working inside Rogue Unit. More than just an informant or a facilitator. *He* was the real alpha.

Worse, if Petrovich was telling the truth about Volkov not knowing Nightshade's identity—and there was no reason to think otherwise—that meant their trail had just gone cold. Even if they went after Volkov, rolled him up, and managed to interrogate him, they would be no closer to finding Nightshade.

He could tell Decker was thinking the same thing.

But before either of them could put it in words, the door burst open, and a man in a leather jacket stood in the doorway, holding a pistol aimed right at them.

THIRTY-ONE

Redd saw the gunman's gaze focus on Petrovich, held down in the chair, with his captors standing fore and aft. He saw the hesitation in the man's eyes. If he took the shot and missed, he might kill his boss.

Redd, however, didn't have cause to hesitate. He lifted the suppressed Glock from behind Petrovich's head and fired three quick shots. Two to the chest, one to the head, a textbook Mozambique drill. The last shot was a little iffy since the gunman was already pitching backward, his unfired gun flying from his hands.

Even with the suppressor, the reports were shockingly loud in the small enclosure. Loud enough to get the attention of anyone else in the vicinity. And Redd didn't doubt that there were other Bratva soldiers nearby. The mere fact that the man had come through the door with weapon drawn was proof enough that Petrovich's bodyguard had come to and sounded the alarm.

It was time to go.

Redd yanked Petrovich to his feet and propelled him toward the doorway, using him as a shield as he moved out into the hall, with Decker right behind him. They stepped out just in time to see more armed men emerging from the door to the stairwell. Decker fired immediately, forcing the front two gunmen to stumble back onto the landing.

"Not getting out that way," shouted Redd, crouching down behind the mobster. "Got any ideas?"

As if to underscore Redd's assessment, a hand holding a pistol poked out from the stairwell doorway, its wielder firing randomly in their general direction. The rounds creased the air overhead, chewing up the ceiling and raining dust and debris down on them. The Bratva gunman wasn't aiming for them, at least Redd didn't think so, but just trying to intimidate them.

Decker returned fire, and the hand with the pistol disappeared. "Fall back to the balcony," he shouted.

Redd complied, dragging a stumbling and swearing Petrovich backward, keeping him between them and the stairwell door as he retreated down the corridor. Another gunman, or maybe the same one, leaned out, trying to get a bead on them, but Decker dropped him with a single well-placed shot.

They reached the double doors a moment later. Decker threw them open, and Redd hauled Petrovich backward through them. The din from the crowd rose up to meet them. A new bout was already underway, the tumult evidently masking the exchange of gunfire.

Redd kept Petrovich positioned in the doorway as a conspicuous deterrent to further shooting from his would-be rescuers. So far, it seemed to be working, but it was only a temporary solution.

Decker moved to the rail and looked down. After a few seconds, he turned to Redd. "If we can get down to the main level, we can use the crowd for cover while we look for an exit."

Redd glanced back. "Care to expand on the first part of that plan? Because I don't recall there being any way off this balcony. I mean, aside from a three-story drop."

Decker shrugged. "That's pretty much the only option."

Redd groaned. A fall from three stories was certainly survivable. He knew because he had done it. When he'd gone through the Army Airborne school—part of his training journey to become a Marine Raider—he'd taken the plunge from a thirty-four-foot jump tower.

No, the landing wouldn't kill them. But it might hurt them. And while a blown knee or a sprained ankle might not be immediately fatal, any injury that hampered their ability to escape the club would kill them just as surely as a broken neck.

"We use the crowd to break our fall," Decker was saying.

Redd blinked. "Wait, what? You want to use those people as a crash pad?"

"It'll work. Trust me."

Redd glanced down again. The spectators were packed in, shoulder to shoulder, fists pumping the air, surging and swaying as they watched two new opponents trying to take each other apart. No one had even so much as glanced their way.

Decker wasn't wrong. Using the spectators to cushion their landing was a viable strategy. And getting down to the floor was their only option. He didn't like it . . . He didn't have to like it. But he would have to do it.

"What about him?" he asked, nodding to Petrovich. The mobster had stopped struggling and was following their conversation with a look of feral intensity. "We can't very well take him along."

Redd half expected Decker to repeat his earlier execution order, this time meaning it, and wasn't really sure how he felt about that. He recalled how Decker had coldly dispatched the man he'd interrogated after the assault on the cabin in the Upper Peninsula, and on an intellectual level, he understood why. These men . . . these gangsters . . . saw mercy as weakness. If he let Petrovich live, all he would really do was make an enemy for life.

Petrovich must've sensed the weight in Redd's silence, because he twisted around, trying to look him in the eye. "Wait," he rasped. "Wait. You don't have to do this."

Decker stared back at Redd, eyes narrowing ever so slightly. Finally, he said, "Whatever lets you sleep at night. But if you let him live, he'll just come after you."

"No!" protested Petrovich. "I swear. On my mother—"

Redd jammed the suppressor hard against Petrovich's skull. "Shut up."

The Russian's pleas softened into faint whimpers. A moment later, the faint ammonia odor of urine filled the air.

Decker didn't press his case, didn't say another word. He just held Redd's gaze, then gave a slight nod. *Your call. I won't stop you. I won't do it for you.*

Redd stared down at the back of the mobster's head a second longer. One pull of the trigger, and the problem would be solved.

He shifted his grip, pulling the Glock back. Petrovich seemed to shrink into himself. "Please—"

Redd brought the butt of the pistol down hard behind the man's ear. Petrovich sagged in his grip, and Redd let him drop like a bag of garbage. He looked over at Decker. "If he comes for me, I'll deal with him. Until then . . ."

Decker shrugged then turned to the balcony rail. "You ready to do this?"

"Not really."

That brought a hint of a smile to the other man's face. "Well, ready or not, we're doing it." He put his hands on the rail and gazed down again. "We should go at the same time. Before they scatter like cockroaches."

Redd joined him then moved down until he found a sufficiently dense cluster of spectators.

"On three," Decker said. "One . . . two . . ."

"'There is no spoon,'" muttered Redd. It was a line from *The Matrix* and a mantra that had served him well during his first parachute jump. A silly little line that helped him overcome the primal fear that had roused itself in anticipation of stepping out the back of a perfectly good C-130.

"What?"

"Three!" Redd shouted and vaulted the rail.

THIRTY-TWO

YELLOWSTONE NATIONAL PARK, WYOMING

Emily sat on a folding camp chair, her boots kicked off, bare toes stretched out toward the warmth. The fire had burned down to a bed of glowing coals. She considered tossing a few more split logs on but decided it was probably better to let it burn down. Besides, she was just too comfortable where she was. Rubble lay at her feet, head down, eyes half lidded but still alert.

Across the fire, Brynn leaned back in her own chair, hoodie pulled up, hands folded in her lap, to all appearances relaxed. Emily was impressed by the girl's ability to push through trauma and keep going. Her resilience really was incredible, albeit probably unhealthy to a degree. Emily was a big believer that everyone needs time to process what they're going through so they can acknowledge it and deal with things appropriately.

Then again, having already lost her mother, Emily knew that Brynn had been through more than most kids her age, and that both she and Mitchell had probably been forced to grow up a lot sooner than Aaron would have liked.

She thought about feeling her way around that conversation but decided against it. They'd have time to talk later. For now, everyone was safe, and Emily took some quiet satisfaction in that. She had brought them all to safety.

The campsite—a primitive, semiofficial spot known as Willow Creek—wasn't on any park maps. It was a legacy spot, known only to a handful of locals and rangers. Matthew had learned about it from a Yellowstone backcountry ranger he'd met the previous year during a joint SAR training exercise. The man had mentioned it offhand as a prime spot to get off the grid, and Matthew had scouted it last fall, thinking it might be ideal for the actual family camping trip they had been planning.

There were no picnic tables, no restrooms, and definitely no reservation slips tacked to a post. Just a flat patch of earth above the creek bank, a fire ring made from river rocks, and enough tree cover to shield them from the view of anyone driving by on the main road.

After leaving Gardiner, they had entered the park, passing under the Roosevelt Arch, and followed the Grand Loop Road east through the northern range of Yellowstone, passing Mammoth Hot Springs and climbing gradually toward the Lamar Valley. It was a stunningly beautiful drive, but there was little time to appreciate it, as they were running out of daylight. While the kids gazed out at bison herds and looked for bears and wolves, Emily kept one eye on the road and the other on the clock.

Just before the turnoff to the Slough Creek Campground—a popular spot that would be bustling in a few more weeks—they turned onto a narrow service spur, just a rutted track lined with dense lodgepole pines and old fire-scarred stumps. A few miles in, they came to a rusted metal gate secured with a weathered padlock. The key was hidden in a nearby fake rock, just as Matthew had described. Beyond the gate, the road wound back into the woods for another two miles, rising gently until it reached the modest clearing above Willow Creek.

They made it just in time, pulling off the gravel road and into the clearing with less than twenty minutes of usable light to spare. They'd set up quickly, with Emily raising the tents while Brynn got the fire going and the boys gathered deadfalls for fuel. Now, with bellies full of hot dogs and s'mores, the boys were zipped in their tent, far from fast asleep but quiet at least, and Lauren was curled up in a sleeping bag in Emily's tent.

That, of course, was not the end of Emily's day. This was Yellowstone, where the wild things were, and while it was fun to look for roaming animals from the relative safety and comfort of a vehicle on the road, it was imperative to avoid doing anything that might invite them into camp. She had stashed their food and trash in bear-proof canisters, setting them well away from the tents and downwind. She'd also wiped down the fire ring and picnic area with unscented wipes, erasing any trace of spilled condiments or greasy fingers that might tempt curious wildlife. It wasn't foolproof—nothing was out here—but it was the best defense that could be mounted against nighttime visitors with sharp claws and powerful noses.

Now, with all that attended to, Emily felt like she could finally take a moment to catch her breath.

She was used to stress in her day job as a nurse practitioner, but today had been one for the books. She'd handled it because she had to, because keeping her family safe was an intrinsic part of who she was, and because, really, there was no one else to do it. But even so, her tank—physically and emotionally—was down to fumes. Here, in the hush of the forest, with the fire's warmth on her skin and the low murmur of the creek nearby, she felt like she might be able to start filling it up. And she would need to, because even though they were out in the middle of nowhere . . . or maybe *because* they were out in the middle of nowhere, she couldn't afford to let down her guard.

She glanced across the fire at Brynn. The girl had handled herself back in Gardiner. Maybe not flawlessly, but she'd made it through, shaken but not broken, and she'd stepped up since.

"You did good today," Emily said.

Brynn shrugged. "Just a campfire and some tents."

"You know that's not what I meant."

Brynn gave a small, sheepish smile but then looked away, staring into the coals. "Do you think it's over? The running, I mean."

Emily didn't answer right away. She wanted to give comfort, to offer reassurance. But she didn't believe it herself. "It will be over when Matty and your father come back and tell us it's over. Hopefully, this pause will last until that happens. Until then, we have to stay on our toes."

Brynn nodded slowly. "Well, I'm glad I'm here. Even if this is just a pause."

Emily looked at her across the fire. "Me too."

Brynn leaned forward, poked at a coal with a stick, stirring up a tiny flare. "I didn't think I'd like camping. Dirt, bugs, no Wi-Fi . . ." She gave a mock shudder. "But this isn't so bad."

"See if you feel that way when you wake up at three a.m. and have to pee."

They both laughed, but then Rubble's head came up, ears pricked, eyes focused on the darkness beyond the firelight. He let out a low growl, and Emily's blood went cold.

Something moved in the darkness, and then a sharp report tore the night asunder.

It was loud, but not as loud as an actual gunshot—though in the moment, Emily was barely able to make the distinction.

Rubble was up, barking at something well beyond the glow of the fire.

There was another loud detonation, and then less than a second later, two more.

Cries of terror erupted from the boys' tent. Junior . . . or maybe Jack . . . Both? A sudden flash painted the trees bloodred, followed by a shriek of sound like tearing metal. Emily's ears rang. Smoke, thick and sulfurous, blew across the campsite.

Fireworks. Someone is shooting fireworks at us!

Brynn had jumped to her feet, eyes wide, fighting back panic.

Emily was already moving. "Stay with the boys!"

She sprinted to her tent, heart hammering. Inside, Lauren was crying, a shrill wail of pure, primal terror. Emily fumbled for the zipper, just as another series of reports cracked right behind her. Rubble yelped as a firecracker detonated beside him.

Emily pulled at the zipper so hard, the tent buckled, almost collapsing, but then it relented, opening halfway, just enough to let her reach in and grab the shotgun. She whirled around, brought the smooth walnut stock to her shoulder, thumbed off the safety catch, and began looking for someone to shoot.

Something wet splashed in her face. She flinched instinctively, starting to raise a hand to wipe it away. For a single confused heartbeat, she thought someone had spit in her face.

Then her world caught fire.

Lips, cheeks, hands—every inch of exposed flesh—flared as if dipped in acid. She squeezed her eyes shut but was too late—her orbs were already ablaze with pain. It was everywhere. Permeating her shirt, burning the skin of her neck and chest. It was in her nose, filling her mouth, constricting her throat.

It was in her lungs.

She tried to scream, to cry out for Brynn, for the kids—*anything*—but managed only a ragged, choking sound.

Bear spray.

She had bought a can of the stuff earlier that day at REI. Designed to discourage grizzlies, it was less concentrated than civilian pepper sprays, but unlike the little key chain mace sprayers, it delivered a massive volume of the capsaicinoid compound from a distance of up to thirty feet. And now it was in her eyes, her pores, her lungs.

She reeled back, one hand clawing at her face—she wanted to claw it completely off—but somehow she kept her other hand on the shotgun. Because whoever had done this to her was still out there, just waiting for her to give up.

And that was something she would never do.

She clenched her jaw, fighting the urge to throw up, and staggered, trying to keep the shotgun pointed out and away, unsure if there was anyone in front of her. Rubble howled somewhere to her left, not his usual plaintive cry but an awful, broken sound. He'd been sprayed too, only he had no idea what was happening to him.

Her gut twisted in sympathy, in fury.

Then through the chaos of Rubble's wails and the kids' screams, she heard a voice—clear, close, and purposeful.

"Forget her. Grab the girl."

THIRTY-THREE

CHICAGO, ILLINOIS

Time seemed to pause. The sound of the crowd dulled to a murmur, and for a heartbeat, Redd felt weightless. Then the world dropped out from under him.

He slammed down like a meteor strike. Feet first, knees bent to absorb the shock, but instead of ground, his boots struck a shoulder, and the person it belonged to seemed to squirt out from under him, shifting his momentum, sending him sprawling into a tangle of limbs and flailing bodies. For a moment, he was tossed about in a wave of humanity, but then the sea parted and he hit the floor.

Yet the pain he'd braced himself for never arrived. He'd have a few bruises to show for his efforts—probably fewer than the unfortunate people who had broken his fall—but he'd taken much harder hits playing high school football. Decker's crazy human-crash-pad plan had worked.

His sense of relief was short-lived. Around him, the victims of his vertical entry were recovering their wits, and they weren't happy about it.

The man Redd had landed atop was on all fours, coughing and swearing, not in Russian but in English with a Chicago accent. An attractive woman in a slinky cocktail dress launched into an obscenity-ridden tirade, swinging her clutch at him like a weapon. Several other men began closing in, fists clenched, voices raised in growing indignation.

Redd showed them his Glock, and everything changed.

Fury turned instantly into fear.

The woman with the clutch shrieked. The men around Redd scrambled backward, shoving past one another in a frantic scramble to get clear. One tripped over a fallen spectator and went down hard, knocking over two more in the process.

Then someone shouted, "Gun!" and the crowd convulsed, a ripple at first quickly building into a wave. Screams rose, wild and disjointed, mixing with the heavy sound of bodies colliding. The fight in the ring halted as spectators turned, reacting to the surge even before they knew what had triggered it. Like dominoes falling in a widening circle, one group shoved the next, feeding confusion into alarm, alarm into terror. People clawed at each other, tried to push through, and when that didn't work, began climbing and trampling over the unlucky ones who had gone down in the crush.

Decker emerged from the chaos, slipping through the panicked masses to join Redd in the widening circle of open floor.

"You good?" Redd shouted.

Decker flashed an upraised thumb then turned his attention to the receding crowd.

"See an exit?"

Decker shook his head. "No. And I don't see any lighted exit signs, which feels like a pretty clear violation of the fire code."

"Add it to the list."

Decker gestured toward the crowd. "I guess we follow them."

Redd holstered the Glock. Dressed as they were, in plate carriers festooned with mag pouches, they wouldn't exactly blend in, but keeping the pistol out of view might knock down their visibility a notch.

They merged with the current of bodies, letting themselves be carried along in the surge. The tactical gear still drew glances, but with the weapon out of sight and the crush of bodies all around, no one challenged them. The crowd seemed to know where they were going, and even though their collective desire to flee the building had created a bottleneck, the mass of bodies was shrinking. Standing at least a head taller than nearly everyone else, Redd could see them trying to squeeze into a narrow corridor opposite Petrovich's balcony.

But not everyone was trying to get out. Among a sea of heads turned away, four faces shone out like stars in the sky—hard faces, searching the crowd.

Looking for them.

Redd's height made him an easy target, even amidst the chaos, and so at almost the same instant that he spotted the men, one of them locked eyes with him.

Then he raised a pistol and fired.

The shot was aimed up at the ceiling but that made little difference to the already terrified masses. Almost in unison, they dove for cover or simply cowered in place, and even before the echo of the report died away, the Bratva gunman had an unobstructed field of fire. The man brought his weapon down, aimed it at Redd, and started shooting.

Redd and Decker had ducked as well, though unlike the others, they were not simply cowering. Both had crouched down, Glocks out, and were returning fire, but with so many civilians in close proximity to the Bratva soldiers, they intentionally shot high. Meanwhile the other three men joined the fray, throwing a hailstorm of lead their way. Their shots were wild, undisciplined, but as J. B. had been fond of saying, even a blind squirrel could eventually find a nut.

Decker tapped Redd's arm, then pointed behind them, to the octagon. "Go!"

Redd didn't need an explanation. When Decker started firing again, Redd bounded up and made a dash for the crudely fashioned fighting cage while bullets continued to stitch the air around him. He slid the last few feet like a runner stealing second, then flipped over and started laying down covering fire for Decker. A half beat later, the other man slid in beside him, just as a round punched a crater into the plywood base of the cage above their heads.

Redd shot out the rest of his magazine, reloaded. Across the floor, the Bratva goons were spreading out as they advanced, shooting on the move.

"Not gonna be able to stay here long," Redd called out.

Decker didn't answer, just leaned out and took a quick glance around the floor. Then he jabbed a finger toward the wall adjacent to the entrance. "There," he said. "Stairs."

Redd followed his line and saw a steel fire door, just like the ones they'd used during their descent from the roof to check each floor.

"That's our exit plan," Decker went on. "Get to the roof. Rappel down."

It was a good plan. But first they would have to make it across fifty feet of open floor to the stairwell entrance.

"You go first," said Decker. "I'll cover."

Redd didn't hesitate. As Decker started firing, he bounded up and began sprinting, his strides weirdly keeping time with the muted thump of Decker's suppressed Glock. Rounds snapped through the air around him—too close—but he kept moving, zigzagging slightly, knowing that the only way out was through.

The steel door was just twenty feet away.

Ten.

And then, it swung open.

Redd's heart stuttered. He reflexively skidded to a halt, boots slipping slightly on concrete slick with spilled drinks, as the door yawned wide and Bratva soldiers appeared. The first man through looked almost as surprised to see Redd as he was to see them, but he quickly overcame his astonishment and brought his pistol up. Redd scrambled backward, firing into the doorway, dropping the first man, but there were three more behind him, already shooting.

Redd twisted away, knowing that he didn't stand a chance against three men at such close range, and made a dash for the relative cover of the octagon. A round sizzled past his ear, and then he felt a mule kick squarely in the center of his back as a bullet pounded into the armor plate. The impact knocked the wind out of him and sent him staggering forward a few steps before sprawling face-first on the concrete, ten feet from the base of the octagon.

More gunfire creased the air above him. Decker and the Bratva gunmen, trading shots. Another of the latter went down, but more were emerging from the stairwell.

Through the fury, Redd heard Decker shouting his name, telling him to move. He managed to find his breath with a welcome gasp, and then gritting his teeth against the pain that now throbbed through his entire body, he began a fast high crawl toward Decker's position, even as the latter kept shooting directly above him. When Redd was within a foot or two, Decker stopped firing and grabbed Redd's collar with one hand, dragging him the last few feet into the questionable cover provided by the plywood base of the fighting cage.

"You hit?"

"Plate caught it," answered Redd through gritted teeth.

Decker gave a terse nod, then looked away, pivoting on his heel as he scanned in every direction, squeezing off several shots. Wincing, Redd got to hands and knees, eased into a crouch, and drew his backup weapon. The Bratva shooters were closing in now from all sides, tightening like a noose.

"This could be a problem!" Decker shouted as he dropped a spent mag and reloaded.

"Tell me about it." Redd snapped off a shot that winged a hostile gunman, then leaned back against the base of the octagon, looking for targets even as he searched for a solution.

They had to get out of this building, and that meant fighting through to an exit. But which one? The main door? The stairwell? He recalled that there was also a side entrance from the alley but had no idea where it was.

He glanced up, still looking for an answer, and that's when he saw it.

The balcony.

Petrovich's perch loomed above, ten, maybe twelve feet away, seeming to hover just a few feet from the chain-link panels that formed the walls of the octagon.

"Aaron! Balcony!"

Decker glanced back, then followed Redd's gaze. Comprehension dawned in his eyes but was replaced by a look of consternation. "We'll be easy targets."

But Redd already had the answer to that. He tore open one of the pouches on his plate carrier and removed an object that looked a little like a small aerosol can, painted olive drab, with a pull ring dangling from the top. Decker understood immediately and took an identical canister from his own rig. They pulled the rings in unison and flung the devices out across the floor—one toward the stairwell door, the other toward the main entrance.

While still in midair, the canisters emitted a distinctive pop and then began gushing white smoke. In seconds, the floor was filled by twin plumes of dense chemical vapor, obscuring their view of the advancing gunmen and, more importantly, hiding them from view.

Redd jammed his pistol into its holster and then launched himself from a crouch, springing up to grab hold of the chain link. The move sent a flare of pain across his back, but he fought through it, gripping the wire and pulling himself up high enough to jam the toes of his boots into the diamond-patterned web of steel.

A random bullet sparked off one of the metal uprights. Another hit the chain link inches from his hand, snapping the wire and sending a stinging vibration through the grid.

Blind squirrel, thought Redd, shaking his head. He kept climbing, pulled himself up onto the top of the cage, and then flung himself across the gap to the balcony.

He easily caught the rail, throwing arms over it a fraction of a second before his chest slammed into the smooth tubular steel. His plate carrier thankfully absorbed most of the impact. He used the last of his momentum to swing one leg up, hook a foot over the top of the rail, and then roll forward, dropping onto the balcony floor in a low crouch. He immediately drew his pistol to provide cover fire for Decker's ascent.

From his elevated vantage point, Redd had an unrestricted view of the chaos they had wrought. The smoke had spread quickly, reducing the floor below to a swirling gray soup. He could see a few wraithlike figures amidst the miasma, Bratva shooters coughing and waving their pistols. One of them seemed intent on reaching the octagon. Redd dropped him with two well-placed shots.

A moment later, Decker's fingers hooked the railing, and he hauled himself up, rolling over the top and dropping in a low crouch beside Redd.

"Stairs?" asked Redd.

"Unless you've got a better idea."

Redd shook his head. "Popping smoke was pretty much all I had."

A hint of a smile lifted the corner of Decker's mouth. He gestured to the balcony door. "Shall we?"

They passed into the corridor where they had earlier waylaid Petrovich and his bodyguard, then raced through the familiar floor layout to reach the stairwell door. Redd grasped the handle and eased the door open an inch.

Shouts rose up from below along with the staccato tap of footsteps. Through the gray haze, he saw blurred shapes ascending, pistols up. The Bratva shooters had evidently figured out where they had gone and were already moving to intercept them.

THIRTY-FOUR

Redd didn't wait for them to come into range. Instead, he yanked another grenade from a pouch on his plate carrier—this one a flash-bang—pulled the pin, and tossed it down the stairwell.

"Flash out!" he shouted, pulling the door shut.

Even with the door shielding him from the blast, the detonation hit like a thunderclap. The door lurched against him, as if someone on the other side had struck it with a battering ram, and the pressure wave vibrated through his body. But what he felt was nothing to what the Bratva shooters in the stairwell would have experienced.

He waited another second, then shoved the door open, moving onto the smoke-filled landing with Decker close behind and bounding up the steps two at a time. There wasn't a hostile to be seen. The stun grenade had effectively flushed them all back down the stairwell.

They reached the rooftop without firing a shot, stepping out into a night that was, in contrast to what they had just left behind, surprisingly peaceful. They did a quick sweep of the rooftop, just to make sure there weren't any Bratva soldiers lurking behind a ventilation cap, and then moved to the edge for a look at the street below.

The pavement in front of the club looked like a street fair. Everyone who had fled the mayhem inside was now milling about outside, no doubt calling for their rides and trying to decide if they were safe or needed to keep running.

"Well, that's not great," Decker muttered.

"Can't stay here," replied Redd.

"No, I don't suppose we can. Okay—we just need to make it a couple blocks."

Aaron stepped back and retrieved the coil of rope he'd used earlier to belay Redd during the fire escape ascent and flung it over the side. He then wrapped a loop of it across his chest and around his waist, gripping the line at the small of his back with his right hand, and moved to the edge.

"See you downstairs," he said, then stepped off the edge.

He went down face-first, an Aussie-style rappel, favored by a lot of operators because, unlike the traditional seated rappel, it let you keep your eyes on the ground, and on any potential threats that might be waiting at the bottom.

It was also fast.

Redd watched as Decker bounded down the brick face in just a few hops, neatly sidestepping the fire escape, using the rope's friction across his torso to slow his descent just enough to avoid injury. At the last possible second before face-planting on the asphalt, he gripped the brake line and flipped upright, landing feetfirst. A quick twist freed him from the line, and he stepped away, making room for Redd.

His arrival did not go unremarked. Several heads turned toward him, fingers pointing, voices raised in recognition and alarm.

Redd snatched the rope, threw a wrap across his chest, and turned toward the edge. He wasn't normally gung-ho about rappelling. Like parachuting, it was a means to an end, something to be endured and survived but not necessarily enjoyed.

But tonight, after everything he and Decker had gone through, going face-first five stories down a rope barely ticked the meter. Gripping the line with his brake hand, he stepped up to the edge and took the plunge.

There is no spoon.

He controlled the descent with short hops, doing his best to stay perpendicular to the wall. The street rushed up, and he let the rope slide a final foot, dropping the last few inches to land in a crouch beside Decker. He freed himself from the line and tossed it aside.

All around them, people milled like the living dead in a horror film. Some pointed. Others just stared warily. No one tried to stop them, but every glance felt like a spotlight. They moved quickly, clearing the throng and cutting diagonally across the street. Redd could see the waiting Durango only two blocks up.

"Leaving so soon?"

Redd froze. So did Decker. The voice was unmistakable.

Petrovich.

From the corner of his eye, Redd saw the Bratva *avtoritet* emerge from the alley, flanked by half a dozen of his men. Every last one of them, Petrovich included, was aiming a gun at them.

Redd did the math.

Draw time: a half second? That was a bit optimistic, especially with the added length of the suppressor.

Enemy reaction time: It took the average person anywhere from three to five tenths of a second to recognize a threat, and then another two to three tenths to actually do something about it. Probably less for these guys, since they already had fingers on triggers.

So, in the time it would take him to draw, acquire, and fire, one or more of the Bratva shooters would get off a shot. If Redd was moving when he drew, the odds were good that they might not hit him with that first shot—good but not great—but in the time it took him to kill one, the others would be able to correct their aim.

Unless they scored a head shot—unlikely but not impossible—his plate carrier might keep him alive long enough to kill a second, but that still left him with a deficit.

There was Decker to consider, of course. Assuming he was able to telepathically read Redd's intent, perfectly synchronize and coordinate his response, they could take down four, maybe even five of the Bratva shooters.

Still not enough.

Decker unexpectedly broke the tense silence. "You really aren't very bright, are you, Petrovich? I was willing to let you walk away from this with your life. Now?" He spread his hands. "Now I am going to have to kill you."

Redd knew that Decker wasn't merely posturing in the face of certain death. There was a method to his seeming madness. If he could keep Petrovich engaged, keep him talking, keep him and his men distracted, it might buy them a crucial fraction of a second while they made their move.

Petrovich took the bait.

"Big words," he said, stalking forward to stand in front of them. He thrust his pistol out until it was mere inches from Decker's face. "But I think *I* am the one who is going to kill *you*."

"You really do like the sound of your own voice, don't you? What, are you hoping I'll beg? Pee all over myself like you did?" Decker shook his head. "Not gonna happen."

Petrovich's face darkened with rage and for a fleeting moment, Redd thought either the Russian would pull his trigger or Decker would make his move, sidestep the pistol—Petrovich had made a huge tactical error getting so close to his foes—and take the gun away from him, but to his astonishment, neither happened. Instead, Petrovich mastered his emotions and took a step back. "On your knees."

Redd shot a glance at Decker, looking to see if the other man would comply. Decker met his eyes and gave a slight nod before slowly sinking down.

Kneeling—the classic execution pose—would limit their mobility when the time came to make a move. On the other hand, it subtly signaled that Petrovich wanted to make a spectacle of killing them, and that just might buy them a few more seconds.

Redd followed his lead.

Petrovich chortled. "I can't wait to see the look on Volkov's face when he finds out I have killed the great Aaron Decker." His eyes flitted over to Redd, lip curling in a dismissive sneer. "And whoever you are."

Decker glanced over at Redd and shrugged. "Told you."

"Guess you were right," admitted Redd. "Live and learn."

"Exactly." Decker nodded and then said one more word. *"Now!"*

THIRTY-FIVE

YELLOWSTONE NATIONAL PARK, WYOMING

Denver Callahan crouched behind the trunk of a stunted lodgepole pine just ten yards from the fire ring, waiting for his chance to move. Smoke swirled over the camp like a battlefield haze, glowing red and orange in the dying firelight. The air stank of sulfur, scorched cloth, and the pungent, eye-stinging vapor of bear spray.

Some of it had blown back his way. Not nearly enough to cause any debilitating effects. Just a faint heat in his eyes and nostrils, not unlike partaking of a particularly choice jalapeño. He'd done the One Chip Challenge on a dare, so this was nothing.

But it wasn't nothing for the woman from the grocery store. He'd sprayed the stuff right in her face, direct hit, full potency. Her and the mutt. Now, she was gasping and staggering, trying to wipe the stuff away and only making it worse.

Payback, baby, he thought. *Teach you to put a shotgun in my face.*

Except she still had the shotgun. Even mostly blind, she had the thing raised, finger on the trigger, ready to blast anything that moved, and that made Denver nervous.

"Circle around and come up from the other side."

Tyler, crouching beside him with a Bic lighter in one hand and a cherry bomb in the other, stared back at him, wide-eyed. "Me?"

"Both of you," said Denver, nodding to include Shane.

Shane gaped at him. "What about Mama Bear?"

"Forget her. Grab the girl."

The girl.

Now there was a choice piece of tail.

When Rick had first put out the word, telling all his street dealers to be on the lookout for a white Chevy Tahoe driven by a woman with a pack of kids, including a seventeen-year-old girl who Rick seemed particularly interested in, Denver considered it just another job, with a nice little payout if he spotted the rig, and a bonus if he could separate the girl. There hadn't been a name or photo, just a general description. So when they'd gotten lucky, spotting the Tahoe as it pulled out of the KFC on North 19th Avenue, he'd only seen dollar signs. The why didn't matter. That was Rick's business.

They'd followed at a discreet distance, just one more truck on the road to Yellowstone, passing and pulling over whenever the Tahoe stopped, all the while daydreaming about what they could do with the bonus Rick had offered if they could grab the girl. By the time the white Chevy pulled into the parking lot of the store in Gardiner, they were sufficiently amped up to make their move.

And then he'd caught a look at her, standing there next to the rig: long legs, dark hair, and that uptight, haughty look that the popular girls in school always had . . .

Oh yeah, they weren't just going to grab her. They were gonna have some fun first.

Maybe she'd even go along with it. Girls like that usually liked to party with older guys, but if not? Hey, she didn't have to be conscious for them to have fun.

Then that woman—the mom or aunt or whatever—came out of nowhere with a freaking shotgun. It was all Denver could do to get them out of there before things went sideways. But he hadn't gone far. And he'd done what he should have done all along and called Rick to report the sighting.

Rick had been too jazzed about the news to care that they'd sat on it for two hours. *"Keep tailing 'em,"* he'd told them.

Well, that was easier said than done. They'd lost track of the Tahoe after Gardiner, so even though they knew it was heading into the park, that still left a lot of places it could be. They had cruised Mammoth Campground, looking for the rig—no luck—and then headed on down the road, feeling their bonus slipping away with each mile they traveled without seeing the Tahoe.

Then Rick had texted with a location. Cell coverage was spotty the farther they got from Mammoth, but the text had gotten through when they'd crested a rise and got line of sight on a distant cell tower. Somehow, Rick—or whoever he was taking orders from—had found the white Tahoe at an unregistered campsite near Slough Creek, and he wanted Denver and his boys to go there and grab the girl.

It was like the universe wanted them to win.

Denver's plan was going perfectly. The fireworks had disoriented both the woman and the dog, and scared the crap out of the kids, which had given him a chance to get in close enough to hose the woman with bear spray. The girl had run to the other tent and hadn't come out.

"She ain't going to be seeing straight for at least an hour," Denver went on. "You hear her? Gasping like a dying cat? Just come up from behind and grab the girl. She ain't gonna shoot in the direction of the tents. And if she even looks your way, I'll hit her again." He held up the half-empty canister of bear spray for emphasis.

Tyler and Shane exchanged a questioning look. Denver reached out and snatched the lighter and cherry bomb from Tyler's hands. "I'll do this one. You two circle wide and get in close. Wait for the pop—then move."

Tyler hesitated, clearly unsure, but a sharp look from Denver got him moving. Shane followed, slinking low through the trees.

Denver watched them disappear into the shadows beyond the firelight, counting the seconds in his head.

Ten . . . fifteen . . . twenty . . .

Close enough.

He flicked the wheel on the Bic, struck a flame, and touched it to the fuse, then lobbed the cherry bomb at the camp, aiming for the fire ring.

He didn't see where it landed but sure as heck heard it go *bang!* A spray of glowing embers shot up into the night air, and he felt the shock wave even from thirty feet away.

The woman screamed, reeled back, falling into the tent, the shotgun all but forgotten. The dog, already staggering and disoriented, let out a fresh high-pitched howl.

Perfect.

Through the smoke and scattered firelight, he caught movement: two shapes—his buds—closing in on the tent where the girl had gone. Shane got there first, unzipped the flap, then stuck his head inside. There was some kind of scuffle, but Shane reappeared dragging the girl by one arm. She was screaming and thrashing, but then Tyler stepped up and grabbed her other arm, effectively immobilizing her.

Suddenly, there was a blur of motion, and Tyler went down screaming as a writhing black shape, like a demon straight from hell, bore into him.

The dog.

Despite the bear spray, the ugly mutt had come to the girl's rescue, and now Tyler was in trouble. To make matters worse, Shane was having trouble managing the girl.

Gotta get in there, Denver thought.

He leapt forward, bear spray ready in his fist, running to help Tyler. He wasn't sure what he would do. Kick the dog, give it another blast of hot sauce . . . He had to do something. But before he could reach them, the dog whirled away from Tyler, its muzzle streaked with blood and foam, and sprang at Shane.

Shane went down hard, shrieking as the animal tore into him. He tried to shield his face, push the dog away, but the mutt was relentless, all snapping jaws and snarling fury. The girl, now free of Shane's grasp, took off, scrambling backward toward the woman.

Tyler wasn't moving.

Forget this, Denver thought. *Forget them.*

Shane and Tyler were good guys, but he wasn't about to let himself get ripped to shreds for them. He turned and went after the girl, caught the back of her hoodie, and yanked her off her feet.

"No!" she screamed, twisting and thrashing, trying to rip free of the restraining garment. He advanced another step, wrapped an arm around her waist, and started dragging her away from the campsite.

Behind him, the woman was shouting, "Let her go!"

Denver didn't even look back. He had the prize he'd come for. If he could just get her back up to the road where his truck waited . . .

The girl twisted again, almost breaking free. Denver cursed, yanked her back, and tightened his grip, which only elicited a cry. "Help!"

"Shut up," he rasped, raising a hand to beat some sense into her.

But before he could deliver the blow, something caught his wrist. He started to turn, and the next thing he knew, he was on the ground, the breath knocked out of him, his face mashed into pine needles. Before he could think to resist, his arms were wrenched behind him, and he felt cold steel biting into his wrists.

Handcuffs.

Handcuffs meant cops. Probably a park ranger.

"Big mistake." The voice was female. Calm. Not the girl, and not the woman either.

Denver squirmed, caught his breath. "Hey! Hey, we didn't do anything. We were just being friendly, and these b—" He caught himself. "These people sicced their dog on us."

"That a fact?" the voice replied, dry as dust. "Because it looked to me like you were assaulting this woman."

Denver tried again. "We were just messing around, you know? Things got out of hand. That's all."

"I'd say so."

"Hey, we're the victims here. That dog tore up my friends. And that woman threatened us with a shotgun. We don't even have any guns."

"That's a lie," panted the girl, still catching her breath. "They tried to kidnap me. They threw firecrackers at a bunch of kids and sprayed pepper spray at us."

Denver tried to sneer but it came out as more of a whimper. "Yeah, well . . . it's your word against ours. What are they gonna charge me with? Misdemeanor assault? I'll plead it down and be out by lunchtime."

He felt the knee in his back press down harder.

"The thing is," the woman said, "this is a national park, which means you just committed a federal crime."

Denver felt his heart rise into his throat. "That's bull. Who are you anyway? Some ranger?"

"Oh, sorry. In all the commotion, I forgot to introduce myself." Something hit the ground next to his head. A small flashlight clicked on, illuminating the object. A wallet . . . No, a badge case. A gold shield with an eagle perched above a circular seal gleamed in the light. Around the edge he saw the words *Department of Justice.* "Special Agent Treadway, FBI. And you're under arrest."

THIRTY-SIX

CHICAGO, ILLINOIS

"Now!"

The word had barely left Decker's mouth when Petrovich's head seemed to burst apart, spraying the pavement behind Decker with blood and brain matter. At almost the same instant, the sharp report of a high-powered rifle split the air. Petrovich toppled forward, hitting the pavement with a dull thud.

Because he was already primed for action, Redd didn't stop to wonder about the source of the miracle bullet. He just moved, rolling left, drawing his pistol, sighting the nearest Bratva gunman—who was already turning away, searching for the unseen sniper—and pulling the trigger twice, landing two head shots. Then he rolled again, searching for his next target.

Decker had rolled the other way, taking out another of the Bratva gunmen, all of whom were now caught in the classic indecision trap, their attention divided between the two men who they had thought were moments away from death and the sniper down the street who had just killed their boss.

A few managed to fire, but the shots were rushed. Rounds sparked off the asphalt all around Redd, but he ignored them, dropping another shooter with a pair of center-mass hits before pivoting away again.

Another Bratva soldier jerked backward as a bullet from the sniper's rifle took him clean through the eye.

Decker put a single round through the heart of the last man standing, and just like that, it was over.

Redd stayed low, scanning for movement, ready to face the next wave of reinforcements from inside the club, but the street had gone deathly quiet. The crowd that had been milling outside the club was gone, fleeing on foot at the first sign of violence.

Decker broke the silence. "Not quite how I thought that was going to go, but I'll take the win."

Redd glanced over at him. "Did you bring a friend to the party that you forgot to tell me about?"

Decker shook his head. "I guess we have a guardian angel."

A block and a half away, the Durango's headlights flicked on, and then the vehicle began rolling toward them, slowing as it reached the scattered bodies of Bratva enforcers and weaving through their midst, coming to a stop alongside Redd and Decker.

The window lowered revealing a silver-haired man with a face that looked like it had been carved from a block of granite and blue-gray eyes that, Redd noted, appeared to be fixed on Decker.

Decker stared back, eyes narrowing in recognition. "Thrasher?"

Something that was almost a smile creased the older man's features. "That was sloppy, Phantom. You're usually a lot more subtle."

Decker shrugged and looked to Redd. "I'm not used to working with a partner."

"Hey," Redd protested. "I was just following your playbook."

The man—Thrasher—nodded his head toward the interior. "Get in. Probably don't want to be anywhere around here when Chicago's finest decide to come investigate."

Redd looked over at Decker. "Aaron, you know this guy?"

Decker nodded slowly.

"Do you trust him?"

Decker was slower to answer, but after several seconds, he shook his head. "Not really, but he's right. We need to go."

Thrasher laughed. "Well, that's gratitude for you."

Decker turned to Redd, gesturing for him to climb aboard, then walked around the front to climb in the passenger seat. Redd, remembering the age-old advice about getting in a car with a stranger, hesitated. Pistol still in hand, he opened the door and looked inside—the older man appeared to be the only occupant—before sliding into the back seat. The strangeness of the situation notwithstanding, he was faintly pleased with the seating arrangement. If this man tried anything, Redd would easily be able to put the gun to the back of his head, or simply pull the trigger.

As soon as they were both in, Thrasher let off the brake and rolled forward slowly until he was clear of the bodies, then accelerated to neighborhood speed.

When they'd gone a couple blocks, Decker turned in his seat and aimed his Glock at Thrasher's head. "Why are you here?"

The suddenness of the move shocked Redd, but following Decker's lead, he brought his own weapon up.

Thrasher didn't flinch, didn't even blink. "What, aren't you even going to introduce me to your friend?"

Without looking away, Decker said, "Matt, this is Thrasher. Thrasher, Matt."

"Is that a call sign?" asked Redd. "Or were your folks big on the skateboard scene back in the day?"

Thrasher laughed. "No, I was the skater, believe it or not."

Redd shot a glance at Decker. "I take it you two used to work together?"

"Thrasher was a targeting officer. He gathered intel on the people we needed to kill. We pulled the trigger."

Redd thought he heard a hint of derision in Decker's tone. "So, you were a spook?"

Thrasher shrugged. "More or less."

"I believe I asked you a question," said Decker, voice hard as cold steel.

Thrasher turned right, heading east along 47th, keeping his eyes on the road. "You can shoot me if you want. But if you're even a little curious about who blew up your life back in Kyiv, you might want to put that gun down and listen."

"I am listening. But you're not saying anything."

Thrasher blew out a breath. "Okay. We'll start at the top and work back. Why am I here? To save the day, obviously."

"That's not an answer. How did you know? Know about the Russians? Know about me? We didn't use names, so how did you find me?"

Thrasher nodded. "Now you're asking the right questions. But it's not going to really make sense unless I start with what happened in Kyiv."

Redd watched the exchange with a mixture of fascination and dread. Decker looked like he was one wrong answer away from pulling the trigger, which was never a good idea when the target was sitting at the controls of a moving vehicle.

"I know what happened in Kyiv," said Decker. "Someone set us up. Someone inside the unit. You know, like maybe a targeting off—"

"That's not the whole story and you know it!"

Decker appeared to consider this for a moment. He lowered the gun. "Go on."

Thrasher nodded. "Even before . . . what happened, there was . . . talk. About target selection. About how it seemed like maybe instead of pulling all the weeds, someone was using us to make more room for the dandelions to grow."

"Cute," muttered Redd.

But Decker was nodding. "We were saying the same thing in operations. Like someone upstairs was using us as their own private hit squad. Prioritizing the elimination of certain targets while ignoring others. It wasn't what we signed up for."

"Problem is, you and your boys in ops weren't very discreet about your reservations."

Decker waved a dismissive hand. "You're not telling me anything I didn't already know. Whoever the traitor was, they sent us into that ambush. And you were the one who handed us the target package that sent us into that death trap, so you'll forgive me if I'm not in a hurry to trust you."

A red light at Ashland gave them a full thirty seconds of silence. Outside, a CTA bus hissed to a stop, the only passenger stepping off into the glow of a liquor store marquee. Thrasher tapped the steering wheel like a man fighting the urge to fill the space with more than words.

"I wasn't the one pushing that target," Thrasher said when they were rolling again. "The finding came down from the tasking authority. I passed it on because that was my job. But what you don't know is that after it . . . *happened*, a lot of folks started asking questions." He paused a moment before adding, "Including yours truly. I couldn't just quit. None of us could. But I started working on my exit strategy. I was already close to retirement, so I didn't draw any heat. When the time came, I packed my stuff in a shoebox and went to live on a beach."

"So happy for you," said Decker, his tone sarcastic and dry.

Thrasher ignored the jibe. "But I kept my ear to the ground just in case . . . well, just in case some of that stink stuck to me. You know how it is in our business. They never really let you leave." He shrugged. "Except, they pretty much did. Never caught even a whiff of smoke. And Rogue Unit? Every now and then, I'd see something in the news that made me think maybe the work was ongoing, but even that got pretty quiet after a while."

Thrasher slowed for a yellow light at Halsted, letting a city truck trundle through the intersection ahead of them, hauling cones and plastic barricades. When the light was green again, he went on. "Then, a couple months ago, something pinged. Not about me, but about Kyiv. And Grigori Volkov. We had a pretty good hunch that Volkov was behind the ambush that . . . well, *killed* you, but we could never tie him to it, and no one upstairs ever gave us the go ahead to build a target package. It was, need I say it, just a little suspicious.

"Anyway, there was chatter coming out of Moscow about a certain 'ghost' from Kyiv, and suddenly, Volkov was very interested in a guy from Eastern Michigan named Aaron Decker. Curious guy that I am, I decided to look into it, and imagine my surprise when I discovered that Aaron Decker was none other than my old buddy Phantom, RIP."

"We were never buddies," Decker shot back.

Redd broke in. "If you knew Volkov was coming for Aaron, why didn't you give him a heads-up?"

Thrasher glanced into the rearview mirror, meeting Redd's stare, and grimaced. "Weren't you paying attention, kid? I'm retired. Keeping my head down. Didn't want to draw that heat if I could help it."

Redd wasn't a fan of being called a kid but ignored the comment. "Sure," he said. "And yet . . . here you are."

Decker nodded his agreement with Redd's line of questioning.

Thrasher sighed. "Yeah, here I am. Look, just 'cause I'm motivated by self-preservation doesn't mean I don't have a conscience. I know there was someone rotten higher up in Rogue Unit, and I always thought it stunk that he got away with it. I just never knew how to go about exposing him. But when I heard that Volkov was sending a hit team to eliminate you, it occurred to me that maybe he was getting his cues from whoever it was that sold you out all those years ago. I realized that if anyone could help me figure out who he is, and just maybe take him down, it might be the one guy who got away.

"You wanted to know how I knew where to be tonight. Well, short answer is I've been tracking your movements for the past few days. I lost track of you after you left your cabin, but I knew sooner or later you'd come looking for Petrovich."

"Wait, you knew about the cabin?" asked Redd.

Thrasher shrugged. "I was there. Saw you roll in like the cavalry."

"You were there . . . and you just watched?"

Thrasher seemed to realize that he'd stepped in it and tried to backpedal. "I was just about to lend a hand when you rolled up and took care of things."

"You could've stepped in at any point," Decker said. "Warned me they were coming. Put a round through one of those hitters, waved a flag . . . anything."

"I was weighing the risk."

"No," Decker snapped. "You were hiding. Watching from the sidelines, hoping I'd solve the problem on my own so you wouldn't have to stick your neck out. That's not caution. That's cowardice."

"It's not—"

"It is," Decker said, cutting him off. "Look, I'm going to find Volkov and kill him. And then I'm going to find the traitor and kill *him*. If you've got something to add, great. But if you're more interested in saving yourself, stay out of my way."

Thrasher's jaw worked. He drove on for another half block before finding his voice. "Nightshade."

The admission caught Redd by surprise. He recalled what Petrovich had said about the mysterious entity who seemed to be orchestrating the hunt for Decker.

"He's afraid of him. And Grigori Volkov isn't afraid of anyone."

Decker looked over at Thrasher. "You know who Nightshade is?"

Thrasher gave him a sidelong glance, then looked forward again. "No. But I'm surprised you've heard of him."

"Petrovich let it slip. Who is he? Some top tier *Vory*?"

"If he was that, I'd know about him." Thrasher shook his head. "Honestly, at this stage you might know more about him than I do. I managed to intercept some calls between Volkov and his man Konstantin. The name came up. He's definitely holding Volkov's leash, but I don't think he's Russian."

"So basically, you've got nothing."

"Nightshade *has* to be the traitor," said Thrasher, with uncharacteristic conviction.

"Agreed. But unless you know who he is, that gets us exactly nowhere."

Thrasher was quiet for another block. "Have you stopped to think about how Volkov was able to find you? Not the first time, but at your place out in the sticks? You left no digital trail. That place was a hundred miles from a surveillance camera and had almost no connection to you."

"Of course I've thought about it. I don't have a clue how he managed to find me there." Decker glanced over at him again. "What are you driving at?"

"Nightshade found you. He gave Volkov the location, and Volkov gave it to Konstantin. But *how* did he find you?"

"I hope that's a rhetorical question. Otherwise, you're wasting my time."

Redd noted the annoyance in Decker's voice, a feeling he shared.

"Nightshade has next-level access," said Thrasher. "Federal level. Beyond classified."

"So, he's a spook. Again, you're not telling me anything new."

"No," Thrasher said. "Not *just* a spook. This goes beyond some case officer with a SIGINT feed running a side hustle. I'm talking unrestricted access to next-gen programs—stuff the rest of the alphabet soup doesn't even know exists."

Redd leaned forward. "Like what?"

Thrasher took a moment to answer. "For a couple years now, there's been talk about an NSA program. It's supposed to be a predictive modeling program. Behavioral profiling combined with machine learning."

Decker frowned. "You're talking algorithms?"

"I'm talking quantum-level AI-enhanced predictive modeling. They take every scrap of data they can find—financials, social media, online purchases . . . anything they can get their hands on, including sealed military records, biometric data—and then create a virtual clone of a subject. Run it through a few million iterations and determine what you're going to do *before* you do it."

He went on, "That cabin—I'm guessing there's not so much as a scrap of paper connecting it to you."

"It belonged to my father-in-law. He was going to leave it to my wife, but . . . I think it's in probate now. But someone would have to dig deep to make that connection."

"The model *does* dig deep. It's got the computing power to trace every person connected to you, and every person connected to them . . . all the way to Kevin Bacon. And it's got access to everything that tells it how *you* think. Military evals, shopping habits, library records. It probably took about five seconds to predict that you would go to that cabin."

When Decker didn't reply, Redd spoke up. "Volkov is in Montana right now. Probably looking for me. But Aaron and I don't have any kind of connection. We met one time. Talked for about thirty seconds. No way is there a record of that."

Thrasher shrugged. "One of Volkov's guys got a look at that truck of yours."

"There have got to be a million black pickups in America."

"And this model can search every one of them. That, and the fact that they pinged you in Duluth, is all it needs to start making predictions."

Redd shook his head, incredulous. "This is for real? It actually exists?"

Thrasher shrugged again. "Officially? Something like this is still the stuff of science fiction. Unofficially . . . like I said, there's talk."

"If this is run out of the NSA," said Decker, "and Nightshade has access to it . . ."

He trailed off, but Thrasher was nodding vigorously. "Right? Using this model to search for you . . . that would leave fingerprints. But maybe Nightshade doesn't care about that because he's above scrutiny. That puts him pretty far up the chain."

"How far up?" Redd asked.

"It's a short list. Cross-reference it with anyone who might have benefited from putting Volkov in play fifteen years ago, and you'll have Nightshade."

Redd watched Decker's reaction, saw his eyes narrow as wheels began turning in his head. Decker was already all in. What choice did he have? Nightshade would keep sending killers after him, and eventually, the law of averages would catch up to him. What was it Margaret Thatcher had said about terrorists?

"They only have to get lucky once."

But what had Thrasher really given them? Talk. Theories. What-ifs. A whole lot of shadows and not much light. Sure, he'd stuck his neck out for them. Taken out Petrovich and very probably saved their lives. But he'd been spare with information.

He's not telling us everything.

Redd leaned forward. "Not good enough. You're holding something back."

"I've told you what I know."

"No, you've given us enough to keep risking our necks, but I think you know more. Something that you know can be traced to *you*." Before Thrasher could protest, Redd pushed on. "You said that someone else pushed you to send Aaron's team into that ambush in Kyiv. Who was it?"

"I told you. It came down from the tasking authority."

Decker, who had been following the exchange with growing interest, spoke up. "Who was it, Thrasher? Last chance."

Thrasher frowned as if answering the question might cause him physical pain. "Switchback."

Decker nodded slowly.

"Switchback?" said Redd. "What's his real name?"

"We didn't use our real names."

"Come on," Redd said. "It's a small community. You really expect me to believe you never tried to figure it out? You're a spook. Information is your oxygen."

Thrasher didn't answer right away. His hands stayed on the wheel, knuckles white against the leather. The hesitation said more than words. "I didn't have a need to know," he said finally. "That was the whole point of the unit's structure. Compartmentalized. I respected that."

"That's a dodge," Redd said.

A nerve in Thrasher's cheek twitched.

"You *do* know," Decker said quietly.

Thrasher gave a long sigh. "Brian Anderson. Retired Special Forces. CIF before he got pulled into our orbit. Now he runs a training outfit in Colorado. High Ground Tactical. Mostly takes government contracts. A few PMCs. That's how I know who he is." He chuckled. "Got his picture right there on his website."

He paused a beat. "But Switchback isn't Nightshade. He was just a cog in the machine, passing along the target."

Decker stared out the windshield for a long moment, then nodded. "Cog or not, he passed along the target. I'm going ask him where he got it."

Thrasher gave a derisive snort. "Good luck getting answers out of him. Leaning on Russian gangsters is one thing. Anderson won't just roll over for you."

Decker didn't blink. "I'll ask nicely."

"Well, do me a favor. Don't tell him where you got his name."

Decker turned to him. "Oh, you're coming with us."

Thrasher opened his mouth to protest but Decker cut him off. "You're already part of this. You don't get to just walk away. So you showed up, pulled the trigger, dropped some names. That doesn't make you a hero, and it doesn't make up for Kyiv. If you really want atonement, then you need to see this through. With us."

Thrasher didn't answer right away. He just stared ahead, eyes on the road for several more seconds before finally muttering, "So much for retirement."

THIRTY-SEVEN

FREMONT COUNTY, COLORADO

Colorado wasn't Montana, but as he drove south on County Road 143, west of Cañon City, Redd felt a lot closer to home than he had at any point during his not-nearly-short-enough visit to Chicago. The dry air, the open sky, the way the Wet Mountains loomed to the southwest—it all felt a lot more like where he belonged.

He had spent a mostly sleepless night in a no-tell motel near the Chicago airport. Sleepless because there was no way of knowing if what was left of the Russian mob in the city might be actively looking for them, and so while they took turns being on watch, Redd found it impossible to completely switch off. Before turning in, they had retrieved Dmitri from the storage unit, blindfolded him, and dumped him in a back alley, so there was at least one Bratva still alive and well in the Windy City.

The night passed without incident, however, and early that morning, they had returned to the airport and boarded Skids's plane. The canny pilot had renegotiated their arrangement, citing the increased fuel consumption associated with an additional passenger. Once a new deal was reached, they'd flown to Colorado

Springs, arriving just after noon. The flight gave them plenty of time to research High Ground Tactical and come up with a plan for approaching its founder.

High Ground Tactical occupied a thousand acres at the edge of Fremont County's red dirt country. A Google Earth satellite view revealed multiple shooting ranges, a mock village, a vehicle track that looked long enough to run NASCAR laps, and a full-spectrum obstacle course. A large central structure probably housed the classrooms and lodgings touted on the website. A quarter mile away, screened off by a small stand of Ponderosa pine, was what Redd guessed to be Anderson's residence. The house was a cowboy palace, sprawling across the hillside in a rough horseshoe layout, all steep rooflines and wide eaves. A wraparound porch traced most of the perimeter, along with multiple decks on upper stories and what looked like a rooftop hot tub on the west wing. A circular drive looped through a large paved motor court, with a detached multibay garage anchoring one side. High Ground Tactical, it seemed, was proving to be a profitable enterprise.

Rather than drop in on Anderson out of the blue—or attempt sneaking into his house, an approach Decker favored—the decision was made to send Redd in alone to make initial contact, while Decker and Thrasher hung back in a second rental waiting for Redd to finish his recon. The plan was to present himself as the weapons and tactics trainer for the Stillwater County Sheriff's Department—a job he actually did on a semiregular basis—looking for a more comprehensive training program for the deputies. As pretexts went, it was believable on the surface, though based on the size of Anderson's operation, Redd guessed an actual training course would use up the sheriff's entire annual budget, and Anderson probably knew it. Still, it was a way to get a foot in the door and hopefully get a feel for how best to proceed.

Redd didn't love the plan. Playacting wasn't his thing, and he'd never had much patience for the kind of games spooks liked to play. But both Decker and Thrasher were former acquaintances of the man they knew as Switchback, and showing up at his front door would raise all kind of alarms for Anderson, even if he was, as Thrasher insisted, just a cog.

"All you have to do," Thrasher had told him, *"is get inside. Shake his hand and look him in the eye. Then come back, and we'll decide what to do next."*

Redd crested a low ridge and saw the gate come into view, a beefy steel setup flanked by high mesh fencing and a double run of barbed wire angled outward.

A wide pullout had been carved from the shoulder to accommodate vehicles waiting for entry, and as he rolled to a stop, the cinder-block gatehouse off to the left disgorged a single guard.

Mid-thirties, likely ex-military, dressed in tan tactical pants and a dark blue polo shirt that didn't even try to hide the SIG riding on his hip, the guy was no rent-a-cop. As he approached the SUV, Redd noted the way he scanned the windows first before leaning in toward the driver's side.

"Afternoon," began Redd, keeping it simple. "I'm Matthew Redd. I called ahead about a site visit."

The guard didn't smile but gave a slight nod. "You're expected. Just follow the road. It'll take you where you need to go."

Redd gave a nod of thanks and eased forward as the gate began to swing open. He followed the road up a small rise, passing the spur that led to the main house, and continued until the road ended in a mostly empty parking lot in front of the main building. The structure itself was everything the satellite image had suggested—big, modern-rustic, built from thick timber beams and corrugated steel with a wide covered porch and dark-tinted windows. A couple of pickups were parked off to the side, and a matte-black Suburban sat directly in front of the entrance, nose facing out, ready for a quick departure.

The front door opened as Redd killed the engine. He recognized the face from the photograph on the website—the very one that had given Anderson away to Thrasher—but the carefully posed headshot did not tell the whole story. While Brian Anderson had to be pushing sixty, every inch of his not-quite-six-foot frame looked ready for war. He had close-cropped gray hair, a salt-and-pepper beard, and a body that had clearly never stopped training. Dressed in the same outfit as the gatekeeper, his broad chest and bulging arms strained the fabric of his polo shirt, and when he strode down the walk, it was with the strutting confidence of a barnyard rooster. Redd got out to meet him, offering a hand, which Anderson attempted, unsuccessfully, to crush into a pulp.

"You're a big fella," Anderson said, sizing Redd up with a glance. "Sheriff's office must feed you boys real good up there in Montana."

"We do all right, sir." The last word was unintentional, uttered purely as a reflex. Three years out of uniform, but he'd slipped right back into military discipline like a bad habit. "It's cattle country, just like here," he went on, hoping that Anderson hadn't picked up on it.

But of course, he had. The older man held both Redd's hand and his eye for a moment longer. "You served?"

There was no point in denying it, so he didn't. "Yes, sir. The Corps."

Anderson chuckled. "That's okay, son. I won't hold it against you." He pointed to the Suburban parked near the front entrance. "Hop in, and I'll give you the full tour."

Redd was mildly surprised at the invitation. He'd expected a standoffish sales pitch in a polished conference room, complete with video presentations, a glossy price list, and a subtly dismissive lecture on how small-town departments didn't usually have the need, much less the budget for the kind of training HGT provided.

Instead, Anderson was treating him like a peer. Perhaps it was the fact of their shared military service. Or maybe Anderson was an inveterate self-promoter, too proud of what he'd built to know that he was probably wasting his time. Whatever his motivations, Redd was happy to let the other man take the lead. It would give him a chance to observe and literally get the lay of the land.

Anderson slid behind the driver's seat and started the Suburban, not bothering to put on his seat belt. Redd was about to reach for his but then noticed that both of the seat belt receivers had little inserts slotted into them to allow the vehicle's occupants to ride unbuckled without setting off the seat belt alarm.

"Your timing's good," Anderson said, one hand resting easy on the wheel as the big SUV rolled forward. "We're between cycles right now. Just wrapped a two-week agency package—FBI HRT and a few folks from Air Marshals. Good group. Didn't break anything."

Redd raised an eyebrow. "Maybe they should have tried harder."

That brought a hearty laugh from Anderson. "I knew there was something about you I liked. We build our courses around real-world scenarios. Not Hollywood BS or fantasy gunfighting. People don't come here to play. They come to learn the skills that keep good men alive in bad places, and that's what we do, over and over again until it's muscle memory. Just like we did it in the Teams."

He steered the Suburban toward an outlet at the parking lot's southern end, which let out onto a service road that wended deeper into the property. From his satellite recon, Redd knew that this road was the main artery from which branch roads led to the various ranges and training sites. Anderson took the first of these spurs, onto another road that eventually brought them to a two-story metal structure big enough to use as an aircraft hangar.

Anderson used a remote to open the roll-up door and pulled inside. "Figured we'd start here."

The building looked like a showroom of working vehicles, everything from SUVs that looked like they might belong in a presidential motorcade, to police interceptors, to "technical"—small pickups modified with heavy machine gun turrets in the bed. There were even a few beat-up sedans. Redd noted the low-slung bump cages, beefed-up roll bars, and extra bracing on the driver's side doors.

"Looks like you've had some fun out here," remarked Redd.

"Fun's not the point, but I'd be lying if I said that it's not a thrill. We run two- and three-day modules, high-speed reverse, J-turns, PIT recovery, barricade breaching—you name it, we've got a module for it. We have contracts with State and Defense, as well as several top-tier PMCs and even a few foreign nationals. Lot of rich Saudi royals who want us to train their protection details. A lot of guys come in thinking they know how to drive under pressure. We disabuse them of that notion in about five minutes."

He continued through the garage, exiting by way of a door on the far side, and out onto the pursuit track where, without any warning to Redd, he put the pedal to the metal.

The Suburban surged forward like a charging bull. Redd felt his body pressed back against the seat as the big SUV howled through the gears. He instinctively pressed his feet to the floor, bracing his body, while fighting the urge to clutch the panic bar.

Anderson glanced over and grinned. "Don't worry," he said, raising his voice to be heard over the roar of the engine. "I know this track better than I know my ex-wife's voicemail password."

They hit the first sweeping curve doing at least sixty. Redd braced a hand against the door as the suspension leaned hard into the turn, tires shrieking in protest as the vehicle began to drift. The Suburban, like most SUVs, was top-heavy and prone to rollover accidents on high-speed turns, but Anderson was treating the big Chevy like it was a street racer.

"Lot of people think it's about horsepower," Anderson said casually, as if reading Redd's mind. "But the real trick is traction and timing. Know where you are on the course. Know what the vehicle can do, and what it can't."

He feathered the brakes coming into the next turn—a tight hairpin—then hammered the gas again as they slalomed into an elaborate chicane consisting of strategically placed shipping containers. Anderson never lost the line, never hesitated.

"Every inch of this track is designed to teach real-world reaction. We simulate everything from embassy extractions to convoy interdictions. High-speed urban evasion. Close-quarters pursuit with contact. Even include a couple of blind turns, just for fun."

They hit one of those now—a sharp left that appeared out of nowhere behind a plywood facade painted to look like a strip mall. Anderson tapped the brakes and drifted the Suburban through almost effortlessly.

"You get a guy behind the wheel in a situation like this," Anderson said over the roar, "adrenaline going, tunnel vision kicking in . . . this is where you find out who's got the touch and who just plays a lot of video games."

Anderson drifted through one last turn that brought the garage into view. The two-mile circuit had taken less than ninety seconds. He let off the gas, coasting the last few yards to the turnoff. "Want to take a spin?" asked Anderson. "Better way to start the day than a cup of coffee."

"I'll stick to coffee," grunted Redd. He enjoyed his truck and liked to drive but wasn't an adrenaline junkie. High-speed tactical driving like this was sometimes necessary, but it wasn't his idea of fun.

"Suit yourself."

Anderson next showed him the rifle range, complete with pop-up targets and sniper lanes, then drove through a mock village so authentic it looked lived in, right down to the weathered storefronts and chain-link schoolyard. Beyond that came a sprawling confidence course that appeared to be spread out over at least an acre or two.

Redd recognized the familiar layout: monkey bars, rope climbs, cargo nets, balance beams, and log hurdles—all the staples of an old-school military obstacle course—but this one also featured a towering steel structure that rose at least fifty feet, with platforms at various heights. Thick ropes for a long commando crawl stretched off one side, suspended above a safety net.

Anderson slowed the Suburban to give him a better look. "Used to be I could run the whole thing in under seven minutes without puking," he said, not quite wistfully. "Now I just stand back and yell at people who aren't puking hard enough."

Redd smiled. "Living the dream."

"We run trainees through this on day one of every multiday course," Anderson went on. "Keeps 'em humble. It's also a good way to spot the quitters early."

He rolled past the last of the stations and nudged the SUV back up to speed. "Anyway, I saved the best for last."

He drove down the road for another quarter mile before pulling off in front of a two-story, windowless concrete building, painted in flat desert tan.

He killed the engine and stepped out, gesturing for Redd to follow. "Doesn't look like much from the outside, I know," he said. "But inside? It's a whole different story."

Redd trailed him to an entrance marked with warning signs reading *Caution: Live Fire Range* and *Training Access Only*. Another sign, posted below a covered red light, said, *Do Not Enter When Light Is On.* Redd knew what the signage meant. The building was a shoot house.

Anderson tapped a code into the digital keypad by the door, and it unlocked with a strident warning bleat. He pushed it open, and the overhead lights came on automatically, illuminating a small anteroom with two doors—one directly ahead and one to the immediate right—as well as a large lockbox on the left wall.

"This is the jewel in our crown," Anderson explained. "Designed it myself . . . Well, conceptually at least. The engineers at Argus Defense up in Denver did the heavy lifting. Same outfit that built the RAVEN-X system for DEVGRU and GSG 9. We were one of the first private facilities cleared to run it. Took a hell of a pitch to get the green light.

"It's modular, configurable. Right now we've got it staged for a small-team raid scenario—two floors, multiple entry points, mixed threats. Targets include everything from compliant civilians to hostage takers to armed opposition. All animatronic. No role players. That way, we can run live fire. There's just no substitute for the real deal when training. The target bots move, react—the bad guys even shoot back."

Redd raised an eyebrow. "Shoot back?"

"Soap rounds, of course," Anderson clarified with a grin. "Compressed-air driven. They sting like hell but won't kill you." He laughed. "Unless you freeze up. Then the embarrassment might. Whole thing's live-fire certified, up to seven-six-two. This is as real as it gets outside of an actual war zone. We've had Tier One units train in here, State Department security details, even a few allied foreign teams. You screw up in here, you'll know it—either from the hit or the scorecard afterward."

"Impressive," said Redd. It wasn't an exaggeration. The shoot houses he'd trained in during his time in the Raiders had utilized some of the technology Anderson was describing, but by the sound of it, the HGT range was next-generation.

Anderson opened a lockbox on the wall and took out a pistol—a SIG P320—empty with the slide locked back, and a standard fifteen-round magazine. He inserted the magazine and released the slide, letting the action ride forward. Then, holding the weapon by the muzzle, he offered it to Redd.

"Give it a try."

Redd stared at the pistol. "Uh, I'm really not sure I have the time."

Anderson laughed. "You can run the whole scenario in under five minutes . . . a lot less if you get scragged. But I'll tell you what. If you can do a clean run . . . kill every hostile, don't shoot any noncombatants, and don't get tagged . . . I'll knock twenty-five percent off our basic small-force LEO training package."

Redd stared at the pistol, then looked Anderson in the eye. He didn't care about the discount and suspected Anderson didn't either. This was a test. A way of establishing dominance, vetting the outsider from Montana. And whether it was ego, instinct, or just the knowledge that their whole plan hinged on getting Anderson to drop his guard, Redd knew he couldn't say no.

He took the pistol. "How many tangos?"

Anderson flashed a wolfish grin. "Wouldn't you love to know." He paused a beat. "Intel says that the leader of an insurgent cell is holed up inside." He opened the lockbox door a little further, and Redd saw an eight-by-ten photograph of a mannequin wearing a latex Osama bin Laden mask.

"This is the guy," Anderson went on, grinning. "He usually travels with a driver and two bodyguards, but there could be others."

"Real world, you'd never do a raid like this singleton with a handgun."

Anderson laughed again. "Fair point. Look, I'm not expecting miracles. Have some fun with it." He turned back to the lockbox and took out a pair of earmuffs and a pair of plastic safety glasses, handing these to Redd as well.

Redd press-checked the SIG, verifying that it had picked up a round, then donned the eye and hearing protection. Anderson clapped him on the shoulder and moved to the door on the right. He opened it, revealing a small booth with a control console and a bank of flat-screen monitors. "I'll be running the show from behind the curtain. Don't worry, I won't make it impossible. That said, if you take a mission-ending injury—real or simulated—the scenario will shut down. The lights will show you the way to the nearest exit, where you'll clear and check before leaving the controlled area. Any questions?"

Redd had lots of questions, foremost being, *Do I really have to do this?* But he shook his head and faced the door. "Let's go."

"In about ten seconds, the lights will go red and that door will unlock. After that, it's your show. Good hunting." Anderson stepped into the control room and pulled the door shut behind him, leaving Redd alone.

He took a deep breath, trying to clear his head of distractions. No matter how realistic or high-tech the training environment, the one thing that could never really be simulated was the consequences of failure. Redd didn't know if the possibility of getting killed actually gave operators an edge in real combat, but he knew that the threat of getting stung by a marker round or failing to complete a shoot house run definitely did not. That was why units in training ran the shoot house over and over and over again until they could almost do it on autopilot.

Running a scenario like this—one designed for an eight-to-ten-man rifle squad—solo and one time only had no training value. Failure was almost certain, and knowing the worst that could happen would be getting smacked by what was essentially an upgraded paintball made it tempting to just accept the inevitable.

He needed to get that idea out of his head, treat this like the real deal, because he sensed that a lot was riding on passing this test and making a good impression with Anderson.

The overhead light abruptly turned bloody red and a loud metallic *thunk* signaled that the inner door was now unlocked. Redd took another deep breath and then reached for the handle.

Showtime.

THIRTY-EIGHT

Without hesitation, Redd swept inside fast and low, entering a foyer just wide enough for a coatrack and a bench. A coat hung from one of the pegs; otherwise, the space was empty, designed only to simulate a compressed entry.

He pivoted left and rolled through the threshold into the next space, a cramped living room mock-up—couch, coffee table, flat-screen dummy on the wall—with a hallway leading deeper into the structure. He swept the angles, his SIG pointing wherever his eyes looked, scanning high to low.

Target left.

A humanoid animatronic popped up from behind the couch. It wore traditional Afghan attire—what the grunts used to call "man-jammies"—but the Kalashnikov rifle in its hands marked it unmistakably as a hostile.

Redd fired. Two quick shots. Center mass. The target toppled, its hydraulic mount folding backward, the AK spitting marker rounds across the ceiling. Redd kept moving.

Target right.

Another figure appeared from the hallway, rifle already spitting marker rounds into the entry point where Redd had been standing a moment before. Redd dropped to a knee, pivoted, and returned fire. Two more rounds. The target folded.

His inner tactical advisor had noted the fact that the second shooter's weapon had been aimed at the entrance—the fatal funnel—where an incoming raid team would, of necessity, be bunched up and most exposed to enemy fire. It strongly suggested that the mannequins were programmed to shoot at fixed locations rather than tracking individual targets. If so, all he needed to do was clear those danger zones as quickly as possible to avoid getting tagged.

Then again, he couldn't count on all the mannequins being programmed the same way.

His inner voice also pointed out that he had fired off four rounds, leaving just eleven. Controlled pairs were SOP for an operation like that, but then so was bringing along plenty of spare magazines. With no idea how many hostiles he would face, he couldn't afford to waste a single round.

He advanced to the hallway then paused. Breathed. Reevaluated. The corridor ahead angled sharply left, creating a deliberate bottleneck no doubt intended to restrict visibility and channel movement into a kill zone. Which meant it was probably wired to hurt him.

No hesitation. He moved down the hall, staying on the safe side, dropped into a controlled slide-step through the narrow gap, slicing the pie with his muzzle.

The room beyond was a kitchen—laminate counters, dummy appliances marked up with real bullet holes, and a central island with breakfast stools. Beyond it, a back door stood slightly ajar—another problem waiting to happen.

Shooter. Rear left, between the refrigerator and a pantry door.

Redd was still turning when he heard the muted *pop-pop* of the compressed air mechanism spitting rounds at him. He ducked reflexively, the rounds marking up the wall behind where he'd been standing, and returned fire.

The round struck the refrigerator. The next hit center mass, and the target went down.

He saw movement behind the island, pivoted—and froze.

A female mannequin crouched beside the island, hands raised in a show of surrender. She wore a head covering and a traditional long garment and appeared to be unarmed. Her mouth was open, as if screaming, but Redd heard no sound.

Then another figure popped up right beside her, AK already swinging toward Redd, with the woman almost directly between them. Redd shifted right, clearing the woman from the arc, and fired one round on the move.

Missed.

He mentally cursed even as he fired again. The second shot struck the dummy low in the gut. Not optimal, but good enough. It collapsed.

He scanned again. The female mannequin hadn't moved, still locked in her preprogrammed panic pose. In the real world, he probably would have put her on the floor, searched her, while one of his teammates provided cover, because you just never knew, but he doubted Anderson was going to throw him a curve like that.

Redd cleared the island and moved toward the kitchen exit, another narrow hallway with a left-hand bend. There was also the matter of that back door. He couldn't afford to pass it up, and yet if he went through to clear whatever lay beyond, he would leave his six unprotected. That was the biggest difference between running solo and with a team. No one to provide security on cleared areas. Every time he advanced, he left a vacuum behind him just begging to be filled. Or at least that was how it worked in the real world. He didn't know how mobile the mannequins were, whether they could move around like automatons, coming in from other rooms to press the attack, or for that matter if Anderson could reactivate the dead, just like respawning enemies in a video game. All he knew for sure was that if he left the kitchen, he'd have to clear it again before moving on.

Can't be helped.

He flattened against the wall, nudged the door open with his boot, muzzle tracking high. It opened onto a simulated mudroom. Washer-dryer set against one wall. Shelves stacked with fake detergent jugs. A rubber mat with boot prints stamped in dusty powder. No movement. No targets. But there was an exterior door, or at least something that was meant to look like one. It had a heavy-duty lockset and a dead bolt.

Another wild card.

Redd stared at it for a long moment—too long—then came to a decision. He reached forward with his off hand and twisted the dead bolt, sealing the door shut.

If the mannequins had the key, he would be screwed, but he was probably overthinking.

He turned and reentered the kitchen tactically, checking behind the island again before heading down the next hallway. It led into a dining room. Hardwood floor, table set for six, a sideboard along the wall, a hanging light fixture above the center.

He glimpsed movement under the table and dove left just as a stream of marker rounds splattered the wall. Redd rolled, came up in a prone position, and fired at the mannequin under the table.

The dummy slumped.

Redd spied movement from the kitchen—

I knew it!

He rolled onto his back, bringing the pistol up just as a shooter mannequin entered from the kitchen hallway. The animatronic was fully articulate, bipedal, *walking.*

And instead of firing blindly, it was dropping the barrel of its Kalashnikov toward Redd, trying to aim directly at him.

Redd fired from the supine position. One shot, center mass. The mannequin shook then toppled backward.

Redd stayed where he was for a moment, panting to catch his breath. Anderson hadn't been exaggerating about the capability of the automated opposition force.

Finally, he rolled to a crouch and scanned the dining room again. Nothing moved. There was another hallway in the opposite corner, and he could see a stairwell ascending.

Stairs were a tactical nightmare, especially when ascending, but there was nothing to be done about it.

He kept to the outside rail, switching his aimpoint from the top of the stairs to the landing above and behind him, moving back and forth constantly. Surprisingly, no attack came. The second-floor landing came into view, and he surged ahead, bounding the last four steps in a single leap and then rolling forward as soon as his feet touched the floor, coming up in a crouch, ready to fire.

No targets.

Ahead was a hallway, with doors to either side. He would have to clear each one of them.

Down to five shots.

He eased up to the first door, pushed it open, but didn't enter right away. In a real-world scenario, everyone in the structure would have heard the shooting and gone on alert, so the likelihood of walking into a bullet . . . and that was how he thought of it now . . . was high indeed.

But like it or not, he had to keep going.

He risked a peek around the corner, exposing himself just long enough to draw fire, and when that didn't happen, he moved inside, gun up.

He found himself in a small bedroom: double mattress, end tables, wardrobe. Two mannequins, both female, were seated on the edge of the bed. No weapons. Hands up.

He scanned the corners. There was no closet, no other doors, and a fake window painted on one wall. He pulled open the wardrobe and stepped back, ready to fire, but the interior was empty. There weren't even any clothes hanging from the rod.

He turned, exited the room tactically, pieing the corner before committing, and moved to the next door. A bathroom. Shower curtain pulled back. No one inside. He moved on.

The next door, opposite the bedroom, opened as he reached for the doorknob.

He dropped to a knee and took aim as a mannequin lunged out, AK already spitting, marker rounds stitching the wall. Redd fired, point-blank, a head shot that knocked the target back, but before it hit the floor, Redd leaped forward, staying behind the "shooter" even as he pushed into the room, looking for any more targets.

The room was meant to look like a home office. Desk, bookshelves, a fake laptop, chairs. No one else inside. In a real raid, this would have been a treasure trove of intel, but he doubted Andersen would mark him down for not grabbing the laptop. He checked under the desk, just in case, then moved back into the hall.

Still clear.

He went wide, back against the wall, checking his six every few steps, and reached the door at the end of the hall. He hadn't seen the primary target yet, so he figured this would be the grand finale.

And he was down to four rounds.

He turned the handle with his off hand, pushed the door open, and rushed through, swinging to the right, clearing the fatal funnel.

It was the main bedroom. Queen-size mattress, workout gear in the corner, an armoire, a closet door half open.

Contact left.

A shooter popped from behind the armoire. Redd was faster. One shot, center mass.

Redd turned, checking the near side of the bed, but keeping an eye on the closet door . . .

Movement. Another mannequin stepped out, AK already popping off rounds, all of which sailed harmlessly over Redd's head and struck the wall behind him. Redd aimed, fired . . .

The mannequin flinched as the 9mm round hit its right shoulder, but kept firing, swinging the AK back and forth, slowly lowering with each pass. Redd corrected, fired again. The mannequin fell back.

He was down to his last round, and still no sign of the primary target. And while in the real world, that frequently happened because of bad or outdated intelligence, Redd didn't think that would be the case here.

He moved to the corner by the door, scanning between the open closet and the far side of the bed . . .

Movement from the closet, a shooter stepping out, AK swinging toward Redd, tracking him. Redd fired. Head shot.

But even as the mannequin fell back, two thoughts went through Redd's head.

Neither of the shooters he'd just scratched was "Osama."

And he had just fired his last round.

As if responding to a premonition, he spun toward the far side of the bed, just as the figure that had been crouching low behind the mattress, out of his line of sight, unfolded, rising to its full height—almost as tall as Redd himself—the barrel of his AK coming up, tracking Redd.

The beard, the turban . . . It was him. The primary target.

Redd then did something that he'd only ever seen people do in movies, something that he'd always thought was the stupidest move in the world. He drew back his arm and flung the empty SIG across the room.

A human might have been able to duck the projectile, but "Osama" wasn't programmed that way. The mannequin didn't even flinch as the empty pistol—a pound and a half of steel and polymer—struck its rubber face squarely between the eyes. The AK in its hands continued moving, continued tracking Redd, because of course, the animatronic target's "brain" and "eyes" weren't in its head. Its movements were guided remotely by a computer in the control room in response to sensors located who knew where.

The rifle started spitting soap rounds.

But Redd had already dropped flat, rolling forward, toward the target. The AK's barrel depressed, trying to reacquire him, but Redd was too quick. He surged up from the roll and slammed into the mannequin like it was a gridiron tackling dummy, driving it back against the wall. The animatronic target shifted but didn't fall. Instead, its feet spread further apart, following some automatic balance protocol, and its servo-powered arms jerked, trying to bring the rifle to bear.

Redd jammed his forearm under the barrel, forcing it up just as the compressor began spitting out a stream of marker rounds, then wrapped his arm around the upper receiver and began to pull. The mannequin resisted. Its servos whined with increased torque as it tried to maintain control, but Redd just gritted his teeth and yanked harder, leaning back, putting his entire body into the motion like he was trying to start a stubborn chainsaw.

The rifle came free with a sharp *crack* as some inner mount snapped. Redd staggered back with the weapon in hand but then widened his stance, slid his hands down to the end of the barrel, drew back, and swung for the fences. The butt of the AK sliced through the air and connected with the mannequin's jawline. The head sheared clean off, rebounded off the wall, and rolled back to land at Redd's feet.

The rest of the mannequin froze mid-motion, arms outstretched. Then its legs buckled, and it folded to the floor.

Redd stood over the wrecked mannequin, chest rising and falling as the adrenaline ebbed away. "Target down," he muttered.

The overhead lights suddenly dimmed, and a klaxon blared, followed by a calm, prerecorded voice: *"Simulation ended. Please clear all weapons and follow the illuminated path to the nearest exit."*

A row of LEDs embedded in the floor began flashing in sequence, tracing a path back out into the hall. Redd dropped the AK and retrieved the spent SIG, dropping the mag even though the locked-back slide was proof enough that it was clear, then started toward the door.

Before he could reach it, however, Brian Anderson strode through the doorway and stalked around the end of the bed. He took one look at the headless mannequin on the floor, then let out a long, theatrical sigh. "I don't know whether to be impressed or seriously pissed off."

Redd just shrugged.

"Do you have any idea how much it's going to cost to replace that unit?"

"More than twenty-five percent off the price of your training package?"

Anderson barked a laugh. He gave Redd a sideways glance. "Well, color me impressed. You must've been one heck of a Marine back in your day."

"I was pretty tough on shoot houses."

"I'll bet you were." Anderson turned to face Redd. "I guess that just leaves one last thing," he said casually. And then, as quick as a striking rattler, he drew a pistol from behind his back, brought it up, and aimed it squarely at Redd's chest.

"Where's Aaron Decker?"

THIRTY-NINE

BOZEMAN, MONTANA

FBI Special Agent Stephanie Treadway savored the last bite of her hamburger as she watched the video feed from the interrogation room. The Calamity Jane, from Backcountry Burger Bar, certainly ranked among the top ten best burgers she had ever eaten, and that was saying something. With her rabbit's metabolism and a generous per diem when traveling, she was on a personal quest to sample—and rigorously evaluate—the best-reviewed burgers in every locale where duty brought her.

And duty had brought her to Montana.

It was actually not her first visit to Big Sky Country. In fact, in the last three years—ever since her boss, Gavin Kline, had begun the somewhat delicate process of reconciling with his biological son, Matthew Redd—she seemed to find her way out west with surprising regularity. What she couldn't quite figure out was whether Kline kept sending her to Montana because he was more than a little overprotective when it came to his son's family or because Redd himself was a trouble magnet.

Probably a little of both.

Trouble had certainly caught up to Redd's family, and her arrival at the remote Willow Creek campsite could not have been more fortuitous. But this time, the trouble had hit a little closer to Treadway's own heart. Although Kline hadn't known it when he told her to *"get to Yellowstone, ASAP,"* Redd's wife and kids were accompanied by Brynn and Mitchell Decker—Aaron Decker's kids.

She'd never say it aloud—not to Kline, and certainly not to Decker—but Treadway had developed . . . feelings . . . for the quiet, dangerous man who sometimes did off-the-books work for her boss.

Okay, she had been crushing hard on him for a while now.

The fact that he was an assassin did not bother her one bit. He wasn't a contract killer or hit man, working for the highest bidder, but more of a renegade knight in the cause of righteousness. She didn't have all the details about his background, but before Kline had recruited her into the Bureau, she'd been CIA, and she knew how the world of covert ops worked. She surmised that Decker had been a wet-work specialist in some secret-squirrel black budget group—a morally inconvenient solution to impossible problems—and while he'd mostly left that life behind, he had shown a willingness to come out of retirement for a good cause. So even though she was sworn to uphold the rule of law, she didn't have a problem with the sort of swift justice Decker delivered. Aside from that, she barely knew him, but somehow that only added to his mystique.

The fact that the punk from Bozeman presently sitting in the interrogation room had terrorized Decker's kids and tried to abduct his daughter made her absolutely livid.

When she'd received the text from Kline telling her to drop everything and head to Yellowstone, she'd been in Portland, following up on a lead in another investigation. That put her on the right side of the Mississippi, but it had still taken her a while to arrange transportation to Bozeman and subsequently to drive to the coordinates inside Yellowstone where Kline had indicated that Redd's family would be camping. She hadn't exactly taken her sweet time getting there, yet she had only just reached the turnoff to the Willow Creek site when the first round of fireworks went off. If she had shown up ten minutes later, Denver would have been in the wind, with Brynn tied up in his back seat. Or worse.

Fortunately, she had shown up when she did, and now Denver and his two dirtbag sidekicks were in custody, the latter under guard at the regional medical facility in Bozeman, badly mauled, but in stable condition. That had been the start of a long night, first waiting for park rangers and additional agents from the Bozeman field office to arrive, then seeing to the processing and transport of the suspects. Emily had been treated for skin and eye irritation, as had Rubble, to the extent that he would let anyone get close, but to Treadway's chagrin, Emily had refused to return to civilization, insisting that her husband wanted her to stay off-grid, and she intended to do just that. The best Treadway could do was convince Emily to allow her and the agents from Bozeman to stand guard throughout the night.

Kline had arrived early that morning, dressed like an L.L.Bean model, accompanied by a dozen shooters from the FBI's legendary Hostage Rescue Team. While the HRT guys melted into the woods, setting up overwatch and sniper positions, Kline had given Treadway her new marching orders. Then he'd gone into the camp to have breakfast with his grandkids while she set to work figuring out why three meth heads from Bozeman had gone after Brynn Decker.

She licked a smear of scallion cream cheese from her thumb and then wiped it clean with a napkin before leaving the observation room and making her way into the interrogation room where one Denver Callahan had been sitting and waiting for the better part of an hour while Treadway finished her lunch.

Interviews with suspects were rarely done solo, but Treadway had told the special agent in charge of the FO that she didn't want an audience. What she was about to do didn't exactly follow FBI protocol, and everyone in the Bureau knew that the acting director had given her latitude to do as she saw fit. In this instance, his orders had been explicit. *"Find out if this was just a case of hooliganism, or if this was a coordinated attack."* Implicit was his standing order, *"Do whatever it takes."*

Denver Callahan sat slouched in the metal chair, one foot bouncing with nervous energy, cuffs still clipped to the table ring. She guessed he was desperate for a bump. His mouth worked like he was trying to suck moisture from his teeth, and every few seconds, he blinked too hard, like the light hurt his eyes. Nevertheless, despite all of that, when she entered the room, he looked up with a sneer. "When am I gonna get my phone call?"

Treadway closed the door behind her and set her paper coffee cup on the table along with a manila file folder, then pulled out the empty chair opposite him with a slow scrape and settled into it. He had been Mirandized of course, but while he *had* demanded a phone call, he had not explicitly requested legal representation, so as far as Treadway was concerned, she was still coloring inside the lines.

If he did say the magic *L* word . . . well, then she would have to get creative.

She took a sip of her coffee, then leaned back in her chair. "I'm going to talk," she said. "And you're going to listen."

"I said, give me my pho—"

"I heard you," she said, almost lackadaisically. "Look, we can pretend this is a formal interview if it makes you feel better. I'll advise you of your rights. Again. We'll log a time stamp. I'll get someone in here to witness. The whole rigamarole. You'll get your phone call eventually, but it won't make a lick of difference because we've got you dead to rights. I doubt the assistant US attorney will even bother offering you a deal."

She paused a beat. "Or you can shut up and listen for a minute. And then, when you've answered a few simple questions, you'll get to call your mom, or whoever, and maybe—maybe—I'll tell the AUSA you were cooperative."

Denver licked his lips. "You can't—"

"I can. And I will. Because, spoiler alert? You're not walking away from this with a slap on the wrist. Your two best buds are in the hospital under federal guard, getting their faces sewed back on, but I guarantee they're already thinking about how they're going to hang this on you. We've got you for assault, attempted kidnapping, use of an explosive device on federal land . . . We're going to make you sound like the second coming of the Unabomber."

She let that hang for a moment, taking another sip of coffee.

Denver shifted in his seat, the swagger fading from his face. "Look, we were just trying to scare 'em. It was a prank. That's all."

Treadway allowed herself a small, humorless smile. "It didn't look that way to me."

Denver clamped his lips shut.

"Here's what I think." Another nice long pause. "I think somebody told you to go after them. To go after that girl. Brynn Decker. You tell me who that is, and suddenly, this doesn't look so bad for you."

She had been watching him closely for a reaction when she said the girl's name. There had been none, and for a fleeting moment, she worried that Denver *was* just a hooligan.

Then he cracked. "It wasn't like that." No sooner were the words past his lips than he seemed to realize he'd made a mistake and clammed up again, but the damage was already done.

Treadway leaned forward. "What *was* it like?"

Denver shook his head. "I want my phone call."

Treadway allowed him another moment to think about his choices before continuing. "I have eyewitness testimony from two of your intended victims. Both heard you say, *'Get the girl.'* That's all we need to turn this into a kidnapping charge."

Denver just glowered at her.

Treadway reached for the folder she'd brought in with her, opening it slowly and sliding the contents—two eight-by-ten photographs that looked like school pictures—to the center of the table, rotating them so they were right side up from Denver's point of view. Denver glanced down at them then just as quickly looked away.

"This is Brynn," she said, tapping one of the photos, and then slid her finger to the other. "And that's Mitchell. Brynn and Mitchell Decker. I noticed you didn't even twitch when I said Brynn's name earlier. That tells me whoever sent you didn't tell you who you were supposed to grab. They just gave you a description. *Seventeen-year-old girl, dark brown hair, traveling with a woman and some kids in a white Tahoe.* Something like that?"

Denver shifted in his seat, an obvious tell.

Treadway gave a little nod. "See, that makes sense to me. You and your friend don't strike me as the sort to stray too far from your street corner in Bozeman. Not unless somebody put you up to it. And somehow, you spotted them, tailed them into the park, and thought you could make the grab."

This time, Denver didn't give her anything.

No matter. It was time to play a wild card. "Poor kid. You don't have a clue who she is, or who her father is, do you?"

Denver glanced quickly at the photograph again, as if he might find the answer to a question he'd promised himself he wouldn't acknowledge.

Treadway shook her head. "Aaron Decker is a killer. I don't mean he's some tatted-up ex-con who's trying to move in on your crank operation. He's an assassin. Like John Wick . . . You've seen *John Wick*, right?" She tapped the pictures. "Somebody wants to hurt Aaron Decker, Denver. And they thought the way to hurt him was to go after his kids. They sent you to do that, and didn't even tell you what you were getting mixed up in."

She sat back in her chair. "What do you think he's going to do about that when he finds out?" When he didn't reply, she added, "Think about what John

Wick did when some dudes hurt his dog. Now imagine they came after his *children*."

Denver was squirming now. The sweat beading on his forehead had nothing to do with his craving for a hit of meth.

"Now," Treadway went on. "There's a chance that Decker's enemy will win this fight . . . I wouldn't take those odds, but it could happen. In which case, the worst that will happen to you is that this will go to trial and you'll go away for at least twenty years. But if Decker survives, he's going to hunt down every person who had anything at all to do with this and . . ." She drew a finger across her throat and made a hissing sound. "You shouldn't have messed with Baba Yaga's puppy, Denver."

"We didn't know any of that!"

Treadway gave a sympathetic nod. "I know."

He swallowed. "You're the FBI. Can't you do something about him?"

Treadway almost winced. She hadn't expected Denver to find the fatal flaw in her ruse. *Maybe he's not as dumb as he looks,* she thought. "Oh, we're trying," she said, improvising. "We've been trying for years. But he's like a ghost. In fact, that's what they used to call him." She cocked her head to the side, suddenly inspired. "He's going to come after whoever it was that sent you to grab his daughter. If we can get there ahead of him, set a trap . . ." She gave an equivocal shrug. "Tell me who sent you, Denver. It's the only chance you've got."

Denver slumped in his chair, deflating like a punctured beach ball. "Rick. Rick Turner."

Treadway had no idea who that was but nodded as if she did. "Smart move."

She swept the pictures back into the folder, stood, and headed for the door.

"Can I get my phone call now?" he asked, his voice so small it was barely audible.

"Were you going to call Rick?"

He didn't answer.

Treadway shook her head. "Maybe not just yet."

FORTY

FREMONT COUNTY, COLORADO

Redd did not allow himself to fixate on the pistol in Anderson's hand. Instead, he immediately brought his eyes up, meeting the man's gaze as he considered how best to respond. It seemed pointless to feign ignorance. Anderson's question had just advanced the narrative.

His thoughts flashed back to the conversation earlier that morning, aboard Skids's plane, when Thrasher had proposed sending Redd in to meet Brian Anderson on his own.

"What if he's Nightshade?" asked Redd.

"So, I take it you're Nightshade," he said, trying to sound unsurprised.

There was a faint twitch in Anderson's cheek, a flicker of interest. "Where did you . . . ?" He trailed off, nodding in understanding. "Ah. The Russians. Of course. They were never very good at keeping their mouths shut."

"That's not a no."

Anderson chuckled. "I'm not Nightshade."

"He's not Nightshade," Thrasher insisted.

"How can you be so sure?" countered Decker. "He's obviously done well for himself. High Ground Tactical is the perfect cover for him."

Thrasher shook his head. "You're thinking too small. Nightshade has access. Global reach. Anderson doesn't have that."

"But what if he's working for Nightshade?"

"But you are working for him," Redd went on, nodding at the pistol in Anderson's hand.

Thrasher brushed aside the question. "I'm telling you, he was never anything but a cog in the machine. Nightshade might have used him, but that's all."

"But what if you're wrong about him?" insisted Redd. "You're asking me to go in without backup. If he is working for Nightshade, then he's going to know that I'm with Aaron."

"Even if he does recognize you," said Decker, "he's not going to make a move. Not yet. He'll want to follow you. Use you to get to me."

A rare miscalculation on Decker's part. Anderson was indeed trying to use Redd to get to Decker but had chosen a more direct route. But it was Thrasher's insistent defense of Anderson that now seemed like the biggest misjudgment.

Had Thrasher betrayed them? Was he working for Nightshade too?

Anderson cocked his head to the side as if trying to decide whether to engage with Redd or simply shoot him. "I asked you a question," he said. "I know you know the answer. But if you're not going to tell me, then you're of no further use to me."

"Still not a no," replied Redd, keeping both his voice and his gaze steady. His mind, however, was whirring like a computer's hard drive, looking for a way out of the situation and berating him for having walked right into this trap.

Anderson seemed to rethink his threat. "You've got brass ones, kid. I'll give you that. Walking in here like you did. Using your own name. That was gutsy. Stupid, but gutsy."

"Shouldn't I use an alias?"

Both Decker and Thrasher had shot the suggestion down.

"Bad idea," said Thrasher. "If he does a routine background check, he's gonna realize you're lying, and that will make him suspicious, even if he's squeaky clean."

"And if he is working for Nightshade," added Decker, "then he'll probably already have your packet. Physical description, photos . . . You're not exactly inconspicuous, Matt."

"Because Nightshade already told you I might be coming," said Redd, nodding. "While we're on the subject, I almost bought your badass-operator schtick.

You've got a good thing going here. A little too good. All of this—" He made a gesture, indicating the shoot house. "You didn't build this all on your own. You had an angel investor. And those government contracts that keep you flush? You're Nightshade's stooge. What I can't figure out is how he knew I'd be coming here. I didn't even know until a few hours ago."

It's Thrasher. Has to be. He gave us Anderson's name. He's the only reason I'm even here.

Now Anderson smiled. "You think I don't know what you're trying to do here? Get me talking? Get me to commit, so Decker will have something to use against me? Maybe try to get me to lead you to *him*? You're wired, of course?"

"Should I at least go in wired?" asked Redd. "Keep an open phone line, so you guys can listen in?"

Thrasher shook his head. "Too risky. He might ask you to give up your phone at the door, and if he realizes that you have an open call, he'll be suspicious and shut down. Even if he's not dirty, which . . . he's not."

"Interesting thing about the shoot house," Anderson went on, not waiting for an answer. "Twelve inches of reinforced concrete sandwiching a half inch of ballistic steel plating stops more than just bullets. This place is one big Faraday cage. No signals in or out. You could be carrying a satellite dish on your back, and it wouldn't make a bit of difference. That's why I decided to have this little conversation here."

Redd cocked his head to the side. "You're not even a little bit worried that when I go radio silent, my friends will know something's up?"

A glimmer of interest flashed in Anderson's eyes. "Friends? Who else has Phantom dragged into this?"

The question threw Redd for a moment. If Thrasher was Nightshade's man, then Anderson would already know the answer to that question.

Did I get that wrong?

This was why Redd hated spy games. You never knew who to trust.

When Redd didn't answer, Anderson waved the question away. "No matter. Actually, that's exactly what I'm hoping for. You're the Judas goat, kid. Staked out as bait for the lion. I've got my men positioned all over the compound, just waiting for Phantom to come running to the rescue. Of course, you could save us all a lot of trouble by just giving him up so we can end this unfortunate business right now."

Redd shook his head. "Sorry to disappoint you, but I'm not wearing a wire. And Aaron's not going to come charging in like the cavalry. That's not how he operates. I'm surprised you don't know that. When I don't come out of here, it's only going to confirm what he already suspects—that you're working for Nightshade. That you were the one who set him up in Kyiv all those years ago. He will come for you, but you won't see it coming."

For the first time since meeting Anderson, Redd saw a hint of uncertainty in his eyes. *No, not uncertainty,* he corrected. *Fear.*

"Who put you onto me? Who are you working with?"

He doesn't know about Thrasher, Redd realized. He fought to maintain his poker face. "You put your picture on the website, genius. Did you think he wouldn't notice?"

The answer seemed to flummox Anderson, so Redd pressed, "Who's Nightshade? Tell me, and I'll tell Aaron, and maybe . . . just maybe I can convince him you're not worth the trouble."

Anderson seemed to weigh Redd's offer for a moment, but then his mouth twisted into a sneer. "You think I'm afraid of Aaron Decker? I don't know how he made it out of Kyiv, but he should have done himself a favor and stayed dead."

He straightened, resolve stiffening his spine, the SIG steadying in his grip, muzzle aimed directly at Redd's heart. "You want to negotiate, I'll make *you* an offer. You're not getting out of this, cowboy; you've gotta know that. But you've got a family to think about."

This time, Redd couldn't hide his reaction.

"That's right. I know all about 'em. You give up Phantom, and that will be the end of it. Refuse, and there will be . . ." He hesitated a beat. "Additional consequences."

The threat sent an electric tingle through Redd's muscles. Rage began to bubble up from his gut, but it wasn't directed at Anderson.

How many times in the last three years had his choices put Emily and the kids in mortal danger? How many times had they been caught in the blowback? And now, despite all his precautions, it had happened again, only this time, it felt even worse. Not only could he not protect his family with his life . . . Even his death wouldn't save them.

"What if you're wrong?" Redd gave Thrasher a hard look. "If he is Nightshade's man and I go in there . . ."

"Not going to happen," replied Thrasher, confidently.

Decker, however, was not so dismissive of the possibility. "I won't lie to you, Matt. I'm sure you can handle this. I'd put money on you against them. I've seen what you can do, and that's good . . . Because if things do somehow go south . . ." He shrugged. "You'll be on your own." He paused a beat, then went on. "But sometimes, that's the best place to be. You can make the hard choices yourself, without having to factor in how that'll impact anyone else."

Redd took a deep breath, exhaled slowly, letting his self-recrimination drain away. He met Anderson's stare.

Hard choices.

"You'll leave my family alone?"

The corner of Anderson's lip began to curl upward in a look of triumph. "They don't need to be part of this."

Redd's shoulders sagged in a defeated slump. "I guess I don't have a choice," he said. He took another breath. "Aaron is . . ."

And then he moved.

FORTY-ONE

Redd lunged forward. He didn't go for Anderson's throat or even the gun. His top priority was to avoid catching a bullet, so any approach vector that kept him in front of the SIG was a no-go. Instead, he aimed for Anderson's left shoulder, hoping more than anything to simply knock him off-balance.

Anderson jerked the trigger a fraction of a second after Redd made his move. His reaction time was nothing short of extraordinary, but while he'd gotten the shot off, he had not been able to adjust his aim. Redd felt only the hot gas from the muzzle flash on the exposed skin of his face. The bullet missed him by six inches.

A second later, Redd made contact, his left shoulder slamming into Anderson. He had expected *some* resistance, but not like what he found. It was like running into a telephone pole. Redd had hit bigger guys to better effect in the past, but that didn't help him now.

Anderson must have anticipated the blow, even if only subconsciously, and shifted his weight at the last moment to brace for the collision. The impact jolted through Redd's shoulder and ribs, reminding him that, not even eighteen hours ago, he'd been shot in the back.

Still, the hit wasn't wasted. Anderson's stance faltered, his weight shifting further as Redd rebounded away, his torso rocking forward. Redd had passed on his weak side, and in order for him to reacquire, Anderson was going to have to pivot.

Which he did.

Just as Redd wanted.

Anticipating the move, Redd spun on his heel, brought his right hand across his body, and slapped hard at Anderson's gun hand, batting the weapon away as it discharged again. He had been hoping to knock the SIG out of the man's hand, but that didn't happen. Instead, Anderson hopped back a step, intuitively recognizing that he'd let Redd get too close, and brought the pistol around for another shot.

Abandoning his original plan to disarm Anderson, Redd opted for plan B—what his Marine drill instructor referred to as a "tactical withdrawal under fire."

He flung himself onto the mattress, bouncing and rolling across, flopping down onto the floor on the opposite side. As he landed, he spun on his back, wedged his shoulder under the frame, and heaved it up, throwing mattress, box springs, and frame toward Anderson.

The big mattress seemed to fill the room, completely eclipsing Anderson from view, but Redd didn't linger to assess the impact of his queen-size missile. He was already scrambling on all fours to reach the hallway, where he hooked right around the doorframe and finally got his feet under him again. Behind him, the noise of Anderson's fight with the furniture diminished as he ran.

He didn't go far, however. As he passed the bathroom mock-up, he quickly ducked inside and pressed himself against the wall. After a moment's consideration, he grabbed the lid off the toilet tank and held it above his head, ready to smash it down on Anderson if he came through the door. Then he waited, holding his breath and willing himself invisible.

The move was a huge gamble. If Anderson guessed what he was doing and cleared the rooms as he went, Redd would be right back where he started, trapped in a confined space against a man with a gun and no qualms about using it. Worse, he would have sacrificed his head start. But if it worked, if he could blindside the other man, disarm him, maybe take him out of the fight entirely, it would be more than worth the risk.

A moment passed. Then another. And then he heard footsteps in the hall. Fast, deliberate. He saw Anderson flash past the open door without slowing.

Redd immediately launched himself into the hallway in pursuit. His timing and technique fell well short of perfect. Anderson saw the motion and spun, trying to bring the pistol around. But his own momentum was working against him, and before he could fix his aim, Redd brought the toilet lid down hard on the extended arm.

The heavy porcelain shattered on impact, leaving Redd holding jagged shards, but the blow knocked the pistol from Anderson's grip, driving him back a step as the SIG clattered to the floor amidst a scattering of broken ceramics.

Anderson recovered quickly, making a desperate grab for the gun, but Redd moved faster, lashing out with one foot to punt the gun down the hallway, and then in the same motion, he threw himself at Anderson.

He caught Anderson just below the sternum, his shoulder slamming in at an awkward angle. Not the clean hit he wanted, but enough to drive the man back into the wall. Before Redd could follow up, something smashed into his temple. Lights burst across his vision. He brought his arms up, covering his head and warding off more blows, even as his knees slammed to the floor.

The first hit had left him more than a little disoriented, but he knew Anderson wasn't going to give him time to recover. Instead of backing off and trying to get to his feet, Redd launched himself from his knees, trying for a low tackle, but Anderson was already twisting, using a judo move to spin Redd face-first into the wall.

The world blinked white for half a second.

In an ordinary house, he probably would have crashed through the drywall and gotten tangled up in the studs, but the shoot house had been designed to withstand endless iterations of close-quarters combat. He bounced off the reinforced panel like a crash test dummy, a bloody faceprint marking the point of impact. Pain radiated from his face down to his spine. His legs went slack and for a second, he wasn't sure he'd be able to get his feet under him again.

Anderson didn't give him the chance to find out.

A sledgehammer fist slammed into the back of Redd's neck, driving him down again. His knees hit hard, but then Anderson grabbed his collar, hauling him up just enough to ram a fist at his face. Redd saw it coming but wasn't fast enough to stop it. His head snapped to the side, the taste of blood filling his mouth.

This isn't working.

It wasn't just that Anderson was strong, but how composed he was. The man wasn't fighting on adrenaline. Wasn't fighting like this was a life-or-death struggle. He was executing his moves with the cold dispassion of a seasoned professional.

If Redd didn't meet him on the same terms, he was going to lose.

And losing meant dying.

Instead of trying to stand his ground, Redd sagged, letting his weight drag Anderson down. Anderson's follow-up punch struck only a glancing blow to the side of Redd's head. It was enough to sting, but it would take a lot more to end the fight.

Shaking off the blow, Redd surged forward, driving into Anderson's legs, finally taking him down. Wasting no time, he mounted his opponent and went on the offensive, driving a fist into Anderson's unprotected midsection. Anderson's abs were about as hard as Redd expected, but he recalled the fate of escape artist Harry Houdini, who many believed sustained internal injuries after taking a punch to the gut when he wasn't ready. The first blow elicited an audible grunt, and Redd knew he'd finally gotten the other man's attention.

He pressed on, hammering fists into Anderson's face and upper body, then rammed an elbow into the man's diaphragm. Realizing Anderson was now desperate to get from beneath Redd's hulking frame, Redd anticipated the man's attempt to lift his hips and shift his weight, and tried to counter by posting an arm for balance, but the hallway was too narrow. His elbow clipped the wall, and that was all the opening Anderson needed. He rolled, bringing Redd with him, and suddenly they were inverted, Redd on his back, Anderson mounting high, a forearm braced across Redd's collarbone.

Wrap this up!

Redd twisted, but Anderson flowed with him, tightening the angle. Redd knew what was coming next but was powerless to prevent it. Anderson's left arm looped under his chin, and his right hand shot behind Redd's head, locking him into a rear naked choke.

It was the classic jiujitsu finishing hold, and Anderson knew how to do it right. Redd tried to tuck his chin, create some space, but Anderson had him locked up tight. His vision constricted. A high whine built in his ears. He twisted, thrashed, but Anderson had his legs wrapped around Redd's torso to keep from being thrown. All he needed to do was hold on.

Redd had only seconds.

With the last shred of will he possessed, he forced himself to ignore the choke hold and focus instead on his body position. He rolled over onto hands and knees, feeling Anderson shift with him, riding him like a bull.

Then Redd pushed off, throwing himself backward, with Anderson caught between him and the wall. He hit with enough force to drive the air from the other man's lungs, but Anderson just squeezed harder.

So Redd did it again. And again.

On the third hit, the grip loosened. Redd sucked air into his lungs, and as the darkness receded, fresh resolve flowed into his muscles. He snaked one hand up between Anderson's forearm and his own jaw, preventing the other man from reestablishing the choke, and then hammered Anderson into the anvil of the wall one more time.

Anderson grunted, and this time the sound was different. Less effort, more pain. The arm around Redd's throat slackened, just a hair, but it was enough. Redd drove his chin down into the crook of the elbow, prying the hold open another inch, and then tore himself free with a desperate twist.

Anderson reacted instantly, snarling like a cornered wolf as he clawed for control. He managed to snag a fistful of Redd's shirt and yanked, dragging Redd sideways, trying to roll him, maybe take his back again. Redd wasn't about to let that happen. He dropped his weight, posting an arm, and then pivoted inside Anderson's grip, seizing the older man's wrist with one hand, pressing his opposite elbow into Anderson's shoulder joint. Then, bracing his heel against the wall, he heaved with all his might, throwing his opponent up and over. Anderson scraped against the ceiling, then thudded into a wall, pinballing back and forth before finally crashing down onto the floor and landing on his back, near the top of the stairs, facing away from Redd.

Redd didn't pause to admire his handiwork. Instead, he closed the distance, ready to rejoin the fight. He might have turned the tide, but Anderson was a long way from giving up.

Redd needed to finish the fight before the old man got his second wind.

Then he saw that Anderson had landed right beside the SIG. It was about a foot from his right hand. Anderson saw it too. He closed his hand over the pistol, then twisted around, flipping over into a prone firing position.

Redd didn't think; he just moved, launching himself forward, diving the last few feet even as Anderson brought the SIG up one-handed. Before he could squeeze off a round, Redd was on him. He landed hard, driving his full weight onto Anderson's back, crushing him flat against the floor. His momentum carried them both forward. Over the edge, onto the stairs.

They went down fast.

Redd stayed on top, chest pressed to Anderson's back, arms gripping the other man's calves like the reins on a horse. The shuddering impacts of Anderson's body hitting treads in rapid succession jolted up through him, but he knew it was nothing to what the other man was feeling.

Sucks for him, Redd thought.

Anderson grunted with each step, his exhalations coming out like the stutter of a machine gun. Halfway down, he managed a sudden, violent twist, throwing his hips to one side and bucking like a bronco. Redd tried to counter, shifting his weight to maintain control, but Anderson somehow got out from under him. Gravity did the rest.

Redd's shoulder slammed into a tread, then his hip. Something cracked against his shin. The world flipped sideways, then upside down, then sideways again. He caught a glimpse of Anderson's elbow, then the blur of ceiling. The impact of the final landing knocked the breath from his lungs and left him sprawled, dazed, halfway into the dining room.

I've got to stop fighting big guys.

Redd's whole body screamed in protest as he struggled to rise, but he knew the aches and pains he was feeling now were nothing to what he'd feel later—if there was a later—thanks to the flood of endorphins telling him, *Get moving, now!*

But it was too late.

Anderson hit him like a linebacker, slamming him backward. They crashed through the dining table, the sturdy oak legs snapping under their combined weight. Redd felt the edge of something gouge his side, but he didn't have time to register the injury before they hit the floor again.

Anderson shoved away, pushing Redd into the tangle of debris. Redd tried to recover, but Anderson gave him another brutal shove that sent him skidding across the floor into the hallway leading back to the kitchen. His shoulder caught the corner, spun him halfway around before he went sprawling into the kitchen. Fighting disorientation, Redd struggled to rise before the next attack came, but Anderson, inexplicably, took a knee.

The reason became apparent when he flipped up the cuff of his pant leg to reveal a compact pistol strapped to an ankle holster.

You gotta be kidding me.

Redd spun and launched himself into the kitchen, veering around the island, leaping over fallen mannequins, making for the hallway leading back to the living room. He half expected to feel a bullet slam into his back—no armor plate this time—but he didn't look back.

He tore into the living room, not bothering to weave around the furniture but scrambling over it. His foot caught the edge of the coffee table as he tried to vault over it, and he sprawled forward but somehow managed to outrun the fall, keeping his feet as he reached the foyer and the front door, still wide-open from his initial entry, and found himself in the sterile anteroom at the entrance to the live-fire range. He reached out a hand to swipe down the lever to open the outside door, expecting to bang through it without slowing.

He hit the door like a freight train—and, shockingly, bounced back like he'd just collided with one. The impact staggered him sideways into the wall with the lockbox. His shoulder took the brunt, but he felt it all the way to his teeth. There was a noticeable dent in the door now, but it hadn't budged.

He approached the door more cautiously, tried the lever again, felt it turn without any resistance. Whatever mechanism held the door shut, it overrode the handle, which meant he was locked inside the shoot house. Trapped. And Anderson was coming.

Redd looked around, frantic for options. The control room door was shut, no help there. Then he saw something he'd missed, mounted to the wall just left of the exit door: a red mushroom-style emergency stop button. There was no label, no explanation, and Redd didn't have the time to ponder its purpose. Either it was an emergency override, or he was cooked. He slammed his palm against it, heard a heavy clunk from inside the door, then tried the lever again, throwing his weight against the door.

A gunshot exploded behind him. Sparks burst off the metal an inch above his right shoulder. But the door was swinging open.

Redd flung himself through just as another report thundered from the shoot house interior, threw himself down onto the gravel, and rolled to the side to take himself out of Anderson's line of sight, then bounded to his feet again. He was out of the building, but not out of danger.

Not by a long shot.

FORTY-TWO

After the artificially dim interior of the shoot house, daylight was almost as painful as the flash of a stun grenade, but Redd didn't let a little thing like near blindness slow him down. Anderson would come out shooting, there was no doubt about that, and the open ground near the structure offered no cover, so his only refuge was distance. Anderson's backup piece wasn't designed for long-range shooting. Past fifty meters, accuracy was a coin toss.

Not that those odds were very comforting.

As his vision cleared, Redd began scanning the distance, looking for something . . . *anything* . . . to improve his chances. He was on Anderson's home turf, and that put him at an already huge disadvantage, but aside from the guard at the gate, he hadn't seen anyone else. If Anderson was telling the truth about having his men out on the perimeter watching for Decker—and there was no reason to think he wasn't—all Redd really needed to do was stay ahead of Anderson long enough to get back to the main building where his rental was parked.

So where am I?

He looked around, trying to get his bearings. His internal compass was still spinning after almost getting his butt handed to him by Anderson in the shoot house, but as he spotted the towers of the confidence course looming before him, one thought went through his head.

Wrong way.

He'd rolled to the left coming out of the shoot house, and now he was heading away from the headquarters building, away from escape. Turning around wasn't an option, not with Anderson almost certainly on his heels.

He glanced back, expecting to see Anderson, huffing and puffing, but instead saw the man flinging open the door of his Suburban.

Of course, Redd thought dismally. *Why run yourself ragged when you've got a two-ton battering ram?*

It would take Anderson a few seconds to get the SUV started and up to speed, but once he did, Redd's head start would evaporate. He might be able to zig and zag creatively, but that would only delay the inevitable. There weren't many places he could go where the Suburban couldn't follow.

But there was one, and he was already a quarter of the way there.

The confidence course.

Its log barriers and rope bridges were hard enough for a human on foot to negotiate. The Suburban would be stopped cold. And the obstacles would give Redd plenty of cover and buy him a little time to figure out what to do next.

That is, if he could make it there.

Redd was exhausted, and as he ran, it dawned on him that Anderson had likely made him go through the full shoot house drill both to size him up and to tire him out before the *real* fun began.

Don't stop! he told himself.

Behind him, the Suburban rumbled to life and then tore out of the shoot house parking lot in a spray of gravel. Redd didn't look back again, just dug deep and poured on the speed.

He had sixty seconds, maybe less.

Redd drove harder. His lungs were starting to burn, his breath coming in ragged bursts. The terrain sloped slightly upward toward the course, just enough to make his quads burn, and still he pushed. Two hundred yards to go.

Behind him, the Suburban's engine roared as it picked up speed.

Just thirty more seconds, Redd begged.

Prayed.

He veered away from the road, running cross-country through the scrub, angling toward a familiar obstacle, one he'd cursed mightily when running a similar course at Camp Pendleton. Called the Weaver—and a few other less savory names—it consisted of several large horizontal logs on an A-frame structure, spaced evenly up one side and down the other. The idea was to weave one's body over and under each successive log, continuing all the way up one side and down the other without touching the ground.

A hundred and fifty yards.

The roar behind him changed in pitch as Anderson steered off road and the big SUV had to labor to maintain its speed on the irregular terrain.

A hundred yards.

You got this, he told himself, pumping arms and legs harder.

The Weaver was just fifty yards away . . . Thirty . . .

Redd could hear the Suburban's tires crushing grit and vegetation as it closed the distance, could almost feel the heat coming off its engine. He juked right a fraction of a second before the SUV would have caught him, its bumper missing him by inches as he closed the last few yards to the structure.

The Suburban skidded hard, the massive vehicle fishtailing slightly as Anderson yanked the wheel to avoid a full collision. The front bumper kissed the bottom log of the Weaver with a thump, and Redd used that moment to vault up onto the A-frame.

He didn't bother weaving. Just climbed, scrambling across one of the logs to reach the opposite side in pure defiance of the design.

Chunks of wood exploded at his feet as Anderson opened fire. Redd leaped the final three feet to make a six-foot drop to the ground on the far side of the structure. He landed in a roll and came up running, sprinting into the obstacle maze, ducking low, using every log, post, and plywood wall to keep himself out of Anderson's sights.

A tall ramp loomed to his left, but it was too exposed, so he veered into a muddy crawl trench topped with barbed wire, dragging himself through the muck with elbows and toes, feeling the barbs tear at his shirt and jeans when he unthinkingly raised up too high.

Then he was clear, emerging out the other side, coated in mud, chest heaving, and spotted his salvation. The tower.

The only way up, aside from the rappelling lines dangling down the opposite side, was by ascending the cargo net that hung down from the top at a slight angle. He'd be exposed while making the climb, but once he reached the top, Anderson would have no choice but to come and get him.

Redd risked a glance back, saw Anderson picking his way across the Weaver, and then made his dash for the net, feeling mud squelching in his boots. When he got there, he reached high, grabbing the thick rope diamonds, and began to climb.

It wasn't like climbing a ladder. There was no rhythm, no solid footing. Each little movement caused the web to swing just a little bit further away, forcing him to hang in a semi-inverted crunch in order to reach the next foothold. The net fought him for every foot of progress, sagging and creaking with each shift, but then, like an oasis in the middle of a desert, the top edge was within reach. Two more steps up, and he was able to heave himself onto the platform.

The top of the tower was a ten-by-ten platform, the floor made of plywood, painted black and covered in grip tape. There was no railing and no roof. Just a vertigo-inducing drop on all sides. He rolled away from the edge, lying on his back and staring up at the sky while he fought to catch his breath.

He'd made it, but it didn't exactly feel like a victory. His decision to climb the tower had been born out of immediate need, with little regard for long-term strategy. He was just trying to reach the one place where Anderson wouldn't have a shot at him. Unfortunately, while he was safe for the moment, he was also stranded.

If Anderson didn't come up, didn't take the bait, then he was effectively treed, and it would be a simple waiting game. Fortunately, Redd knew something Anderson didn't.

Decker clapped him on the shoulder. "Relax. If things go south, we'll come for you. Count on that."

"But you just said . . ."

"I know what I just said. And if things get hairy, that needs to be your mindset. No one coming to save you. But if Anderson does make a move against you, I think that's going to be pretty conclusive evidence that he's Nightshade or at the very least working for him. Either way, you better believe I'm going to want to have a talk with him."

Of course, Decker didn't know that Anderson had set a trap for him, but as long as Anderson had his men lying in ambush, he wouldn't be able to call them in to back him up, which evened the playing field a bit. Still, unless something changed, either Anderson would have to come up or Redd would have to come down.

And he was already thinking about how to do that to best effect.

Redd crawled to the nearest edge and cautiously peeked over, looking down at the obstacle course. No sign of Anderson there, so he shifted to the opposite side. Nothing.

Where is he?

Redd made another quick check, rising to a crouch, scanning all the places where Anderson might conceivably be hiding. With a handgun, his chances of sniping Redd from the ground weren't great. Not impossible, but not great. No, if Anderson wanted him dead, he would have to come up—

A faint rasping sound—wood sliding against wood—caused him to turn around just as a section of the floor at the center of the platform burst open and Anderson erupted from the revealed opening like a demonic jack-in-the-box.

A trapdoor, Redd realized. *Of course.*

Anderson and his cadre of instructors wouldn't want to have to climb the cargo net every time they led a rappelling event. While Redd was busy struggling up the rope ladder, Anderson had been humping it up a stairway hidden behind the tower walls.

His hands were empty, the pistol evidently left behind. In such close quarters, it would have either been a decisive advantage or a liability, particularly since he didn't know where Redd would be when he emerged. It proved a fortuitous decision as Redd *was* behind the trapdoor when it opened.

Anderson kept his stance compact, knees bent, torso hunched slightly forward, as if moving through a low tunnel, and spun to face Redd. Redd took a reflexive step backward, barely catching himself at the edge, as Anderson came at him swinging. Redd twisted aside, throwing himself flat to avoid both his foe's reach and any chance of toppling over.

Anderson pivoted toward him, knocking the trapdoor closed and throwing a weak jab that did little damage. Redd resisted the urge to flinch away, mindful of the yawning drop less than a step behind him. Anderson, who now had his weight behind him, threw another punch, which Redd batted away, but the impact rolled him back, and the mere awareness of how close he was to the edge caused him to flail for a handhold. Anderson advanced, trying to claim the space and push Redd even closer to the edge, so Redd did the only thing he could and rolled into Anderson, trying to take the man's feet out from under him. But Anderson just leaned forward and dropped onto him. His weight hit hard, compressing Redd's ribs, pinning him flat to the boards. Redd twisted, got an arm inside, and jammed it into Anderson's throat, levering space. When the older man tried to swat it away, Redd went with it, snaking his hips, rolling them both into a clinch.

After a moment, they broke apart by mutual need, rolling away from each other, rising fast but staying low. Anderson feinted left. Redd didn't fall for it. He stepped in instead and shot a fist into the other man's ribs. Anderson grunted but retaliated with another jab. Redd ducked under it and rammed his fist into Anderson's sternum, driving the other man back two steps, closer to the edge.

Redd closed the distance, not giving his foe any room to maneuver or any time to recover, throwing rapid-fire punches at Anderson's face. The first hit connected solidly, splitting the man's lip and releasing a spray of blood, but Anderson immediately turtled, bringing his hands up to guard his head. He weathered the next few blows, then charged forward, plowing into Redd's unprotected middle.

Redd just managed to pivot away, avoiding the full force of Anderson's charge, but the glancing impact still knocked him sideways a step. He glanced down, saw how close he was to the edge, and windmilled frantically to shift his weight in the other direction, even as Anderson spun around and lobbed a haymaker at his head. Redd just managed to block the swing, countering with a punch that snapped Anderson's head back.

But the man didn't go down. He just took a step back, spat a gobbet of blood on the floor at Redd's feet, and came at him again.

This guy's nuts.

Redd stood his ground, leaned forward, and started throwing punches. Despite the punishment Anderson had meted out, he felt like he was catching his second wind. His strikes were focused. He had height and reach on the older man, and he was finally using it. When Anderson blocked high, Redd aimed for the solar plexus. When Anderson tried to punch back, Redd simply leaned to the side and hit harder.

And yet, Anderson was still on his feet. Bloody and battered, but undiminished. They were too evenly matched, in both ability and stamina. But the real problem, Redd realized, was the fighting space. He didn't mind fighting up close and personal, but the sixty-foot drop that awaited just a few feet in every direction was making him hold back, play it safe. A single misstep, a missed throw or overcommitment, could easily prove fatal. If he was going to end this fight decisively, he needed to find a better answer.

Redd closed with Anderson again, fired a shot at his ribs, then another, and another. Anderson leaned in, going for the clinch, but Redd shifted away, moving toward the opposite edge of the platform. As he did, he glanced down, saw a pair of two-inch manila ropes stretching out a good hundred feet in a slow descent to ground level. The fixed lines were used for an event called the commando crawl, where a person had to slide down the top of the rope, or if they lost their balance, hang upside down from it. There was a rope safety net directly beneath it to catch anyone who failed, and that gave Redd an idea. The presence of the net meant that falling from that side of the tower would likely be survivable.

It occurred to him that the rope ladder he'd climbed to get to the tower might serve a similar function, allowing for a slower, possibly even controlled descent from the platform.

He mentally marked those sides of the tower as "yellow zones." Better not to fall at all, but if he had to risk it, those would be the places to take that chance.

The side with the fixed rappel lines remained firmly "red," as did the other side, which seemed to serve no utilitarian purpose at all.

Anderson came at him again, feinting short jabs, clearly trying to corral Redd, maneuvering him toward an edge. One of the red zones, as luck would have it. Redd ducked a swing and countered with an upper-body shot, which Anderson absorbed and then threw a kick into Redd's thigh.

Redd winced at the impact, feeling a jolt like electricity sizzle through the muscle. He staggered backward, favoring the leg, and felt the heel of his boot rock back over empty air. He glanced back—a mistake—and saw only the yawning drop. A wave of vertigo roiled his gut. He had come within inches of stepping off the rappelling wall.

He managed to shift his weight forward, onto the leg Anderson had just kicked, and once again threw himself at the other man, surreptitiously shifting to the right, trying to put the commando crawl station at his back.

Anderson refused to give ground, instead lunging at Redd again. Redd pivoted, narrowly dodging a sweeping punch that would have sent him over, and answered with a hook to Anderson's jaw. The older man's head snapped to the side, but he came right back, eyes crimson with fury.

Another punch from Anderson clipped Redd's cheek, rattling his teeth, but Redd managed to bury a shot under Anderson's arm, hearing the man grunt as the air rushed out of him.

The tower floor creaked underfoot as they traded strikes, each one a gamble so near the edge. Anderson tried driving forward again, trying to shove Redd back over the corner. Redd was struggling to put the commando crawl station at his back. It was almost as if Anderson realized what he was attempting and was intent on denying him the safety net.

Then Redd's heel caught something—one of the fixed rappel line anchors bolted into the tower floor—and he felt his weight shifting backward. The moment stretched like taffy, a single desperate thought surging through his head.

No!

FORTY-THREE

Redd twisted his body, trying to bring himself closer to the wall even as he fell. His hands shot out, scrabbling for anything. The fingers of one hand grazed the edge. The other found the rope attached to the anchor ring he'd just tripped over. He caught himself.

Barely.

Pain jolted through his shoulders as his full weight came down on the tenuous holds. His arms quivered, the strain of the dead hang burning through his biceps and forearms. His feet pedaled uselessly, trying to find a foothold on the smooth wall. He had a hand on the rappelling rope, but it was hardly a lifeline. Even if he managed to get both hands on it, he wouldn't be able to do much more than hang there. Up or down, he needed to trap the rope between his feet, add some friction.

Anderson's face loomed above him, a bloody but triumphant grin on his face. He knelt there, leaning closer. "Last chance. Tell me where to find Decker."

Redd smiled. "Big mistake."

Before Anderson could register Redd's response, Redd let go of the edge, reached down and gathered a loop of rope, then swung it upward, around the older man's neck. Anderson's eyes widened in shock, one hand darting up too late to stop the rope from tightening around his throat.

There was no need for Redd to pull it tight. All he had to do was hold on and let gravity do the rest. As his own weight came down on the rope, it pulled Anderson forward, yanking him over the edge. He struck Redd as he fell past, the collision nearly breaking Redd's high hold. He felt the rope burn against his palm as he slid a full foot, but then Anderson was under him, his body caught in the rope, stopping Redd's fall instantly.

Beneath Redd, Anderson was thrashing, both hands clawing at the rope around his neck in a futile effort to relieve the crushing pressure. His boots kicked against the air, twisting, swinging away and then into the side of the tower, but his efforts only seemed to cinch the impromptu noose tighter. The fact that Redd was practically sitting on his shoulders probably didn't help his efforts.

With a moment to breathe, Redd considered his options. Rappelling down would require him to either bypass Anderson or somehow loosen the loop from which he was hanging and let him drop. Either choice posed its own set of challenges, but both almost certainly ended with Anderson dead.

Which would not really have troubled Redd at all, except for one small detail: Anderson knew who Nightshade was.

Redd spared a glance down. Anderson's face was purple, eyes bulging, spit and foam on his lips as he clawed at the rope. He was seconds away from unconsciousness, and if Redd didn't do something—and soon—any answers he might have would die with him.

The only alternative to going down and, realistically, the only way to keep Anderson alive, was for Redd to climb back up to the top of the tower and then drag the beaten man up after him.

Aaron's going to owe me a huge favor.

The edge of the tower was barely six feet above him. If he stood on Anderson's shoulders and reached up, Redd could get both hands on the edge, though he didn't like his chances of being able to pull himself up from where he was. Instead, he adjusted his hold on the rope and, ignoring the fire in his left hand, reached up, gripping it with both hands. He then wrapped the rope once around his left boot, pinning it in place with his right, trapping the line between the instep of one boot and the arch of the other, and pushed down with his legs. Using his legs rather than his arms, he quickly propelled himself up the rope until he was able to grasp the anchor atop the tower and pull himself the rest of the way up.

He wanted nothing more than to just collapse and take in his victory. To lay there in the sun for an hour or two and do absolutely nothing. But he knew the whole ordeal was far from over, so he forced himself to keep moving, crawling back to the edge to look down at the now motionless form of Brian Anderson.

Fearing that he might already have waited too long, he grabbed hold of the rope with both hands, bent his knees with his heels braced against the edge, and started pulling. Anderson was a solid two forty at least, all deadweight now, but Redd—who was a good twenty-five pounds heavier than that—let his legs do the work, dragging the man up tug-of-war style.

Drive, breathe, reset.

He grunted, bracing and pulling again, his thighs and calves screaming with each drive backward. Each time he shifted for a new grip, he worried the rope would slip from his hands, that Anderson would slip free and fall, or worse, that the limp weight at the other end was already a corpse.

Finally, Anderson's shoulders crested the edge. Redd quickly worked his way back down the rope, then grabbed the man under the arms and heaved him the rest of the way, rolling Anderson onto the platform like a landed fish. The man just lay there, unmoving, limbs slack, head lolling to the side. The rope was tight around his neck, a smear of blood seeping out from under the cordage.

Redd's fingers, trembling and numb, fumbled with the line, slick with sweat and blood. The rope was as solid and unyielding as a tree branch, but after a few seconds, Redd felt it give. As it slid away, Anderson's chest heaved and he sucked in a ragged gasp.

Redd sagged back in relief.

Still alive.

He doubted Anderson had any fight left in him, but just in case, Redd rolled the man onto his stomach, yanked his arms behind his back, and used the rope to hog-tie him. Only then did Redd finally surrender to collapse. He lay there beside his beaten foe, every muscle quivering with exhaustion, and stared up at the sky.

If there was ever a time to offer up a prayer of gratitude, this was it.

But even as his lips started to form the words, a familiar rasp of wood surfaces rubbing together broke into his reverie. He sat up, darting a glancc in the direction of the trapdoor even as it started to rise, and spun into a crouch, poised, if not entirely prepared, to meet whatever new threat was coming for him.

The cover was thrown back, and a man's head rose into view.

Redd almost collapsed again when he saw who it was. "Aaron."

Decker regarded him from under a raised eyebrow, then looked past him, taking in the hog-tied captive. "Looks like my timing was perfect."

Redd nearly choked on a laugh. "Actually, ten minutes ago would have been perfect."

Decker shrugged and climbed out onto the platform, making room for Thrasher, who hauled himself up with considerably less grace.

Thrasher gave Redd an appraising stare. "You look like you got beat up."

Redd gestured to Anderson. "Check out the other guy, though." He turned to Decker. "How'd you guys get here? Anderson said he set a trap for you."

Decker's expression didn't change. "Did he? We must have missed it."

"We came in through the front gate, actually," said Thrasher. "The guard gave us a little trouble, but we gave him the rest of the day off."

"When we heard the shooting, we realized you were in trouble," Decker continued. "Spotted you up here and came running to the rescue." He looked down at Anderson. "Not that you needed it."

Anderson craned his neck to stare back up at him. "Phantom," he whispered, his voice still hoarse.

Decker's expression remained utterly calm, but Redd saw a glimmer of cold fire in his eyes. "Switchback."

Anderson tried to sneer, but it looked more like a pained grimace. "Should've stayed dead."

Redd felt the temperature drop a few degrees.

Decker knelt beside Anderson, then reached under the flap of his shirt and drew his pistol, slow and deliberate. He didn't point it at Anderson, but its presence was enough to send the message. "You remember Kyiv?"

Anderson's nostrils flared, but he didn't answer.

"Three good men died." Decker's tone remained calm, but Redd could see the slight tremor in the gun barrel, could hear the tightly leashed rage threading each syllable. "Because of you. Their blood calls out for vengeance."

Anderson worked his mouth, still saying nothing, but the defiance in his eyes was wavering, replaced by something like fear.

"But it wasn't your idea, was it?" Decker went on. "Someone told you to send us into that ambush. Who was it?"

"You were asking too many questions," Anderson muttered. "Couldn't trust you anymore."

"Who was it?" Decker asked again, his tone edging up. "Who's Nightshade?"

"Forget it," hissed Anderson. "If you're going to kill me, kill me. I'm done talking to you."

Decker's head cocked slightly to the side, and then with a look of something that was almost resignation, he placed the suppressor of the pistol against Anderson's forehead.

Redd stepped forward. "Aaron, wait."

Decker didn't look at him. His finger curled around the trigger. "Last chance, Switchback. Who is Nightshade?"

Anderson let out a strained, rasping laugh, his eyes defiant even as they glistened with fear. "Go to hell."

"Aaron!" Redd snapped, kneeling beside Decker. "There's a better way."

"He's not going to talk, Matt. We're wasting our time here."

"Phantom's right," said Thrasher. "Maybe if we had a couple weeks, we could wring it out of him, but we don't have that kind of time."

Anderson tilted his head to the side. "Thrasher? Is that you, old buddy? You're mixed up in this?" He shook his head sadly. "Boy, you've really stepped in it. But there's an easy way to fix it. You know what I'm talking about."

Redd ignored both of them, focusing on Decker. "He's no good to you dead."

"He's not going to talk," Decker said again.

"He doesn't need to. We can use him. Hand him over to Gavin. Let the Bureau take him apart. His financials. His government contracts. There's a thread there that connects him to Nightshade."

Decker seemed to recoil at the idea. "The FBI can't touch him, Matt. Whoever he is, he's above the law. I'm the only one who can end this."

"Maybe that's true. Maybe Nightshade is too powerful or too connected or whatever . . . Maybe he'll never see the inside of a courtroom. But that doesn't mean the FBI can't help us figure out who he is. Nightshade *is* a criminal. He's been working with the Russians and who knows who else. But he—" Redd pointed at Anderson. "He's not above the law. He might be willing to die for Nightshade, but maybe he'll think twice about spending the rest of his life in a supermax prison."

"Good luck with that," Anderson said defiantly. "You've got nothing. A lot of unsubstantiated accusations."

Redd held Decker's gaze. "We've got him for what happened in Kyiv. You can testify to it. So can Thrasher. That's enough to move this forward."

Thrasher shook his head. "Not gonna happen, kid. Rogue Unit operations were way beyond top secret. They're a political third rail. Worse than that, everything we did was illegal. Even if you could find a prosecutor willing to take it to trial, or a judge to hear the case, me and Aaron would be admitting to numerous extrajudicial killings."

"So, make a deal. Full immunity in exchange for telling it all. Gavin can make that happen." He looked meaningfully down at Anderson. "I imagine he might even offer you the same deal. Immunity in exchange for Nightshade."

Anderson's eyes narrowed slightly, a microreaction, but it was there. "Gavin Kline," Redd added, though he suspected Anderson already knew. "Acting director of the FBI. You might say he's a personal friend."

This time, Anderson didn't react, but Redd sensed that he'd made an inroad. "You don't have to go to prison for Nightshade. You don't have to die for him." He made an expansive gesture. "You don't have to give all of this up. I can call him right now."

Redd wasn't bluffing. Getting Anderson to roll on Nightshade was their best chance of ending this nightmare, and if that meant letting Anderson escape justice, then so be it. He patted his pockets, searching for a phone he didn't have, then turned to Thrasher. "Let me use your phone."

Thrasher frowned but took his phone from a pocket, unlocked it, and handed it over. Redd dialed Kline's private number from memory and held the phone to his ear, his thoughts racing as he considered how to even begin explaining the situation to Kline. Decker's insistence that he not loop Gavin into the search for the traitor would complicate things a bit, but Redd didn't need a legally binding plea agreement. Thrasher had been right when he'd said that none of this would ever be adjudicated in a court of law.

The call went immediately to voicemail. Redd hid his disappointment as he listened to the greeting and considered his next play. Waiting for Kline to get back to him was hardly ideal. Redd was barely keeping Decker in check as it was.

"Please record your message after the tone."

Redd didn't wait for the beep. "Hey, Gavin. It's me." He paused, as if listening to a reply. "Good, good. Listen, I'm here with Aaron."

Out of the corner of his eye, he saw Decker's lips turn down in a frown.

"Yeah. We've, uh . . . Actually, we've made some progress on that problem I told you about . . . Right. That's the one. Listen, I can't go into all the details over the phone, but . . ." He looked Anderson in the eye. "We've found someone who might have the answers we're looking for."

Anderson's eyes narrowed with something that almost looked like curiosity.

Redd kept going. "The thing is, I need to be able to offer him something . . . No, I was thinking more along the lines of immunity . . . I know it's a big ask . . ."

An automated voice cut in. *"If you are satisfied with your message, press one now."*

Redd ignored the prompt. "Gavin, this guy's a small fish, but he can give us Nightshade . . . We can end this . . . No, don't worry about that. Aaron will take care of it . . ."

There was a double beep as the call disconnected. Redd kept going.

"I just need you to back my play . . . I've never asked you for anything, Gavin, but I'm asking for this." Saying it aloud felt strange, even if Kline would never hear the words, but Redd felt the personal touch might help sell the illusion. He waited a beat, then nodded. "Thanks, Gavin. I'll call you back when I have an answer."

He thumbed the already dark screen as if to end the call, then nodded at Decker. "He's got our back." He turned to Anderson. "So, what's it gonna be? You want to give us a name? Or should we do this Aaron's way?"

Anderson was quiet for a long moment, his eyes moving between Redd and Decker. He finally settled on Redd. "He told me you were Kline's kid." He coughed. "Wasn't sure I believed it."

Redd's pulse quickened. His relationship to Kline was not exactly a state secret, but neither was it public knowledge. Still, if Nightshade had the kind of access Thrasher had suggested, it was hardly a surprise that he knew. He forced himself to stay calm. "Believe it," he said. "And believe me when I say this is the best deal you're ever going to get."

"Still," Anderson went on, "I'm a little surprised you were able to reach him."

"He takes my calls."

Anderson's eyes darkened, a vicious glint cutting through the pain in his face. "Because last I heard, your daddy was out of cell range. In Yellowstone." He paused a beat. "With your family."

The words landed like a punch, leaving Redd weak in the knees. Behind him, Decker went utterly still, the tension in the air turning razor-sharp.

Anderson's lips twisted into a feral smirk. "You didn't really think you would be able to hide them away, did you? You can't escape him. He's going to kill them, and then he's going to find you and—"

Decker moved, too fast for Redd to even think about stopping him. He dropped down beside Anderson and gave him a shove, rolling him like a sack of potatoes toward the edge of the platform.

Anderson's eyes went wide, a strangled "No, wait—" tearing free as he went over the edge. His scream echoed as he disappeared over the side, then cut off abruptly.

Redd stared at the empty space where Anderson had been, too astonished to move. Thrasher just gaped at both men, eyes wide in disbelief. "I didn't know," he whispered. "You gotta believe me."

Redd ignored him, turning to Decker, his voice low and urgent. "We need to get to Yellowstone."

"Yeah."

Redd nodded toward the edge of the platform. "What about him?"

Decker frowned, then both men took a step forward and looked down.

Anderson had fallen, but he hadn't gone far. The rappelling rope Redd had used to bind him hand and foot was still attached to the anchor hard point, arresting his fall and leaving him dangling upside down, about eight feet below them.

"I suppose we should bring him along. Maybe he'll give us something useful after all." Decker paused. "And if not, I can always kill him later."

FORTY-FOUR

BOZEMAN, MONTANA

Treadway cruised slowly through the cracked asphalt lot of the strip mall, trying to decide where to park her government-issue Malibu. Finding a space wasn't the problem. There was nothing but space.

A shuttered vape shop sat at one end, windows papered over with a *For Lease* sign slowly peeling away from the glass. Next to it was a nail salon, Diamond Tips. A neon sign in the window indicated the salon was open for business, but there were no cars parked out front. A payday loan storefront occupied the other anchor slot, its green neon sign advertising *LOANS UP TO $500*, but it too looked as quiet as a cemetery.

Judging by the parking lot, it was a wonder that any of the businesses occupying the storefronts were able to make rent. However, as Treadway knew all too well, looks could be deceiving. Businesses like these often relied on . . . alternative revenue streams. Treadway knew at least one of the businesses was a front for methamphetamine traffic, which was why she had been hesitant to even pull into the lot in a vehicle that screamed *fed*. She would have preferred to rent something a little less obvious, but time wasn't something she had in abundance.

She chose to park in front of the payday loan place and strolled down to the storefront with blacked-out windows on which various stylized images had been painted, as well as the words *Tattooes & Peircings* and the name *White Buffalo Ink*.

According to Denver Callahan, White Buffalo Ink was the front from which his supplier, Rick Turner, operated, dispensing half-gram bags of crystal and laundering the proceeds. It was Turner who had put the word out to his dealers to be on the lookout for Emily Redd's Tahoe, and in particular, two kids matching the description of Brynn and Mitchell Decker.

Treadway had debated just having Turner picked up and brought in for questioning, but that would have brought a lot more attention to what she was doing, which in turn would have made it a lot harder for her to do things her own way, especially if Turner lawyered up, which seemed likely given his rap sheet. A mid-level meth dealer, with a couple priors for distribution—nothing big enough to put him away for long—he was clearly a lot more intelligent than the kids he sent out to peddle his stuff.

It was unclear where Turner got his supply, but he was almost certainly connected. Nobody moved weight on their own, not for long. And it stood to reason that whatever criminal organization controlled him was also responsible for putting the word out on Emily Redd and the Decker kids. The trick would be getting Turner to tell her who that was.

As she reached for the door handle, she checked her reflection in the glass. She didn't have time for a full costume change, so she'd been obliged to work with what she had. Washed-out jeans, a fitted black tee under a slate-gray hoodie, hair scraped into a loose ponytail that let a few rebellious strands frame her face. Just enough lip balm for a hint of shine. She pulled the zipper of her hoodie down just a notch, letting herself look a little vulnerable, and then pulled the door open.

The place was small, dim, with a strong smell of cannabis. The walls were lined with framed photos of tattoos—skulls, snakes, wolves, the Virgin Mary. An old, threadbare sofa lined one wall, a battered coffee table in front of it, strewn with old copies of *Inked*. A pair of adjustable tattoo chairs looked to be in surprisingly good shape. A curtain hung over a doorway at the back.

There was a glass display counter showcasing body jewelry to her immediate left, and behind it, a man looked up from his phone. She recognized him instantly from his mug shots. Rick Turner. Late thirties, lean, with a shaved head, full tattoo sleeves on both arms, and what looked like barbed wire crawling out from the collar of his black T-shirt.

For a split second, Turner's eyes narrowed in surprise at the arrival of a stranger in his empty shop. But then he smiled, a slow, predatory curve of the lips that was meant to be charming, the kind of smile that probably worked on the girls who wandered in off the street looking for a cheap piercing or a discount tattoo.

"Hello," he said, setting his phone down on the counter. "What can I do for you today?"

Treadway let herself smile back, warm and just a little shy, stepping closer as if she were uncertain about what she was looking for. She let her eyes drift to the display case, feigning a look at the jewelry on offer while taking in the man behind it, reading his body language, already laying out the angles she could play.

"Hi," she said, letting a little breathiness slip into her voice. "Do you do walk-ins? Or do I need to make an appointment?"

"Well, I guess it depends on what you're interested in."

Treadway let her gaze flick to the empty chairs and back to him, then gave a small shrug, twisting her lips in a thoughtful almost pout. "I want something . . . discreet."

She watched the flicker of interest in his eyes. "I can be discreet," he said, voice dropping into a drawl. "Ink is usually by appointment only, but I can call my guy and see if he's free to come in. If you want a piercing . . ." He flashed a coy smile. "I can take care of that for you."

She glanced at the curtain separating the front from the back, then looked him in the eye again, dropping her voice to a conspiratorial whisper. "A friend of mine told me this is the place to come when you're looking for something . . . special." She let the last word hang, inviting him to fill in the blank.

Turner's smile froze, and his eyes narrowed. "You want a piercing or not?"

She tilted her head, giving him a bashful grin. "I was hoping for something a little more fun than that." She let her hand slip into the pocket of her jeans, brushing the roll of twenties she'd prepared, letting just the edge of a bill peek out before she tucked it back in.

The smile was gone. "We don't sell fun here, sweetheart. Go find your fun somewhere else."

She let a hurt look flicker across her face. "Look, I just need a little something, okay? Just to take the edge off. I'm not looking to cause trouble."

"Get out." His voice dropped, hard now, all pretense of charm gone.

Treadway let out a breath, stepping back, her shoulders slumping as if she were about to give up. "All right, then. I guess we'll have to do this another way." She reached into her pocket again, but this time it wasn't for cash. She pulled her badge and flipped it open.

"I knew it." Turner's face hardened into a scowl. "You got a warrant?" He reached for his phone again, holding it up. "Because I told you to leave, and if you don't have a warrant, you're trespassing, and I'm calling my lawyer."

Treadway shook her head sadly. "Rick, if you want to do this the hard way, I can do the hard way. I can call in a team, get a warrant, and we can turn this place upside down. I can put you in cuffs and perp walk you into the federal building for questioning. You can call your lawyer, sure, but it won't look good. Not for you, not for your business."

His lip curled, but he didn't say anything. His fingers drummed on his phone.

She leaned forward, her voice dropping, calm but with an edge that cut. "Or we can have a quiet conversation right now. Just you and me." She shrugged. "Your choice."

"I got nothing to say."

Treadway's eyes didn't leave his. "I think I know what the problem is, Rick. You think this is about you dealing crank." She shook her head. "I don't care about that. It's not my department. This is about something bigger. Something I don't think you want to be a part of."

He thrust his jaw forward, signaling his refusal to say another word.

She tapped her badge with a fingertip. "This is about conspiracy to commit kidnapping."

The accusation sufficed to break his self-imposed vow of silence. "I don't know what you're talking about."

"Don't you? Your boy Denver already pointed the finger at you. Told us that you were the one who put out the word to watch for a lady driving a white Tahoe with a bunch of kids. He even said you were the one who told him to grab the girl. She's seventeen, Rick. Did you know that? Do you know what we do to people who go after kids?"

A flicker of something—guilt, fear, realization—flashed across Turner's face before he masked it with a sneer. He held the phone closer to his face, stabbing his finger at the screen. "I'm calling my lawyer."

Treadway shook her head, letting the disappointment show. "Rick, Rick, Rick. This is your chance to get out ahead of something that's going to bury you. I don't think you wanted anything to do with kidnapping. You've got a good thing going here. Why ruin it with a major felony? That idea came from further up the food chain, am I right?"

She let that linger for a moment before continuing. "But the thing is, Denver and the others have already rolled on you. It's up to you whether you want to take the fall for this or point me somewhere else."

Rick's jaw twitched, but he didn't say a word. The defiance was still there, but Treadway saw something else flicker across his face, a shadow that had nothing to do with fear of jail or federal charges.

He's not scared of me, she realized. *He's scared of them.*

Treadway let out a slow breath, schooling her expression to mild disappointment. "Okay, Rick. I get it. You think staying quiet is going to protect you. Maybe it will." She shrugged, then took a step closer, lowering her voice to a conversational murmur. "But what happens when I take you in for questioning and then turn you out again, thanking you for being so cooperative?"

His eyes widened in alarm. "I told you, I don't have anything to say to you."

"But they won't know that." She tilted her head. "You must work for some scary people, Rick. Who is it? Neo-Nazis? Cartel? Bikers? The Russians?"

A nerve in his cheek twitched.

Gotcha.

Treadway felt her pulse quicken.

The Russians.

She wasn't sure what she'd been expecting to find in this dead-end strip mall in Bozeman, but it hadn't been that.

What does the Russian mob want with Decker's kids?

There was no good answer to that question.

She nodded slowly, still holding Rick's gaze. "So you're working for the Russian mob. No wonder you're scared."

"I never said that."

"It's okay, Rick," she soothed. "You don't have to say it."

Treadway debated her options. She could push him. Lean in, promise him protection, spin him a fairy tale about witness relocation and second chances.

But really, what more could he tell her? She had what she needed.

"Thanks, Rick," she said, putting her badge away.

His eyes widened. "Wait—no—I didn't say—"

She was already turning, moving for the door.

"You can't—" he shouted, scrambling up behind the counter. "I never said that! You hear me? I never said that!"

She didn't look back.

When she was behind the wheel of her Malibu, she took out her phone and dialed Kline's personal number. The director needed to know who was behind this. Who they were really dealing with.

The call immediately went to voicemail.

"Yellowstone." She said it like it was a curse, then started the car and tore out of the parking lot.

FORTY-FIVE

GARDINER, MONTANA

Two dusty SUVs rolled up the gravel track and pulled to a stop in front of the cabin where Volkov, Skvortsov, and a small contingent of Bratva soldiers from Chicago had spent the previous night and most of the day, sitting idle, waiting for guidance from Nightshade.

The appearance of the vehicles, while expected, sent a ripple of nervous energy through the Bratva men. They were used to being the toughest dogs on the street, so the arrival of a dozen hitters from Sibir Z—men with combat experience—must have seemed like a personal affront. For his part, Volkov didn't much care what the two groups thought of each other, as long as the job got done.

The men that got out of the vehicles did not look like mercenaries. They wore ordinary civilian attire—jeans and flannel shirts—which was better than camouflage for blending in with the seasonal workers and tourists who would be occupying the park. But the way they moved—quiet, disciplined, coiled like snakes ready to strike—revealed the truth of who they were.

Skvortsov approached one of the men and clasped his hand, pulling him into a quick, one-armed embrace with a solid clap on the back. "Sasha. You made good time."

Sasha's expression was dour. "We are . . . motivated."

The last word was full of menace, and Volkov knew exactly why. These men knew of the fate that had befallen their comrades in Michigan and were eager to avenge them.

Skvortsov shot a glance at Volkov before replying. "All in good time, Sasha."

Sasha cocked his head to the side. "What are we waiting for?"

It was a question Volkov had asked himself repeatedly since making the long drive from Chicago to Montana.

Nightshade had put them on the trail of Decker's accomplice, Matthew Redd, and surmised that the men were headed to Redd's home in Montana. But then, while they were still en route, Nightshade had called with new information.

"Decker has already left Montana."

Volkov's heart had sunk a little. His greatest fear had been that Decker, realizing that he was now the hunted, would be impossible to track. "Where is he going?"

"It doesn't matter. What matters is that he left his children there. He thinks they will be safe, but he's wrong. Take his children, and he will come to you."

Of course, it hadn't been as easy as that. Redd's wife, evidently recognizing the potential risk, had taken off with Decker's children. Volkov had countered by having Petrovich put the word out to his network of street-level operatives to be on the lookout for Emily Redd, and in short order, they had pinpointed her location in Yellowstone National Park.

And then one of those operatives had screwed up royally, botching an attempt to abduct Decker's daughter. Now the FBI was crawling all over the park, providing direct security for the families.

It was yet another spectacular failure in the hunt for Aaron Decker, and Volkov had already exhausted his reserve of second chances. Yet, when Nightshade had contacted him again, there had been no anger in his voice. *"Patience, Grigori. This is a chess game. When all the pieces are in place, I will give you the signal."*

That was it. No threats. No rage. And somehow, that was worse.

"This is a chess game."

A chess game that Nightshade was playing. But what did that mean for Volkov? Was he just a pawn to be sacrificed when the time was right?

He had no illusions about what would be expected of him.

When Nightshade gave the signal, Volkov would go into the park and take Decker's children, no matter how many guns were pointed at him.

He'd sent scouts in to get the lay of the land and knew that there were at least half a dozen FBI agents patrolling the vicinity of the campsite. Just getting close would mean walking into a hornet's nest, and Volkov had no doubt it would end in blood. His men's blood. Federal agents' blood. Maybe his own.

It was madness. And yet, Volkov would do it.

Because this was the only path to redemption, and because if he failed, he was dead anyway.

They had been here ever since, in a rented cabin near the park entrance, where they could still get cell reception as long as they were outside, waiting for Nightshade to give the signal. Volkov hoped that with the addition of reinforcements from Sibir Z, the odds of success might improve, but what then?

Even if they succeeded—took the children, lured Decker to his death—the FBI would not simply pack up and leave. They would come, in numbers Volkov couldn't match, and there would be no escaping the blowback. Once Nightshade's business with Decker was concluded, Volkov would face the fallout alone.

But what else could he do? This was the path he would have to walk. There was no turning from it now.

Skvortsov was explaining the plan to Sasha, only in his version, once the primary objective was completed, they would melt away into the woods, travel cross-country to Canada, and from there, make their way back to Eastern Europe.

It was a nice fantasy. And some of them might even make it out of the country, slipping across the border before the net closed. But no border would save Volkov.

The FBI would never stop hunting him, not after what they were about to do. And if they couldn't reach him legally, Volkov had no doubt they would send someone very much like Aaron Decker to exact the blood price.

He felt a vibration in his pocket, and his blood went cold. The world seemed to fold in on him. The sounds of Skvortsov's briefing and the rustle of pine branches moving in the wind were drowned out by the pounding of his pulse in his ears. He took his phone from his pocket, dreading what he would see.

And there it was. A text message from Nightshade.

Execute.

FORTY-SIX

YELLOWSTONE NATIONAL PARK, WYOMING

Gavin Kline held his granddaughter, rocking her gently as he watched the boys playing some sort of game that involved batting a pine cone around with sticks. Mitchell Decker and Jack seemed to have mostly perfected their technique, while Little Matty seemed content to simply hammer the ground with his stick as Rubble, Matthew's friendly but protective rottweiler, chased after the pine cone every time one of the boys sent it scudding into the woods.

It was all so perfect that Kline could almost believe this was an ordinary family outing. That they weren't currently being watched over by HRT operators, armed with assault rifles. That less than twenty-four hours earlier, this campsite had not been the scene of a terrifying attack.

He had broached the subject with Emily just once, shortly after arriving, not so much to make her relive the events of the previous night as to determine whether it had anything to do with the trouble Matthew had talked about, trouble that he now understood also involved Aaron Decker. Kline wasn't a great believer in coincidences. Emily hadn't really been able to shed much light on the situation, except to say that a threat from Decker's past had resurfaced. He and Matthew had gone off to deal with it, and then Matthew had called her and warned her to flee.

Kline suspected that the source of the threat to Decker was the same entity that had nearly killed him in Kyiv all those years ago, forcing him to fake his death and go underground. He knew that Decker probably had his reasons for playing his cards close to his vest, but maybe if Decker and Matthew had trusted Kline enough to loop him in on the situation, the ugliness of the previous night could have been avoided altogether.

Still, Kline reminded himself, what mattered was that they were safe now. Treadway was working the investigation, and if there was a thread leading to Decker's enemies, she would find it and pull it. For now, the only thing Gavin Kline needed to do was spend time with his family.

Lauren gurgled in his arms, one chubby hand clutching the fabric of his camp shirt.

"You're a natural," Emily told him.

Kline chuckled softly, thinking that nothing could be further from the truth.

Just then, Brynn, who was busy at the camp stove, boiling water for hot cocoa, called out, "Okay, come and get it."

The boys cheered, sticks clattering to the ground as they abandoned their pine cone game without hesitation. Little Matty let out a whoop that was almost as big as he was, charging ahead with Jack and Mitchell close behind, all three of them jostling for position as they crowded around Brynn, who began passing out Styrofoam cups filled with rehydrated Swiss Miss cocoa and miniature marshmallows.

"Easy, guys," she said. "It's hot, so sip it slowly."

Kline just watched, letting himself savor the moment. It was all so ordinary, so achingly normal. The sort of thing he'd never imagined himself enjoying.

He had never wanted a family. Had willingly passed up the opportunity when it had presented itself, allowing another man to raise his son. He thought of family life as an anchor. Some people needed to be anchored to weather life's storms, but anchored ships didn't go anywhere.

But standing here now, holding his granddaughter's chubby hand, watching the kids play, he found himself wondering if being anchored was so terrible after all.

"Want some?" Brynn called out, looking their way.

Emily raised her hand in a *no thank you* gesture, then turned to Kline. "You want?"

Before Kline could answer, he glimpsed movement from the corner of his eye and turned to see two black SUVs rolling slowly down the gravel road toward them. When the vehicles were still about a hundred yards out, a pair of HRT operators, guarding the perimeter, stepped into the road, rifles low but ready, palms raised to halt the vehicles. Curious, Kline watched as one of them approached the vehicle and began speaking with the driver. After a brief exchange, the HRT agent straightened and stepped aside, calling out something that Kline couldn't make out. The two SUVs rolled forward again, continuing toward the campsite.

Emily glanced at Kline. "Friends of yours?"

"I'm not sure," he replied, gently passing Lauren back to her and starting toward the road. He was more curious than concerned. Whoever was riding in the SUVs, they had passed muster with the HRT boys, so they clearly weren't a threat.

The vehicles halted, and a quartet of men in standard black suits got out, quickly moving to take up positions fore and aft of the vehicles, scanning the area with the discerning eye of professional bodyguards. Kline's first thought was that they must be Secret Service, but he couldn't imagine anyone on that relatively short list of Secret Service protectees who might have cause to visit him out here. Or for that matter, even knew where to find him.

Then another man emerged from the second vehicle, and the mystery was solved. The men in suits weren't Secret Service but their counterparts from the Pentagon Force Protection Agency, and the visitor they were protecting was none other than the secretary of defense.

Kline's first thought was that it had to be about the conversation they'd had the previous day in his office. A quick follow-up with updates about Russian organized crime, concerns about "an uptick in coordinated activity."

Still, an unannounced visit to the Hoover Building was one thing. Flying out west and tracking Kline down in the middle of nowhere . . . That was a whole new level of concern.

"Mr. Secretary," Kline said, stepping forward with a hand extended. "I think it goes without saying that you're just about the last person I expected."

The SecDef accepted the handclasp, but his expression was anything but welcoming. His posture seemed unusually tense as he scanned the campsite before bringing his gaze back to Kline. "You're a hard man to reach, Director."

"I'm taking some personal time," replied Kline. It was more or less true. "That said, if you needed to reach me, I'm sure the Bureau could have found a way to put us in touch. You didn't need to come all the way out here."

"I'll get right to the point, Director. Earlier this morning, we intercepted signal traffic indicating that an action was imminent."

"What sort of action?"

"Violent action."

"Where?" Kline asked.

"Here."

"Wyoming?"

The SecDef's eyes narrowed. "Yellowstone. Here."

Kline's breath caught, though on some level he wasn't surprised.

The timing of the attack on Emily and the kids, Matthew and Decker vanishing to deal with whatever shadow from Decker's past had resurfaced, the sudden spike in chatter the SecDef's people had flagged . . . Of course, it was all connected.

"And the fact that you're here," the secretary went on, "either means you knew about this and didn't share it with me . . . or you're the target."

"I didn't know," Kline said slowly. "Or I should say, I didn't realize there was a connection. Now I'm starting to."

He glanced back toward the campsite. Emily, still holding Lauren, was watching them intently.

"Well, I'm not going to pretend to understand what this is all about," the SecDef was saying. "But I think the best course of action is to immediately move you to a safe location."

"We've taken precautions." Kline gestured to the HRT agents up the road. "Those guys are just the ones you can see."

The SecDef's expression hardened, a grim finality in his voice. "If what we're hearing is even close to accurate, whatever precautions you've taken aren't going to be enough. The Russians are coming. And they're bringing an army."

Kline stood there for a moment, weighing the SecDef's words.

"Bringing an army."

Of course, the head of America's military organization would see it in those terms—as a war.

But what if he was right?

If it had just been his own life in the balance, Kline might have been tempted to stand his ground, meet the enemy head-on. But the Russians weren't coming for him. They were coming for Emily and the kids . . . coming for Brynn and Mitchell Decker.

No way was he going to take chances with their lives.

"Okay," Kline said quietly. "You've made your point."

The SecDef gave a small nod, his relief hidden beneath the severity of his expression. "We need to get you all somewhere safe. Now."

Kline exhaled, steadying himself, already shifting out of grandpa mode and into cop mode. "All right. I'll give the family the news."

He turned, striding quickly back toward the campsite, scanning the tree line the way the HRT operators had been doing all morning, looking for threats. When he reached Emily, he did his best to project calm, even though he knew she would see through him. "We're going to relocate," he said. "Pack the kids up. Leave everything else behind. I'll send someone to retrieve it."

"What's wrong?" She looked past him toward the black SUVs, the men in suits, and the secretary of defense, all looking around anxiously.

"It's just a precaution," he said. "I'll explain on the way."

She pursed her lips, clearly wanting more information, but then nodded and turned away. "Brynn, we're going for a little ride. Can you get the boys loaded up?"

Satisfied that Emily was on board, Kline jogged back up the road, passing the SecDef, and waved one of the HRT agents over to update him. The man started toward him.

"We're moving out—" Kline began but was cut off by a loud crack. The sudden noise startled him, but it was only when he saw the operator collapse forward, a hole the size of Kline's pinky finger punched through the back of his Kevlar helmet, that Kline realized what had just happened.

"Sniper!" he shouted, backpedaling away from the fallen man. He spun and sprinted for the nearest cover—the SecDef's SUV—reaching it even as another round slammed into the vehicle's rear window. The ballistic glass spiderwebbed, a white bloom radiating from the point of impact, but the glass held. Kline zigged to the left, continuing along the side of the vehicle. Ahead, the Pentagon security team was already bundling the SecDef into the rear of the SUV. Kline only had one thought—to get his family out of harm's way—but as he passed the SUV, one of the bodyguards grabbed him by the collar and forcibly propelled him toward the still-open door the SecDef had just used. The secretary pulled him into the spacious interior and shouted for the driver to go. Then, before Kline could protest, the SecDef addressed him.

"We're going to get all of you to safety," he said, as the SUV began rolling forward, passing the lead vehicle, which had turned sideways to provide a degree of cover for the people in the campsite beyond. The SecDef's driver continued forward, pulling up to the campsite, where Emily and Brynn were still in the process of rounding everyone up. When the SUV stopped, the secretary gripped Kline's shoulder. "Stay with your family. We'll provide front and rear security."

Kline nodded, still trying to process the sudden escalation. The SecDef's warning had not come a moment too soon.

The secretary held his gaze a moment longer, then turned to the man sitting in the right-side seat. "Give him your radio."

The Pentagon bodyguard immediately unclipped his handset and handed it over to Kline, who recognized it as a standard military issue PRC-148 Multiband Inter/Intra Team Radio—MBITR. Kline accepted the radio, then threw the door open, half falling out of the vehicle.

He heard the crack of gunfire coming from up the road—the rest of the HRT team engaging with the as-yet-unseen hostiles. Mindful of the sniper, whose location and angle of fire remained unknown, Kline moved at a crouch toward the Tahoe, where Emily and Brynn were still in the process of shoving the boys inside. Rubble was barking wildly, hackles raised, but thankfully stayed close to his charges.

"Just get in!" Kline shouted. "Stay on the floor until I tell you otherwise."

Emily shot him a questioning look but heeded his admonition, boosting Little Matty inside and into Mitchell's waiting arms before climbing in after him, all the while hugging Lauren to her breast. Brynn and Jack climbed inside as well, the boy turning and coaxing Rubble to join them. As soon as the rottie was aboard, Kline closed the rear door and slid into the driver's seat, starting the engine.

"Everybody, stay down!" he shouted, then keyed the MBITR. "This is Kline. We're set!"

As soon as he released the push-to-talk, he heard the SecDef's reply. "Roger. Pull up ahead of us and follow the leader."

Even as the message came in, the SecDef's SUV began moving, cutting a tight arc to face back up the road, but did not immediately advance. The other vehicle in the blocking position also began moving, rolling back onto the road, leaving plenty of room for Kline to pull in behind.

Kline depressed the accelerator, pulling away from the campsite and steering the Tahoe onto the road, pulling close to the lead SUV, which began rolling forward as soon as they got to within a few car lengths, accelerating quickly to lead them all off the X. The big SUV's tires threw up a prodigious dust cloud, all but obscuring it from view. Kline had to fight the urge to back off, giving the other vehicle some space, and instead, maintained pressure on the gas pedal, keeping the other vehicle's bumper in view. The trailing SUV carrying the SecDef quickly closed in from behind, forming a tight formation, with the up-armored vehicles bracketing the thin-skinned Tahoe.

As they passed the body of the HRT agent felled by the sniper, Kline felt a lump of emotion rise into his throat. The man had died protecting them, protecting *his* family, and the rest of his team was fighting even now, holding the line, sacrificing themselves so that Kline could get the others out of harm's way.

He swallowed hard, bringing his eyes back to the road, vowing that their sacrifice would not be in vain.

The lead SUV picked up speed, and Kline matched it, feeling the Tahoe's suspension shudder across the washboard ruts in the road. Over the din, he could hear the sharp reports of rifle fire erupting from the tree line.

There was a sudden crack as one of the rounds struck the rear right window, transforming the glass into a cascade of pebble-sized fragments that rattled onto the seats and floorboards.

Kline ducked reflexively, then glanced back to check on his passengers, who were still huddled in the footwell. Emily and Brynn were covering the children with their bodies. Rubble was the only voice of complaint, letting out a low wail as the interior filled with dust, sucked in through the window opening.

He returned his attention forward, but through the haze of dust, he glimpsed a pair of figures crouched behind trees at the roadside. They wore jeans and flannel and might have looked like ordinary hikers if not for the black plate carriers strapped over their shirts and the carbines they held at the high ready, tracking the Tahoe as it passed.

Over the low rumble of road noise, Kline heard multiple overlapping reports and knew that they were entering the kill zone, where the hostiles had massed in an effort to cut off their escape.

He felt the jolt as a bullet struck the rear quarter panel and hunched forward, almost leaning against the steering wheel, keeping steady pressure on the accelerator. Another round glanced off the windshield. The glass held together, but a spiderweb pattern of cracks radiated from the point of impact. More bullets found the Tahoe, the noise of the impacts rattling like a jackhammer. Without the SecDef's armored SUVs drawing some of the fire, Emily's Chevy would have already been torn apart.

One round shattered the window beside him, showering him in jewel-like fragments of glass. Another glanced off the windshield, multiplying the web of cracks, but still the glass held. The steering wheel shuddered in Kline's hands as he kept the Tahoe tight on the lead vehicle's tail.

And then, as suddenly as it had begun, the sound of gunfire diminished and ceased altogether. Kline waited a few seconds before slowly raising his head.

A moment later, he felt a hard jolt as first the front wheels then the rear transitioned from the gravel road onto pavement. The ride immediately smoothed as they hit the highway. The lead SUV made a sharp left and began picking up speed. Kline, caught by surprise, hauled the wheel over, skidding into the turn, the Tahoe's tires shrieking across the pavement. Behind them, the SecDef's vehicle completed the turn and charged ahead to resume the formation.

It was only then, as they accelerated away, that the dust cloud finally dissipated, the wind sweeping through the Tahoe's interior and clearing the air. Still blinking the grit from his eyes, Kline risked a glance back, seeing Emily and Brynn still crouched over the children, Rubble wedged in beside them, eyes wide and panting.

"Everyone okay back there?" he called, voice rough with dust and tension.

For a moment there was nothing but the quiet rush of air through the shattered windows and the hum of the tires on the pavement, the silence somehow more unsettling than the chaos they'd just passed through.

Then Emily's voice came, clear and steady. "We're all okay. Thank God."

"Thank God," Kline echoed, exhaling.

He turned his eyes back to the road, the dust gone now, the path ahead clear. The convoy pressed on, heading deeper into the park. But even as they sped away, Kline knew the Russians weren't finished with them yet.

FORTY-SEVEN

Redd gazed out the small side window at a patchwork of dark timber, winding rivers, and pale meadows dusted with the last stubborn patches of snow. From eighteen thousand feet above, the world's original national park looked both wild and tranquil.

But Redd knew better.

Anderson's words still rang in his memory.

"He's going to kill them, and then he's going to find you . . ."

Redd had to force himself to breathe. Emily and the kids were down there, tucked away in those trees where he had sent them, trusting his promise that they would be safe. But that was a promise he couldn't keep. Nightshade knew where they were, knew also that Kline was with them. For all Redd knew, Nightshade might already have made a move against them, and there was nothing he could do to get to them faster.

It had been a mad dash back to Colorado Springs. Redd kept the rental's speedometer pinned at exactly ten miles over the limit, fighting the urge to go faster. Decker sat in the passenger seat, quiet but restless, clearly as anxious as Redd to rejoin his family. Thrasher had taken the other rental, along with a still-bound-and-gagged Anderson, and headed for an undisclosed location, where he hoped to persuade his former teammate to flip on Nightshade.

Skids had them in the air within minutes of their arrival at the field, heading north, but Yellowstone still felt impossibly distant. They flew VFR to avoid having to file a flight plan, not to hide their movements, but simply in the interest of saving time. Every minute that they weren't there for their loved ones was an ordeal.

The miles and hours slipped by, the landscape unrolling beneath them in slow motion, each passing ridge and river a reminder of how far they still had to go.

Decker leaned back in his seat, arms folded across his chest, eyes half lidded. "We're not going to make this thing fly any faster by worrying. The best thing we can do for them right now is to make sure that we're physically and mentally sharp when we get there. And after what you went through today, you probably need rest more than I do."

Redd knew Decker was right, but he just couldn't switch off. Rest felt like a luxury he couldn't afford, even though his aching body disagreed.

Finally, Skids's voice called back from the cockpit. "We're ten minutes out. I'm going to start depressurizing now."

The words snapped Redd from his restless vigil. He felt the shift in his center of gravity as Skids began descending, and he had to repeatedly pop his ears as cabin pressure equalized with the outside air. Gradually, the plane lowered from cruising altitude down to around ten thousand feet, which seemed very close given the park's mean elevation of around eight thousand feet.

Redd and Decker spent the remaining minutes strapping into their newly acquired parachute rigs. On their way back from High Ground Tactical, they had made a quick stop at a skydiving outfitter in Cañon City, where Decker—who had kept his FAA Master Rigger certification current—purchased a pair of Performance Design Spectre canopies, which he'd personally inspected and packed into Sun Path Javelin Odyssey containers while Redd looked on uneasily. He had been less than enthused when Decker suggested that they could save a lot of time by jumping directly into the park rather than trying to find a place to land nearby and then procuring vehicles to drive the rest of the way. He wasn't afraid of making a jump—he'd done plenty of them in the Marines and agreed that it was probably the fastest way to get to Emily and the kids—but that didn't mean he was excited at the prospect.

Skids had taken a lot more convincing. The Cessna 414 wasn't designed as a parachuting platform. Everything about it was wrong for a jump: the narrow cabin, the low side door, the slipstream that could catch a jumper wrong and slam them against the tail or pull them under the stabilizer. It was pressurized, which meant he'd have to descend and fully depressurize before opening the door, and even then, there was the risk of cabin turbulence when the door was opened at one hundred knots. And Skids had made it clear he wasn't keen on putting the plane on autopilot while he crawled back to man the door for two lunatics wanting to hurl themselves into the Wyoming backcountry.

In the end, of course, money had talked, and Skids happily pocketed another cash bonus, admitting that he was kind of looking forward to tossing them out of the plane, even if they were wearing parachutes and going of their own free will.

"I'm not saying this hasn't been fun," he'd said. "But if I never see you guys again, it will be too soon."

After gearing up, the two men safety checked each other, ensuring that all the straps and buckles were secure and that their weapons, now openly holstered, weren't going to work loose during the drop. Redd had traded in the suppressed Glock for his prized Korth NXS. If things got hairy down on the ground, he wanted the stopping power of a Magnum rather than the quiet anonymity of the 9mm semiauto.

At the two-minute mark, Skids locked in the autopilot and came back to join them. "You yahoos sure you want to go through with this?"

Redd didn't reply, because truthfully, he wasn't at all sure, but Decker flashed a thumbs-up, and Skids accepted that as good enough. He braced himself against the frame, pulled the latch, and with a sharp yank, the door cracked open, instantly filling the cabin with a rush of cold air and noise.

Skids glanced at his watch, then back at them, shouting over the wind. "Get ready. On my mark!"

Decker stepped up to the opening. Redd was right behind him. Below, the ground looked very close.

This is it.

Redd took a breath, steadying himself, forcing the noise in his head to go silent.

Skids raised three fingers, then two, then one.

"Go!"

Decker launched himself through the narrow doorway without hesitation, angling his body as he cleared the slipstream, pulling his arms in tight to avoid being spun sideways or slammed into the tail.

"No spoon," Redd whispered and then followed.

The rush of freezing air stole his breath as he dropped into the slipstream. He remembered to tuck his knees and elbows to reduce drag and clear the aircraft. The wind roared in his ears, tearing at his cheeks, the cold biting through his clothes as he felt the unmistakable drop in his gut while Yellowstone rushed up to meet him.

He didn't want to feel the rush, but it came anyway.

His heart hammered, the air roaring past like a living thing, the clarity of the moment pressing every other worry from his mind.

The feeling didn't last long.

Just ten seconds after leaving the aircraft, Decker deployed his chute. As his canopy blossomed open, Redd reached back, found the pilot chute handle, and yanked it out, throwing it into the slipstream. It caught the rushing air, simultaneously pulling him into the correct body position and yanking the container open and dragging the deployment bag clear. Redd tilted his head back, watching the lines snake out in a blur. If they got fouled or the canopy failed to inflate, he would have only seconds to either fix the problem or jettison the chute and pop the reserve.

But the deployment was clean. The canopy ballooned open, and he was jerked upright. It felt as if the very hand of God had snatched him out of freefall, though compared to his military jumps, the shock was quite mild. In an instant, the rushing sound faded into the quiet hiss of canopy flight.

They'd chosen to freefall for only ten seconds to buy themselves more altitude under canopy, giving them time to steer, to correct for wind, and to line up precisely over the campsite rather than risk a long trek if they missed the mark. It was a calculation that made sense in the plane, and now, suspended beneath the open canopy, Redd was grateful for it.

The ground, which had seemed like a green blur a moment ago, sharpened into detail as he descended. Redd worked the toggles, shifting his body weight to slip left and then right as needed, making minor corrections as he searched for the landmarks that would guide them to the campsite.

He quickly found the bend of Willow Creek and the gray ribbon of Grand Loop Road cutting across the landscape. Once he spotted the dusty snake of the gravel access road that led into the campsite, he began a corkscrew descent, turning circles around the spot where he knew the camp lay. As he drifted lower, more details emerged. He saw a pair of tents—little more than brightly colored geometric patterns peeking through the trees—right where he would have positioned them. Further out, near the junction with the highway, he saw a pair of parked vehicles—black SUVs, though it was impossible to determine their make from the air. He guessed they were federal motor pool rigs. Hadn't Gavin promised to send agents to watch over Emily and the kids?

Then a tingle of apprehension shot up his spine.

Where was Emily's vehicle?

His thoughts spun with possibilities, both dire and mundane. He tried to convince himself of the latter. Maybe they had all gone sightseeing, driven out to see Old Faithful.

I'm coming, Em.

Ahead and below, he saw Decker's canopy angling toward a clearing maybe two hundred yards from the camp. Redd followed, adjusting course to align himself with Decker's approach.

They dropped lower, passing the tops of the trees. Redd felt the familiar tension of anticipation in his legs and shoulders. Landing was the worst part of any jump.

At ten feet, he flared the canopy, pulling down hard on the toggles, letting the forward speed bleed away as he shifted his feet into landing position, knees bent, body loose, ready to roll if he caught uneven ground. He hit, hard enough to feel it but controlled, letting his knees flex, taking two quick steps before the canopy collapsed behind him.

Redd turned immediately, grabbing the risers and pulling the canopy toward him, bundling it against his chest to keep it from reinflating and catching the wind. When he had the chute in its stuff sack, he pulled off his goggles, oriented himself in the direction of the camp, and started running through the woods.

"Em!" Some part of him knew she wasn't there, knew shouting her name wouldn't make a bit of difference, but he couldn't stop himself. "Emily!"

Decker was beside him, moving like a shadow, quiet and controlled, eyes scanning ahead even as Redd crashed through the brush. Redd sensed the other man's disapproval. They were approaching an unknown situation. There was no reason to give up the element of surprise by announcing their presence, but Decker made no attempt to silence him. The lives of his loved ones were on the line too.

Then the trees thinned, and they broke through onto the edge of the campsite. Redd skidded to a stop, taking in the scene. The tents were still there, fabric rippling in the gentle breeze. Three folding chairs were arranged to one side of the cold fire pit. A blue enamel pot sat on a camp stove nearby.

At first glance everything looked neat and orderly, as if waiting for the return of the campers. But then Redd noticed a scattering of white Styrofoam cups on the ground. Emily would never have allowed the kids to leave their trash out in the open like that.

"Something's wrong."

Suddenly, Decker was grabbing his arm. "Matt, look."

Redd followed the line of Decker's finger and saw it. A shape on the roadside, maybe seventy-five yards away.

A body.

FORTY-EIGHT

Redd hauled out the NXS and started running toward the discovery. Decker, Glock in hand, kept pace, scanning in all directions for possible threats. As they drew close, Redd saw that the figure—lying face down—was in full combat gear, but it wasn't until they were standing over the body that they saw a bullet hole in the man's Kevlar helmet and the dark pool of blood spreading out from under. There was a patch affixed to the back of the man's plate carrier—three letters: *FBI.*

The sight stole the last vestiges of hope from Redd's heart. They were too late. Nightshade had come for their families.

Decker had rolled the body over and was saying something.

"What?" Redd was barely able to get the question out.

"He's still warm," Decker repeated, looking up at Redd. "This can't have happened too long ago. An hour at most."

Redd sucked in a breath, trying to anchor himself, to think.

Decker rose, gripped Redd's biceps. "Matt, we don't know what this means. Emily's truck isn't here. It could mean they made it out when the shooting started."

Redd seized on the explanation like a lifeline. The presence of an FBI agent, even a dead one, meant that Gavin had followed up on his promise to keep an eye on his family, and that he had brought backup. Clearly, something had happened, but the fact that the Tahoe was gone seemed to support Decker's explanation. He managed a nod. "Yeah, okay."

Decker released his arm, then knelt over the fallen agent, retrieving his weapon—a Heckler & Koch HK416—and carefully removing the man's plate carrier, along with its supply of spare magazines, draping it over his own shoulders. "Let's head up to the highway," he said when he was finished. "Maybe we'll be able to get a better idea of what happened."

Redd nodded again, trying to keep the panic beast at bay, and fell in beside Decker as they started down the gravel road at a steady jog. A few hundred yards further along, Redd spotted a scattering of spent brass scattered in the dirt.

He knelt, picking up one of the casings, rolling it between his fingers.

"Five-five-six," he murmured.

"Matt," said Decker, moving off a few yards. "Over here."

Redd stood to follow and saw another body, partially concealed behind a tree. Like the first, he wore FBI kit, but unlike the man felled by a single shot, this agent had sustained several wounds before going down.

"They put up a fight," Decker said quietly, his voice calm, steady. "Maybe bought the others time to make it out."

Redd swallowed hard, trying to convince himself that Decker was right, that these men hadn't died for nothing. That Emily and the kids had made it out.

A sound—faint at first but quickly growing louder—intruded into the quiet whisper of the woods. It was the sound of gravel crunching under tires. Redd, still gripping his NXS, knelt down, trying to keep a low profile as he watched the road. Beside him, Decker raised the 416 to his shoulder and waited for the approaching vehicle to appear. The sound grew louder, and then through the trees they saw it, a silver Chevrolet Malibu.

"That's government issue," Decker said, lowering his weapon.

Redd was inclined to agree. The Malibu was a favorite fleet vehicle in federal motor pools, which meant there was a very good chance it was being driven by one of Gavin's agents.

He rose from his hiding place and started toward the road, keeping the NXS drawn but pointed down to avoid giving the appearance of a threat.

The driver of the Malibu braked suddenly, skidding on the loose gravel, and then the door flew open and a dark-haired woman stepped out: Special Agent Stephanie Treadway, Gavin Kline's protégé.

Redd started to call out to her, but she spoke first. "Aaron!"

From beside Redd, Decker replied, "Steph?"

The casual familiarity caught Redd by surprise. He glanced over at Decker. "You two know each other?"

But Decker was already running ahead.

Treadway watched him, a noticeable flush touching her cheeks. Her arms hovered awkwardly for a moment, as if she couldn't decide whether to cross them, reach for him, or just stand there.

Decker halted a few steps away, looking similarly uncertain about what to do with himself. They stared at each other, neither seeming to know what to say. Then, in perfect unison, they both blurted, "What are you doing here?"

The words collided, hanging in the air. A half smile tugged at the corner of Treadway's mouth before she bit it back, tucking a loose strand of hair behind her ear, her gaze dropping for a moment before meeting his again.

Redd stopped a few paces back, taking it all in. "Okay," he muttered. "I guess that answers my question." Then, louder, he said, "Where's Emily?"

Treadway's eyes widened at the question, then her forehead creased in concern. "She's not here?"

Redd shot a glance at Decker, who fielded the question. "There's no one here."

Treadway's eyes began darting back and forth as if processing this revelation.

"You know something," Redd prompted.

She nodded. "I just came in from Bozeman. I was running down a lead on the guys that tried to kidnap Brynn—"

"Brynn was kidnapped?" Decker broke in.

Treadway shook her head. "*No*. We stopped them. But they were taking orders from the Russian mob."

"Russians," muttered Decker. "Volkov."

"Nightshade must still be using him to hunt you down," Redd said.

Treadway listened to the exchange with a bewildered look. "You knew about them? I just found out. Only I couldn't reach Gavin because there's no cell coverage out here—"

"How much backup did he bring?" Redd asked, cutting her off.

"I don't know exact numbers. I got here last night but then went to handle things in Bozeman. Gavin arrived this morning and was staying with your family."

"We found two bodies. FBI agents."

Treadway went pale. "Let me think." She swallowed. "I'm pretty sure Gavin brought an HRT team with him. Beyond that, I can't say for sure."

Redd felt his own panic rising again but forced it down. "Emily's truck is gone. There's no sign of Gavin or anyone else."

"We think they might have made a run for it," added Decker. "Do you have any idea where they might have gone? Was there an evac plan?"

Treadway shook her head. "If there was, nobody told me. I didn't pass them on the way in. Maybe they went the other way?"

Redd reviewed his mental map of the park. Yellowstone could be a trap as easily as it could be a sanctuary. It was vast, but there were only so many ways in and out. And if they'd made it back to Grand Loop Road, they would only have two options. Left or right.

East or west.

West would take them back toward Mammoth and the North Entrance. If Gavin had just wanted to get out of the park, that was the logical choice. The shortest distance to civilization and cell phone reception where they could call for reinforcements. But Volkov might have anticipated that possibility and left some of his men behind as a blocking force just in case his quarry slipped through the net. Redd didn't know if his father knew his way around the park, but he'd know enough to avoid a choke point.

That left east.

East on the Grand Loop meant following the road toward Tower Junction where they could either turn onto the Northeast Entrance Road, head through the Lamar Valley, and if they stayed the course, eventually reach Cody, or alternately, they could head south into Yellowstone's interior and some of the park's most popular attractions, like Old Faithful and Norris Geyser Basin, where they would not only likely find crowds but also a cell signal. Either way, heading east would give him a lot more options.

"That's probably what they did," agreed Redd.

"Volkov won't give up," said Decker. "We need to go after them."

Treadway nodded and jerked her thumb back at the Malibu. "Hop in."

They climbed into the Malibu, with Redd consciously choosing the back seat, allowing Decker to sit up front with Treadway. As soon as they were all in, Treadway attempted to turn the car around without driving off the road, a move that required several back-and-forth adjustments—somehow making a three-point turn into a seven-point turn. She finally got the Malibu turned around but headed down the road at a snail's pace. Redd clenched his fists and kept his mouth shut. He hated being a passenger under the best of circumstances, hated not being in control, not being able to *do* something. The fact that Emily and his kids were out there, in danger, only made it worse.

They broke through the tree line onto the Grand Loop, the broad sweep of the road curving away through the pines. Up ahead, two black SUVs were parked on the shoulder.

"Stop," Redd shouted.

Treadway braked hard, the Malibu sliding forward on the gravel. Redd was out the door before the car had fully rocked back, running toward the nearest SUV.

The vehicle, a newer-model Ford Expedition, was empty, but the engine was quietly running. It was a common practice for law enforcement agents to leave their vehicles powered up and idling for quick deployment.

He turned and waved to Treadway and Decker. "Come on. Let's go."

Treadway leaned out the open window of the Malibu. "Why? We're already rolling."

Redd shook his head. "This rig can go places your ride can't."

Decker, signaling his agreement, was already out, moving toward the waiting Expedition. With an audible sigh of frustration, Treadway twisted the wheel, pulling the Malibu off onto the shoulder. Decker circled around the front of the Expedition but stopped dead in his tracks when he got to the other side.

"What is it?" asked Redd.

Decker looked up and met his gaze, then shook his head. Redd had a sinking feeling, already guessing the answer, but jogged around to have a look. Beside the Expedition, half concealed in the brush, lay the body of another FBI agent, helmet askew, eyes open but unseeing.

Redd heard a gasp behind him and turned to find Treadway, looking down in horror at the dead agent. "Oh, my gosh."

Redd turned to her and, marshaling his emotions, said simply, "Get in."

Treadway looked like she wanted to say something but instead just nodded and, stepping carefully past the grisly discovery, opened the rear passenger door. Redd went back to the driver's side and got in, shifting the Expedition into drive and pulling away as soon as Decker and Treadway were aboard.

Just being behind the wheel made him feel a little better. He hadn't been exaggerating about the superior capabilities of the four-wheel-drive-equipped Expedition. While the Grand Loop Road was paved, there were places in the park, especially at this time of year, where some extra traction and ground clearance might come in handy. But the real reason he had made the switch was to get himself into the driver's seat.

Still, as the big SUV picked up speed, racing down the Grand Loop Road heading east, Redd was all too aware of an unspoken reality. He didn't know how much of a head start Emily and Gavin had, but he did know that he was going to have to go through the Russians to get to them.

FORTY-NINE

Grigori Volkov sat in the passenger seat of the lead Yukon, watching the trees slide past beyond the fogged window. They had been climbing steadily for several miles now, the meadows giving way to thick pine forests and scattered snowdrifts that deepened as they gained elevation. Spring meant nothing up here; winter still had its claws in the pass.

Behind them, the second Yukon, driven by Sasha and carrying the rest of the Sibir Z mercenaries, trailed closely, while the third vehicle, a Toyota Land Cruiser bearing the Chicago mobsters, struggled to keep up. The road they were on was officially closed for the season, but that hadn't stopped Decker's family and their protectors from taking it, and it wasn't going to stop Volkov either.

They hadn't yet made visual contact with their quarry, who had a good ten-minute head start on them. It had taken that long to mop up the last of the FBI tactical team. The Americans had fought hard—two of Skvortsov's men had been wounded, though not seriously—but in the end, the numbers hadn't been on their side. The delay translated into a lead that would be hard to close, but Skvortsov, who sat in the driver's seat, was confident that they would catch up. "It is only a matter of time," he promised.

Volkov had no doubt that they would, as long as Skvortsov didn't get them all killed first. The mercenary leader drove the Yukon like he was playing a video game, racing into curves without slowing, letting the heavy vehicle drift until the four-wheel drive caught hold and snapped them back on course. After the first few times, Volkov stopped watching the road, but that didn't stop him from feeling it in his gut. Every slide, every shift.

The sharp electronic chirp of the Iridium Extreme satellite phone in the center console came as a welcome distraction. Skvortsov's team had brought several of the devices with them to maintain comms in an environment where traditional line-of-sight devices were all but useless. The magnetic antennas attached to the Yukon's roof allowed for clear satellite communication even here, deep in the park's interior.

Volkov grabbed the handset and hit the button to receive the call. *"Da?"*

There was a brief pause in which the only sound was the faint hiss of the electronic ether, then, "It's Ivan. At the North Entrance."

Ivan was one of Petrovich's enforcers. Volkov had left him and another of the Chicagoans behind, ostensibly to monitor the park entrance in case their quarry managed to slip through and head for that exit. The reality was that he was trying to reduce some of the friction between Petrovich's men and Skvortsov's mercenaries. The latter were professionals who trained for scenarios like this and worked as a unit. The Bratva men, while tough and loyal, would just get in the way.

Volkov couldn't imagine what news Ivan might have.

"We just saw something," Ivan went on. "Two men came down using parachutes."

"Parachutes?" A tingling sensation ran up the back of his neck. "Where?"

"Near your location, I think."

Volkov doubted Ivan knew their location; he probably meant the location of the campsite. If so, there could only be one explanation.

Decker.

It had to be him.

"Take his children and he will come to you," Nightshade had said.

They didn't even have to take them; the threat alone had sufficed to bring Decker out of hiding.

"What do you want us to do?" Ivan was saying.

Volkov hadn't figured that out yet, so he said, "Stand by. I will call back," then ended the call.

"Problem?" Skvortsov asked, not taking his eyes off the road as he negotiated another bend.

"Decker is here."

Now Skvortsov looked. "You are certain?"

"Two men just parachuted into the park." Volkov shook his head. "It is him. And his friend, Redd."

"Parachuted?" Skvortsov gave a short humorless laugh. "He's got some stones. I'll give him that." He paused a beat. "So, what do you want to do? Turn around?"

Volkov hesitated. That was the obvious answer. Decker's family had only ever been bait for the trap. Now, they were nothing more than a loose end, and whether or not they survived was irrelevant. Decker was the priority.

But what if Decker somehow slipped the trap again? He'd done it before, so many times that it seemed imprudent to assume he would not. "If we do that," Volkov said slowly, "and Decker gets past us, then we lose him *and* the bait."

Skvortsov snorted. "You're overthinking. We will just have to make sure he doesn't get past us."

Volkov looked ahead, watching the snowy road curve into the trees, then made his decision. "Stop here."

Skvortsov shot him a quick glance but did as ordered, tapping the brakes to signal his intention to the trailing vehicles before slowing to a full stop.

Volkov turned in his seat to face Skvortsov fully. "I want you to go on. Take your best men. I'll stay behind with the rest and deal with Decker myself."

Skvortsov narrowed his gaze, as if he was trying to decide if he was somehow being cheated. "Are you sure that's what you want to do?"

"Now who is overthinking?" said Volkov, laughing. "We will take care of Decker and his friend. You need to hunt down the others and deal with them, hopefully before they can send for reinforcements." Then, as if it might incentivize the mercenary, he added, "You'll be able to travel faster on your own."

Skvortsov accepted this with a hearty laugh, then got out and went back to discuss the plan with his men in the second Yukon. He took only one man to occupy Volkov's seat in the lead vehicle and put Sasha in charge of the rest of the force, directing him to follow Volkov's instructions. Then he returned to his vehicle and sped off.

Volkov watched him depart, then turned to Sasha. "Decker is probably already on his way here. We need to find a place to set an ambush. A choke point. Someplace Decker won't be able to get past."

Sasha smiled. "I know just the place."

FIFTY

Redd tapped the brakes as they rolled up on Tower Junction. There wasn't much in the way of signage—just one of the ubiquitous Park Service low-profile direction and mileage markers. Off to the right the Tower-Roosevelt service station remained shuttered, awaiting the official start of the tourist season, but a few cars were parked at the adjacent restroom facility, their occupants stretching their legs and taking a break, unaware that a deadly gun battle had taken place just down the road. Both the signs and the Expedition's live onboard GPS map showed the four-way junction that lay just ahead, and the choice they now faced.

To the right, a spur road led up to Roosevelt Lodge, though a barrier across the road indicated that it, like the service station, was still closed for the season. To the left was the Northeast Entrance Road, which all of the cars sharing the road with them were either turning onto or coming from. The GPS showed it veering away north and turning east, across the Yellowstone River and continuing on through the hills and mountains of the eastern limits of the park. Straight ahead, the Grand Loop Road continued onward, but nobody was taking it.

The road south was officially closed for the season. While the park had mostly thawed out, the Park Service did not plow or maintain the road through Dunraven Pass during the offseason, and sections of it were likely still snowed in. The short stretch of it visible from the intersection provided visual confirmation of the route's long dormancy. Wind and snowmelt had carried dirt, gravel, and other debris across the pavement in sweeping fans. The edges of the road were ragged, crumbling where frost and water had done their slow work through the winter.

But as Redd slowed the Expedition to a crawl, he could see that the steel barriers blocking the road had been knocked askew, creating an opening large enough for a vehicle to pass through.

Redd brought the Expedition to a full stop, letting it idle as he studied the empty stretch of road ahead.

Decker glanced over at him. "Which way?"

"That's the question," replied Redd. "My gut says they took the Loop."

"Sign says the road's closed. Probably a good reason for that."

"It's going to open in a couple weeks. The snow is mostly gone. And Emily's rig has four-wheel drive."

Decker gave an equivocal hum. "If we guess wrong, we'll lose any chance of catching up to them."

Treadway, who had been sitting quietly in the back, suddenly called out, "Hold on. I got a text from Gavin. It says, *Heading to Norris Geyser Basin. Send backup.*"

Redd felt an immediate sense of relief swell in his chest.

They made it out.

He tapped the GPS screen, scrolling down, dragging the map south until it was centered over a white smear that stood out in stark contrast to the green and brown of the surrounding forests.

Norris Geyser Basin.

Although it looked like a snowfield in the satellite display, Redd knew he was actually looking at vast silica flats where steam vents and boiling pools had created a mineral crust. The basin was one of the most heavily visited sections of the park. Tourists flocked there to see the geysers and the rainbow-colored hot springs. It was beautiful, but it was dangerous too. The pools were hot enough to strip flesh from bone. The hidden vents and fumaroles could erupt unexpectedly, and despite many posted warnings about the peril, it wasn't unusual for some reckless visitor to step off the boardwalk and break through the eggshell-thin mineral crust to be swallowed whole.

Even at this time of year, the basin would be busy, which was likely why Kline had chosen to make a run for it, hoping to find a degree of cover in the crowd.

Provided, of course, that the Russians cared about not making a public spectacle, which was by no means guaranteed.

There were two ways to reach the basin. They could backtrack to Mammoth and then head south on Highway 89, which was currently the only officially open route. Or they could do what Kline and Emily had done and continue on Grand Loop, risking Dunraven Pass. The first route guaranteed that they would get there, but it would take longer. Grand Loop Road, for all its uncertain risks, was still the fastest way.

"That's it then," he said and started forward again, steering the Expedition into the gap between the askew barrier and the roadside, and then putting the pedal down, accelerating down the barren road.

Behind him, Treadway cursed aloud. "Can't get a call out. Not enough bars. I'm surprised the text got through."

"When did he send it?" asked Decker.

Treadway swiped the screen a few times. "Looks like . . . about half an hour ago."

"Probably sent it from right here," muttered Decker, then glanced over at Redd. "Half an hour is quite a lead."

"Not on these roads," replied Redd. "They probably haven't made it to the basin yet. And hopefully Gavin didn't just send one text. With any luck, half the Bozeman field office will already be waiting for them when they get there."

The road climbed gently, following the gray thread of the Yellowstone River off to their left. With no traffic to dodge, Redd used every inch of the road, swinging wide on the curves. He wanted to wring out every bit of speed while he still could, before the conditions at higher elevations forced him to drive more cautiously.

Through breaks in the trees, Redd caught glimpses of the water far below, sunlight flashing on the black current as it wound through the gorge. A low stone barrier edged the roadside, marking the line between pavement and a fatal drop.

To the right, the forest seemed to be creeping toward the river, the upslope so steep in places that small rockslides had tumbled down onto the asphalt, encroaching into the lanes.

As they passed the pullout for the Calcite Springs Overlook, Redd spotted a vehicle—a red Toyota Land Cruiser—sitting in the parking lot.

It might have just been a rogue tourist, flaunting the *Road Closed* signs, but then again . . .

He glanced in the rearview, watching the unmoving vehicle as it receded behind them. "Aaron, did you catch that?"

Decker was already craning his head around, looking back. "Yeah."

There was enough concern in that lone syllable to assure Redd that he wasn't being paranoid. He spared another glance in the mirror, but the Cruiser was already hidden from view, as they rounded a corner—

Redd barely had time to slam on the brakes as a big green SUV appeared directly ahead of them, parked sideways across the road, blocking both lanes. There was no way around it. To the right was a sheer cliff wall. To the left, a stone guardrail and a drop-off beyond. The antilock braking kept him from skidding but extended the stopping distance to bring them within ten yards of the unmoving vehicle.

Because sighting the Land Cruiser had already primed his early warning system, Redd didn't wait for what he knew would happen next. Even before his brain consciously registered the armed figures stepping out from either end of the blocking vehicle, he shifted the transmission into reverse, hit the gas, and shouted, "Down!"

The world exploded in noise. Rifle reports. The sharp crack of rounds striking the hood and windshield, the glass starring with multiple impacts, then collapsing completely. The interior was suddenly alive with the vicious snap of supersonic rounds creasing the air.

But the Expedition was already surging backward, away from the trap, and as the distance increased, Decker slid his HK onto the glass-strewn dashboard and started returning fire. The first report set Redd's ears ringing. Everything after sounded as if his head was stuffed with wool. He kept his head low, eyes on the display from the backup camera, trying to mentally coordinate his control of the steering wheel with the fact that everything was flipped.

Thankfully, the blind corner worked both ways, and in a matter of just a second or two, they were back around the bend, out of the attackers' line of fire. Then Redd saw the red Land Cruiser appear in the display, charging up from the rear. Almost in the instant he spotted it, the other vehicle cut the road, skidding to a stop diagonally to block the escape route.

Redd didn't brake, didn't slow. He just gently moved the steering wheel, lining up the virtual backup path in the camera display with the Land Cruiser's rear quarter, and kept his foot pressed hard on the gas.

A moment later, the Expedition slammed into the Land Cruiser's tail with a heavy crunch. The collision snapped Redd's head forward. He felt the steering wheel fighting his grip as the rebound energy shunted the Expedition away from the impact and toward the upslope to the right. Redd felt a shudder rumble through the SUV's frame as the right tires dragged through loose rock and dirt at the road's edge, but from the corner of his eye, he saw the Cruiser's shattered rear corner spinning away, opening a path. Redd fought the wheel, steering the Expedition back onto the road.

Ahead, half a dozen men were spilling out of the Land Cruiser, rifles already coming up, but Decker was ready for them, loosing bursts from his 416. Ejected brass rebounded off the side window, flying everywhere, but Decker held steady, driving the hostiles down behind their vehicle while Redd kept the Expedition on course.

The turnoff to the overlook, where the Land Cruiser had been lurking, was rapidly drawing close. It was the perfect place for a quick turnabout, but as he contemplated the maneuver, Redd thought about what to do afterward.

Right now, he was just reacting to contact, getting clear of the ambush by the only available route. But it wasn't getting him any closer to Emily and the kids. He needed to get to Norris Basin, and the quickest way there was still Grand Loop Road, through Dunraven Pass.

He scanned the surrounding terrain, looking for a solution. From the overlook parking lot, there appeared to be a broad footpath on the river side, but he also knew that only a few hundred yards further up, the river passed through a narrow gorge, with no way past or around it. On the opposite side of the road, however, the story was very different. Unlike the sheer cliffs the Russians had used to box them in, here the slope met the road in a low rise of bare earth and scattered rock, like a ramp leading into the trees. Above, the slope remained shallow, studded with trees spaced wide enough for the Expedition to slip through.

Still, as inviting as the slope appeared, it did not necessarily represent a solution to the problem, not unless it afforded a route that would get him past the blockade and back onto the road.

As he came even with the overlook turnoff, he shifted his foot to the brake and steered backward into it, bringing the Expedition to a full stop. He quickly shifted into drive, changing the view on the display screen back to the GPS map, which not only showed the road, but also a top-down view of the surrounding terrain, and that showed the upslope area as a vast, treeless expanse, covering the low flank of the mountain to the west, skirting above the section of cliff where the Russians had set their trap and almost . . . *almost* rejoining the road again further south.

It'll do, he thought.

He dropped the transmission into neutral and spun the drive mode dial to 4L. The shift took a beat, but he heard the satisfying *thunk* as the transfer case engaged. In the time it took for that to happen, the Land Cruiser began turning around, even as the gunmen who had been riding in it advanced on foot, taking shots down the road at the momentarily idled Expedition. Turned broadside to the road as they were, Decker had no shot.

"Matt, what are we waiting for?" he shouted.

Redd didn't answer. He just slammed the gear selector to drive and applied steady pressure.

One didn't stomp the pedal when driving in low-range four-wheel drive. It was a system designed for power, not speed. The engine dropped into a low growl, the whole frame vibrating as it rolled forward across the asphalt and then began climbing the dirt at the base of the slope. The Expedition tilted up like an airplane taking off, throwing its occupants back into their seats, momentarily silencing Decker's protests. The incline wasn't steep, but the soil was loose, the tires spinning a little before catching. Redd kept steady pressure on the pedal, letting the low range do its work, the SUV creeping up the rise, slipping, then clawing forward, gaining ground. Finally the slope leveled out, the tires finding firmer ground, and the rig began picking up speed.

I'm coming, Em. Just hold on.

He checked the GPS again, looking for a way back to the road. There appeared to be nothing but open ground ahead, and if he stayed on a more or less southward course, he would eventually get there, but if there was one thing he'd learned from years of humping through the woods, both as a Marine and a hunter, it was that the map was not the territory. What looked like flat terrain on a map or satellite image might be broken by hills and gullies that didn't show up on a flat projection. And unlike a photograph from space, the landscape was always changing.

Still, the way ahead looked clear, and if it stayed that way, they just might make it.

Beside him, Decker breathed a soft curse, then unbuckled his seat belt. Redd started to ask what he was doing but glimpsed movement in the side mirror. The Land Cruiser had come up the hill after them.

It was slewing wildly, throwing up tails of loose earth as the driver fought for traction. Redd could tell the driver hadn't shifted into low range, and he was paying for it, but despite that, the Cruiser was making forward progress.

Decker squeezed through the gap between the seats and moved all the way to the Expedition's rear cargo area. Once there, he smashed out what was left of the rear window with the butt of his HK, then took aim at the Cruiser. Treadway joined him, steadying her aim on the back of the rear seat, and a moment later, the interior of the Expedition was filled with noise and smoke.

Redd tuned it out, keeping the wheel steady, eyes on the slope, but intermittently checking the GPS, looking for a line back to the road. For the moment, the GPS was in agreement with what he was seeing. And if that trend held true, in about five hundred more yards, he would come to a creek crossing and a loosely spaced stand of trees. If he could get through that, he'd hit what looked like a campground access road, which he would in turn be able to follow back to the main highway, well beyond the ambush site.

There were only about a hundred things that could go wrong with the plan, so he was optimistic.

The creek came up faster than he expected, and unlike what the satellite image appeared to show, there wasn't a gentle slope down to a placid stream. Instead, there was a three-foot drop into a torrent.

Redd barely had time to shout, "Hang on!" before the Expedition's front end rolled off the edge, dropping hard into the water.

The impact slammed through the suspension, throwing Decker and Treadway around like the last few nuts in the can. Frigid water exploded up over the hood, drenching Redd. Nevertheless, he kept the throttle steady, letting the tires churn through the water. For a moment, the current was in control, dragging them sideways, but then the front tires found the far bank. Redd kept steady pressure on the gas pedal and rocked the steering wheel back and forth, trying to line the Expedition up on the far bank.

Then they were through, climbing up the low rise onto solid ground. He slalomed through the lodgepole pines, low branches scraping at the sides, and then the trees thinned, and he saw blessed asphalt directly ahead.

He let off the gas, tapped the brake, and shifted into neutral, and as the SUV coasted onto the pavement, he spun the dial back to 4H. Strictly speaking, disengaging low range while moving was a very bad idea, but then so were most of the things he'd done in the last few minutes. As soon as he heard the *thunk* and saw the indicator light go green, he shifted back into drive and hit the gas.

Mud and dirt flew up into the air behind the Expedition as Redd accelerated down the narrow access road. The GPS showed the road winding through the trees for about four hundred yards before rejoining the Loop.

Perfect.

But then in the mirror, he saw the Land Cruiser burst out from the trees, clawing its way onto the pavement. Somehow, despite uneven terrain and the creek crossing, the other driver had found a shortcut and was just a hundred yards behind them. And now, gunmen were leaning out from the windows on both sides of the other vehicle.

Muzzle flashes flickered, simultaneous with the sharp cracks of rifle fire and rounds snapping through the interior of the Expedition. The shooters were riding on relatively smooth asphalt now, steady enough to aim and close enough to matter.

Decker and Treadway were still trying to recover their wits after getting bounced around during the creek crossing and were slow to return fire. All Redd could do was keep the pedal to the floor.

He could see the dot on the GPS closing in on the Loop Road, and then it was there in front of him, at the base of a low decline. He took the turn at speed, swinging wide, the tires shrieking as the Expedition drifted across the pavement.

Too late, he saw a dark shape appear in his periphery. The big SUV that had blocked the road earlier was attempting to cut them off again. Its front end seemed to fill the window frame, the big red letters—*GMC*—so close that Redd could have reached out to touch them.

Time stretched, cold adrenaline flooding his veins, sharpening everything.

There was no time to brake, no time to swerve.

That was probably what saved them.

The Expedition shot past the oncoming vehicle without making contact.

Redd felt the tires juddering across the gravel on the far shoulder and hauled the wheel over, steering back onto the road.

In the mirror he saw a flash of color as the Land Cruiser burst out of the intersection a fraction of a second later and heard the shriek of brakes as the driver tried to avoid hitting the GMC.

Too late.

The Cruiser clipped the big SUV's rear bumper. The GMC was knocked sideways, and then both vehicles were spinning out of control. The gunmen who had been leaning out of the Cruiser were flung into the air, and the vehicle's momentum sent it hurtling across the road and down the far embankment into a stand of lodgepoles. The shockwave from the collision vibrated the air in the Expedition's interior. The GMC managed to stay on the pavement, rocking to a stop in the middle of the road. Redd lost sight of it a moment later as the Expedition rounded a bend.

The adrenaline drained all at once, leaving him feeling utterly spent. Whether it was that or the rush of air coming in through the gap where the windshield had been and chilling his soaked body, he felt himself start to shiver.

With a conscious effort, he cleared his throat and called back, "Everyone okay?"

Behind him, Decker stirred and grunted, "I'll live."

"Jury's still out," moaned Treadway, but then added, "Let's not do that again, okay?"

Redd managed a wan smile. "Good thing we switched rides. Couldn't have done that in your Malibu."

Treadway rolled her eyes. "No one likes a showoff, Redd."

FIFTY-ONE

Gavin Kline had never been to Yellowstone before, but he'd seen plenty of pictures and documentaries depicting its unique geothermal features. So when the SecDef radioed early in their frantic journey away from the besieged campsite that they were heading to Norris Geyser Basin, he imagined the journey taking them into a surreal alien landscape, shrouded in steam with bubbling mud pots and eerily colored hot springs. But as they neared the turnoff to the basin, there was little indication, aside from a pervasive smell of rotten eggs, that anything had changed. Since escaping the pass—a fraught journey through miles of unplowed snowdrifts—the landscape had not changed much at all. Just mile after mile of forested hills.

Kline hadn't questioned the SecDef's choice of the geyser basin as a rally point. With a carful of frightened kids, and an unknown number of hostile shooters on their tail, he was just grateful for the assistance. But as they slipped and slid over roads that hadn't seen a single vehicle in months, he wondered what had really motivated the decision.

On the map, there was a certain logic to taking the road through the pass because it was a loop—hence the name—that would eventually bring them back around to the North Entrance, the quickest route to Bozeman, but that didn't explain the stop.

Kline figured the secretary knew something he didn't.

The ascent of the pass had been treacherous, but thankfully the SecDef's Suburban, which had moved to the front of the convoy, bore the brunt, packing down the snow for the trailing vehicles. It had been a slow process, and more than once, the protective detail had been obliged to dig the big SUV out. Eventually, the hard work paid off, and once they began the descent, they were able to make good time.

Up ahead, the secretary's Suburban slowed and then stopped, joining a line of cars waiting their turn at a four-way intersection. After nearly an hour of forward motion, sometimes slow but always constant, stopping left him feeling vulnerable. He checked the mirrors, looking for signs of pursuit, but saw only the trailing Suburban.

As he had done several times since starting out, Kline checked his phone and was pleased to see that he had a couple bars of signal. He thumbed to his text messages and saw that Treadway had read the one he'd sent almost an hour earlier before tackling the pass but had not replied.

He tried calling her, but it went straight to voicemail. He ended the call without leaving a message and instead tried the special agent in charge of the Bozeman field office.

"This is Director Kline," he said when the call connected. "I need immediate tactical support at Norris Geyser Basin in Yellowstone Park. We are moving with the secretary of defense and civilians under threat. I need air and ground assets en route ASAP."

"I'll get right on it, sir," the SAC replied, but then added, "It's going to take some time."

Kline let the Tahoe roll forward, advancing slowly toward the intersection. Off to the roadside, a park service sign indicated *NORRIS GEYSERS* straight ahead. Below it, alongside an arrow pointing to the right, the sign read, *MAMMOTH.* "How much time?"

"Best case . . . maybe forty-five minutes to get a chopper to you. Road teams will take longer."

"Forty-five?" Kline couldn't believe his ears. Was the park really so remote that it would take the better part of an hour for a *helicopter* to reach them?

"It will take that long to find a bird and get our agents in the air."

After leaving the campsite behind, there had been no further encounters with the Russians, but that didn't mean they weren't coming. "Do what you can," he said. "We'll hold them off—"

A double beep sounded in his ear, indicating that the call had terminated. A quick check showed that he'd lost the signal again. He set the phone in the center console. Ahead, the SecDef's SUV passed through the intersection, going straight down a narrow two-lane road that vanished into the surrounding woods. Kline dutifully braked at the stop sign, but then rushed through, following the other vehicle.

"No help coming?" Emily said from the passenger seat.

Kline glanced over at her. "Oh, it's on the way. It just won't be here in time."

She took the news in stride, just as she had everything else that had happened to them in the last hour. Kline had been nothing but impressed with his daughter-in-law's cool head. She had been a steady presence throughout, soothing the kids and keeping them calm in the face of what had to be the most frightening experience of their lives. No panic, no drama.

"You think they're going to try again?" she asked, pitching her voice low.

Kline glanced in the rearview mirror and saw Brynn Decker looking back, watching him, waiting for his answer.

"I don't think they're going to give up. Not now."

"So, what's the plan?"

"Stay alive." He almost added, *And pray that a certain six-foot-three, two-hundred-sixty-pound former Marine Raider magically shows up,* but didn't.

A nerve in Emily's cheek twitched. "That's not an answer, Gavin."

He looked over, saw the steel in her eyes, and nodded. She was right, of course, and she deserved better. "Let me coordinate with the SecDef. We'll figure something out."

"He's got . . . what, five or six men with him? The Russians are going to roll right over them."

Kline kept his gaze forward. "If it comes down to it, I'll hold them off while you take the kids and get out."

"Sacrifice yourself buying us time to run," she replied. "Just like your agents did."

"If that's what it takes."

"And when they get past you, then what?" She shook her head. "I'm tired of running, Gavin. Brynn can take the kids. I'll stand with you."

Brynn spoke up immediately. "I'm not running either. Give me a gun. I'll fight."

Kline sighed. "Let's not get too far ahead of ourselves. Let me talk to the secretary. We'll come up with a plan."

The road wound through the forest for about a quarter mile, eventually bringing them to a surprisingly small parking area. The SecDef's Suburban pulled forward then stopped, blocking in several parked cars. Kline stopped right behind him.

A moment later, the MBITR chirped. "Director Kline, would you join me for a moment?"

Kline glanced over at Emily, giving her a reassuring nod, and said, "Be right back."

He stepped out, wrinkling his nose at the strong sulfur odor, and moved up to the lead vehicle. As he approached, one of the secretary's bodyguards opened the rear door to admit him. The secretary remained seated inside. Kline climbed in, and the door was shut behind him.

"Mr. Secretary," Kline began, "I managed to get a call through to the Bozeman FO. Reinforcements are on the way, but we're going to be on our own until they get here. ETA forty-five minutes."

The SecDef regarded him coolly for a moment. "Director, what do you know about the nature of this threat?"

Kline blinked. "As I told you earlier, this wasn't on our radar. And forgive me for saying it, but I think right now a better use of our time would be discussing how to prepare for it."

"And we will," the SecDef said, voice even. "But first, tell me what you know."

"Only what you've told me." But even as he said it, Kline knew that wasn't the whole story.

Before he could qualify his statement, however, the SecDef asked another question. "Does the name Nightshade mean anything to you?"

Kline shook his head. "Doesn't ring a bell. Who is it?"

"The name's come up in our intel relating to the Russian activity. Beyond that, we're in the dark."

Kline absorbed that, then decided to play a card of his own. "Has the name Aaron Decker come up in your intel?"

That seemed to catch the SecDef off guard. "*Decker?* No. Why?"

Kline drew a breath. "I think he's the real target here. Years ago, he was an operator in a deep-black assassination unit. Someone inside his unit was working with the Russians. They burned him, tried to kill him, and forced him underground. His kids are with my daughter-in-law, and last night, one of my agents stopped an attempted kidnapping of his daughter. I'm pretty sure this attack was an effort to get to Decker's kids so they can use them as leverage against him. I think whoever's behind this is the same person who betrayed him back then. And I think it might be this Nightshade you're talking about."

"Where is this Decker? Are you in contact with him?" The SecDef shot him a hard stare. "Am I to believe it's a coincidence that his children happened to be staying with your daughter-in-law?"

Kline hesitated. If he admitted to his relationship with Decker, such as it was, he would be opening himself up to inestimable political and possibly even criminal consequences. "Decker is . . ." He groped for a description that would answer the question without giving too much away. "An asset."

"You're keeping a former deep-black assassin as a stringer," mused the secretary. "I underestimated you, Director."

Kline started to protest, but the other man waved him away. "Don't sweat it. We're all just trying to get the job done."

"If we get—" Kline stopped himself. "*When* we get through this mess, I'll open a formal investigation into this Nightshade. We can find a workaround to incorporate your intel without compromising your network."

The SecDef's eyes narrowed, but then he nodded. "Yes. You should do that."

"On that note," Kline went on, "we need to talk about our more immediate problem."

The secretary's reply was swift and unequivocal. "We're going to stay put."

Kline frowned. "You think that's wise?"

"Even if the Russians followed us up the pass, they can't know we came in here. They'll be looking for us on the highways, trying to intercept us heading north."

"I'd feel better if we were moving."

Before the SecDef could answer, his radio crackled to life. *"Sir, there's a suspicious vehicle coming up on our six."*

Both men turned to look out the window and saw a green GMC Yukon, its front and sides streaked with drying mud, slowly rolling up alongside the three idle vehicles. The glare coming off the windshield hid its occupants from view, but Kline didn't need to see inside the vehicle to know that his worst fears had just been realized.

"They found us," he snarled, as if the words were a curse.

Kline reached for the door handle. He had to get back to the Tahoe . . . had to warn Emily . . . protect the kids.

The secretary grabbed the MBITR and keyed the push-to-talk. "Protect Director Kline and his family."

Even as he said it, his driver craned his head around to face him. "Sir, we have to get you out of here. You're the principal."

Kline didn't stick around to hear who won the argument. He flung open the door and as he turned to move back to the Tahoe, he saw the Yukon swing in front of the SecDef's ride, cutting off that exit route. A heartbeat later, the first crack of gunfire broke the calm.

Kline ducked instinctively as rounds snapped past, and threw himself behind the big Suburban, cutting in front of the Tahoe's front end to approach on the far side. On the sidewalk, just beyond the line of parked vehicles, visitors were scattering, dropping bags and backpacks, and running for cover.

Kline went to the front passenger door and wasn't surprised at all to find Emily already in the back seat, directing the kids to get down on the floor. Brynn and Mitchell were helping, while Jack had his arms around Rubble, who was barking and snarling wildly. Kline threw himself over the console and slid down behind the steering wheel, keeping his head below the dashboard. There was enough room between the vehicles for him to pull out of the line, but with the Russians to the front, there was little question of which way he would have to go.

He shifted the gear lever into reverse and cranked the wheel hard to the left, but as he started to depress the accelerator, a burst of gunfire raked across the side of the Tahoe. The entire vehicle lurched and then tilted sideways. On the dashboard, a tire pressure alert flashed, confirming what Kline already knew to be true. The burst had shredded the front left tire. They weren't going anywhere.

Kline risked a quick peek and saw three gunmen break from the cover of the Yukon, swinging wide to his left in an apparent flanking maneuver. In a matter of seconds, they would be able to direct their fire into the side of the Tahoe.

Behind him, the men from the SecDef's protective detail were using the rear armored vehicle for cover, firing back at the Russian gunmen with short controlled bursts from compact machine pistols. One of them came up on the Tahoe's passenger side and pulled open the rear door. "Everyone out," he ordered. "We need to get you into the Suburban."

Kline seized on this solution. With its armor package and run-flat tires, the second Suburban would afford a lot more protection than the thin-skinned, already-disabled Tahoe. He met Emily's questioning gaze and nodded. "Do it."

More rounds sparked off the Tahoe's front end. One thumped into the door, penetrating through the base of the driver's seat, missing Kline's backside by mere inches.

Too close.

Kline squirmed out from behind the wheel, crawling over the console and exiting out the passenger door, staying low as he moved back to help the bodyguard evacuate the others. Brynn was already out, holding Lauren in her arms. Mitchell was pulling Little Matty along, but Emily was still huddled on the floor, trying to stay calm as she urged Jack to move.

"Come on, honey," she said, her voice almost inaudible over the din of more rounds striking the Tahoe. "We can't stay here. Rubble won't leave if you don't, so you have to do this for him."

The appeal seemed to work. The boy, shaking with fright, released his hold on the rottweiler and crawled through the door, joining the others, who were hunkered down with Kline and the bodyguard. As soon as his feet touched the ground, however, Jack turned and coaxed the dog forward. "C'mon, boy."

Rubble bounded out, almost knocking Jack down.

Kline turned to Emily, extending a hand. "Time to go!"

Emily needed no urging, but before climbing out, she grabbed her shotgun. It wouldn't be much good against men wielding assault weapons, but Kline supposed it was better than throwing stones. Then another idea hit him.

"Hey, why don't you let the dog go hunt?" Gavin had seen Redd's rottie rush into several fights in the past and was well aware of just how capable the massive K9 was when it came to tearing limbs off bad guys.

Emily shook her head. "He's the last line of defense for the kids. He stays with us."

Kline shrugged.

"Into the Suburban!" shouted the bodyguard. "We're going to get you—"

A loud boom reverberated through the air. It was a sound Kline knew well, though he never thought he'd hear it in one of America's national parks. "RPG!" he shouted. "Down!"

He threw his arms wide, trying to cover the children with his body, even as the projectile completed its short journey and detonated with a second, much louder concussion. A wave of heat and pressure slammed him flat, knocking him down partly atop Mitchell and Little Matty. The Tahoe was shoved sideways almost a full foot, rocking on its suspension.

For a moment, Kline didn't move. Couldn't move. His ears rang, the world narrowing to a high electric whine. Dust and grit rained down on him, the smell of hot metal and burning rubber filling his nostrils. Finally, after what felt like forever, he managed to raise his head.

The passenger side doors of the Suburban had been blown open, and black smoke was boiling out of it. Kline immediately grasped that the armored SUV had been the target of the RPG—a weapon designed specifically to burn holes through tank armor. The plating had largely shielded them from the worst effects of the detonation, but the vehicle was toast.

No refuge there.

Something moved off to his left. He turned his head just in time to see the other Suburban, holding the SecDef, buck forward, ramming the Yukon aside and accelerating away.

Kline felt a cold weight settle in his chest as he watched it go. He understood why, recalling the last thing he'd heard the driver say. The primary duty of the protective detail was the safety of the secretary, but the sight of the vehicle speeding away filled him with despair.

They were on their own now.

Beside him, the bodyguard who had tried to herd them into the rear SUV raised his head, face streaked with grime and blood, and began looking around. Kline swept his gaze over the rest of the group. All looked dazed, and the baby in Brynn's arms was bright red, mouth open in a scream that Kline couldn't hear. Then he found Emily, likewise stunned but struggling to regain her wits.

He reached out, grabbed her arm, and pointed to the nearby woods. "Run!"

FIFTY-TWO

"What's that?" Decker shot a finger out through the empty frame where the windshield had been, pointing to something above the distant treetops.

Redd followed the other man's gaze until he saw it too, a column of thick black smoke rising skyward.

"That's no geyser," said Redd, pressing harder on the accelerator. The Expedition was already moving well in excess of the suggested speed limit, but somehow it didn't feel fast enough.

They had made good time across the pass. Faster than Redd would have thought possible, following in the tracks of the vehicles that preceded them—the Tahoe with Emily, Kline, and the kids, and at least one other, no doubt carrying more Russian killers. The earlier traffic had blazed a path for them, knocking down drifts and packing the snow, allowing them to practically fly up and over the pass, surely gaining on the others. But the black smoke rising into the sky told him it still wasn't enough.

Up ahead, traffic appeared to be backed up at a four-way stop. The GPS showed their destination, the Norris Geyser Basin, on the other side, but there was a line of cars several hundred yards long clogging the road. Redd swung into the opposite lane, laying on the horn and flashing his headlights as he charged past the unmoving vehicles. Oncoming cars hastily pulled over to get out of his way.

As they neared the intersection, Redd saw not only cars but people on foot streaming out of the narrow road on the opposite side. Redd held down the horn, surging through without stopping, braking only to avoid hitting fleeing pedestrians. The smoke column now loomed large above them, the harsh smell of burning metal and plastic permeating the open interior of the Expedition. Then the trees seemed to part, and the source of the smoke was revealed.

Redd saw right away that the burning vehicle was not Emily's Tahoe, but something larger. Smoke and flames poured from the windows, and there was a fist-sized hole in the rear quarter panel, just above the passenger-side wheel well. Redd had seen damage like that before. It was the sort of thing caused by anti-tank weapons.

Three bodies lay near the rear of the vehicle, all wearing dark suits, one of them holding a machine pistol in an outflung hand.

Fifty or so yards ahead, a green Yukon—identical to the one that had blocked the road in the ambush on the other side of the pass—sat askew and, to all appearances, abandoned.

"What happened here?" wondered Decker.

"Those guys don't look like Bureau," said Treadway, staring at the bodies.

Redd thought the men looked like Secret Service, but before he could voice this opinion, he saw something that turned his blood to ice and stomped the brake, bringing the Expedition to a full stop.

Just beyond the burning wreck, barely visible through a shroud of smoke and convection waves, was Emily's Tahoe.

Or what was left of it.

The windows had been shot out, and the side panels and fenders were riddled with holes. The front tire was shredded, sitting on its rim.

Decker, in a rare display of emotion, let out a strangled cry and threw his door open, braving the heat from the fire and running to the Tahoe, peering in through its shattered windows. Redd was right behind him.

The vehicle was empty.

"They're not here," said Decker. "Where are they?"

Redd didn't have an answer, but he knew one thing. He gripped Decker's shoulder. "They're alive, Aaron. We'll find them."

Then, as if to punctuate his assertion, the rapid-fire reports of an automatic weapon—distant but distinctive—cracked from somewhere beyond the trees.

Both men looked up, orienting on the source of the noise like bloodhounds, and then took off running toward it. The shots, like a scattering of sonic breadcrumbs, brought them to a gravel path wending through the lodgepoles to a large stone-and-log structure housing the geyser museum. As they continued past it, the trees thinned, revealing the stark, almost lunar landscape of the Norris Geyser Basin.

Steam hissed from fissures in the ground, gauzy plumes of vapor drifting across the barren, blistered landscape. The basin lay spread out before them, the ground shimmering under a pale mineral crust, mottled with hues of white and gray, etched by trickling rivulets of superheated water carving their way across the terrain. Here and there, the water gathered in pools, some a brilliant blue or milky green, others the hue of sulfur.

Another burst of gunfire drew Redd's attention, and his searching eyes were drawn to movement. Northwest of their position, maybe two hundred yards out, a group of figures—five men? Six?—were running along the boardwalk that spanned the basin. Farther along the loop, maybe a hundred yards ahead of the men, was a second group, and even though they were too far out for him to make out much in the way of detail, Redd knew them.

"It's them," he shouted and bolted forward again, running down the gravel path, leaping down a flight of stone steps and veering onto the trail. Decker was right on his heels.

A body lay supine near the base of the stairs, a man in a black suit, machine pistol still clutched in one hand, face and body riddled with bloody holes. One of the protection agents from the destroyed Suburban, Redd surmised. His position suggested he'd died making a stand against an oncoming and overwhelming enemy force.

Redd ran on.

The path ducked through a stand of lodgepoles, and then they emerged onto the boardwalk. The air was thick and damp, and Redd felt a metallic taste at the back of his throat. The planks underfoot were slick with moisture. Before him, the basin looked like a World War I battlefield, desolate and smoking. He scanned the path ahead, finding the two groups now moving west along the trail loop. The pursued were maintaining their lead, but the pursuers were pausing intermittently to take shots at them, the reports echoing across the basin floor. They all seemed impossibly out of reach.

Redd pushed himself harder, legs pumping, feet pounding along the slick boardwalk, seemingly floating above the alien world. The air felt like acid vapor, stinging his eyes, burning his lungs, but he didn't hold back.

It was a race he had to win because the alternative was unthinkable.

A mechanical growl cut through his despair. He glanced back and saw the Expedition, with Treadway at the wheel, surging across the basin, running parallel to the boardwalk. Steam swirled in its wake, rising from the twin grooves of mineral crust crushed and broken by its massive tires. It slowed, pulling alongside Redd and Decker, matching their pace, and then he heard Treadway's shout. "Get in!"

Redd skidded to a halt and leaped down off the boardwalk, opening the rear door of the Expedition and pulling himself inside. Decker circled around and climbed in the front passenger door, shouting, "Go! Go!" even before he was in his seat.

"Hang on." Treadway punched the gas, veering away from the boardwalk and heading straight across the basin.

The ride was anything but smooth. Despite the appearance of a more or less flat expanse of earth, the terrain was soft and irregular, the brittle crust cracking under the Expedition's weight. Steam boiled from nearby vents, some of it dense enough to momentarily blind them. One wheel dropped suddenly, the tire spinning in soft, hot mud. Treadway worked the steering wheel back and forth, keeping the pedal to the floor until the vehicle lurched free and shot forward again.

Through the steam, the running figures on the boardwalk came into view, now moving east where the boardwalk skirted the base of a wooded hill that rose above the basin. They were close enough that Redd could see them distinctly. His heart soared when he saw Emily, running with Matthew Junior in her arms. Brynn Decker held a smaller bundled shape—surely Lauren—while her brother, Mitchell, ran out ahead of them all, with Rubble bounding forward at his side. Gavin was bringing up the rear, carrying Jack.

Alive! All of them!

But the Russians—six men in jeans and flannel, carrying assault weapons—were closing fast.

Decker leaned forward on the dashboard, extending his HK416 through the window, and commenced firing. One flannel-clad man staggered and collapsed off the boardwalk. The others, only now realizing that a new player had entered the arena, leaped from the boardwalk and scrambled for cover in the tree line, then began returning fire.

Bullets snapped past the Expedition, creasing the air around them. Decker held his position, targeting the faintly visible puffs of smoke that betrayed the shooters' positions.

"Forget them," Redd snapped. "Get to my family!"

Treadway nodded and cranked the wheel to the right, slewing the vehicle toward the boardwalk. Redd could see Kline and Emily, still running, but glancing back as the Expedition loomed closer. It was only as they pulled up alongside the fleeing group that understanding and then relief dawned in their faces.

Treadway braked and spun the wheel, swinging the Expedition broadside, nose up against the boardwalk to provide some temporary cover. Emily and the others needed no urging. They leaped from the planks and dove behind the SUV.

Redd was already out, sweeping Emily into his arms, with Junior pressed between them. Jack squirmed loose from Kline's grasp and threw his arms around Redd's legs, while Rubble ran in tight excited circles around them. Decker exited the vehicle almost as quickly and was nearly bowled over by Mitchell and Brynn, still cradling Lauren. Kline just stood back, watching the reunion with a crooked smile. Redd reached out with his free arm and pulled him into the huddle.

The moment didn't last.

A burst of enemy fire hammered into the opposite flank of the Expedition. Treadway had ducked down behind the front end, aiming her pistol toward the woods where the Russians were hiding. Redd instinctively pulled Emily down into a crouch, even as he drew the NXS from its holster, preparing to return fire.

Decker, who had likewise borne his children down, was now leaning across the hood of the vehicle, sighting down the barrel of his 416. He squeezed off several shots then turned to Redd. "Get them out of here. I've got this."

Redd heard the conflict in Decker's plea. He wanted to win. To end the threat and destroy his enemies once and for all, but more than that, he wanted to protect his family. It was the dilemma every warrior faced, especially when the danger was at the doorstep.

It was, after all, what Decker had asked of him in the first place.

"Keep them safe until this is over."

But war—and this was a war—was a numbers game, and right now, if they stuck together, the numbers were just about even. A least one of the Russians was down. The rest were pinned down. This was not the time to divide their forces.

He glanced over at Emily, crouching low, comforting the kids, but still holding on to her shotgun . . . At Jack, looking up at him with those big trusting eyes . . . At Brynn and Mitchell, who he barely knew, but would nonetheless give his life for. They were all in danger here, yes, but if he did as Decker insisted, led them away from the battlefield, subtracted himself from the equation, could Decker still win the day?

And if he couldn't, what would that mean for the rest of them?

"No," Redd said, turning back to Decker. "If we stay together, we can finish it."

"Matt, just—"

"They came after my family too. I'm not leaving until they're dead."

Before Decker could argue further, Kline joined in. "He's right, Aaron. I got a call out to the Bozeman FO. Backup is on the way. We just have to hold out a little longer."

Decker looked between them, eyes narrowing . . . calculating.

"Keep them safe until this is over."

And then the equation changed.

Across the basin, maybe two hundred yards out, another vehicle—a dark green SUV—nosed through a veil of steam, crawling over the scarred crust Treadway had plowed through only moments earlier.

Redd's heart fell. This was the SUV that had ambushed them on the other side of the pass, the one they'd left behind, and that meant the number of enemy shooters had almost certainly doubled.

He turned to Decker, saw the grim look in the other man's eyes, but it was Kline who said what Decker didn't need to. "Go, Matt. Get them out of here while you still can."

Redd turned to Emily. "We have to go."

Emily just nodded.

He turned and scooped Jack up in his arms. Emily still had Junior, and Brynn was holding Lauren. He'd just have to hope that Mitchell and Rubble could keep up. He glanced over to check on the approaching SUV and realized that it had halted its approach while still more than a hundred yards out.

Then he saw a figure crouched down beside an open door, hefting something onto his shoulder. Not a rifle, but something bigger . . .

Redd barely had time to shout, "RPG!" before the launcher flashed.

FIFTY-THREE

From the passenger seat of the Yukon, Grigori Volkov watched as the RPG-7 round streaked across the desolate plain and struck Decker's SUV. The grenade detonated with a flash and an eruption of smoke, the sound—a tremendous boom—reaching his ears almost a full second later.

As the dust began to settle, he raised a pair of binoculars to his eyes, finding first the smoking remains of the vehicle and then the prone figures scattered behind it. For a fleeting second, he thought perhaps the explosive projectile had finished them off, but then he saw movement—first one, then another, and then all of them rose and began running up the low hill into the woods.

"Idiot," he muttered, lowering the binoculars.

Sasha glanced over from the driver's seat. "I told you."

Sasha had indeed warned him that the RPG-7 wasn't an effective antipersonnel weapon. Yes, there would be an overpressure wave and some shrapnel, but the explosion wouldn't be catastrophic like in the movies.

"At least we took their vehicle away." He gestured forward. "Go."

Sasha complied and the Yukon resumed crawling across the geothermal basin. As they neared the wreckage, Volkov saw Skvortsov and three of his men emerge from the woods and begin advancing. The mercenary had taken five men along with him in pursuit of Decker's family. Now his group was down to four.

Volkov's vehicle was carrying eight men—nine, if he counted himself. In addition to the six mercenaries from Sibir Z, they had added two Bratva soldiers, the only survivors of the wreck of the Land Cruiser on the other side of the pass. One had a shattered collarbone; the other had caught a bullet to his upper chest and didn't appear long for the world. Two more of the men riding with him had sustained wounds during the fight with the FBI agents at the campsite. None of them were fit to fight on foot, but all could still pull a trigger.

Thirteen shooters against . . . how many? Decker and his friend, and maybe two or three others who could hold a gun. Four or five total, and a bunch of children.

It would suffice.

He glanced at the GPS display, which showed a top-down view of the area around them. The stand of trees where their quarry had disappeared was little more than an island poking up out of the austere, moonlike landscape. Decker and the others would not be able to hide there for long.

Volkov turned in his seat and addressed the occupants of his crowded vehicle. "Everyone who can walk, get out now."

Sasha looked over at him, questioning, and Volkov nodded. "You too. I'll drive."

As the able-bodied men began piling out, Volkov opened his door and moved to join Skvortsov. "Mikhail, have your men sweep through the forest. I'll drive around and catch them as they come out."

A fierce grin broke across Skvortsov's face as he turned and relayed these orders to his men. They quickly assembled into a picket line, spaced out at ten-yard intervals, and then as one began moving north, into the woods where Decker and the others had fled. There was some risk, of course. If Decker and Redd turned to fight, some of Skvortsov's men would die, but the others would converge on the shooters and deliver swift vengeance. If they were smart, though, Decker and Redd would flee rather than fight, and if they did, Volkov would be ready for them.

He circled around to the driver's side of the idling Yukon and slid in. Behind him, the four wounded but capable fighters had their windows rolled down and their weapons pointing out. Volkov put the vehicle in gear and steered away from the boardwalk, heading east on a course that would take them around the wooded patch.

The ground beneath the tires appeared solid, but Volkov had been paying attention when Sasha drove in. He kept the Yukon's speed down, barely faster than a walking pace, letting the vehicle feel its way across the brittle basin. But as he swept wide to avoid a suspicious patch of orange-stained runoff, the right front wheel broke through and dropped with a bone-jarring jolt. Steam hissed upward, fogging the windshield. Volkov gritted his teeth and kept pressure on the throttle. The tire spun once, twice, then found purchase and yanked the vehicle forward.

Behind him, one of the wounded men cursed in Russian. Volkov silenced him with a look and pressed on, eyes flicking between the brittle ground and the GPS display.

Up ahead, the boardwalk gave way to a dirt path that ran along the base of the rise, continuing west past the end of the wooded section. Volkov turned onto it, rolling over the split rail border placed by park personnel to delineate the trail, and began climbing the eastern flank of the forest island. From somewhere in the woods came the *pop-pop* of sporadic gunfire.

At the crest, Volkov surveyed the landscape on the far side of the rise. Ahead and to the right, another vast geyser basin sprawled out before him. Steam drifted like smoke across the pitted landscape, dotted with glinting pools and a bleached mineral crust. As he began the descent, Volkov kept an eye on the tree line to his left, watching for any sign of Decker and the others. When he reached the northeast corner of the woods, he stopped and began scanning the basin for any sign of their prey. A moment later, he spotted a line of figures breaking from the edge of the trees to the west, running out across the open terrain, heading northwest. He reached for the binoculars and brought them into focus. He immediately identified Decker's big friend—Matthew Redd—his hulking frame towering above the others. The woman beside him had to be the wife. He saw several children as well, but no Decker.

He continued watching, debating whether to take off in pursuit of the group or wait for Skvortsov to finish his sweep. The choice was made for him when the mercenary leader emerged from the woods followed a moment later by two of his men, and then, further down the way, another pair helping a third who appeared to be unable to walk on his own.

That's six, thought Volkov. *Where are the other two?*

Skvortsov, spying the waiting Yukon, began jogging toward it. Volkov leaned out his window. "Redd and the others came out, but not Decker. Did you kill him?"

Skvortsov spat into the dirt. "He killed two of my men. Wounded another. Then vanished."

"Then he's still in the woods."

"If we go back in there," Skvortsov warned, "he'll wipe us out. He's not human, Grigori. He's a ghost."

Volkov narrowed his eyes, recalling what Konstantin had said about Decker all those months ago. He also remembered Nightshade's counsel: *"Take his children, and he will come to you."*

He looked back at Skvortsov. "Take three men with you and go after the others. Kill the man—Redd. Bring the others back alive if you can."

"And Decker?"

"Decker will come after you," assured Volkov. "And when he does, we'll have him."

FIFTY-FOUR

DANGER: THERMAL AREA
Boiling Water
Unstable Ground
DO NOT ENTER

Redd felt more than a twinge of apprehension as he passed the sign, but he didn't slow. Whatever natural hazards lay ahead, they were nowhere near as certain as a bullet. Nevertheless, he did look over his shoulder at the others—Emily and Brynn still carrying the youngest children, Mitchell and Rubble trotting along behind them.

Ahead, to the northwest, across the shimmering expanse, he spotted the distant edge of the basin, fringed with lodgepole pines. That was where he had to lead them all. He didn't know what he would find there—a road, a trail, or nothing at all—but all that mattered was that it was away from here. Away from the men who were trying to kill them.

"From here on out, we're going to move single file," he said. "Follow exactly in my steps. Got it?"

Emily nodded and shifted over until she was a few steps directly behind him. Brynn's eyes widened a little, but she complied, as did her brother.

"We're going to be all right," Redd added. "Just stay behind me, and don't wander off." He noticed Rubble starting to do exactly that and called to him. "Here, boy."

The rottie's ears perked up and he raced across the mineral crust to Redd's side.

Redd glanced down at Jack, still in his arms, unusually quiet since they fled into the woods. "You think you can keep Rubble out of trouble?"

A faint smile touched the boy's lips. "That rhymed."

"It sure did." Redd chuckled. "Can you do it?"

"I'll try."

Redd eased him to the ground, and Jack immediately threw one arm around the dog's neck. "We have to walk behind Dad, Rubble. Be good, okay?"

Satisfied, Redd turned his attention to the landscape ahead and began moving forward, testing the ground with each tentative step.

Every footfall was deliberate. Boot lowered gently, then a little pressure, and a little more before committing his full weight. He avoided ground that looked cracked or soft, steering clear of any venting steam or heavy mineral accumulations.

The first twenty yards passed without incident.

Thirty yards.

Fifty.

In the distance, glinting pools—some a milky turquoise, others the color of rust—dotted the landscape. As they neared one of the larger pools, he noticed that his feet felt warmer. Just a little at first, like walking over hot asphalt on a summer day. But then it got hotter. Worse, he felt a definite vibration rising up through the soil, like water circulating in a radiator.

Exactly like that.

He scanned the terrain ahead, looking for a path through the nightmare. Then Emily called out to him.

"Matty. Behind us!"

He turned, followed her line of sight, and saw them—four figures moving across the desolate terrain at a jog, bearing down on them.

Of course it couldn't be easy.

He looked forward again, toward the distant stand of trees, blurry through the heat shimmer.

Two hundred more yards? Three?

It might as well have been a mile.

"Em, you've gotta take the lead. Stay on this line as best you can. Go slow and trust your gut."

"What about you?"

"I'll bring up the rear. Don't worry. I'll be right behind you."

She hesitated, looking first at the landscape ahead and then at the men behind, then nodded.

As she passed Redd, Jack looked up at him expectantly, so he ruffled the boy's hair. "Go on. Follow your mom."

He waited until Brynn and Mitchell passed to draw his NXS from its holster, then turned to face the approaching threat.

FIFTY-FIVE

Volkov glassed the tree line with mounting impatience. It was a mood shared by all the men who had stayed behind with him. Three of them were hunkered down outside the idling Yukon, rifles aimed toward the woods. Three more—the ones whose injuries had left them completely nonambulatory—were inside with him, windows lowered, weapons ready.

The air above the basin roiled with heat and steam. Skvortsov and his men were barely visible now, even with the binos, and soon they would catch up to the fleeing group. Decker had to know that, had to know that his family was in danger.

So what was he waiting for?

As if in answer, a shot rang out from the woods. One of the men in the back seat let out a yelp of pain. Someone else cried out, "Sniper," and then all of them opened fire, shooting into the woods.

Suddenly feeling very exposed, Volkov hunched over, trying to stay out of the sniper's line of sight. After a moment, the fusillade ceased. A pall of smoke hung in the air above the vehicle. Volkov raised his head, peering cautiously into the woods.

Did we get him?

Someone in the back seat uttered a curse. Volkov glanced over his shoulder and saw that Pavel, the man who had been sitting directly behind him, was now slumped forward, unmoving and unresponsive to the ministrations of his seatmate, Oleg.

"Is he okay?" Volkov asked.

"No, he's not okay," snarled Oleg. "He's dead."

Volkov swallowed nervously. The sniper could just as easily have targeted *him.*

Another shot rang out.

Volkov ducked again, his heart hammering in his chest.

Forget this, he thought and crawled over the center console, shoving against the door with his feet. One of the wounded mercenaries was sitting in the passenger seat, but Volkov paid him no heed. He just clawed his way past the man, shoved open the door, and dropped to the ground in an awkward sprawl as the men around him opened fire a second time, unloading their weapons into the trees.

Volkov crawled behind the front tire. He recalled hearing somewhere that a car's wheels offered more protection from gunfire than the doors. A few feet away, one of the mercenaries—Yura—leaned out from around the front end and loosed a fully automatic burst. Another—Anton—was shooting from just behind the rear bumper.

Yura flinched and flopped onto the ground, unmoving.

Volkov gasped. This wasn't how it was supposed to happen. He hugged his legs to his chest, shrinking behind the wheel, trying to make himself less of a target.

Anton shouted, "There! I see him," and unleashed a burst from his weapon. A half second later, his body jerked, and he fell to the ground as if all his bones had turned to liquid inside him.

That was when Volkov realized that the world had gone completely quiet.

"Yura?" he called out.

There was no reply.

"Oleg? Are you there?"

Nothing. He risked looking up into the still-open door of the Yukon. The man he'd crawled over in his haste to escape was hanging out the door, held upright only by the cross-strap of his seat belt, bloodstains spreading across his chest.

In the back seat, Oleg was sprawled out, unmoving, blood dripping down into the footwell.

Dead. All dead.

Except him.

It's not possible.

How could this have happened? He had the numbers on his side. He was supposed to win. To redeem himself. To be the one who finally delivered Decker's head to Nightshade. Instead, he was going to be Decker's next victim.

He squeezed his eyes shut, willing the terror to pass.

No. Not like this.

He opened his eyes again and began looking for a weapon. Yura lay just a few feet away, the stock of his rifle jutting out from under his unmoving form. If he could just get to it . . .

"Don't."

He froze, his outstretched hand mere inches from the rifle. The voice had come from behind him.

"Turn around."

His breath caught in his chest, the realization that he was about to die hitting like a blow to the gut. Panic seized him.

Not like this. Please, not like this.

But then a different emotion stirred within him. Pride. Rage.

Dignity.

Slowly, very slowly, he rolled over to face his executioner.

Aaron Decker stood just a few steps away, a suppressed pistol in his outstretched hand, aimed squarely at Volkov's chest. Volkov stared at the gun for a moment, then met Decker's cold stare.

"If you're going to kill me," he rasped, "just do it."

"Not yet," replied Decker. "First, you're going to tell me who Nightshade is."

FIFTY-SIX

Treadway lay prone at the base of a stunted lodgepole, sighting down the barrel of the rifle she'd liberated from one of the flannel-clad gunmen—his need for material objects of any sort was forever ended. Aside from Decker, who stood on the far side of the vehicle, and whose head and shoulders were just visible through its open windows, there was no sign of life around the Russians' SUV.

We did it.

She knew better than to celebrate victory prematurely, though. These Russian mobsters were like cockroaches. Just when you thought you had eradicated them, more came crawling out of the sewer.

"Steph," whispered Kline, who was similarly concealed about ten yards off to her right. "Check two o'clock."

She swung her attention in the indicated direction and saw two men making their way along the loop trail from the east. They weren't running, but their strides were quick and purposeful, their ultimate destination clear.

One was dressed in a black suit that looked comically out of place in this desolate landscape. She recalled the bodies they had seen in the parking lot, the men who looked like Secret Service agents, and intuited that the man was one of their number. Like them, he was carrying a compact machine pistol, held at the low ready. The other man was older, wearing a much better suit, though without a tie, his dress shirt open at the collar. He looked vaguely familiar, but in this context, she couldn't place him.

Treadway wasn't sure whether to put her sights on them or not. "Friendlies?" she whispered.

She saw Decker turn toward the newcomers, a questioning look on his face. The older man raised a hand in greeting and spoke, but Treadway couldn't make out what was said.

"I should say so," replied Kline. "It's the SecDef."

Treadway glanced over at her boss. "What's *he* doing here?"

"Long story," Kline said. "He came out to warn us about the attack. Some DOD shadow outfit intercepted signal traffic. He took off when the shooting started. His bodyguard's idea. I didn't expect to see him again. But at least he's on our—"

The crack of a gunshot cut him off.

Treadway whipped her gaze back toward the SUV. Decker wasn't there anymore. And that wasn't the only thing that had changed. The secretary of defense now had a pistol in his hand, and as Treadway watched aghast, he calmly turned and shot his own bodyguard—a single round to the head.

Treadway recoiled in shock as she realized where the first shot had surely gone.

Aaron!

Kline was already on his feet, his face emotionless, rifle at the ready, as he moved out. "Cover me."

Shaking off her astonishment, Treadway bounded up and moved out behind her boss, but in that instant, the SecDef stepped behind the SUV and knelt, removing himself from view.

A third shot rang out.

Kline reached the back end of the Yukon a moment later, motioned for her to circle wide, and then cut around the rear corner of the SUV, leveling his weapon at the secretary of defense.

"Drop it."

Treadway, a few steps behind Kline, saw the secretary kneeling over a body—one of the Russians—pressing a pistol into the dead man's slack hand. Decker lay sprawled on the ground a few feet away, a puddle of blood beneath his head.

No! Aaron!

The secretary turned at the sound of Kline's voice, face twisting in a look of surprise. "Director Kline?" he said, voice full of forced relief. "You made it. About time."

Bang!

Treadway jumped when Kline pulled the trigger. The secretary fell back, slumping awkwardly atop the dead Russian, a red mist settling over them both.

"Target down, Steph. We're clear here."

For a moment, Treadway stood frozen, the echo of the shot ringing in her ears, her brain struggling to make sense of what had just happened.

Then she was on the ground, kneeling over Decker.

He lay unmoving, blood streaming from the right side of his head, staining the white crust under him.

"Aaron . . . no. No, no. No!"

She touched his cheek. Still warm, but his skin was pale beneath the blood. So much blood.

Then Kline was there, kneeling beside her. She pressed two fingers against Decker's neck. "I got a pulse. He's alive!"

Kline didn't respond. He just tore off his shirt, wadded it up, and put it in her hands. "Hold this over the wound. Hard pressure."

She did, holding the makeshift bandage against the wound, pressing against it with one hand, cradling his head with the other.

"Don't you leave me," she whispered. "Don't you dare."

Kline gripped Decker's hand. "Hang on, Aaron. Help is coming."

Treadway's arms shook with adrenaline and fear, but she held tight, praying for the bleeding to stop.

Praying for him to stay.

FIFTY-SEVEN

Redd braced himself in a shooter's stance and took careful aim. The heat shimmer made the approaching figures waver, and at more than fifty yards' distance, he couldn't trust his eyes. But he didn't dare let them get any closer. Keeping the sights squarely center-mass on the nearest target, he took a breath and squeezed the trigger.

The NXS boomed like a cannon. The recoil brought the weapon up, momentarily spoiling his sight picture. When the barrel came back down, he saw one less Russian on his feet.

The others reacted quickly, scattering, but also raising their rifles.

Redd didn't wait around to see more. He turned and ran to catch up to his family, expecting at any moment to hear the crack of supersonic rounds streaking by.

Emily was making steady progress, advancing nearly thirty yards since he'd given her the lead. He didn't try to overtake the single-file procession but turned to face the pursuing Russians once more.

The Russians had changed tactics. They were now fanned out, moving low and careful across the basin, giving him three targets to focus on—and affording them three different angles of fire. Smart tactics under normal circumstances.

But these weren't normal circumstances. They were moving through a geothermal minefield.

What puzzled him was why they hadn't returned fire yet. With automatic rifles, the Russians didn't have to worry about accuracy. They could spray and pray.

So what were they waiting for?

Then it hit him.

Decker's kids.

The Russians probably still wanted to take them alive, use them as leverage. That explained the shift in their tactics. The two men on the outside were going to try to flank him, find an angle that would let them shoot at him without hitting Brynn or Mitchell by mistake. How long they would show restraint would probably depend on how much of a threat they judged Redd to be.

He leveled the NXS again, taking aim at the man on the left and squeezing off another shot, the force of the blast straining his forearms as he fought the vertical recoil.

The Russian flinched but didn't go down. Instead, he ducked and kept moving, zigzagging. Redd fired again but to no better effect. He muttered a rare curse. *He* didn't have unlimited firepower. Squinting into the heat haze, he tried to lead the man, anticipate his next shift—

Suddenly, the man was gone, engulfed in a cloud of steam. The eruption lasted only a second or two, but when the vapor dissipated, the Russian was simply gone.

Then he was back, exploding into view with a great splash. Half of him, anyway. From the waist down, he was submerged in a pool of water, previously hidden beneath the mineral crust. Even from a distance, Redd could see the surprised look on the man's face transform into something else.

The man's skin had turned bright red, but even through the heat distortion, Redd could see mottled patches of white blossoming all over. The Russian let out an unearthly shriek and began clawing at the water. He tried to heave himself sideways, to reach the broken edge of the crust, but then he vanished again, swallowed by the pool. Whorls of vapor rolled off the surface, but the man didn't come up a second time.

Redd swallowed hard, bile rising in the back of his throat. His gaze swept the basin floor around him, suddenly alive to every suspicious glint of moisture, every subtle sag in the crust, every whisper of rising steam. One wrong step, and he might be the next one boiled alive.

Or Emily. Or the kids.

He started forward again, searching for the trail of footprints that would show the path the others had taken. The safe path? He could only hope so. A burst of steam erupted to his right. Close, too close. He felt its hot dragon breath on his face, but he didn't break stride.

Somewhere behind him, the remaining Russians were still moving, but cautiously now. Redd could feel it. They'd seen what happened. Whatever their orders had been, capture or kill, this place didn't care. The basin didn't play favorites.

What a rough way to go.

Emily was about twenty yards ahead, still carrying Matthew Jr., with Jack and Rubble close behind. Brynn had Lauren in her arms, her stride dogged but unsteady. Mitchell, bringing up the rear of their line, was hyperfocused on his sister's feet, careful to step exactly where she did. Redd quickly closed the gap, slowing only when he was a few steps behind the boy.

The ground was beginning to change. The mineral crust was yielding to the gritty native soil as they climbed a gentle rise toward another stand of lodgepole pine. Steam still drifted between the trees, thin and spectral, but Redd no longer felt the heat underfoot.

"Go!" he called out. "We're clear. Move!"

Emily didn't need to be told twice. She broke into a run, Jack at her side. Rubble dashed ahead barking excitedly. They reached the trees and pushed through. Redd scanned the woods as they ran, searching—hoping—for a road or a ranger station. A refuge.

They crested the low hill, and as they descended, the woods thinned, depositing them abruptly on the bank of a river. It wasn't a major waterway, only about ten yards across, shallow, but running fast. Redd could see the small eddies created as it flowed around rocks and deadfalls. Upriver, the flow narrowed slightly, picking up speed where it bent around a gravel bar. No sign of a ford. No bridge. Nothing but whitewater and fallen trees. Downriver, it widened and slowed, but the banks steepened and choked with brush. On the far side, there were just more trees.

Behind them, the woods seemed almost serene, but Redd didn't believe it for a second. The Russians would still be coming. If they didn't make a move now, the choice would be taken from them.

He turned toward the river again. Ten yards across, and he could see the smooth rocks lining the bed. Not even knee-deep.

Still, he knew better than to underestimate it.

Even shallow water, moving fast, could knock a grown man off his feet. As much as six hundred pounds of lateral force. It didn't take a deep river to drown someone. And the kids, shorter and with considerably less mass, would be especially vulnerable.

On the other hand, danger was a great equalizer.

He turned and addressed the group. "We're going to cross here. It's not very deep, but the current is fast enough to knock you down and sweep you away if you aren't careful."

Emily gave him a cautious look. "Matty, are you sure about this?"

He nodded. "I'm going to take you across one at a time, buddy-style. We'll lock arms and move together. That will give us added stability. You first, Em."

She shook her head. "Not a chance. Take the kids before me. I'll go when they're safe."

"I *need* you on the other side to help receive them as I bring them across. Trust me, okay?"

After a brief pause, Emily finally reached her hand toward Redd. "Fine."

"Just hang on to Junior and follow my lead," he said as he took her hand in his. "Just like dancing."

She arched an eyebrow. "Since when do you know anything about dancing?"

"You know me," said Redd, "full of surprises." Then he added, "Let me show you."

She took his hand, and they moved down to the water's edge. Redd stepped into the flow first. The water splashed around his boots, and though it didn't even come up to his ankles, he could feel the weight of it. He turned, facing downstream, and shifted his hands, placing one on either side of Emily's torso, under her arms. He could feel the tension in her muscles, but her face showed only determination and trust.

"Okay," he said. "Left foot first. Small steps."

They moved as one, sliding sideways. He planted his feet carefully, avoiding or kicking aside slippery, unstable rocks. The water splashed up around his ankles, soaking his jeans. It was frigid, but that was easy enough to ignore as long as it didn't come above his waist.

They soon fell into a rhythm, much like the dance he had suggested, their combined footing creating the stability that one person would not have had.

Nevertheless, as they reached the middle of the flow, Redd could feel the current trying to take his feet out from under him. The water, a low, barely audible murmur on the shore, hissed like a viper as it rushed around his calves.

Emily was knee-deep now, her face grim and determined, her eyes locked on his.

"Almost there," he said. "You're doing great."

Another step.

And another.

Then the pull began to weaken. The water still swirled around them, but it was only at ankle level, and then not even that high.

"Last one," Redd breathed, lifting her out of the water and depositing her on dry land.

They were across.

Emily exhaled in a shuddering breath, Junior still safe in her arms. Redd nodded to her. "Be right back."

He turned and strode back out into the river, but without a partner to supply added stability, the force of the current hit harder, slewing around his legs with a ferocity that caught him off guard. He faced upstream, leaning into the current, widening his stance and lowering his center of gravity, but could feel the flow trying to take his feet out from under him. By the time he reached the midpoint, he felt like he was barely making any headway.

Then one foot slipped off a rock, and the other was swept back, dropping him face-first into the river.

The cold punched the air from his lungs, water flooding his mouth, eyes, nose. He broke the surface again, coughing, arms flailing, trying to remember the swift-water self-rescue techniques he'd learned. The current had already carried him several yards downstream before he managed to roll over and regain some semblance of control.

On the near shore, Rubble was pacing him, barking frantically. Redd tried to call out to the dog, warn him to stay, but when he opened his mouth, the river swept in, choking off his cry. Rubble, heedless of his own safety, charged in after him.

"Rubble, no!" Redd choked.

The warning came too late. The current caught the rottie, carrying him away. For a moment, the dog was almost within Redd's reach, but then Redd felt himself dragging along the bottom, slowing, while Rubble's furious dog paddle was taking him further out.

Unable to reach his best four-legged friend, Redd clawed his way back up onto the bank. Rubble would be fine, he knew. He would find calmer water downstream, make it out and run back up the shore to rejoin them.

At least it was what he told himself, what he had to believe. Right now, there were other people counting on him.

He hauled himself onto shore, dripping and gasping, his soaked shirt clinging to him like ice, and began running back to where the children waited. Jack was openly sobbing, crying out Rubble's name. Mitchell was trying to comfort him, while Brynn rocked back and forth, Lauren clutched tight to her chest.

There was no time to be gentle about things, not with the Russians closing the distance between them. "Jack. It's okay, buddy. Rubble will be fine. We're all going to be fine. It's just water." He turned to Brynn. "I'm going to take Mitchell and Jack next."

"No!" cried Jack. "I'm scared."

We don't have time for this, Redd thought, but he could never say that aloud. Not when Jack had just watched Rubble get swept away by the water.

Taking a deep breath, Redd changed gears. "Okay, buddy. Jack and Mitchell, you'll go last so that you can watch me go across again and see that it's no big deal. Just have to be careful. I'll be right back for you guys, okay?"

Both boys nodded.

Turning back to Brynn, Redd said, "We have to do this, and we have to go *now*."

She swallowed, then nodded.

"Just hang on to Lauren. Let me do the rest."

Another nod.

He stepped off, planting his feet in the riverbed again, and brought his hands under Brynn's arms as he had with Emily. He could feel her trembling.

"You've got this," he told her. "You're tougher than you think."

She didn't answer right away. Her arms tightened protectively around Lauren, and she managed a weak smile. "I know," she admitted. "My dad tells me that all the time."

"Eyes on me," Redd said gently. "Just like you saw me do before. One step at a time. We move together."

She nodded once, tighter this time, and they began. Redd could feel her body instinctively resisting his guidance. She didn't have Emily's fortitude, not yet, but she would get there. He didn't rush her.

Halfway across, she slipped, let out a cry, but Redd caught her, holding her steady while she regained her footing.

And then the bank was within reach. Emily was there, reaching out to take the girl's hand and pull her to safety. Redd released her and turned back again for the boys.

This time, it felt as if the river didn't fight him quite as hard. Or maybe he was figuring out all its little tricks. He stayed low, kept his center of gravity over his feet, and made it across without losing his footing even once.

He splashed up onto shore and knelt beside the boys. "Okay, listen up," he said. "I'm going to carry you both across. I know you're scared. That's okay. But I need you to hold on tight. No sudden moves. Just wrap your arms around me and don't let go."

Mitchell gave a stiff nod, teeth clenched. Jack hesitated, his face still wet with tears. "Is Rubble okay?"

"He's fine," Redd said, with a confidence he didn't entirely possess. "He's a better swimmer than any of us. He'll find a calm spot in the water, jump out, and be back soon. Right now, I just need you to help me get across."

That did the trick. Jack wrapped his arms around Redd's neck, hugging him so fiercely that Redd thought about asking him to ease up a bit, but then decided against it.

With both boys hugging him, Redd stood and stepped back into the current. Without a partner to brace him, and with a lot of extra weight up top, this would be the most challenging crossing yet. He kept his stance wide, knees bent, lowering himself into the river. At the midpoint, the water lapped at his thighs, caught the dangling feet of his precious cargo. He felt both boys tighten their already-fierce grip.

Redd gritted his teeth and pushed forward. One foot. Then the other. He was almost there. Maybe four steps from the shallows. He could see Emily waiting, one hand stretched out as if beckoning him home.

Then he heard her shout, "Matty! Behind you!"

He turned his head and saw them.

The Russians.

They burst from the woods at a dead run, still carrying their assault rifles but making no effort to use them. Instead, they barreled down the bank and splashed into the water without hesitation. The lead man hit the river like a missile, aimed straight at Redd.

His hasty entrance did him no favors. He slipped and fell, sending a plume of spray into the air, but his momentum carried him forward, toward his intended target. Redd tried to sidestep, to keep moving, but it was too late. As the man went down a second time, one hand snaked out under the surface and caught Redd's ankle, yanking it out from under him. His remaining foot slipped, and he barely had time to shout, "Hold on!" before splashing into the water.

The river took them all.

Redd fought to keep his grip on the boys and raise them above the surface, but the cold, rushing water was an irresistible, unrelenting force, trying to peel them away. He twisted, trying to get his feet back under him, but the Russian still had his foot and was dragging him along.

He surfaced again, coughing, but was pulled back under almost immediately. He could feel the boys slipping away from him and knew that if he tried to hang on to them, they would all surely drown, so with a great heave, he thrust them up out of the current, flinging them toward the far bank. The effort pushed him under once more, but without the additional weight, he was quickly buoyed up. He saw Mitchell splash down in the shallows, half swimming, half flailing until he got his hands under him and crawled up onto the bank.

But Jack was gone.

FIFTY-EIGHT

Skvortsov stumbled through the current, boots dragging against the rocks below, the cold biting up to his thighs. The river fought him with every step, tugging at his legs, slipping underfoot like the tentacles of some demonic sea creature.

Downstream, Sasha was locked in a savage struggle with the big American. They were rolling, half submerged, as the river dragged them away.

Skvortsov hesitated.

He and Sasha had fought together in Chechnya, in Donbas, in gun battles and bar fights. If there was anyone he trusted to handle himself in a brawl, it was his old friend.

But the American—Redd—was *big*. And he'd proven exceptionally resilient.

Skvortsov shook his head. In taking down Redd, Sasha had cleared the way for him to accomplish the mission Volkov had given him. Decker's children were unguarded.

Yet somehow that triumph, now within his grasp, tasted like ashes. When Volkov's man—Konstantin—had first contracted Sibir Z to eliminate Aaron Decker, it had sounded like easy money. Not in his darkest nightmares could he have imagined what the assignment would cost him.

The hunt had brought them halfway across the continent and taken the lives of some of his best men.

Good men.

Friends.

He would win in the end, of course, but it would be a Pyrrhic victory. *A Russian victory.* Just like in the Great Patriotic War, when men like his grandfather had defeated the Nazis by simply hurling millions of bodies at them.

That was how Russia always won. Not with finesse or tactics, but with sacrifice.

A dozen men . . . two dozen . . . to kill one?

If that's what it takes.

He didn't know what would happen after this. Surely by now, the American law enforcement agencies would be alerted, maybe even their military, swooping in to cut off all avenues of escape.

But that didn't matter. All that mattered was finishing the mission.

Winning.

He pushed forward, through the final yards of water, and flung himself up onto the muddy bank with a guttural growl. He would drag Decker's children back with him, put a gun to their heads, deliver an ultimatum—

He froze.

The woman—Redd's wife—stood before him, the butt of a double-barreled shotgun pressed tight to her shoulder, aimed down at him.

No.

He started to raise a hand . . .

And saw her finger tighten on the trigger.

FIFTY-NINE

Redd thrashed against the current, trying to kick free, but the Russian's grip on his leg was like an iron band. The water twisted around them both, churning white and loud in his ears, drowning out everything else. He got his head above the surface, sucked in a breath, and then went under again.

Their bodies slammed together and separated again. Redd tried to gain leverage, but there was no solid footing, no way to use his superior size against his foe.

And through it all, he searched desperately for Jack.

He caught a glimpse of the boy being swept along like a rag doll, thrashing to keep his head above water. He dipped under for a moment then bobbed up again, eyes meeting Redd's, his mouth forming a word that Redd couldn't hear.

Dad.

Redd roared in answer, trying to kick free, but in that instant, the Russian caught hold of his belt buckle and began crawling up his body like a ladder, forcing Redd's head underwater once more. They broke the surface, gasping, only to collide again. Redd pushed at the other man, trying to shove him away.

"Jack!"

Then, through the tumult, he spied a blur of motion, a dark shape splashing into the water.

Rubble.

The rottie hit the water at full speed, once again charging in without hesitation, head low, paddling furiously.

Jack was barely afloat now, going under again, his arms flailing weakly, but Rubble closed the distance fast, powerful limbs cleaving through the current, his jaws closing on Jack's outflung arm, dragging the boy toward the bank.

The sight shot through Redd like a jolt of adrenaline. He didn't know if Jack was okay—he prayed that he was, that Rubble had gotten to him in time—but now it was out of his hands, and time to give the Russian his undivided attention.

He slammed his forehead into the Russian's face, hearing . . . *feeling* the crunch as the man's nose cartilage snapped. The man's grip on him loosened, but instead of thrusting him away, Redd wrapped both arms around his foe, rolling him over, holding him under the surface.

He felt the man's struggles, felt the stones of the riverbed striking his crossed arms as the current dragged them both along. He was so focused on holding the man under and ending the fight that he didn't see the lodgepole that had fallen half across the river until it was almost too late.

Whitewater guides and swift-water rescue teams called them *strainers*—fallen logs and other obstacles that let water pass through but caught solid objects—like human bodies—and held them under.

Redd reacted instinctively, letting go of the Russian and throwing his arms up, trying to catch the tree trunk before he was dragged under. He succeeded, but only partially. Even as his arms hooked over the rough bark, his legs and lower body were dragged under, held fast by the constant pressure of the current.

Suddenly free of Redd's grasp, the Russian bobbed to the surface just in time to strike the trunk, and then he was gone, dragged under into the tangle of branches.

Redd's situation wasn't much better. The river hammered him against the trunk like a battering ram, pinning his chest to the wet bark, his legs trailing behind in the hydraulic grip. He tried pulling himself up, wriggling his torso onto the trunk, but the current wouldn't let go. It was taking everything he had just to hold his position.

The cold was making him sluggish, fatigue battering down the door. He had to do something different, or he would simply run out of gas.

He twisted his upper torso sideways, trying to align his body with the trunk.

That allowed him to roll his left shoulder up onto the tree but meant sacrificing the grip of his right arm.

Redd knew that he had one shot to get it right.

He wrenched himself up, driving his hip into the trunk and then leaning into it, twisting until his left knee was against the submerged bough, sliding across the rough bark, inch by agonizing inch until—miraculously—the leg was out of the water, rolling over the top of the strainer. He let it dip into the water on the far side, and then, with one more mighty push, rolled his body over the top, crashing through the branches to plunge once more into the flow.

The current caught him again, but he was clear of the strainer now. He rolled onto his back, angled his body toward the far bank, and with a few hard kicks, propelled himself into the shallows. When he finally pulled himself up onto shore, he wanted nothing more than to simply collapse, but he knew he couldn't afford the luxury of rest. Not until he knew his family was safe. So instead, he dragged himself upright and began shambling along the riverbank, feeling, and probably looking, like a zombie from a horror film.

He had no idea how far the river had taken him. Probably no more than fifty yards, but it seemed like miles.

"Jack!" he shouted, his voice cracking. "Jack!"

No answer. Just the river, quiet now that he was free of its relentless grasp. The terrain along the bank was uneven, cluttered with slick rocks and tangles of brush. His boots squelched with each stride, the saturated fabric of his jeans dragging like anchors around his calves, but the thought of Jack spurred him onward.

Then he heard a faint woof.

"Rubble?"

The rottie answered with a louder bark and then seemed to explode through the vegetation at the riverbank, leaping up to put his forepaws on Redd's shoulders.

Who's a good boy?

Joy and fear rose to a crescendo in Redd's chest as he hugged the dog. "Where's Jack, boy? Take me to Jack."

Rubble barked twice and then dropped down and charged back up the shore. Redd raced after him, dreading the moment when he would find Jack's pale, motionless body on the riverbank, but then Jack was there, standing before him, hair plastered to his forehead, clothes soaked, shivering . . . but moving. Breathing.

Alive.

Redd dropped to his knees, hands shaking as he pulled Jack close.

"I got you, buddy," he whispered. "I got you. You're safe now."

Jack clung to him, still sobbing, but this time with tears of joy. Redd held on tight.

Rubble barked again, excited. Redd looked up and saw Emily running down the riverbank toward them, followed by Brynn, still carrying Lauren, and Mitchell, holding Junior's hand. The worry in her face transformed into joy when she saw them, and a moment later, she was there, joining the embrace, breathless with relief.

After a few seconds, which seemed both too long and far too brief, Redd managed to croak, "The Russian?"

Emily shook her head. "He won't be a problem."

Something about the way she said it made him smile.

His smile faded when he heard a strange but familiar sound, a low mechanical thrum carrying faintly above the rush of the river, but getting louder.

A helicopter.

Redd tensed, envisioning another wave of Russian shooters. He turned to Emily, ready to tell her that they needed to get moving. She too was looking skyward, but her expression was one of relief.

"Gavin said reinforcements were on the way," she explained.

Redd remained unconvinced until he saw the familiar outline of a UH-60 Black Hawk cruising low over the treetops to the north. "Reinforcements," he murmured. "Perfect timing."

Emily laughed, hugging him tighter. "That means it's over, right?"

He pulled her close, one arm around her shoulders, Jack still clinging to his side, Junior toddling over to join them.

"I sure hope so," he whispered.

SIXTY

The rotor wash stirred the treetops as the Black Hawk passed overhead and then dropped lower, bobbing back and forth as its pilot brought it down to within a few feet of the boardwalk trail. The planks would never support the weight of the aircraft, and the pilot evidently knew better than to trust any seemingly open terrain in the basin, so instead he held the ship at a hover, close enough for its occupants—a dozen FBI agents wearing plate carriers and bump helmets over everyday clothes—to drop from its open doors. As soon as the last man was down and had moved out from under the shadow of the spinning top rotor, the Black Hawk lifted off, clawing its way back into the sky.

A hundred yards away, Acting Director Gavin Kline rose from where he'd been kneeling at Aaron Decker's side and began jogging up the trail to meet the new arrivals, all of whom were moving in a haphazard formation, like men who had watched one too many action-adventure movies. He was grateful for their arrival, even if the threat that had initiated their urgent dispatch was no longer extant. There was still one thing they could do for him.

When the lead agent recognized him, he motioned for the others to lower their weapons and come forward to meet him. Kline didn't waste time with introductions. "I've got a man down. He needs immediate medevac."

The agent nodded and then glanced over his shoulder. "Medic!"

A young man attired in the latest-issue digital-camouflage Army battle uniform and carrying a heavy black backpack and a holstered pistol instead of an assault rifle pushed through the formation and approached Kline, who simply pointed back in the direction of the Yukon, where Treadway still knelt beside Decker. Kline surmised he was a National Guard medic, on loan along with the helicopter.

The man who had given the order stepped forward. "Director Kline, I'm Ken Boudreaux, assistant special agent in charge, Bozeman FO. Sorry it took so long to get here. Better late than never, right?"

Kline returned a stony stare. "You're going to bring that bird back for medical transport, correct?"

Boudreaux swallowed nervously then keyed his mic. "Fox One, we've got a priority medevac. Return to the LZ, ASAP. Over."

Kline nodded his approval.

Boudreaux, somewhat encouraged by this response, went on. "Sir, what's the current tactical situation?"

"The immediate threat here has been neutralized, but I need you to find my son and his family. They're somewhere out there." He half turned, waving in a generally westward direction, wishing he could be more specific. "I don't know if there are any hostiles still out there."

"We'll find them," Boudreaux assured him. He turned and began relaying instructions to the rest of the group.

Kline watched them move out with a heavy heart. The Russian assault had been thwarted and a traitor exposed, but it hardly felt like a victory. Aaron Decker was critically wounded and might not survive. Matthew and his family were unaccounted for. At least half a dozen FBI agents were dead. And right now, he had more questions than answers.

"Director?"

Kline blinked and saw ASAC Boudreaux holding out a satellite phone. "The attorney general called just before we left and instructed me to give this to you. He wants you to call immediately."

Kline waved a dismissive hand. "I'll call when I have something to tell him."

"Sir"—Boudreaux's tone was respectful but firm—"he was very insistent."

Kline sighed and took the phone. As he tapped in the AG's private number, he began walking back to rejoin Treadway and check on Decker.

He had meant what he said about wanting to delay making the call until he had something to report. His boss was sure to demand answers that he just didn't have and wasn't likely to accept *I don't know* for an answer.

His relationship with the new attorney general had always been professionally cordial, but distant. The AG was a political appointee and as such more interested in image than results. He made no secret of the fact that he saw Kline as a placeholder and made little effort to seek Kline's input in policy decisions that affected the day-to-day operations of the Bureau, much less longer-term crime-fighting priorities.

But he was still Kline's boss.

He waited for the call to connect.

"Gavin. What on earth is going on there? I'm hearing reports of a mass shooting in Yellowstone? And I'm told the secretary of defense is there . . . with *you*?"

"The situation is still fluid, sir," replied Kline. "I'll tell you everything when I get back to DC."

"You'll tell me *now*. I need to know what's going on there so I can start doing damage control."

And there it is, thought Kline.

He glanced down at the National Guard medic preparing Decker for transport, at Treadway, still cradling Decker's head in her hands, at the bodies scattered around them.

"All right," he said at last. "Here's the gist. The secretary of defense was a traitor, working with a Russian gangster. He orchestrated a paramilitary strike inside a national park, targeting an American citizen who was under my personal protection."

The silence on the line went on so long that Kline thought the call might have dropped. "Sir, are you still there?"

"Did you just accuse the *secretary of defense* of being a traitor?"

"I did. And when I get back to DC, I'll bring you the proof."

Another long pause followed. "Where's the SecDef now?"

"Dead."

Another silence, and when the AG spoke again, his tone was more subdued. "I want you to hold off on launching any formal investigation until I've had time to brief the president. And, need I say it, I don't want a whisper of this in the press. Do you get me, Kline?"

Kline shook his head. Containment. Optics. Politics. Business as usual.

The truth didn't matter.

He glanced over at the SecDef's body again, remembering the impulse that had prompted him to pull the trigger. Kline had been around Washington, DC, long enough to know that, while it was rough justice, it was the only way justice would be served—period.

And maybe that was more important than the truth.

"Understood, sir," he said and ended the call. He turned, looking for Boudreaux. "Why isn't that chopper back here yet?"

The ASAC, who was just a few steps away, talking to someone on his radio, met Kline's stare and nodded. "It's on its way now, sir. And the pilot reports that he's got eyes on a group of people moving along the river west of here. Looks like a family." He paused a beat, listening as another update from the aircraft was transmitted to his earpiece, and then grinned. "They've even got a dog with them."

Despite everything else, Kline allowed himself a smile. He closed his eyes, feeling the tightness in his chest loosening. Maybe it was going to be okay after all.

SIXTY-ONE

WASHINGTON, DC

A Secret Service agent was waiting for Gavin Kline as he stepped through the West Executive entrance of the White House.

"Director Kline," she greeted him. "This way, please."

He retrieved his portfolio—a slim leather folder embossed with the FBI seal—from the X-ray screener and fell into step behind her. The escort was standard procedure, though Kline could easily have found his way without assistance. Since taking on the role of acting director of the FBI, he'd visited the Executive Mansion on several occasions for National Security briefings and other routine business.

Today's meeting, however, would be anything but routine.

The press had been howling for answers for forty-eight hours now, ever since word of the incident at Yellowstone first got out, much of the initial carnage captured on cell phone video from numerous park goers. A mass casualty event in a national park, with federal agents among the dead, and no official statement?

Kline had done his best to adhere to the AG's orders to keep a lid on things, but *it's an evolving situation* wasn't going to cut it much longer. And it wasn't just the press demanding action. His own people were at a loss to understand why *nobody* seemed to be actively investigating the events of that day. Oh, forensic teams were combing the park, collecting evidence, removing the bodies, but the formal structure of the investigation had not been established. There was no lead agent, no hierarchy. No mission.

Kline followed the agent down a narrow corridor paneled in cream and mahogany, lined with historical portraits and framed presidential photographs. He kept his eyes forward, but his thoughts spiraled.

He knew what this was. You didn't summon the director of the FBI to the White House for answers. You summoned him to fall in line. The fact that this meeting wasn't happening at Main Justice—the Robert F. Kennedy Building—was telling in itself. This wasn't about law enforcement. This was about optics. He wasn't here to speak truth to power. He was here to find out what truth power had chosen.

He thought about the leather folder tucked under his arm, the revelations it contained. There was enough information in that portfolio to completely upend the "official" version, but he knew it would probably never see the light of day.

He had a sense of how this would play out. The AG would supply the narrative—prepackaged, patriotic, palatable. The secretary of defense would not be remembered as a traitor who conspired with Russian gangsters to assassinate a US citizen, but as someone who had died in service to his country, shielding civilians from foreign terror on American soil. A hero's death.

He realized with a start that they had passed the stairwell leading down to the Situation Room. "We're not going downstairs?"

"No, sir," the agent said. "This way."

She led him past the Roosevelt Room and stopped in front of another door which, while familiar, he had never passed through. "Wait, this is—"

The agent opened the door without fanfare and motioned for him to enter the Oval Office. The attorney general was waiting inside, along with the White House chief of staff and, sitting behind the Resolute Desk, the president of the United States. Kline stepped across the threshold, spine straight, heart heavy.

"Gavin," began the AG. "Thanks for agreeing to meet with us."

Kline raised a hand to forestall any ritual exchange of pleasantries. "Let me save us all some time, gentlemen," he began, looking only at the AG. "I've observed your explicit direction to hold off on launching a formal investigation into the events that occurred in Yellowstone Park two days ago, but I think you should have some context."

He held up the portfolio. "This contains information obtained by Aaron Decker, the man whose family was under my personal protection and who was cold-bloodedly murdered by the secretary of defense."

There were a few untruths in this statement, not the least of which was the origin of the information he was about to share. It hadn't come from Decker, but rather from Matthew, by way of an as-yet-unidentified source. In the grand scheme of things, the specific provenance of the material mattered less than its substance.

"Decker," he went on, "was a former paramilitary operator—an assassin, to put it plainly—working for an off-the-books unit operating in Eastern Europe and the Middle East back in the 2010s. Decker learned that his unit had been co-opted by a traitor—a man known as Nightshade who was manipulating the target lists, using sanctioned killings to advance his own criminal schemes. When Decker's team started to question some of the targets, Nightshade sent them and his team into an ambush, which Decker alone survived, faking his own death to avoid further attempts on his life.

"A few months ago, however, Nightshade learned that Decker was still alive and tapped one of his criminal allies—a Russian gangster named Grigori Volkov—to finish what he'd started fifteen years ago. In the process of trying to elude Volkov's assassins, Decker identified one of Nightshade's inner circle—a former Army officer and now a DOD contractor named Brian Anderson."

He waved the portfolio again. "This contains the full transcript of Anderson's debrief in which he not only identifies Nightshade as the man you"—he cast his gaze at the president—"appointed as secretary of defense but also goes into some detail about his history of leveraging top secret intelligence and even operational assets to advance his personal wealth and influence."

The AG chose that moment to break in. "The uncorroborated, and I'm guessing *coerced* testimony of an alleged co-conspirator is hardly sufficient basis to make accusations of this magnitude."

"That may be true from a *legal* standpoint," countered Kline. "I personally witnessed the secretary murder not only Aaron Decker, but also one of his own protective agents as well as Grigori Volkov, so I think *my* testimony would suffice to at least begin an investigation. But as to the merits of this evidence . . ."

He waved the portfolio again. "Among other things, it details Nightshade's use of DOD assets—specifically a predictive AI algorithm running on a top-secret quantum computer at Fort Meade—to hunt down Decker. I imagine a review of the security access logs will confirm that the secretary made in-person visits to Fort Meade on the days in question."

Kline took a step forward and thrust the portfolio toward the AG, who took it, almost reflexively and, hesitantly, opened it.

"It may not be the proverbial smoking gun," Kline went on. "But it more than satisfies the burden of proof as far as I'm concerned. Do with it what you will."

Having said his piece, Kline felt lighter. Maybe nothing would change, maybe the truth didn't matter, but he'd done his job. He might be finished in Washington, but he would walk away proud. He turned and started for the door.

"Director," the AG called out. "What's this?"

Kline looked back and saw the man holding up the unsealed envelope Kline had tucked into the portfolio along with the transcript of Anderson's interrogation. "My resignation. I assumed you'd be wanting it."

The other men all shared a glance.

"Sit down, Director."

The directive came not from the AG, but from the president, who had up until that moment regarded his visitor with stony silence.

Kline blinked. "Excuse me, Mr. President?"

"I said, sit down." The president's manner was firm but rather than conveying anger, there was a hint of something like amusement in his tone. "You've had your say. Now it's time for you to shut up and listen."

Kline swallowed and took a seat on one of the divans arranged around the presidential seal in the center of the room.

The president leaned back in his chair. "Quite the can of worms you've just kicked over." There was no anger in his voice. "There are very real consequences to airing this scandal in public. The media will have a field day. My opponents in Congress and our foreign enemies will eat this up with a spoon."

Kline said nothing. This was exactly what he'd expected. The rehearsed concern. The talk of optics. Of political calculus. He waited for the pivot, when national security would be invoked, when the specter of public panic would be raised as justification for burying the truth.

"I understand, sir," Kline said, trying to hide his contempt. "Rest assured, I have no intention of going public with this. Once I step down, what you do with the information is your decision."

"You misunderstand me, Gavin. Can I call you Gavin?"

Kline blinked, surprised, and nodded.

"I'm not trying to muzzle you. You've exposed a rotten apple in my administration, and while I'd rather keep this in-house, I am grateful." He paused, letting the statement sink in. "I want you to conduct your investigation. Discreetly, if possible. But thoroughly. If there are other rotten apples in the barrel, I want you to find them."

Kline studied the man's expression, searching for guile. He didn't see any, but the president was, after all, a politician. "I appreciate your trust, Mr. President. But I don't think I'm the man for that job. Not anymore."

"I disagree," the president said, with a faint smile. "Regardless, you opened the can of worms, so it's your mess to clean up." Before Kline could protest, the president went on. "I'm beginning to realize that the vacancy in the leadership of the Bureau is part of the problem. We've all been expecting you to keep the ship on course with one hand tied behind your back. That stops today. I've put forward your nomination. I want you to be the director of the FBI."

Kline stared at him, blindsided. Stunned.

The president waited a beat, then continued. "I've already spoken with the Senate majority leader. We're going to get your confirmation fast-tracked."

"Mr. President, you don't need to buy my silence."

The president's expression didn't change, but he glanced over to the attorney general, who in turn handed the portfolio back to Kline.

"I don't want a puppet or a yes-man, Gavin," the president said. "I want you to do your job."

Kline stared back for a long moment. "I'm going to hold you to that, Mr. President."

"See to it that you do," said the president. "But one word of advice. Or maybe more of a request, depending on how you look at it."

"Sir?"

"It seems that in recent years there has been an uptick in—how should I say this?—large *events* occurring in and around Montana. From what I'm told, it's not an area where such events normally occur."

Matthew . . .

Kline nodded, wondering how much POTUS really knew about Redd or their relationship as father and son. Would that personal connection matter? On the one hand, the president himself was a known family man, who at various stages even allowed his own children to take part in his campaign. On the other, his tone was hard to read, and Kline couldn't be sure this wasn't the man's way of telling him to put a leash on Redd.

Like that'll ever happen.

His answer came a moment later.

"I trust you can get creative, if needed, to make sure we have . . . *someone* . . . capable of handling anything that may pop up in the future . . . you know, out west."

Kline fought to hold back a smile. "I think I can figure something out, Mr. President."

"Good deal. Well then, that'll be all, Director."

With a smile and a nod, Kline took the portfolio.

Somehow, the weight of it felt different now.

Epilogue

STILLWATER COUNTY, MONTANA

Redd knelt over the big Igloo cooler, stuffing bottles of craft ale and cans of assorted soft drinks into the waiting nest of ice cubes. The kitchen was filled with delicious aromas—the lasagna and baked beans in the oven and the pies cooling on the counter—but Redd could still pick up a hint of savory smoke wafting in from the back porch. Lauren was in her playpen in the living room. Jack and Matthew Junior were playing out back, supervised by the ever-vigilant Rubble.

Behind him, Emily was busy making final preparations, which mostly consisted of turning in circles, trying to figure out whether she'd overlooked anything.

She hadn't, of course. Emily was . . . perfect.

Weeks had passed since the events at Yellowstone, and life was finally starting to feel normal again. There were still a few reminders of what had happened. Emily had been driving J. B.'s old pickup to work, at least until they settled on a replacement for the Tahoe. Jack had had a few bad dreams . . .

Poor kid, thought Redd. *He's gone through so much.*

But the boy was resilient, and if anything, the trials they had endured had reinforced the family bond.

Redd decided he couldn't stuff anything more into the cooler, so he hefted it in his arms and started for the back door. As he was trying to figure out how to open the door without setting the cooler down, he was distracted by a voice coming from the living room, a news broadcast playing on the television.

". . . continuing questions surround the violent gang war that erupted in Yellowstone National Park almost three weeks ago. Officials say that they're still trying to get to the bottom of what happened, though sources inside the FBI have revealed that many of the dead were foreign nationals with ties to organized crime."

His curiosity piqued, Redd set the cooler down and leaned into the living room to take a look.

The screen was presently displaying a cell phone video of people running to the accompaniment of distant gunfire.

"Several federal agents are also listed among the dead along with this man . . ." The video cut to a still image of a familiar face—a driver's license or passport photo, Redd guessed. *"Aaron Decker of Richland, Michigan, who, according to sources, was a federal witness under FBI protection. No further details have been released."*

"You'd think they could have found a better photo of him," said Emily, who had come up behind him.

Redd gave a half smile. "Good luck. Aaron and cameras have never mixed."

"Good point."

Redd heard Rubble barking and glanced out the front window to see a silver pickup rolling up the drive. "Mikey and Liz are here."

He stepped out onto the front porch, calling Rubble back just as the silver Dodge rolled to a stop in front of the barn. The driver's door opened and Mikey got out. Redd watched as his best friend's gaze shifted to the Raptor, which, although still drivable, had sustained considerable cosmetic damage during the tangle with the Bratva killers from Duluth.

Mikey sighed. "You're killin' me, Matt."

Redd raised his hands. "You think that's bad, you should see Emily's rig."

"I just can't leave you unsupervised for a minute, can I?"

"I don't suppose it matters, but it wasn't me this time."

"That a fact?" Mikey walked around the front of the truck to get a better look.

"You'll get the full story after supper," promised Redd.

Mikey turned back to him, regarding him with a dour expression for a moment, then shook his head. "Ah, you know I can't stay mad at you, bro." He threw his arms open wide. "Bring it in, big guy."

Redd laughed and embraced his friend in a hug that was no less awkward because of the size difference. "So how's your mother-in-law?"

"Doing really well, actually. Liz got things set up so she has some help at the house a few days a week, but she's already made a lot of progress."

"I'm glad to hear that."

Behind them, Liz finished unbuckling Lucas from his car seat. When the boy saw Redd, he let out a squeal of delight. "Uncy Matt! Where's Junior?"

"He's out back, bud," replied Redd. "You know the way."

As Lucas headed around the outside of the house, Mikey gave the Raptor one last shake of the head, then turned to help Liz unload several bags of groceries.

"We brought dessert," Liz said. "And Mikey insisted on more potato salad, even though Emily said she had enough to feed an army."

"You say that like it's a bad thing," retorted a grinning Mikey. "Matt needs a lot of food. We wouldn't want his weight to dip into the two-fifties or anything crazy," he joked.

Redd grabbed the last couple bags from the cab and followed his friends up to the house. While Liz went to work setting out their contribution to the feast, Redd took Mikey out onto the back porch to watch the kids play. Redd took two Coke Zeros from the cooler, cracked them open and handed one to Mikey.

They tapped cans together and Mikey took a generous swig. "Hey, did you hear about what happened in Yellowstone? Crazy, right?"

Redd smiled around a sip. "Crazy."

He was spared an uncomfortable conversation when Rubble lifted his head, ears perked, and gave an alert woof.

"More company," Redd announced.

They passed through the house and stepped out onto the front porch just as a familiar-looking Chevrolet Malibu rolled to a stop next to Mikey's truck. The engine cut out, and a moment later all of its doors were thrown open in unison.

The first person out was Mitchell Decker, who was nearly bowled over by Rubble. Laughing, he threw his arms around the dog and then waved to Redd.

"The boys are all out back playing," Redd told him. "Take Rubble with you."

With Rubble beside him, Mitchell made a beeline for the backyard, calling out Jack's name as he went.

Brynn got out the other side and flashed a radiant smile. "Hello again, Mr. Redd."

Redd nodded. "Hello, Brynn." He turned to indicate Mikey. "This is my best friend, Mikey." He lowered his voice to a conspiratorial whisper. "Don't tell him about the time I let you drive my truck."

Brynn grimaced but Redd gave her a wink, then turned to the pair that got out of the front seat of the Malibu. "Mikey, I think you remember Special Agent Treadway—"

"How could I forget?" said Mikey.

The last time Mikey and Treadway had been together, they'd fought side by side in the Wellington courthouse against a small army sent to kill Redd.

"Better circumstances this time, thank goodness," said Treadway with a laugh. "And please, it's just Stephanie."

The man who got out on the passenger's side stood there for a moment as if he didn't quite trust his legs to hold him up. He wore a ball cap that only partially hid the buzzed patch above his temple, or the line of a recent and still-healing surgical incision.

"And this," Redd went on, "is Aaron. He's . . . a friend."

Mikey stared for half a second, then stuck out his hand. "Any friend of Matt's," he said. "Let me grab you something to drink."

"You look pretty good for a dead guy," Redd joked once Mikey had turned away.

Decker managed a smile. "Yeah, well . . . dying sucked a lot more the second time than it did the first."

In truth, Aaron Decker very nearly *had* died this time. While Nightshade's bullet had only grazed him, it had still done plenty of damage, cracking his skull and creating significant trauma. Emergency surgery to relieve intracranial pressure had saved his life, even though, officially, he was listed among the dead at Yellowstone.

With the full scope of Nightshade's network still uncertain, the best way to ensure Decker's safety, not to mention avoid the political fallout of prosecuting a man who had technically spent the past two decades as a rogue assassin, was to let the world believe he was dead. A ghost once more.

"So, probably not going back to Michigan anytime soon, huh?" asked Redd.

"Doubtful. I'm supposed to be dead, remember? No, we'll need to start a new life, but for now, we just want to lay low. Figured Montana was as good a place as any to spend the summer."

Redd laughed knowingly. "Careful. This place has a way of growing on you."

Treadway came up and put an arm around Decker's waist. "You feeling okay? Doc said you might be a little unsteady."

"I'm fine, Steph," Decker growled.

Redd pretended not to notice the open display of affection.

Now that's a couple I never saw together . . .

Treadway turned to Redd. "Is Gavin here yet?"

"We're expecting him anytime." He turned, noticing a dark government-issue Suburban coming up the drive. "Speak of the devil."

"I'll tell him you said that," laughed Treadway.

"He already knows." Redd watched the SUV pull up. "Go on inside. I'll catch up."

As the Suburban came to a stop, Redd went over to meet its sole occupant, and as Kline got out, he extended a hand. "Director Kline."

Kline regarded the offer suspiciously, but as he reached out to accept the handclasp, Redd pulled him into a hug.

Kline seemed surprised at first but then returned his son's embrace.

"Seriously," Redd added as they separated. "Congratulations. You deserved this."

Kline smiled ruefully. "It remains to be seen whether it's a reward or a punishment."

Redd chuckled. "You'll make it work. Come on, let's get some food in you."

"I am starving," Kline said. "But first . . . can I have a word in private?"

Redd looked at him sideways. Things had been good between them since Yellowstone. Better than they'd ever been, really. Especially after everything Gavin had done to protect Emily and the kids. Redd had begun to see him not just as the father he'd never really known, but as the kind of man he could respect.

Still, he hoped Kline wasn't going to get all sentimental.

"Sure," he said. "We can take the long way around."

He led Kline along the edge of the corral fence, away from the house. For a long moment, Kline said nothing, just gazed out across the pasture. Finally, he said, "You've really taken to this life."

"Surprises me more than anyone."

"I guess I'll get to the point. I want you to work for me. At the Bureau . . . Or more specifically, I want you working for me *from here*."

Stopping, Redd couldn't help but laugh.

"What's so funny?"

"It's just, this isn't the first time you've driven up, got out of your car, and offered me a job on the spot." Redd saw the recognition spark in Kline's eyes.

"You're right. But this isn't anything like before."

"You want me to become an FBI agent," said Redd, skeptically.

"A different kind of agent. Something new. Officially, you would be a special assignment officer. An agent-at-large. Kind of like what Stephanie is doing for me right now, only this would be your beat." He made a sweeping gesture.

"Montana?"

"The West," Kline clarified. "The Bureau takes a very one-size-fits-all approach to crime. We really don't get rural America. I want you to be our eyes and ears out here, and our boots on the ground. No cubicle, no reporting to a senior agent. You would answer to me and *only* me. And you won't have to uproot your family. You can stay here and keep running the ranch. Honestly, Matt, you're already doing this job. I'm just giving you a paycheck, a badge, and the legal cover to keep doing it.

"You'd still have to get your creds through the Academy," Kline went on, speaking quickly, not giving Redd the space to answer, "but we can put you through an accelerated course. No probationary period, no desk duty. Your commission would be issued under an executive waiver. I can do that now."

Redd rubbed his chin thoughtfully. "Government salary, huh?"

"Yeah. You won't be rich, but it'll take some stress off trying to make ends meet ranching on your own up here. And the benefits are good." Kline lifted a hand. "Don't answer yet. Think it over. Sleep on it. Talk to Emily—"

Redd didn't need to do any of that. "I'm in."

"You're in? Really . . . just like that?"

"You said it yourself: I'm already doing the job." Redd wanted to add, *And to be honest, I enjoy getting to spend time with you, Dad,* but he wasn't anywhere near ready to let those words flow from his mouth. Instead, he just said, "Besides, I like the people I work with."

Kline smiled. "Let's get some food."

As everyone settled in around a large picnic table out back, Redd spotted Jack sitting by himself on the porch step. "Jack, come on, buddy. Let's eat."

"Hey, what you got there, pal?" asked Mikey as Jack plopped down next to him. "That a journal or something?"

Jack had a small, A5-size notebook in one hand, and a dull pencil in the other. "Just a story I was writing."

"A story, huh? Can I see it?" Mikey took the notebook from the boy and held it up. *"Umm, someone saves . . ."*

"*Daddy saves*," offered Jack, looking embarrassed that his penmanship wasn't legible.

"Don't worry about it, Jack," said Redd, "Mikey can barely read."

"Or type," said Liz. "He voice texts everything. I can't tell you how often I get a whole paragraph, all one sentence, no grammar or punctuation."

"His talking isn't much better," said Emily, piling on their friend. "Remember when we pulled up to that coffee place one time, and he tried to order a strawberry punch mocktail, but it came out, '*strawberry munch pocktail*'?"

The table erupted in laughter.

"I feel like that checks out," said Treadway.

"Whoa, friendly fire, bro," said Mikey, holding his hands up in mock surrender. He turned to Jack. "So, this story is about your dad here?"

Jack nodded.

"Well, you know, as your daddy's best friend, if you're writing about Matt and he's the hero, make sure you write me in as the sidekick. I'll be the fan-favorite character."

Everyone laughed again.

"Not for nothing," said Redd, pulling Junior onto his lap, "but I'm pretty sure Aaron would be the fan-favorite side character."

"Agreed," said Decker. "I'm definitely way cooler."

"That's debatable," shot Brynn, eager to get in on the harmless ribbing.

"Hey," yelled Mikey, "I've had your back in every adventure so far, Matt."

Multiple glances shot around the table, smiles and more laughter filling the air.

Redd finally spoke up. "Yes. Thank you, Mikey."

But that wasn't enough for his most trusted friend, who was beginning to realize that he'd missed more than just a few get-togethers while they were out of town.

"What? What'd I miss?"

Liz shot a palm to her forehead. "Babe! *Think* about it."

Everyone eyed Mikey, waiting for the moment when the lightbulb would turn on and he'd put two and two together. Several seconds later, it finally happened.

"Wait . . . *Daddy Saves . . . Yellowstone*," Mikey said, looking again at the title. "Your dad saved Yellowstone? Matt, that was *you*?"

Redd shrugged. "Like you said, crazy."

"It was *all* of you," Mikey said, his voice full of shock. His eyebrows were so high on his forehead that they looked like they were going to touch his hairline. "Oh, c'mon. Somebody better tell me the story. And I want all the details. Don't skip anything!"

"Deal," said Redd. "But first . . . let's eat."

As everyone began passing dishes and scooping food onto their plates, Redd paused a beat amongst the dinnertime chaos to soak in the moment. He looked around at Kline, Decker, Treadway, Brynn, Mitchell, and then over to Mikey, Liz, Lucas, and finally to his own children. He couldn't believe how much they'd grown. He hugged Junior as his eyes swept across Jack and Lauren. Redd was so caught up in the moment that he nearly jumped when his eyes moved to Emily, who was—unlike everyone else—sitting still, silently watching *him*.

Their eyes met, and for the briefest of moments, they shared a loving glance.

This, Redd thought, surrounded by his closest friends and family, *is living.*

And he planned to do a lot more of it.

Acknowledgments

First and foremost, I want to thank my Lord and Savior, Jesus Christ, who has blessed me far beyond anything I've ever deserved.

To any of my readers who don't personally know Jesus, I just want to invite you to pray and accept Him as your Savior. I'm constantly stuck by just how ordinary the twelve men were that Jesus called to follow Him and be His disciples. But therein lies the beauty of grace and God's plan for salvation. The Creator of the world is willing to meet us even at our darkest, deepest depths. We don't have to *earn* that because, frankly, we are all unworthy and undeserving. Salvation is a gift, one that will inevitably change you once you accept it—but accepting it is the first step, and if you're reading this and haven't done that, I'd encourage you not to wait a second longer. "For the wages of sin is death," wrote the Apostle Paul in Romans 6:23, and I could never express with words alone just how thankful I am that that debt was paid in full by the blood of Jesus Christ. (If you're reading this and would like to talk about the gospel, or if you need someone to pray for you, please reach out to me at Ryan@TheRealBookSpy.com.)

While writing *Target Down*, I decided to dedicate this book to **Bryan Tema**, the lead pastor at Gracespring Bible Church. *My* pastor. In 2023, I made the decision to really rededicate my life to living for Jesus, but finding a church home proved difficult. Then, in 2024, the Lord led us to Gracespring, and oh, what a blessing it's been for my family. Our church, while big, has the feel of a smaller church, and that is because of Bryan, who takes time to talk to everyone who comes through the doors. Not only is he a brilliant teacher, from whom I've learned so much about God's Word, but Bryan is a truly remarkable shepherd. I've never had a pastor who's also been a friend and mentor, someone I could reach out to as needed for prayer, support, or questions. Now I do. Bryan, I love you, brother, and I cannot thank you enough for all of your encouragement this past year. (And to Bryan's wife, **Tammy Tema**, thank you for always being such a positive, energetic, and loving force within our church family.)

To **Kenneth Price**, our spiritual formation pastor, thank you. Much like Bryan above, Kenneth has become a friend, and someone else I can—and have, regularly—gone to for any number of reasons. In addition to being a gifted preacher, Kenneth is multitalented with both the written word *and* music. We're lucky to have him at Gracespring, and I'm thankful to call him a friend.

To my buddy **Eric Kuhn**, the church troublemaker, I love you, man, even if you are a Vikings fan. Or don't know how to vacuum properly. But seriously, thank you for being one of the first smiling faces to really welcome us to Gracespring. Eric has a loud, infectious laugh, and once he gets going, it's impossible not to join in. He's also a talented writer, and to be frank, has the personality and smarts to excel in any career field he might have chosen. Eric, count me among those who are incredibly thankful that you chose *this* career, my friend.

To our dear friends **David** and **Julie Johns**, thank you so much for loving my family and being such an encouragement to us.

I'd also like to thank **Patty Cramer**, **Jim Mitchell**, **Preston Hoxworth**, **Michelle Williams**, **Sean Solitro**, **Anita Ollia**, **Matt Koenig**, and my friends **Abraham Cook** and **Brandon Fuller** for everything they do to keep our church running smoothly.

About halfway through writing *Target Down*, my children and I witnessed a horrific multicar accident. I'll spare readers the details, but it was awful. Shaken and a little in shock after witnessing such horrors, I went up to our church. As it would turn out, all the pastors were out that day, but both **Lauren Doorlag** (who is such a bright light in a dark world) and **Kylie Whitman** (one of the most talented artists I've ever met) were there, and they took the time to talk to me, pray with me, and just *be* there. Lauren and Kylie, you don't know how much that meant to me. From the bottom of my heart, thank you for that, and for *so* much more.

All week long, I look forward to **Michael Johnson** (our worship pastor) and his team leading us in worship on Sunday mornings, and they never disappoint.

Michael, you guys are all so talented—and your song selection is always perfect. **Reina Jenkins**, in particular, has become a celebrity of sorts in our home. My only gripe is that both she and **Mikayla Tema** regularly ruin songs for me, because after they sing one, I can never go back and listen to the original artist's recording. You both have so much talent. Thank you for sharing it with us!

To **Ginger Tiffany**, along with her kids, **Grant** and **Brooke**, thank you. I mean, where do I even start? My daughter, who suffers from anxiety, had her first-ever sleepover with Ginger and Brooke. My son, who had never really made a real friend, is now BFFs with Grant—a teen with the body of Goliath, the heart of David, and the appetite of both Shaggy and Scooby-Doo. Ginger, seriously, thank you. Melissa and I appreciate you so much. Getting to know your family and spending time with you all has been one of the biggest blessings for us.

Speaking of BFFs, a huge thank-you once again to **Mikey** and **Emily Derhammer**. I'm a big believer in "blood makes you relatives, but you choose your family," and I'm forever thankful you guys continue to choose us again and again. We love you, Lainey, and Bodie so much.

To my partners-in-crime on our HUB Sundays, **Ida Wetters** (and her husband, **Rick Wetters**, the most even-keeled man I've ever met) and **Lynn Demink**, thank you for being so welcoming to Melissa and me when we joined. Go white team!

Special shout-out to **Bryce Anderson** (I'd note that he's a pilot, but I don't want him to get a big head) and **Josh Tema**, both of whom have become friends, for their willingness to be part of the Safety Team.

To my agent, **John Talbot**, thank you for always being there to support me and offer sound, sage advice. John, your friendship means so much to me, and I am forever thankful for all the work you've put into making my dreams of being an author come true. I wouldn't be where I am today without you, nor would this journey be the same without your constant, steady encouragement. Here's to many more books together!

It's hard to believe that this is the fifth Matthew Redd adventure. Time flies. It still seems like just yesterday *Fields of Fire* was hitting bookstores. To **everyone at Tyndale**, thank you for believing in me and supporting me every step of the way. **Karen Watson** has been my biggest advocate and supporter, and I will forever be thankful, Karen, that you took a chance on me and Matty Redd. Thank you for all that you've done for me in the last five years.

As I've long said, when it comes to publishing a book, I'm really only in charge of the writing. Everything else—from the packaging and artwork to the marketing and publicity plans—falls on the wonderful, talented people at Tyndale. To that end, I would like to thank **Dean Renninger**, the artist behind all of my covers, along with **Andrea Garcia** and **Natalie Wierenga**. Andrea (marketing) and Natalie (publicity) lead the charge when it comes to making sure people know a new book is coming out, and I'm incredibly thankful to both of you for all you've done for me and this series over the last several years.

A special thank-you, also, to **Stephanie Broene**, **Elizabeth Jackson**, and **Andrea Martin**.

And finally, from my Tyndale family, I would like to thank my amazing, patient, and brilliant editor, **Sarah Rische**—the only person who might know Redd better than me. While it's true that I *could* write these books without Sarah, it's also true—and I can say this with absolute certainty—that I would mess up so many small details without her, including the age and physical appearance of my own characters. Whether I'm incorrectly adding snow to summer scenes or aging Redd's children several years ahead by accident, Sarah has long been a steady constant for me on the editing and revising side of this job, and I cannot imagine telling one of Redd's stories without her.

To my wife, **Melissa Steck**, thank you for always being my better half. You really are the glue that holds our whole family together. And while I get a lot of recognition publicly for what I do as a writer, *none* of it would be possible without you. From running all the errands and handling all the grocery shopping, to caring for our children and making sure their needs are met day in and day out, rain or shine, regardless of how you feel or how little sleep you get, you always show up for your family. I love you endlessly.

To **Brynn**, **Ryan Junior**, **Rylee**, and **Mitchell**, I am so thankful that I get to be your dad. You four are what drives me every single day to get up and work hard. I love you all more than you will ever know. (And to Mitchell . . . Daddy finally put you in one of my books. Sorry it took this long!)

Early in *Target Down*, Redd mentions getting baptized, which was a late addition to the story. Why? Because after I finished writing it, in late August of 2025, I got to help baptize my son, **Junior**, my wife, **Melissa**, and my closest, most trusted, best friend in the world, **Mikey**. What a perfect day, and I am forever thankful that we all got to share it together.

Lastly, to my readers, thank you for allowing me the opportunity to live out my dream as an author. I never imagined that *this* would be my career, and yet, here we are. It's surreal, even still, and I am so appreciative of everyone who's bought one of my books, taken the time to email me, or left a review online. I know that Redd ends this book in a happy place, but fear not, this isn't the end for him. Next summer, there's fixing to be more trouble brewing up in Montana, and you can expect the whole gang—including Mikey *and* Decker—to show up. No spoilers, but trust me when I say that Matthew Redd's toughest challenge is yet to come . . . and I think this next book is going to shock a lot of people.

So, get ready. I'll see you in 2027!

About the Author

RYAN STECK is an editor, an author, and the founder and editor in chief of The Real Book Spy. Ryan has been named an "Online Influencer" by Amazon. TheRealBookSpy.com has been endorsed by #1 *New York Times* bestselling authors Mark Greaney, C. J. Box, Kyle Mills, Daniel Silva, Brad Thor, and many others. A resident of Michigan, along with his wife and their six kids, Steck cheers on his beloved Detroit Tigers and Lions during the rare moments when he's not reading or talking about books on social media. He can be reached via email at ryan@therealbookspy.com.